F*CKED UP FAIRY TALES

F*CKED UP FAIRY TALES

*Sinful Cinderellas,
Prince Alarmings,
and Other
Timeless Classics*

Liz Gotauco

Illustrations by Jade A. Gotauco

W. W. NORTON & COMPANY
Independent Publishers Since 1923

This is a work of fiction. Names, characters, places, and incidents are the products of the author's imagination or are used fictitiously. Any resemblance to actual events, locales, or persons, living or dead, is entirely coincidental.

Copyright © 2025 by Liz Gotauco
Illustrations by Jade A. Gotauco

All rights reserved
Printed in the United States of America
First Edition

For information about permission to reproduce selections from this book, write to Permissions, W. W. Norton & Company, Inc., 500 Fifth Avenue, New York, NY 10110

For information about special discounts for bulk purchases, please contact W. W. Norton Special Sales at specialsales@wwnorton.com or 800-233-4830

Manufacturing by Versa Press
Book design by Lovedog Studio
Production manager: Delaney Adams

Library of Congress Cataloging-in-Publication Data is available.

ISBN 978-1-324-10633-3

W. W. Norton & Company, Inc., 500 Fifth Avenue,
New York, NY 10110
www.wwnorton.com

W. W. Norton & Company Ltd., 15 Carlisle Street,
London W1D 3BS

1 2 3 4 5 6 7 8 9 0

*For Mom and Dad,
who never feared the people
I'd meet or lessons I'd learn between
the covers of a book*

Contents

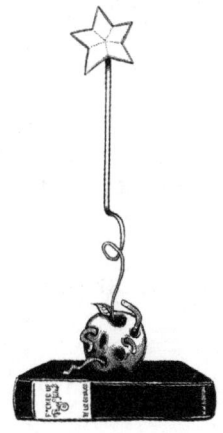

Introduction — xi

Trigger Warnings — xxiv

Part 1
F*CKED UP FAMILY TREES

Daddy's Little Donkey-Skin
(Charles Perrault's "Peau d'Âne") — 3

The Devil Made Her Do It
(The Grimms' "The Juniper Tree") — 17

Thumberella
(India's "Bâpkhâdi") — 31

Snakes Who Cannot Shed Their Kin
(Lithuania's "Eglė, the Queen of Serpents") — 44

Blanca Rosa, Mother of Thieves
(A Chilean Snow White)   63

Part 2
SWIPE RIGHT TO YOUR HAPPY ENDING

Love Is for the Birds
(Oscar Wilde's "The Nightingale and the Rose")   79

Love Is Like a Tree
(The Xhosa's "Kamiyo of the River," South Africa)   87

Love Is a Revolution
(A Filipino Myth of Mount Makiling)   94

Love Is a Family Affair
(Vietnam's "Hon Vong Phu")   109

Love Is Dead
("The Finger," a Jewish Folktale)   120

Part 3
SO . . . YOU MARRIED AN ANIMAL

Till There Was Mew
(Madame d'Aulnoy's "The White Cat")   131

When a Bird Loves a Woman
(The Tzotzil Mayan's "The Buzzard Husband," Mexico)   150

Mule Be in My Heart
(Tunisia's "The Donkey's Head")   159

My Carp Will Go On
(Haiti's "Tezen")   178

Master and Serpent
  (Denmark's "King Lindworm")   195

Part 4
WHAT'S YOUR BODY COUNT?

The X-Treme Sport of Giant Killing
  (Scotland's "Molly Whuppie")   217

How to Trick Friends and Execute People
  (Hans Christian Andersen's
  "Little Claus and Big Claus")   228

Never Cross a Cinderella
  (Korea's "Kongjwi and Patjwi")   241

Skin-Deep
  (Giambattista Basile's "The Flayed Old Woman")   255

No Small Peat
  (Germany's "The Maid of Wildenloh")   267

Part 5
CRAPPILY EVER AFTER

Good Soup
  (A Japanese Folktale)   283

The Stench of Embarrassment
  (A Tale from *Arabian Nights*)   289

It Snot What You Think
  (Korea's "Origin of the Common Cold")   298

Kalendrin, the Party Princess
(A Muria Period Piece, India) 303

The Pongo's Prophecy
(The Quechua's Poopy Parable, Peru) 316

References 325

Recommended Reading 337

Acknowledgments 339

Introduction

Disney's *The Little Mermaid* was released on VHS in May 1990. This little black plastic brick transformed me. Under the spell of Ariel, I was no longer an awkward eight-year-old kid; instead, I was a graceful sixteen-year-old mermaid, grown-up enough to wear a seashell bra! I no longer paddled Aunt Carol's pool in suburban Rhode Island; I flicked my fins across the sparkling Mediterranean! (Or Caribbean? It's hard to say.) I belted my all-consuming love of Prince Eric from the steps in the shallow end, now an outcropping above the waves. I tossed my majestic ginger mane (a tangled brown mop with uneven bangs) as the ocean and the orchestra crashed behind me (drenching my sunbathing mother).

My mother, luckily more of a buoying fairy godmother than a vengeful sea witch, toweled me off and handed me a beautifully illustrated, oversized anthology of Hans Christian Andersen tales. "Wait till you see how Ariel's story *really* ends." I wrenched open the book to the OG "The Little Mermaid," and my adoration transferred seamlessly to the page. While I was scandalized that there was no singing crab, bestie fish, or dopey seagull, I was shocked and thrilled to discover the pain and despair the nameless little mermaid endured. The sea witch literally cut out the kid's tongue to take her voice; the mermaid felt blades tearing through the soles of her feet with every step; and on top of all that, the prince married some *other* lady, and Ariel threw herself into the ocean and *died?!* I gaped at my mother . . . then devoured "The Snow Queen," "The Tinderbox," and "The Steadfast Tin Soldier."

Like a warm fluffy cat, these old fairy tales dug their claws into me and wouldn't let go. Oooh, it hurts, but gimme more! I had no idea sad stories could be so satisfying. Not only did Andersen's "Little Mermaid" introduce me to big feels, but it provoked big questions in my little brain. How far would I go for love? And where do you go if you never arrive at that destination? Why was the movie so different from the book version? If Mr. Disney made a movie musical of "The Tinderbox" (and I really hoped he would), would he change the gory climax with the entire royal family dashed to pieces on the cobblestones of Copenhagen? If I were in charge of the movie, that would definitely stay in!

As I got older, I frequently revisited this collection of fairy tales and found that, unlike many of my childhood rereads, the stories grew with me, becoming meaningful in new ways. As an unpopular teen, I felt the mermaid's longing to escape a humdrum existence for a more romantic and fulfilling one. As a new adult trying to start a theatrical career, I understood the mermaid's drive to belong in an unreachable world, as well as her devastation when that world rejected her. Later, picking up the pieces after my broken engagement, I found solace in the mermaid's story: Why do women suffer so much pain in pursuit of our goals? Why is this poor kid in love with a man who treats her like a child? Why had I never realized that the mermaid had greater motivations in mind than true love? The prince was merely a vehicle toward gaining an immortal soul, after all. Maybe my life was also bigger than my failed relationship.

I treasure fairy tales for their constancy. As a kid of divorce, I moved with my parents from apartment to apartment and relationship to relationship. After college, I tumbled between odd jobs and creative projects. As an adult I've tried to corral my identity through hobbies picked up and dropped; I took piano and guitar lessons, I collected teapots, I wrote fanfic, I tried jogging, I became a cosplayer, I sang in cover bands. The list grew (and so did my debt). I've been told, "The only thing constant is change." Well, I fucking loathe that phrase. Fairy tales have always been there, and I know they will continue to be, whenever I need them.

Stories have been there for me my whole life, but the practice of storytelling solidified them as my life's work. From the moment I could read aloud from the page, I moved from just consuming stories to reinterpreting and sharing them. When my fifth-grade teacher noticed my penchant for the melodramatic, she recommended the local community theater, where I discovered the joy of telling stories onstage. To earn extra bucks after college, I took a job directing for a local youth theater, gratified to be fostering storytelling skills in others. I had no business in show business, but my theatrical toolkit easily transferred to my next role as a storyteller (and story consumer, and story maker) when I became a children's librarian.

One of the joys of librarianship is seeing how stories impact people. Something I learned very quickly about reading to young children is that they are very self-absorbed. As they should be! They are trying to make sense of so much new information and so many new experiences every day. When I run a storytime and invite kids to reflect on the books, they do so through their own lenses. "I have a dog too!" or "I like the lady in the pink dress, cuz I like pink." Sometimes they just want to tell you it's their birthday in seven months.

Now that you are laughing at a child's expense, go look in a mirror; because grown-ass people engage with stories in the same way. At least, they do with fairy tales.

When the COVID-19 pandemic shut down libraries and everything else, my outlets for storytelling suddenly vanished. So, I opened a TikTok account at the age of thirty-eight and began sharing my favorite old, weird fairy tales. My retellings were fast and loose. I dug up the strangest stories I could, improvising my way through them in the same way I shared them with friends over a pint. Then my nineties kid resurfaced, turning my storytelling into a mash-up of VH1's *Pop-Up Video* and *Mystery Science Theater*, flush with fun facts and wry commentary. If you're surprised to hear that people want to listen to a middle-aged librarian perform fairy tales on an app otherwise known for dancing, skin care tutorials, and pissing off Congress, I was surprised myself. Come to find out, I wasn't the only person finding consolation in fairy tales. Writer and historian Rebecca Solnit was also reading fairy tales online, because, as she said in an interview with *High Country News*, we were collectively finding ourselves "in the middle of a fairy tale." We were Hansel being fattened by the witch (or, in our case, a lot of sourdough bread), we were Briar Rose sleeping the day away, while social-distancing with thorny brambles and face shields. We were Cinderella, stuck at home sanitizing our groceries and dreaming of the ball. Maybe we needed to feel six years old again and taken care of; or maybe our isolation amplified our desire to relate to each other. I noticed how my online community reacted to my grown-up storytime the same way kids do at the library: by self-inserting. I'd share "The Sun, the Moon, and Talia," in which the king leaves his wife for a sleeping beauty, and someone would say, "My ex also left me for a 'less complicated' girl." I'd retell "Jack and the Beanstalk" and viewers would comment, "I'd probably sell a cow for magic beans if I ran out of my meds." "The Princess and the Pea," once an example of uber-pampered royalty, had an audience relating to her obvious sensory issues. I delighted in other adults rediscovering tales they grew up on within the frame of their modern experience, all the while puzzling over what made my adult and child storytime experiences so similar. Does hearing a story aloud awaken the instinct to connect to it personally? Have we never fully grown out of being little narcissists? Or do simple stories, like picture books and fairy tales, invite us to insert ourselves into them?

Maybe it's bigger than that. Fairy tales are a genre of folklore. Fairy tales are hard to define, but they are essentially fictional narratives that usually include magic or supernatural elements. Folklore is even tougher to define, even for those who've earned their Ph.D. in the subject. I like the definition proposed by scholar Lynne S. McNeill: "informally transmitted traditional culture," a deceptively simple phrase that contains multitudes. Within that definition, folklore is the stuff we share with each other that builds culture and shapes our identities. Folklore cannot proliferate without personal connection and reinterpretation, which makes it far more expansive than just Greek mythology and Pecos Bill. Telling someone a joke is folklore. Trying out a Keara Wilson dance with your friends is folklore. These are moments of personal connection over shared culture. Telling the joke with your own spin or adapting the dance to include your friends' secret handshake is folkloric reinterpretation. The way we do these things today is often by forwarding a tweet or a video and adding our own commentary to it. Thus memes function as modern digital folklore through both personal connection *and* reinterpretation. Sure, 2013's "Side Eyeing Chloe" is an inherently funny GIF on its own, but it wouldn't have lasted into Chloe's teen years if we weren't constantly texting it to friends to react to their mom's new boyfriend or that awkward thing their professor said. Fairy tales endure and persist for the same reason. In fact, you could argue that fairy tales are some of our first memes.

Think about it: Like memes, most widely known fairy tales do not have just one version. Look at "Cinderella." Before Hollywood rebooted her tale dozens of times over, storytellers of the past developed countless versions. We've *tried* to count them: British folklorist Marian Roalfe Cox recorded over three hundred versions in her 1893 Cinderella anthology. About sixty years later, ethnology professor Anna Birgitta Rooth reported up to five hundred versions in *The Cinderella Cycle*. But more have since been discovered, and today folklorists estimate that more than a thousand Cinderellas have emerged up and down both hemispheres! How did one soot-covered lady inspire so many twists on her story?

The answer is largely by word of mouth, what we call the oral tradition. Some tired wet nurse in medieval times told a Cinderella story to the young scullery maids as they cleaned. The maids grew up and shared it with their own children, modifying the plot with their own jokes or simply changing details they couldn't recall, like a game of Telephone. At the same time, the lord's kids were re-creating the story with their own privileged spin. Cindy made her way to merchants, soldiers, migrants, and more who brought her across borders. Hundreds of other fairy tales have gotten this around-the-world treatment. Many nations have their own white-as-snow and red-as-blood ladies, their own ogre-slaying tricksters, their own little lost children outwitting hungry witches. In this way, fairy tales were a lot like TikToks, Snap-Chats, and Instagram. Our ancestors shared their favorite stories socially, much like you and I forward a video we love to family and friends. Each subsequent storyteller then added in their own local color or inside jokes, just as we use a trending sound or image in our own videos but reinterpret it through our own experience. Folklorist Jack Zipes sums it up quite nicely in his 2008 study of "The Frog Prince" as a meme: "Memes change, shape shift, and have their own specific evolutionary history, as can be seen clearly in the evolution of certain folk and fairy tales." Across the globe, we found as much to relate to in Cinderella as we do in Evil Kermit; their basic hook is the same. Your Cinderella may wear Air Jordans while mine is in Louboutins; your Evil Kermit wants you to Insta-stalk your ex and mine wants me to skip my cousin's baby shower. Either way, we both feel the allure of wealth, exclusivity, and giving in to the dark voices in our heads.

A big difference between fairy tales and memes is that these days the latter are perpetually popular among adults, but fairy tales are largely regarded as a form used to teach and entertain children. Sure, writers like Gregory Maguire and Helen Oyeyemi retell tales for adult readers to acclaim. Disney adults will always stan a princess story. But when I share a dark, sexy, or bizarre old fairy tale, my audience often asks, "What's the moral of this?" or "People read this horrifying story to their children?" Fairy tales do help kids make their way in the world, and at one point in European history they were adapted with this very idea in mind: to teach children the morals their societies preached. Listen to your mother, do not wander off the path, be kind and gentle for love to prevail. While fairy tales were used as cautionary tales as far back as the Middle Ages, the use of them as such accelerated in Europe as notions of child-rearing (and with it, children's literature) were formalized. In seventeenth century France, Charles Perrault popularized several of our most well-known fairy tales today ("Little Red Riding Hood," "Cinderella," "Sleeping Beauty"). Some of his success was assessing how the popular stories shared among the peasantry could be distorted to instruct women and children of the middle and upper classes. In doing so, he reframed some of their messages and instilled his own biases against women and poor folk. (In the meantime, his female contemporaries were subverting those very ideas with much more fun but now largely forgotten fairy tales.)

Jacob and Wilhelm Grimm accidentally revolutionized how we regard fairy tales; they initially were more concerned with documenting Germanic culture than with teaching little children how to be quiet and pious. But a misconception about their collection led their audience to share their tales with children. Realizing this would mean a lot more buck for their bang, the Grimms leaned into it and purposefully adjusted the stories for a child audience. Victorians ran with this example, and the practice of steamrolling the adult out of fairy tales continued in children's books, and eventually on the big screen under the Disney name. Since Hollywood is less interested in people and more interested in profits and conformity, they've kept regurgitating these stories, reinforcing a childlike, very white, and very heteronormative perception of fairy tales.

My mission has been to break those bonds. I love telling fairy tales to adults, because when you push past the Disney of it all, fairy tales are about people and situations that are messy as fuck. They provide comfort and relevance to our modern adult lives, especially when you dig into the sprawling diversity of the tales and the uncomfortable situations they interrogate. Snow White isn't always #TradWife material; in Lebanon, they have a version where Snow scares off ghouls. I love that take because women have had to defend themselves from monsters since day one. In Puerto Rico, Snow marries one of the dwarves, because love and attraction are more nuanced than the one version of Prince Charming we usually get. Oh yeah, and she isn't always white as snow, because she's existed in the imaginations of the global majority long before the Grimms popularized the "skin as white as snow" trope! Men have fallen in love with dead-ish ladies not just in Germany, but in Romania and Egypt and Gabon and India and Argentina and Louisiana. Disney never went woke; women of all shades do not want to be left alone with strange men, alive or dead!

I have tracked down hundreds of twists on popular fairy tales in search of the ones that will resonate most with modern adults, seeking connections and universalities. Tracing different versions of fairy tales is a delight because discovering them is a lot like being the hero *in* a fairy tale. The experience is like a Hansel and Gretel story: You start with a tale you love, and then you follow its bread crumbs through the woods to find new versions, using a handy system called the Aarne-Thompson-Uther Index (or the

ATU Index), a sort of card catalog for folktales. Each tale has a number assigned to it, and we use those numbers to track down how the tale has developed around the world. You may think these crumbs will lead home to a fairy tale's origins. But time, like the birds, has eaten up the path, leaving most fairy tale origins a mystery.

Other tales are on their way to being lost. Like dying languages, they have grown rare because they are told so infrequently. Some tales only exist handwritten in archival boxes, where modern folklorists and storytellers sometimes unearth rare gems. Two of my favorite such researchers are Dr. Csenge Zalka, who was the first to translate a nineteenth century folktale from the Carpathian Mountains featuring a disabled princess (whose disability is not demonized or cured), and Pete Jordi Wood, whose mission is to locate the queerness in folktales that once made them "too obscene" to print.

That being said, certain stories last not only because a folklorist deemed them worthy to be in a book, but because they become cultural touchpoints. We see this reflected again in digital folklore. Some memes are one-hit wonders and others can't stop giving farewell tours: your Rickrolls, your "It's Gonna Be May," your "THIS IS FINE." These timeless memes are the Cinderellas and Snow Whites of our age. All of us, regardless of language, generation, and experience, fiercely relate to a cartoon dog just trying to enjoy his morning coffee while the world burns down around him. It helps us laugh at our own fear. But while you're taking that feeling and doomscrolling, I'm spiraling into the dark web of fairy tales: where a Celtic Snow White's *biological* mother tries to eat her heart and liver; where Little Red Riding Hood accidentally eats her own grandma; and where a Greek Cinderella watches her sisters kill and eat their mother. (Is anyone else hungry, or is it just me?)

The reason I like paging through weird and gory fairy tales as much as weird and gory Reddit threads is that fairy tales bridge all the gaps doomscrolling creates. Fairy tales are a vital art form for a society of adults who find themselves perpetually divided and isolated. I share these old stories online to remind folks that there were never any "good old days"—we've always feared being able to feed our children or finding ourselves in bed with an ogre. Yeah, kids are probably online too much (frankly, so are you), but fears of brain rot aren't new—consider the number of fools in everyone's folklore. When we reconnect with fairy tales, we find a way to hold hands with our frazzled neighbors and anxious ancestors across oceans and backward in time. You have an awkward relationship with your dad's second, much younger wife? So did some kid in Italy four hundred years ago. You saw a lady shoplift diapers from Walmart? Who cares? Corporate giants are still hoarding record profits, while us Jacks are forced to live off increasingly expensive beans. For four thousand years, we've entertained the idea of animals marrying people. Yes, there is evidence that "Beauty and the Beast" stories are actually that old! (Think about that next time you're contemplating the widely acknowledged sex appeal of Disney's foxy Robin Hood.) During a time when dating apps present overwhelming options, it is sorta comforting to know that way before the birth of Christ, some single lady like me also wondered if she should pack it up and just enter a lifelong commitment with her dog.

In reading the following selection of fairy tales, you too may recognize both your ancestors and contemporaries as kin. I'll start us off where we all begin: bearing the brunt of our parents' dysfunction. In Part 1, "F*cked Up Family Trees," we'll judge whether we could forgive and forget the sins of our fathers in France's "Peau d'Âne." In "Bâpkhâdi," we'll sort out the cycle of childhood abandonment, and we'll cringe at "The Juniper Tree," a family drama of biblical proportions. In-law fighting gets deadly in Lithuania's "Eglė, the Queen of Serpents," and "Blanca Rosa and the Forty Thieves," a Chilean-Spanish tale, reminds us of the superiority of found family.

In parts 2 and 3, we move on to romance and marriage. We'll meet the literal monsters we fear waiting for us on the other side of a dating app across three different continents. You'll read how Oscar Wilde warned us about parasocial relationships well before we had a term for that weird phenomena. We'll meet horrifying bachelors in both South Africa and South Asia. We'll deal with the uncomfortable skeletons in our partner's closet in Vietnam's "Hon Vong Phu." And if fucking an animated fox isn't your thing, you can dally with a sweet fish, a floating donkey head, a loyal buzzard, a kinky serpent, and the world's most eligible cat.

In Parts 4 and 5, we'll binge on humanity's base instincts. In the section "What's Your Body Count?" we'll focus on violence, starting in Scotland, where Molly Whuppie forces us to face the barbarous side of heroism. In Hans Christian Andersen's "Big Claus and Little Claus," we'll leave the mermaids in the ocean and read how long it's been in fashion to value profits over people. Korea's "Kongjwi and Patjwi" uses Cinderella to shine a light on themes of brutality begetting more brutality. In Italy's "The Flayed Old Woman," we'll indulge in the ongoing battle between aging and beauty, and society's obsession with true crime shows its folk origins in Germany's "The Maid of Wildenloh." Lastly, in Part 5, "Crappily Ever After," we'll cringe at some delightfully disgusting folktales. As long as people have been pissing, shitting, menstruating, and ejaculating, we've had fairy tales about it! The next time Netflix recommends *The Human Centipede 3*, you can comfort yourself with the assurance that human storytelling has always been raunchy and squeamish AF!

By the time you close this book (no doubt to open your phone), I think you'll agree with me: The true magic of fairy tales is that they never go out of style, because they'll always reflect the people who are reading them. At some point in your life, you might have been the persecuted princess, unfairly struggling while lazy colleagues flourish. Maybe you were the lonely child sent to stay with your scary grandmother for a weekend while your parents "worked through some things." Perhaps you've been someone else's fairy godmother, hyping them up for their big event. Maybe you've even been the jealous stepsister. (I know I have.) Within these pages, you will find characters going through the exact same things and coming out of them much worse than you did. So tuck in for some gleeful schadenfreude, and remember: You never needed a magic wand or a handsome prince to make your life a fairy tale. You're already living one!

A Quick Note

I use the term *fairy tales* loosely. But in this book, you'll read a variety of different story types. Each of these definitions paraphrase folklorists and all-around cool ladies Drs. Jeana Jorgensen, Sara Cleto, and Brittany Warman.

Folktales: Fictional narratives largely spread through oral storytelling. An umbrella term that includes fairy tales, fables, narrative jokes, fabliaux (bawdy tales: think Chaucer), and formulaic tales (think "The Little Red Hen").

Fairy Tales: Fictional narratives with magical or transformative elements. Some are folktales, handed down through the oral tradition ("Hansel and Gretel" or "Cinderella"), while some are literary fairy tales, which are original narratives inspired by folklore ("The Little Mermaid" or "The Happy Prince").

Myths: Ancient narratives regarded as truth by specific societies, including sacred stories and origin and creation tales ("Cupid and Psyche" or trickster stories).

Legends: Narratives, often tied to a real person, place, or thing, that may or may not be told as truthful. They range in scope and setting from old legends such as that of King Arthur, to urban legends such as the 2016 creepy clown sightings.

Trigger Warnings

"Daddy's Little Donkey-Skin"—Attempted incest, death of an animal.

"The Devil Made Her Do It"—Dead moms, abortion, gory filicide, desecration of a corpse, cannibalism. (It's the grimmest of Grimm!)

"Thumberella"—Poverty, abandonment, infanticide, breastfeeding tweens. (Wow!)

"Snakes Who Cannot Shed Their Kin"—Child abuse, gruesome murder, and, like, a billion snakes!

"Blanca Rosa, Mother of Thieves"—Death of an animal (again), desecration of corpse (you saw that coming), a fairytale roofie. (Jesus!)

"Love Is for the Birds"—Suicide of an animal. (SORRY!)

"Love Is Like a Tree"—Honestly, this one's not too bad. Oh wait: Suicide of a tree?

"Love Is a Family Affair"—Accidental incest. (Oops).

"Love Is a Revolution"—Murder and more murder!

"Love Is Dead"—Desecration of a corpse AGAIN.

"Till There Was Mew"—Death of an animal, but it's not so bad!

"When a Bird Loves a Woman"—Death of an animal, but he had it coming!

"Mule Be in My Heart"—A king beats up an old lady. (Does specificity make it better or worse?)

"My Carp Will Go On"—Murder and once again: suicide, maybe?

"Master and Serpent"—Implied sexual violence, off-page gore. (Why do I like these stories?)

"The X-Treme Sport of Giant Killing"—Death of animals, but this time it's really bad . . .

"How to Trick Friends and Execute People"—More dead animals. (It's a folklore thing.) Plus, murder and suicide but, like, it's funny, I guess?

"Never Cross a Cinderella"—Cannibalism and murder, blah blah blah.

"Skin-Deep"—Domestic abuse, more body horror.

"No Small Peat"—*Kill Bill* but it's the Middle Ages.

"Good Soup"—Pee. (Well, that's harmless.)

"The Stench of Embarrassment"—Farts. (That's it? What a lark!)

"It Snot What You Think"—Molestation by ghost, semen in awkward places. (Aw man, things were going so well.)

"Kalendrin, the Party Princess"—Recreational drugs and alcohol on your period. (Just another Friday night at my house.)

"The Pongo's Prophecy"—Poop, but you'll love it.

So . . . who's still here?

Part 1

F*CKED UP
FAMILY TREES

*Blood is thicker,
if more dysfunctional,
than water.*

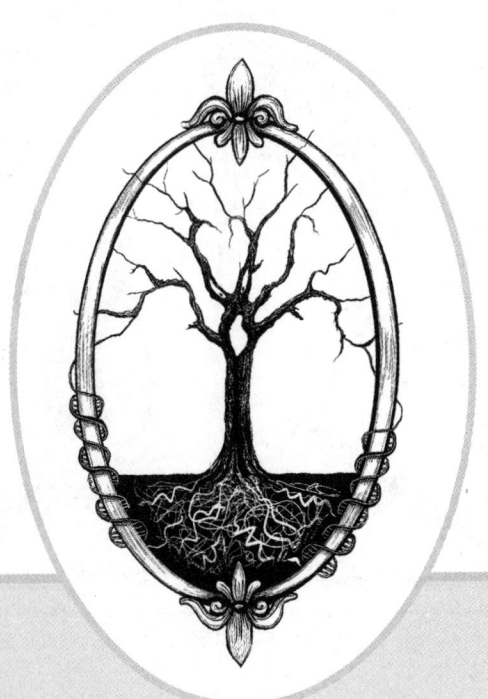

DADDY'S LITTLE DONKEY-SKIN

(CHARLES PERRAULT'S "PEAU D'ÂNE")

ONCE UPON A TIME, THERE WAS A DONKEY WHO pooped gold coins.

Customarily, this tale would introduce the royal family first. But here at *F*cked Up Fairy Tales*, we don't bury the lede.

The donkey belonged to the royal family. He was treated like a king himself; he occupied a very fancy stall, had an ass-ortment of ass-istants, and one ass-umes he brought in a lot of tourism dollars as the kingdom's most adorable slot machine. His only assignment was to fund the royal coffers with his bankable buttocks.

I will stop ass-ailing you with these superior posterior puns. After a few more:

The kingdom was happy and successful, with money literally coming out the wazoo. The palace safe-deposit boxes contained a veritable buttload of coin! Limitless gold poop nuggets provided a sprawling offering of public services. Sure, neighboring countries and petty thieves attempted to force the donkey-bank from the king's hands. But all he had to do was feed the animal a laxative, and boom! His public safety needs were paid in full.

Andrew Lang made the donkey's superpower more palatable to his Victorian audience in *The Grey Fairy Book* (1900). He changed the donkey's mode of payout to its very big ears, rather than what must have been a very sore butthole.

The king stayed grounded and likable despite his endless wealth. He was a benevolent leader and adored by his subjects. His wisdom and kindness extended to his court and staff. His queen was the most beautiful woman in the land, with charm to boot. Their daughter was the reflection of her. This royal family was flying high.

So, when tragedy struck, it struck hard.

The queen suddenly came down with a mysterious and incurable illness. Every ounce of donkey dung was invested in the country's best doctors and the latest innovative medical treatments. But the queen knew she would never recover. One night, close to the end, she called her husband to her bedside.

"My dear," she uttered, her voice still melodious in malady, "it is time to have a difficult conversation: You will soon be a widower. I know you will lead our nation through a beautiful and appropriate mourning period. But when that is done, you must remarry."

The king was inconsolable. "Don't speak of such things! I'd rather follow you into the grave than find a second-rate second wife!"

"Now, now," the queen murmured, stroking his hair. "You must consider the future. We need an heir to the throne."

The king looked up. "Our daughter is intelligent and responsible. Could she not rule after I am gone?"

The royal couple considered this for a moment. Then they burst into laughter at the thought of a girl in charge. The queen wiped tears of mirth from her eyes. "Oh dear, you do know how to make a dying woman smile. But please, promise me you'll only marry a woman whose beauty and charm exceeds my own. I want nothing less for you."

The king made this promise, and, thus contented, the queen took her final breath.

The queen didn't actually give a fuck about her husband or heirs. She couldn't stomach the idea of him remarrying and thought she could prevent it. Hubris, thy name is this lady!

To say the king greatly mourned his wife is an incredible understatement. He sank into a deep depression, wandering the halls, refusing meals, and skipping meetings. This man had not only lost his wife, but the Greatest Wife of All! So, without modern psychology and SSRIs, the king quite literally lost his mind with grief.

The royal council intervened as the king's mourning dragged on. They pressured him to vet potential mates. The king pushed back, explaining the promise he had made to his wife. His councillors sent along portraits of possible matches anyway. The king declared the portraits an insult to the late queen.

"Look," his councillors implored, "we're in a real bind here. Your daughter is of marrying age and has a list of suitors a mile long, seeing as she is just as gorgeous and personable as your late wife. But we can't marry her off to another kingdom without making sure you secure yourself an heir!"

A light bulb went off in the king's addled brain. "You're right. My daughter *is* the picture of my wife, inside and out." He cocked his head, considering. "In fact, you could even argue she is *more* attractive, having youth on her side." He smiled for the first time since he'd lost his wife. "Bring her here!"

The princess was summoned to the council's chambers at once. "Are you all right, Father?" she asked, taking his hands. "How can I help?"

The king observed his daughter's luminous skin, the golden locks streaming over her delicate shoulders, the tawny eyes wide with sympathy, so like his deceased wife's. Suddenly he imagined himself back in his prime, courting the love of his life. "Call the calligrapher," he ordered. "Tell the royal tailors to rustle up their best bridal lace and book the finest lute player in the land! I have found my queen!"

The councillors were repulsed, and the princess was horrified. She protested, "Dad, you can't marry me. It's a sin against God! And it's gross, Dad! It's just gross!"

This example of a man trying to date ~~a woman young enough to be~~ **his daughter opens dozens of similar fairy tales.** The story is a great indicator that we have always feared the truth of sexual abuse: that it often comes from the people we think we know. Despite its scary situation, it is one of my favorite fairy tale types, because it usually features its heroine saving herself. The Grimms' "Allerleirauh," Giovanni Francesco Straparola's "Doralice," and Giambattista Basile's "The She-Bear" are other great examples.

The king couldn't be convinced otherwise. He was so deep in his inadvertently incestuous fantasy that he couldn't comprehend his daughter's negative reaction. He brought in a priest (one more interested in ascending the court than ascending to heaven) to assure her that everything was fine. The councillors gave up the fight. So, the princess confided in her most powerful ally: her fairy godmother, the Lilac Fairy.

Fairy godmothers are very common in French fairy tales of this period. Just like real godmothers, their usefulness varies.

The princess took a sheep-drawn carriage **(yes, you read that correctly)** to her godmother's home. Lilac was disgusted. "You came to the right person!" she assured the girl. "We fairies get you mortals out of all kinds of messes. **(And into them.)** What you need to do is make your marriage contingent on an impossible demand."

"What do I ask for?" the princess worried. "What on earth is too difficult for the most powerful man in the kingdom to obtain?"

"Something magical, of course!" The fairy snapped her fingers. "I've got it! Demand he commission a gown for you; a gown the color of the sky!"

The princess narrowed her eyes doubtfully. "In other words, a blue gown? A blue gown is an impossible demand?"

"No, no!" The girl's godmother laughed. "The sky is not merely blue: It is a myriad of ever-changing colors! Cornflower, slate, or ash by day, navy and ebony by night! No mortal has the power to make a gown the color of the sky."

The princess was convinced. Upon returning home, she demanded a sky-colored gown before she could even consider agreeing to her father's proposal.

Well, I don't know how he did it, but the king came through. He assembled the best tailors in the land and ordered them to figure this gown out, upon penalty of death! **(It seems his grief also screwed up his formerly peaceful ruling style.)** The tailors were so terrified, they managed to produce the sky-colored gown in a mere two days.

This stinks of a deal with the devil, who frequently pops up to offer his services in these types of fairy-tale situations. I smell a companion novella!

The princess wasted no time driving her sheep back to her fairy godmother's to share the bad news. "So, what do we do now?"

The Lilac Fairy instantly had a new suggestion. "Ask him for a gown the color of the moon."

The princess tried to clean out her ears in a delicate manner. "I'm sorry, did I hear you right? You want me to do the exact same thing we just tried?"

"I think my mistake was picking something we can plainly see," the fairy replied. "But the moon? No one knows what it really looks like! No one is setting foot on that thing for another three hundred years!"

"Really?" the princess asked.

"Oops." Lilac blushed. "Forget I said anything."

Not one day later, the royal tailors produced the moon gown. Its dusky raw silk shone silver at night. The silhouette even changed shape when the princess moved, reflecting light in smaller and larger slivers.

The princess drove her sheep back to Lilac's house. "He did it again!" she said, with an accusatory note coloring her tone.

"No matter!" the Lilac Fairy breezed. "Ask him for a gown the color of the sun."

I honestly think my non-fairy godmother Aunt Sue would have come up with a better plan.

"You're joking," the princess snapped.

"Look!" Lilac was getting frazzled too. "At the very least it will buy me some time to figure out another escape!"

The king's tailors put together a haute couture piece, hand-sewn with gold and diamonds, that emitted blinding sunbeams. It was at this very moment in history that sunglasses were invented.

Later that evening at the royal palace, Lilac said to the princess, "I think I've been going about this all wrong!" The princess swallowed a retort and nodded.

"My mistake was having you demand your father *produce* something. What you need to do is demand he *destroy* something. Something he cares about. Something he relies on for his power and wealth. His greatest ass-et, if you know what I mean." She winked.

The princess felt a rush of hope. "His gold-shitting donkey!"

"His gold-shitting donkey!" her godmother affirmed. "Demand that the king slay the animal and give you its skin. It doesn't matter how head-over-heels he has fallen for you. No man will sacrifice his bottom line for a piece of ass!"

The princess set out to see her dad. "I have a good feeling about this!"

The fairy waved and called after her, "If he gives you that donkey-skin, I'll eat my foot."

I think you know what happened next. Open up, Lilac!

* * *

AFTER THE ass-ass-ination of the donkey **(okay, I'm done)**, an escape plan was the only option left for the princess. The Lilac Fairy used her magical abilities to help the girl out. **(Finally!)** "First off, you need a disguise," she instructed. "Let's not waste this poor animal's sacrifice. Use the donkey-skin as a cloak. No one would believe a princess would wear something so hideous."

The fairy gathered the princess's belongings, including the celestial gowns, into a magical trunk. "Take my magic wand," the fairy continued, "and make haste on foot until you can walk no longer. I will make sure you are invisible to your father and his men while you are within the bounds of the kingdom."

Seems like this talent could have been used earlier. It would've saved time, money, and the donkey.

"Your belongings will follow you unseen underground. When you need them, tap the ground with the wand three times, and they will appear." The princess dirtied her royally pampered skin with soot, kissed her godmother goodbye, and left the palace by moonlight.

The princess traversed a long distance before she attempted to seek shelter. The kindness of strangers only went so far. The wild appearance of her donkey-skin garment combined with days on the road made people pity her enough to feed her, but not so much that they wanted to open their doors to her. It wasn't until she reached a town a few kingdoms over that she met a farmer's wife willing to put her up—if she was willing to work.

"I've been looking for someone to take the rougher jobs off my hands," the farmer's wife told her. "You'll manage the fowl and the pigs and take care of the dishes. The only room available is rather cramped, but you don't seem like the type to put on airs."

Not anymore! the princess thought.

The princess was put into the kitchen, where she gratefully took on her assortment of odd jobs. However, she had trouble making friends. She was so mocked by the farmhands, they didn't bother to learn her name. They called her "Donkey-Skin," and considered her the most disgusting girl in the kingdom.

Long gone are the days when we named people after their favorite clothes. I suppose "Pretty Yoga Pants," "Mr. Shorts-in-Winter," and "Little Bluey Sweatshirt" don't have the same ring to them.

The men of the staff harassed her with crude jokes until they got tired of their own wisecracks. But the princess remained pleasant and was a hard worker. So, the farmer's wife became her guardian (and you don't mess with a farm woman).

After a time, Donkey-Skin developed a routine for herself. She'd dutifully finish her work, then treat herself to some me-time by a private fountain where she could bathe and feel bad for herself. On Sundays she'd stay home and tap the ground with her magic wand to summon her chest of belongings. Then she'd spend the time playing dress-up, fondly recalling the days when she didn't have to disguise herself in the hide of a sacrificial animal. She had to admit that the three gowns her godmother had pitched looked fantastic on her. The sky gown matched whatever time of day she was wearing it; the moon gown bathed her in a silvery glow; and the sun gown? Well, that was just baller.

One day, however, the princess wasn't the only one enjoying her solo fashion show. You see, the farm was situated between the royal palace and the woods where the prince liked to hunt. The young man would occasionally stop by the farmhouse to rest and sup on his way home. On one of these visits, he decided to explore the property. When he came to the door of Donkey-Skin's hovel, he leaned down and peered through the keyhole. Imagine his shock when he saw a princess in a sun-shining golden gown!

Imagine his greater surprise when he went blind in one eye.

As he packed up for the rest of his ride home, the prince asked the farmer's wife, "Who are you hosting in the tiny room near the stables?"

If the farmer's wife was curious why the heir to the throne was snooping around her barn, she didn't show it. "I believe you're referring to Donkey-Skin's hovel."

The prince's nose wrinkled. "What a frightful name. That can't be the beautiful woman I saw."

"You have a peculiar opinion of what's beautiful!" the farmer's wife retorted.

Both parties left this conversation more confused than when they had begun it. The prince went home, but he couldn't get the image of the dazzling princess out of his mind. He cursed himself for not barging in and introducing himself like any other fairy-tale prince would. "Pathetic, respectful bore!" He vowed to himself he'd go back the next day to meet her. But lovesickness struck him so hard, he was bedridden with a fever the following morning.

Our princess goes through hell or high water to avoid marrying her father, but this guy is bedridden at the mere idea of not getting the girl. Is this what "Charming" looks like?

The royal family became consumed with the prince's mysterious ailment. Doctors, mystical healers, all were brought in to diagnose the young man. Common treatments didn't help. "Perhaps it's not a sickness of the mind, but of the heart," they suggested.

The queen mom began pressing her son for his heart's desire. "Is it the crown you want? If so, your father will immediately abdicate! Is it a princess you desire? No matter who she is, we will make the union happen! I'll do anything to spare your life, my child!"

The prince took a shuddering breath. "Tell Donkey-Skin to bake me a cake."

A scuffle of laughter broke out from the royal guards minding the doorway. "Excuse me?" the queen snapped. "What is so funny?"

"Nothing, Your Majesty," one replied, apologizing. "It just surprised us, is all. Donkey-Skin is the most bizarre woman in the kingdom."

"I don't care if she's a wart on the jester's left butt cheek!" the queen clapped back. "If my ailing son wants her to bake a cake, she'll bake it immediately!"

It's hard to say if the princess knew much of this besotted prince prior to his request for cake. Perhaps she had seen him riding. Perhaps she heard him outside the day he took a looksee, and opened the door a crack to catch him sneaking away. Or maybe she was just tired of chasing geese around all day and saw an out. Whatever the reason, she threw herself into making the best cake she could, right in her tiny hovel. She even dressed up to do the baking, donning a silver corsage, a very fancy green petticoat with silver trimmings, and a little gold-and-emerald ring on her hand.

Petticoats refer to a waist-down undergarment, so I thought the princess was indulging in some topless housekeeping. But petticoats also referred to a full-body shift when this was written in the seventeenth century. Either way, she's baking in her lingerie.

When the cake was delivered to the prince, he seized it, smushing it into his mouth with the haste of a toddler on his first birthday. Then he sputtered and spat something into his hand. It was the princess's tiny golden ring.

The prince put the ring under his pillow, only taking it out to study when he was alone. The ring was clearly made for the fingers of a fine lady. How did it get into Donkey-Skin's cake?

The prince's doctors figured out that the prince was suffering from lovesickness. His parents pestered their son for the name of the girl he was pining for. "It doesn't matter if she's of the lowest rank," the queen assured him. "If it will make you happy, we'll embrace her as your wife!"

The prince handed his mother the ring. "I wish to marry the woman who fits this ring."

Yes! This is a Cinderella tale. Cinderella is one of our most variable folktales, and the princess doesn't always sport a glass or gold slipper. Nose-piercings, diamond anklets, and magical bracelets have also been worn by the maiden.

The royal family papered the town with advertisements in search of a bride who fit the ring. They began with all princesses in traveling distance. When none of them fit, they summoned the duchesses, marquesses, baronesses, and all the other "esses." All tried whatever they could to slim their fingers, but none could shove their digits past the first knuckle. Next up, the peasant girls were brought in; obviously they were all too fat-fingered as well.

Tiny fingers, tiny feet. Most Cinderellas continue the tradition of fat-shaming women (particularly the poor ones), no matter the accessory!

Finally, after they had exhausted all other girls, the prince spoke up. "You haven't brought Donkey-Skin."

The prince's servants laughed. "Of course we didn't. She's the grossest!"

"But she made me the cake where I found the ring," the prince reasoned. It was good reasoning.

While this hullabaloo was happening, the princess was readying herself for the inevitable summons. Once again, she pulled on her fancy petticoat and corsage, then hid those designer pieces under her donkey-skin cloak. She was ushered to the prince's bedside as everyone in the court hid their snickers behind handkerchiefs. Even the prince, who had a suspicion that Donkey-Skin was The One, was taken aback at how grotesque she was in person. "You're the girl who lives in the tiny hovel at the farm?"

The princess nodded, and the donkey's head nodded along with her. "I am."

The prince grimaced. "Well, let's get this over with."

The princess let her sleeve fall back, and the entire court gasped at the flawlessly smooth, slim fingers exposed. The prince slid the emerald ring onto her hand with no trouble at all. And in a show of fashionable timing not even Met Gala Queen Rihanna herself could compete with, the princess let the donkey-skin shimmy from her shoulders, revealing her true wealth and beauty (... and underwear. So, Rihanna dressed by Thierry Mugler).

The girl was immediately smothered in embraces from both the prince and his parents. All hurriedly proposed marriage. Before the princess could even open her mouth to accept, the ceiling opened, and the Lilac Fairy descended into the room upon a chariot woven from wildflowers. "Have I got some gossip for you!" she declared, revealing the whole skeevy backstory. "But it all worked out!" she concluded. "You shall live Happily Ever After!"

This moment indicates to me that the Lilac Fairy knew the girl's fate this whole time. All-knowing fairies and prophecies are also common motifs in French fairy tales. Frustrating for a princess trying to escape a bad situation. But a hell of an entrance for the fairy with all the secrets!

But whatever became of Donkey-Skin's father?

In the time that had passed, the man had come back into possession of his wits. He eventually gave up on the promise he'd made his late wife and remarried a perfectly lovely widow. Then he received an invitation to a wedding a few kingdoms over. The bride's name was not disclosed, adding a little mystery to the event!

When the king laid eyes on the bride, he immediately recognized his daughter. He burst into tears as the princess embraced him. "I had no idea I'd be attending your wedding!" he told her.

"I know," the Lilac Fairy interjected. "That was my idea."

Of course it was!

✳ ✳ ✳

SOURCE: Charles Perrault, *The Fairy Tales of Charles Perrault*.

Wanna read more French fairy tales? Try *Beauties, Beasts and Enchantment: Classic French Fairy Tales*, edited and translated by Jack Zipes.

THE DEVIL MADE HER DO IT

The Grimms' "The Juniper Tree"

Long, long ago—about two thousand years ago, in fact—

[*record scratch*] What? The Grimms rarely attach dates to their story, making this a jarring opening. The time frame implies a biblical setting—and the plot might as well be from Revelations.

—there lived a wealthy merchant and his wife Mariah. The couple had everything they could possibly want, but for one thing: a child. Mariah prayed from dawn to dusk, but every month she was visited by the Red Sea with no sign of it parting.

Childless couples introduce hundreds of fairy tale plots. The sheer number of times I've read this exposition is exhausting. Though not as exhausting as navigating all the appointments, expenses, calendars, not-always-sexy sexual positions, and insecurities that accompany a difficult conception.

One snowy day, Mariah was standing beneath the twisted juniper tree outside her home, peeling an apple. The knife slipped and pierced her finger. A few drops of blood hit the stark white snow. The warm colors against the bright expanse reminded the woman of her one desire. "My greatest wish is for a child as red as blood and white as snow!" she lamented.

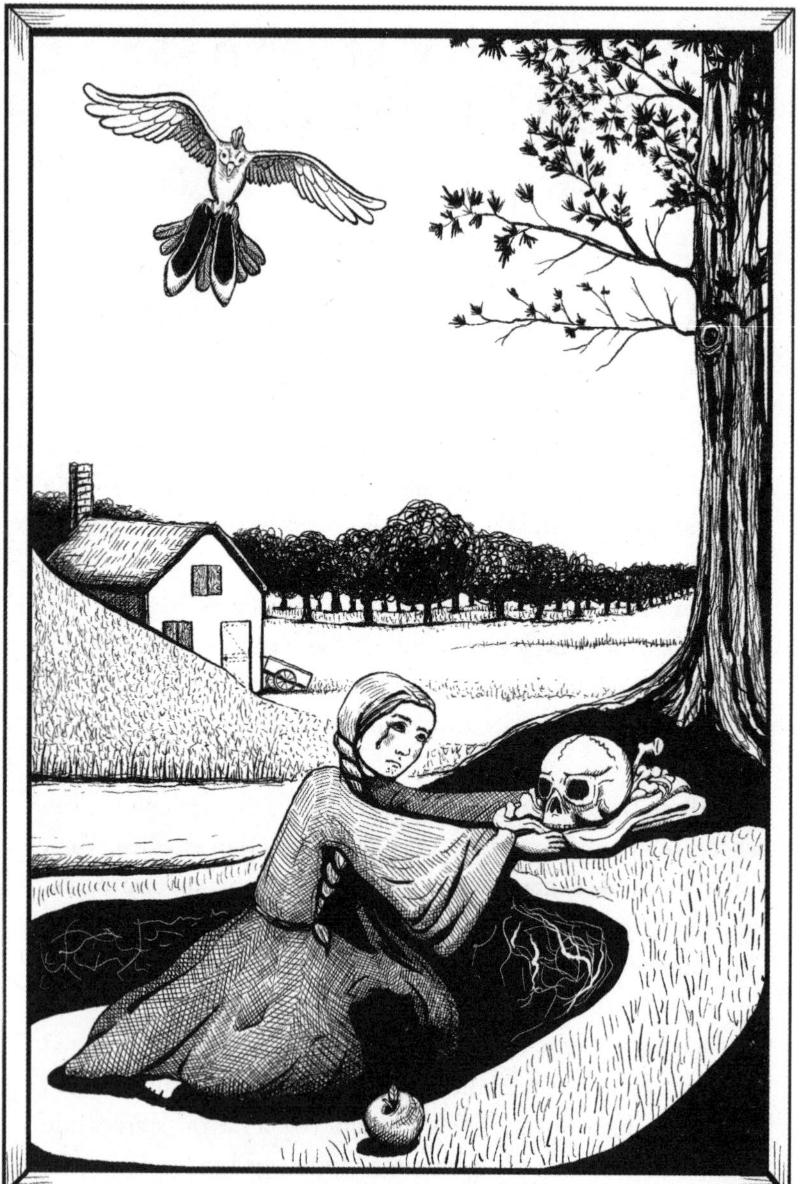

Did we just take a sharp turn into Snow White? Yes and no. This tale shares some themes with Snow White, as you'll see. But yearning for children and lovers as white as snow and red as blood pops up in lots of tales, such as Norway's "Twelve Wild Ducks" and Giambattista Basile's "The Crow." General imagery of blood on white is also pervasive; see "The Goose Girl" and "Faithful John." A predominant interpretation of this symbolism is Francisco Vaz da Silva's theory that this color contrast symbolizes the stages of a woman's life, especially in regard to sexual attraction and fertility: the blood of birth, menstruation, deflowerment, and the flush of youth.

As soon as Mariah uttered the words, her shoulders relaxed, her jaw unclenched, and she felt certain she'd get her wish. Her woman's intuition was right: she became pregnant.

A month passed; the snow melted, and the baby was the size of a wee poppy seed. The grass grew in the second month, and the baby grew to raspberry-size; flowers bloomed in the third month, and the baby bloomed into a perfect little plum. Birdsong ushered in month five, and Mariah sang lullabies to the pear in her womb. The trees fruited in month six, and the fruit baby grew to the size of, well, a vegetable! A real *corny* kid, you might say.

During this sixth month, Mariah had second thoughts. She worried her child might have been conceived by unnatural means. She and her husband had been trying for ages to get pregnant; suddenly she makes one wish under a juniper tree and it comes true?* What were the chances of that?

Not to mention, she spilled blood to do it, eating The Most Tempting Fruit. That's a demon baby secured by blood magic!

---

* *Juniper berries were historically used as both birth control and abortifacients.*

In month seven, the baby continued on its veggie track, growing to cauliflower-size. Mariah privately consulted a midwife, and returned to the juniper tree, which was now bursting with berries. She stood, entranced by the bursts of blue among the sharp needles. She remembered the wise woman's advice and fingered a berry. She hesitantly laid one on her tongue and swallowed. She ate two more, then a mouthful, then a handful. She stopped only when she couldn't reach the rest. Then she sat under the tree and wept at what she'd done.

One day during the eighth month, Mariah cradled her belly, now round with a kicking squash. The baby survived, and not only that, refused to choose from a fruit/vegetable binary. Baby said, "I can be both!" However, Mariah was sick and bedridden. She grasped her husband's hand one night. "If I die, bury me under the juniper tree!" The merchant, unaware of her poisonous picnic, chalked the macabre request up to mood swings.

In the ninth month, the leaves rusted and fell, and unto Mariah a watermelon-sized child was born. A boy as white as snow and red as blood, just as she specified. Mariah took one look at him, named him Jonas, then made her Exodus, dying of joy.

Best-case scenario, where fairy tale death is concerned.

The merchant fulfilled his wife's last wish, burying her beneath the looming juniper tree. He grieved for a long time. But eventually he found love again, with an ebony-haired woman named Heddie. Heddie also bore a child, with less seasonal world-building: a little girl she named Marlene. The siblings grew close. But as the boy approached adolescence, Heddie increasingly resented her stepson. She couldn't contain her antipathy; she took it out on Jonas, who went from snow-white to black-and-blue.

The Brothers Grimm launched the "wicked stepmother" into stock character status. Some of their most famous folktales began with villainous *mothers*, such as early versions of "Snow White" and "Hansel and Gretel." But as Wilhelm revised the tales over the years, he changed the bad moms to bad stepmoms for a couple of reasons: (1) he was revising the tales with children in mind, and felt they'd be less scarred by a mean stepmother than an abusive mother; and (2) the folktales were meant to represent German culture, and he didn't want people walking away thinking German motherhood could be so nasty.

Heddie's resentment was fueled by Jonas's likely inheritance. She grew paranoid that her husband would leave his riches to the boy and none to their daughter. By Jonas's tenth year, Heddie's resentment grew so powerful, it caught the attention of humanity's most famous shit-stirrer: Lucifer, THE EVIL ONE.

"The Evil One" is a moniker for the devil that we should bring back. Lucifer was so full of himself, he got thrown out of heaven. There's no way his diva theatrics ended there. That guy would one hundred percent make everyone in hell call him THE EVIL ONE.

One day, Heddie picked apples **(the Most Tempting Fruit!)** while the children were at school. She dropped one and it rolled away from her. As she bent to retrieve it, she heard someone drawl, "Wouldn't you love to see that boy's head roll?"
Heddie looked up. She found a tiny man sitting on her left shoulder. "Who are you?"
The man bowed with flourish. "I'm Lucifer; THE EVIL ONE."
Heddie looked at her right shoulder. It was empty. That seemed like a bad sign.

"It would be so easy, Heddie!" Lucifer continued. "Kids die all the time! Just one little accident, and Marlene's future would be secured."

Heddie considered this as she brought her basket of apples to the house. She deposited all but one in a large trunk.

"Have you ever noticed the heavy lid and sharp iron lock on that trunk?" It was Lucifer, using Heddie's earring as a swing set. "Sure would be a shame if a careless little boy got caught under it."

Heddie stared at the trunk, imagining the lid crashing down on Jonas's neck. It was a tempting idea. She took a large bite out of her apple and chewed. She stared at the trunk with a creepy little grin.

The open-and-shut of the front door broke her trance. Marlene ran inside. Jonas tiptoed after, trying to pass through the house unnoticed.

"Oh, apples! I want one!" Marlene said, running forward.

"Not yet!" Heddie caught her by the arm. "Your brother gets his pick first. Change out of your school clothes and clean your room." Marlene rushed off obediently. Jonas looked up at Heddie with wide eyes.

She gestured to the trunk and put on her sweetest smile. "Don't you want an apple?"

Jonas wasn't hungry. As he hesitated, Heddie scowled. He nodded quickly. "Yes, thank you, Stepmother!"

"Then get it yourself!" Heddie pointed at the trunk. "I'm not your maid!"

The prevalence of evil stepmothers in the Grimms' tales is an interesting commentary both on their era and the difficulty in stepparenting. Stepmothers were common before medical advances slowed maternity mortality rates. Dads weren't the homemakers, so they remarried quickly to provide for their kids. Even the nicest stepparent faces bumps in the road when blending families. Murder is one way to deal with that? (My lawyer is advising me to stress that this is a joke.)

Jonas sensed something was off. Still, he tentatively knelt in front of the massive trunk and peered over the side.

"What are you waiting for?" Lucifer hissed in Heddie's ear. "Do it!"

Heddie slammed the lid of the trunk down with a *bang!* The boy's body slid down the side, leaving his head among the apples. Lucifer MWA-HA-HA'd and disappeared.

Lucifer is like that one friend who only pops into the group chat to start drama.

The sound of Marlene singing brought Heddie down to earth. Her plan didn't seem so simple now that the boy was bleeding out in the kitchen. She cleaned up as best she could and propped Jonas's body up on a chair. Then she retrieved his head and an apple from the trunk, wiped the apple clean, and perched it in his limp hand. She balanced the boy's head on his neck, but she still had the problem of the gaping neck wound. So she pulled the white scarf she was wearing off her head and tied it around his neck. He'd lost so much blood, the scarf didn't stain.

This is the worst prequel to *Weekend at Bernie's* I have ever read.

"Mama?" Marlene poked her head into the room. "Can I have that apple now?"

Heddie gestured to the boy. "Your brother picked one for you, go ahead and ask him." She pumped water into a pot.

Marlene walked to the table. "Jonas, may I have that apple?" She took in her brother's pale, silent form, and crept to her mother's side. "Mama, he's not answering me." She frowned. "He doesn't look so good."

"He's just ignoring you. Rude little boy!" Heddie put the pot on the fire. "Ask him again, and if he won't hand it over, box his ears for sassing you." She gave Marlene a sharp look.

Heddie offers the rare representation of wicked stepmother *and* wicked mother!

The little girl approached her brother. "Jonas? Can I have the apple?" When he didn't answer, she looked back at her mother. Heddie gave her a nod. So she cuffed Jonas's ear. His head flopped to the floor.

Marlene screamed and ran back to Heddie, burying her face in the woman's skirt. "Mama! I knocked Jonas's head off!" she bawled.

"Oh, Marlene!" Heddie reprimanded, as if the kid had merely made a mess of her lunch. "You have to be more careful!" She huffed as the girl began to hyperventilate. "Now, now, there's no use crying over spilled brother. Let's pick up his pieces. I'll have to cook him into our dinner!"

She thrust a wooden spoon into Marlene's hand and pushed her toward the hearth. "If you're going to cry so much, cry over the pot. It'll save us the salt!" She glowered. "And don't you *dare* tell your father what happened here today!"

Therapy would prevent a lot of fairy tale plots. But a lifetime of therapy wouldn't help this poor kid.

Heddie quickly diced up her slain stepson and dropped him in the pot with some onions and herbs. By the time the boy's father arrived home, a stew was simmering. "That smells fantastic!" the merchant said.

I know what's coming, but it floors me every time.

He sat down at the table. "Where's Jonas? It's not like him to miss dinner."

Heddie set a bowl in front of him, full to the brim with his boiled offspring. "He asked if he could visit your brother for a month or two."

The merchant furrowed his brow. "He should have at least said goodbye first." He lifted his spoon to his lips but stopped as Marlene burst into fresh tears. "It's okay, honey, he'll be back before you know it," he reassured her. Marlene was not reassured.

I wish I could tell you that Dad refused his stew. I wish Marlene spilled the beans, or that Dad noticed Heddie's reluctance to chow down, but no. Dad dug into that meal and, boy, did he fuckin' love it. He ate and he ate and he ate, oblivious to Marlene's aghast weeping. He ate and he ate and he ate, so ravenous that he refused to share. He ate and he ate and he ate, so damn feral, he threw the bones under the table! "This stew is all mine!"

"It sure is!" Heddie deadpanned as her husband scarfed the last of the morbid meal.

In his essay "On Fairy-Stories," J. R. R. Tolkien condemned his contemporaries for removing the cannibalism from Grimm, suggesting that dark plot points have a time-traveling effect on the young reader, alleviating the horror and elevating the form to mythical stature. He also argued that fairy tales shouldn't be dismissed as kids' stuff. Tolkien's my boy!

Marlene was told to clean up, because she couldn't catch a fuckin' break. She tenderly collected the bones of her brother and wrapped them in her favorite accessory, a silk shawl. She lay the wrapped bones underneath the juniper tree atop his mother's grave. This ritual soothed her. In fact, she forgot the events of the entire evening, as if the act whisked away her suffering.

I guess you don't need therapy with a fluoxetine tree in your front yard.

As she sat content, the gnarly limbs of the juniper tree began to writhe. A mist gathered in the center of its branches and condensed into a flame. A large bird with a coat of many colors flew from the burning ~~bush~~ tree. The sight of the bird cheered Marlene so much, she skipped into the house singing merrily, as if she didn't come from a family of killers and cannibals.

But the bird knew! The next day, he soared to the center of town with vengeance on his mind. First, he needed to get people talking. He started at the goldsmith's, perching on his window ledge. He sang:

My mother, she killed me,
My father, he ate me,
My sister Marlene
With a tear and a sigh
Sank down on one knee
Laid my bones 'neath our tree.
Tweet, tweet! What a beautiful bird-boy am I!

The bird sang of his brutal murder so prettily that the goldsmith rose in a haze, wandering from the delicate gold chain he'd buffed.

I'm starting to think this town is built over a gas leak.

He was so rapt, he didn't even notice when one of his shoes fell off.

This is the worst version of Cinderella I have ever read.

"I've never heard that ditty before!" he marveled. "Sing it again, bird!"

"I don't take requests for free!" the bird replied, asserting the very first instance of piano bar etiquette. "But I'll sing it again if you'll give me that beautiful gold chain you just finished!"

The goldsmith retrieved the necklace and handed it over. The bird curled his talons around it, and sang his song:

My mother, she killed me,
My father, he ate me,
My sister Marlene
With a tear and a sigh
Sank down on one knee
Laid my bones 'neath our tree.
Tweet, tweet! What a beautiful bird-boy am I!

I love this braggadocio at the end. He's a regular Ghostface Killah. (Ghostbird Killah? I'll workshop it.)

The bird flew to the shoemaker, and sang,

My mother, she killed me,
My father, he ate—

I'm not doing this every time.

The shoemaker was so moved by the song that he gathered his

family to listen. He tried to hit repeat, but the bird said, "You gotta upgrade to a paid membership! That beautiful pair of red shoes in your window will earn you an encore."

Fairy Tale Facts: Red shoes in fairy tales are never a good sign. Hans Christian Andersen took that idea and ran with it. Red-hot iron shoes killed Snow White's stepmother. Avoid red shoes at all costs!

The shoemaker paid the bird with the red shoes, which the animal grasped in his other foot.

He flew to the noisy mill, where twenty apprentices shaped a millstone. *Clickity-clack, clickity-clack,* the mill went. The bird took a minute to bob to the beat, then spit his rhymes. One by one, the millers drifted over, and at the end, they gave the bird the slow clap. "Again! Again!"

"Give me that millstone, and I'll not only sing it again, I'll release the EP!"

The millers handed it over. Yes, they placed an actual millstone around the bird's neck!

Is this fucker Big Bird or what? Even that Muppet would need the strength of a pro wrestler to carry this off.

The bird repeated his song, then flew home. Inside, his family was back around the table. Marlene had relapsed into misery. Heddie paced. "Do you hear thunder in the distance?" Dread pulsed in her veins.

"Nope!" the merchant replied. "The sun is shining and I'm feeling fat and happy!" He pointed. "Oh look! A bird! Does he look familiar to you?"

The bird perched himself in the juniper tree and sang once again:

My mother, she killed me,

Heddie choked on air laden with cinnamon.* Her blood pounded in her ears.

My father, he ate me,

"Now, there's a plot twist!" the merchant said with a laugh. "And delivered with such panache! I gotta get a front seat to this concert." He stepped outside.

My sister Marlene
With a tear and a sigh
Sank down on one knee
Laid my bones 'neath our tree.
Tweet, tweet! What a beautiful bird-boy am I!

The bird dropped the golden chain. It landed around his father's neck, nothin' but net! The merchant beamed. "A natural talent and generous? This is my favorite bird ever!"

The bird repeated his verse. (**They got the Family and Friends discount.**) Heddie rushed to close the shutters, then slid down the wall, trembling. But Marlene had seen the flash of gold fall from the bird's grasp. Curiosity led her outside, where she received the fancy red shoes. She beamed and slipped them on, the melancholy wiped from her memory once again.

Not so much for Heddie. "Lord, forgive me!" She wailed from inside, curled up like a little fruit-shaped fetus.

"Mama, come on out!" Marlene suggested. "You'll feel better, I'm sure of it!"

---

* *A spice associated with the phoenix.*

Perhaps the kid was right, Heddie thought. She couldn't feel worse than she did now! She pulled her body up heavily and stumbled out the door, cowering as the bird flew toward her, the enormous millstone around his swole neck.

Tweet, tweet! What a beautiful bird-boy am I!

He dropped the millstone, flattening his stepmother and ending his song with a literal *bang!*

The bird returned to his perch in the juniper tree. Its branches contorted and mist billowed from its center. The tree burst into flame, consuming the bird. When the fire died out, there stood Jonas, beaming as if he'd never been decapitated, dismembered, cooked in a stew, eaten whole by his own father, reborn into a bird, burned alive, and resurrected. "So, what's for lunch?"

"I can tell you this much," Marlene replied. "It's vegetarian!"*

* * *

SOURCE: Maria Tatar, editor and translator, *The Annotated Brothers Grimm*.

Want to revisit the Grimms? My favorite translators are Ms. Tatar and Jack Zipes.

---

* *The Grimms collected this tale from German Romanticist Philipp Otto Runge, who was inspired by a folktale. Its roots extend to other locales: in Hungary, "The Crow's Nest"; in England, "The Rose Tree." In Romania, the tale begins like "Hansel and Gretel," then segues into the boy's murder. Sometimes the siblings are reversed, sometimes the dead one is never resurrected, and occasionally the father kills his wife when he learns what she's done. The Grimms wrote the superior version, with its song, its curious use of the juniper tree, and its wacky cast of characters.*

THUMBERELLA

INDIA'S "BÂPKHÂDI"

Once upon a time, a man gave birth to a little girl from his thumb.

Let me explain: The guy was a hermit, devoted to Shiva. His devotion was admirable, but rejecting monetary gain was hard to justify when he had such a large family to support—a wife and six daughters. He'd go door-to-door in his neighborhood, begging for rice. Eventually, the neighbors tired of feeding so many mouths. So the hermit took his begging to the next community over. Maybe these folks were averse to strangers, for some lady there poured boiling hot rice from the pot into his bare hand!

The hermit rushed home so his wife could nurse his burn. A large blister had grown on his thumb. The man braced himself and asked his wife to break it. His wife found a needle and took her husband's hand in hers. As she brought the needle closer to the wound, a child's voice spoke to her. "Please be gentle with that needle, Mommy!"

The woman narrowed her eyes at her husband. "What did you say?"

The hermit shrugged. "It wasn't me."

"The kids are pranking us," his wife surmised. She went back in with the needle.

"Mommy, please!" the voice cried out again. "When you break the blister, be careful!"

The woman was bewildered, but she followed the voice's directions, gingerly piercing the tough skin of the blister. The parents gaped as a little girl emerged from the wound.

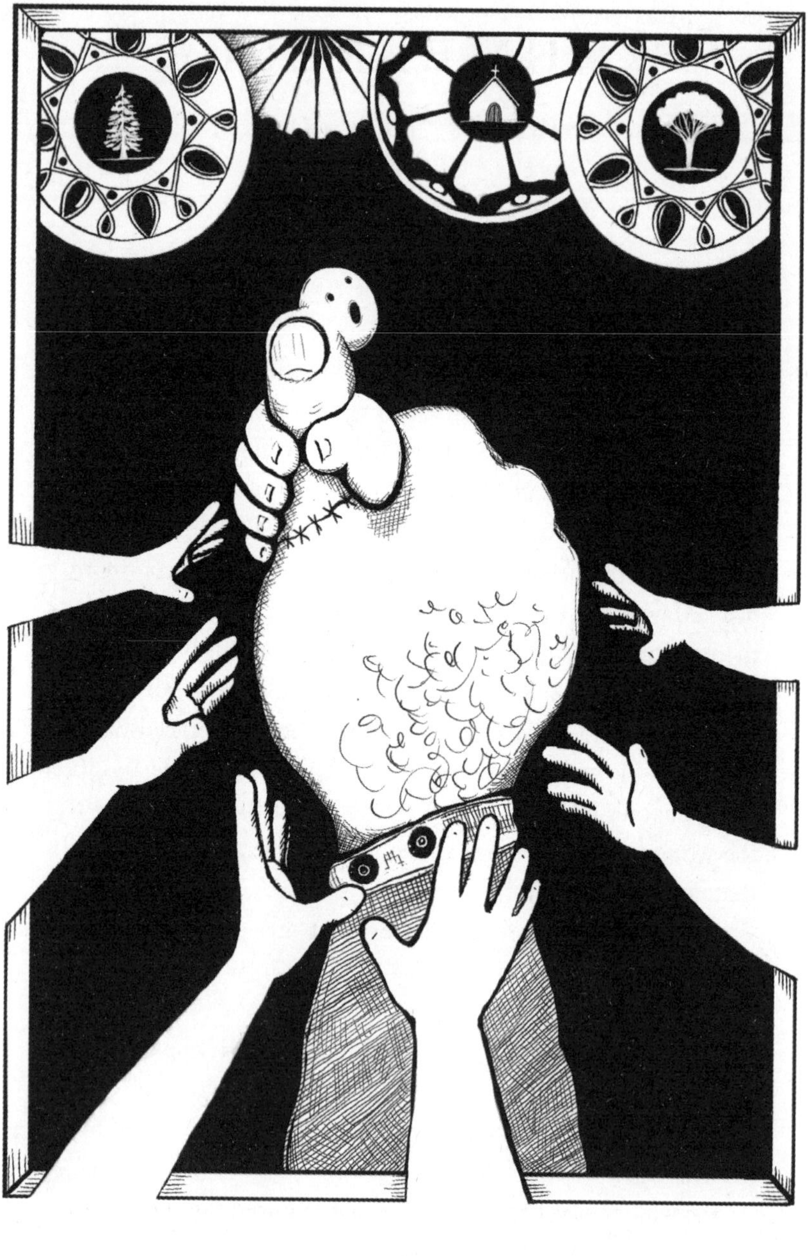

Imagine giving vaginal birth to six kids and then your husband pops one out from a blister. You get a torn perineum and postpartum depression, and all he needs is a Band-Aid.

"What the hell is this?" the hermit's wife asked. "You go out for food, and you come back with a child?"

"Hey, I don't know where she came from! I don't even know how she got in there!"

"Maybe you should tell me where that thumb has been!"

The little girl swung her head from parent to parent.

"Why would I purposefully impregnate my thumb?" The hermit dropped his head in his hands. "We can't afford a seventh child, never mind another girl! How will we survive?"

"Figure it out!" his wife ordered. "That little girl is *your* child. You'll have to make do!"

Sources do not specify if our little thumb girl is tiny like Thumbelina. Later she seems to be average-sized, so maybe that blister was bigger on the inside.

Back on his neighborhood rounds the hermit went. Most of his efforts went right into the mouths of the children, and he began to tire of this. One day, he asked his wife to do something a little fancier with their daily haul. "How about some puran poli?"

His wife sighed. "I'll make some, but you know those little girls will sneak that flatbread right off the platter and into their mouths before you get home to enjoy it."

"Just lock the children in the other room while you cook. Then we can all eat together."

So, this is what the hermit's wife did. She tried her best to cook quietly. But in such a small home, there's only so much you can keep from half a dozen bored and nosy children. As soon as the scent of the poli wafted into the girls' room, they began plotting a way to snatch it.

"Mom," one called, "I need to go to the bathroom!"

These days it's hard to imagine a scatological reference in a fairy tale, but there is folklore precedent for children using the toilet as an escape plan; see early versions of "Little Red Riding Hood."

The poor mother let one kid out to use the bathroom, but not long after that another one piped up with the same issue. Then the third, and the fourth, and pretty soon all seven girls were doing the tiptoe dance. Amid the melee, each clever kid grabbed a flatbread or yoinked a fingerful of sweet filling. By the time everyone was locked back up, there was no dinner left. So the hermit's wife scooped some ashes out of the hearth and made bread out of those, hoping her hungry hubby wouldn't be able to tell the difference.

Her hoax was not as successful as her children's. The hermit spat out his ashy bread with a twisted face. His temper darkened. He was hangry, and the feeling pushed him to tempt karma. "That's it!" he hissed. "Tonight, I'm leaving those seven brats in the forest. They've been nothing but a burden since they were born."

"I spy 'Hansel and Gretel'!" you are shouting. Good job, reader!

The hermit told his daughters that they'd been invited to visit an uncle. The girls had never heard of any extended family, but they were excited for the surprise trip. As their father led them into the forest, they were all grins and chatter. Then began the "Are we there yets" and the nonstop potty breaks—reminding the hermit why he was doing this in the first place. At last, when the moon was high, their father set up camp.

"It's a long way off to your uncle's yet," he explained. "We'll sleep here overnight."

The older girls settled down. The youngest, the little thumb girl, was restless. You see, the girl couldn't get to sleep unless she was sucking her father's thumb.

Clearly, she's yearning to be back in the womb.

Nine times out of ten, she'd wake back up if he tried to extract himself. So while his kiddo suckled away, the beggar weighed his escape options: (1) gamble on his youngest sleeping through his hasty exit, (2) abandon this selfish plan and take everyone home, or (3) cut off his thumb and bail on his children. He picked the third thing.

The "Hansel and Gretel" abandonment plot is a gut-punch for children who self-blame. It doesn't matter how many times Mom and Dad tell you the divorce isn't your fault; *you* remember how you'd crawl into their bed and keep them apart. Did that act of physical separation lead to their marital separation? . . . Wow, my own book is triggering me.

When the girls awoke the next morning, they were mystified by their father's disappearance. It was only when the youngest rose and spat out her father's disembodied thumb that the girls thought they'd figured things out. "You nasty little ogress!" the oldest sister sneered at the kid. "You've eaten up Papa!"

The youngest protested, but the blood on her mouth (not to mention the odd circumstance of her birth) was enough evidence for the rest of her sisters. They renamed her "Bâpkhâdi" and told her she was no longer welcome to travel with them.

Bâpkhâdi is Marathi for "eater of the father." Not as pretty a fairy tale name as France's "Cendrillon" ("Little Ashes"), but not as offensive as "Little Saddleslut." (Thanks for that one, Greece.)

Bâpkhâdi secretly followed her sisters, easily tracking them as they gabbed and complained. Eventually the sisters stumbled on an impressive house at the opposite edge of the woods. They knocked at the door, but no one answered. The eldest sisters bickered over the ethics of breaking in, but hunger won out. And anyway, the front door opened easily.

"Hello?" they called, bracing themselves around every corner for a child-eating witch or bone-crushing giant. Lucky for them, the house was not only unoccupied but well stocked. The kitchen was full of rice, preserves, and spices. A large courtyard revealed a veggie garden. The house was dusty but spacious and furnished beautifully. It had six bedrooms, with closets full of gorgeous garments, as if the place had magically materialized just for them. Maybe it did!

The girls haggled over who got which room. Eventually they decided the eldest could choose first, then the next eldest, and so forth.

"What about me?" a voice piped up. Bâpkhâdi waved from an open window.

The six older girls huddled for a quick conference. "The upside of letting her stay is we can make her do all the housework," the eldest pointed out. "The downside is that she might eat us too." They decided to risk it and assigned their despised sister a tiny closet.

Bâpkhâdi opened the peeling door, revealing grimy walls, cobwebs, and nothing else. The eldest shrugged. "You're lucky we let you live here at all, you nasty little cannibal!"

Bâpkhâdi sighed, but what could she do? She retired to her little room, closing the door behind her. She turned the lock, thankful that she at least had some privacy. When the lock clicked, the dingy room melted away, and in its place was the most luxurious space in the house! The floor was a rainbow of glass tiles, leading to tall arched windows overlooking a tropical seaside view. She slid open paneled doors to find an expansive closet of Paithani saris in peacock-blues shot through with gold, gowns of glittering plum-colored Mashru silks, rows of soft leather sandals, and a dozen drawers of golden jewelry and hair ornaments. The room even led to a hidden stable housing a horse in every color. Suck on that, sisters! Wisely, Bâpkhâdi kept her dream house a secret, remaining in rags as long as her family treated her like a servant.

"Wait, now the story feels like 'Cinderella'!" Right again, reader! Many "Cinderellas" feature the motif of kids being abandoned in the woods. Clearly, we have always loved a crossover episode.

Each Sunday, the older sisters dressed up to attend church.* They would always invite Bâpkhâdi, but she would demur, so they thought! As soon as her sisters left, Bâpkhâdi would don embroidered robes and beaded sandals from her secret stash, hop on a horse, and beat them to church. When the sisters arrived, they observed a very fancy lady with fabulous shoes being oohed and aahed over, but they didn't recognize her as their raggedy sis. By the time the gals got home, Bâpkhâdi had ditched her Sunday clothes and was prepping dinner at the hearth.

---

* *The term* church *in a Hindu tale is puzzling. Missionaries did their damnedest to convert India starting from the moment the Portuguese landed in the sixteenth century, but it is possible* church *is just a stand-in word for a temple or other space of worship. Another point to consider: in her stellar essay "The Colonizer-Folklorist," scholar Sadhana Naithani notes that some popular Indian folktales depicted the lives of their British invaders. Could that be the case here? Our only version was written down by a British officer for a British audience, now further interpreted by an American TikTokking librarian. May I offer you a grain of salt?*

Yes, the sisters are young adults now. This sort of time-jump is common in fairy tales. Cinderella gets to skip her awkward teen years, unlike the rest of us plebes.

During one escapade, Bâpkhâdi dropped a golden shoe on the way home. The sandal caught the eye of another swanky parishioner: the king's son. The prince picked it up and, upon returning home, tethered his horse and plopped down in the stable to puzzle over his find. He was very drawn to the shoe. Very, very drawn to it.

One wonders how the story of Cinderella would have unfolded if storybook princes had access to WikiFeet.

He imagined the type of woman who wore a sandal so grand. He was certain she must be the loveliest princess and decided none other could compete for his hand. But how the hell could he find her?

Unaccustomed to not getting what he wanted immediately, the prince staged a hunger strike, refusing to leave the stables. He lay among the horse dung until the stable hands came to feed the animals.

Disney really let us down by making Prince Charming such a dud. Where is my scene where he makes love to a shoe, then throws a diva fit until he finds his lady?

The king was summoned. He took in the sight of his wan and weepy son and declared, "What brought this on? Did someone lay a hand on you? I swear, I'll take the rogue's hands! Did someone drop-kick you? I swear, I will take the scoundrel's legs! Did a man even look at you the wrong way? I swear, I will take the villain's eyes!"

"The only part of me that is grievously injured is *my heart!*" the prince whined. He tossed his father the slipper. "If I cannot find the owner of this shoe, I will *literally die*." He threw back his head and wailed.

He and Donkey-Skin's beau need a support group.

The king assured his emo son that he would send men out to all corners of the kingdom to locate the mystery woman. The hunt for the lady commenced! For several days, the king's men shoved the shoe on many eager contestants, with no luck. At last, they arrived at the home of Bâpkhâdi and her sisters. The first six got their chance. As an afterthought, they called Bâpkhâdi into the room for a turn. The ladies were shocked when the sandal easily slid on their grody little sister's foot.

No Happily Ever After yet, though! Many "Cinderellas" include a second half. Storytellers of the past knew that a betrothal was only the beginning of a woman's story. Revenge, betrayal, and attempted infanticide must follow. You know, the everyday concerns of wifehood.

The wedding of Bâpkhâdi and the prince was an extravagant affair. As a family perk, Bâpkhâdi's six sisters were invited to live at the palace. The catch was they would now be Bâpkhâdi's attendants. This role reversal incited a dark grudge among the women, but they weren't about to turn down the invitation. They submitted to their new life, waiting for a chance to steal the prince's affections.

Their opportunity arose when two events converged: Bâpkhâdi became pregnant, and the prince decided to take a long sailing trip.

That's one way to avoid midnight snack runs and sympathy contractions.

Ignorant of his in-laws' nefarious schemes, the prince gave the sisters the following instructions. "Bâpkhâdi's well-being should be your first priority. There is no need to alert me when the child is born; a higher power will do that. If I am blessed with a son, the heavens will make it rain gold upon my ship. Should I be blessed with a daughter, it will merely be a silver rain, for obvious reasons."

And here you thought zealously heteronormative Americans popularized the gender reveal!

Nine months later, the prince was thrilled to receive a, um, golden shower. A son was born! He threw a party onboard, distributing bonuses of besan ladoo, karanji, and other delectable sweets. It should have been a happy occasion for Bâpkhâdi as well. But her sisters took advantage of her vulnerable position. They blindfolded her for the birth and postpartum care and swapped out her baby with a large pestle. As for the child? The sisters buried him alive under a large pine tree.

When the prince arrived home, he was shocked when his wife's sisters produced a swaddled pestle instead of an infant son. Now, Bâpkhâdi was an intelligent girl. She knew her sisters had done a terrible deed, but, like many stoic princesses before her, she remained silent.

This plot point is a *third* fairy tale type in this sprawling story, called "The Three Golden Children." Occasionally the villain stages things to look like the mother ate her kids. Curious that this isn't the case here, particularly since Bâpkhâdi was already accused of cannibalism. That's the direction I'd pick for a Bollywood epic I have no business directing.

A couple of years passed, and Bâpkhâdi became pregnant a second time. Her husband abandoned her again to party on his yacht with the boys, leaving the dastardly sisters free to interfere. The prince celebrated when he received a second... golden rain, we'll call it. But back home things were not so celebratory. Bâpkhâdi was blindfolded, and the baby boy was swapped out for a hand broom and buried under a fig tree. The prince was frustrated to once again find a household item rocking in a cradle, with no explanation.

Another couple of years later, Bâpkhâdi got pregnant again and her husband fled to the seas once more. Bâpkhâdi gave birth to a girl, who was promptly buried alive beneath the church. The prince rejoiced at his silver deluge and hurried home to meet his daughter. This time, the sisters handed him another broom in a diaper. (**Another broom? Now they're just getting lazy.**) They also told the prince a lot of lies about his wife. Mainly the "she ate our father" story. The slander horrified the gullible prince so much that he imprisoned Bâpkhâdi, and took all six sisters as his new wives.* Bâpkhâdi was locked up, dressed in rags, and served fish guts for meals. Things were looking extremely bleak for the persecuted princess.

Ten years passed. Reader, you will be happy to note that the three babies were saved by heavenly intervention. Yes, the Almighty himself dug up those poor babies before they could suffocate underground. They grew to be small children, who survived by begging on the streets. (**Apparently God was too busy to go the extra mile and give them a trust fund.**) As they went house to house, they recited their life story to anyone who opened their door:

---

* Polygamy is a common feature of Indian folktales (as is infighting between jealous wives). The fact that the prince is seemingly monogamous when he marries Bâpkhâdi is more unusual.

At birth we were buried alive, yes! all three,
Under the church and a pine and fig tree.
Our father, the prince, is out of his mind.
He threw Mother out, to a dungeon confined.

The children collected alms and made their way to the palace with their haunting nursery rhyme. The prince overheard them singing at the door, and the story perplexed him. He approached and asked them to repeat the verse. He asked for it again and again.

I'm gonna make it a point to sing any future accusations or confessions. Presenting information that way is much more compelling!

Soon his sister-wives were listening too. They realized what the prince couldn't get through his dense noggin: these children were definitely Bâpkhâdi's. Quickly, the women offered the children alms to get rid of them. But the kids refused to take anything from the six sisters. This puzzled the prince further. "Why do you refuse money from my wives? You are obviously in need of it."

Each of the children spoke in turn. "Bring us your first wife, the one you imprisoned—like a chump!"

"Then hang seven curtains between her and us to see an incredible magic trick!"

"Maybe then you'll finally get it!"

The prince was mesmerized and ordered that Bâpkhâdi be retrieved and the seven curtains hung immediately. As the prince watched, milk burst forth from Bâpkhâdi's breasts **(SURPRISE)** in three streams **(there's a *Ghostbusters* joke here somewhere)**, blasting forward with such force that it penetrated all seven curtains and landed with uncanny aim into the mouths of the three children.

Welp. I guess in Bâpkhâdi's case, breast really was best.

The prince pried the true story out of the six sister-wives, then asked Bâpkhâdi why she never stood up for herself. "I was blindfolded for each ordeal and had no way to defend myself."

In fairy tales like "The Six Swans," the princess has a compelling reason to remain silent—she must do so to break a curse. But in many more fairy tales, princesses suffer in silence for no reason. Either way, it's one of the worst tropes in fairy tales.

Bâpkhâdi and her children were restored to their rightful states of wealth and comfort. All lived to old age. The six sisters, however, received little mercy. The prince ordered their hair and noses to be cut off, and that they be banished on the backs of donkeys.

The donkeys took the women far from the palace, and fast. It seemed as if they would never stop running. Several hours into their journey, the sisters cried out to the inexhaustible animals, "Where on earth are you taking us?"

"To the ends of the earth!" the donkeys howled. "You royally fucked up; now we too must suffer!"

#JusticeforDonkeys!

* * *

SOURCE: Geo. Fr. D'Penha, "Folk-lore in Salsette."

Want to read more Indian folktales? Try *Tales of India: Folk Tales from Bengal, Punjab, and Tamil Nadu* by Svabhu Kohli.

SNAKES WHO CANNOT SHED THEIR KIN

Lithuania's "Eglė, the Queen of Serpents"

Long ago lived an old couple and their gargantuan family. We're talking enough kids to launch a reality show sure to age terribly. These folks had twelve sons and three daughters. The youngest and prettiest of the three was named Eglė.

In fairy tales, you either get one perfect snow-white child or three dozen terrible children plus one hot baby.

In Eglė's seventeenth year, the three sisters strolled to the lake one summer's day for a skinny-dip. They swam until they'd pruned up, then scurried back to shore. Eglė reached to grab her shift, but her hand landed on something slick and scaly. She screamed bloody murder as she realized she'd grabbed an enormous green-ringed snake tangled up in her garments.

Eglė's fright had a domino effect; soon all three young ladies were wailing and flailing across the shore, tits out and terrified. The snake nestled back into Eglė's shift. Then he spoke: "Assss amusing as this whole scene is, I assure you, I mean no harm. My name is Zilvynas. I came to asssk Eglė to marry me!"

The girls gaped. "That snake just spoke like a man!" the eldest cried.

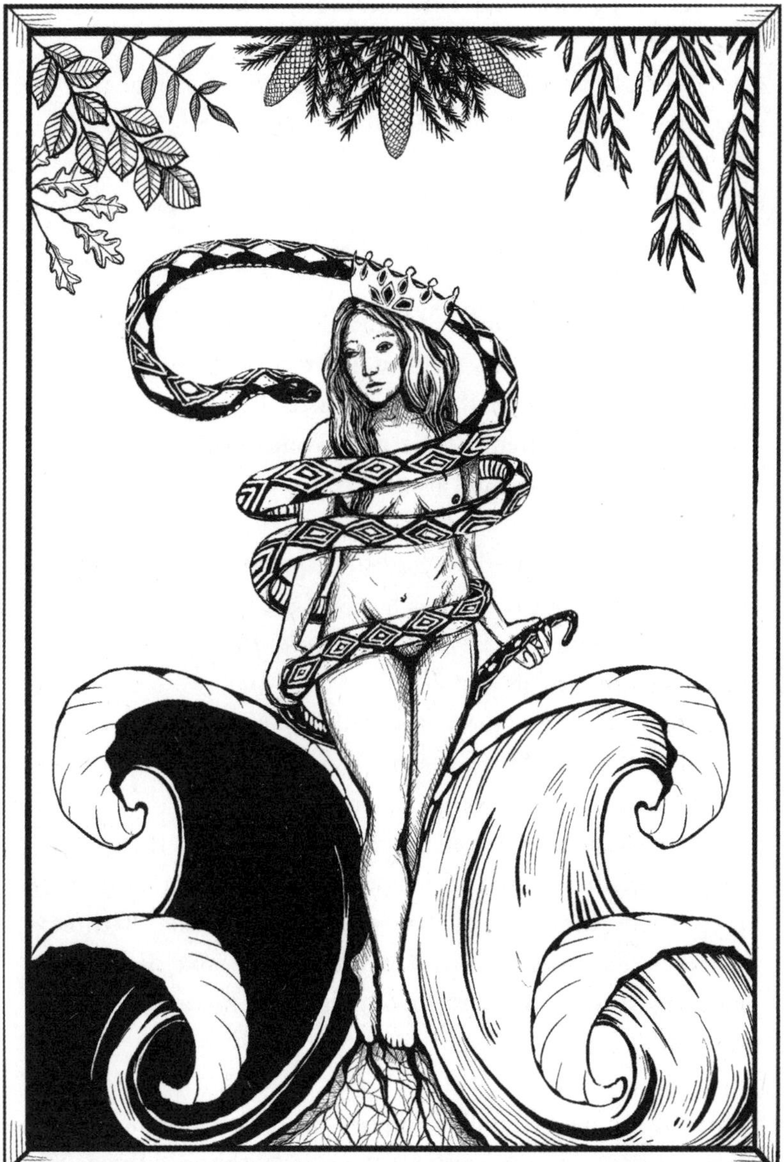

"You slimy creep!" said the next. The older girls dashed for their clothes.

Poor Eglė stretched her arms around herself as modestly as possible. "Let me get dressed and then we can talk about marriage!" she bargained.

"Nuh-uh." The snake blew a raspberry. "I'm not moving until you say yesss! Say Yesss to Get Dressed!"

The grass snake was revered in Baltic mythology. A superstition declared that if you accidentally stumbled upon a snake, it meant a marriage or birth in your future. The superstition does not specify how often the marriage comes with the threat of being stranded naked and afraid.

Eglė's sisters flocked to her side, spreading their skirts as shields. They spoke to her in a hush. "Eglė, just tell the creature you'll marry him to get your clothes back. Then we'll run home and ghost the wriggly perv!"

Eglė agreed to wed the reptile. Satisfied, he released her undies and slid into the lake. Eglė shook out her dress a few times for good measure before covering up and racing home.

A couple of days passed quietly. The girls kept the uncomfortable event a secret, and figured they'd gotten away with their trick. They neglected to remember the rule of threes, however. For on the third day, the family woke up to their mother's shriek. "Snakes! Thousands of snakes are swarming the yard!"

Three is the magic number in fairy tales. Folklorist Vladimir Propp defined this narrative device as "trebling." Three is a beloved number in mathematics, mythology, and art. Author Kate Forsyth chalks that up to nature's love of pattern-making, since three is the smallest number required to create a pattern.

This tale really leans into the tradition, so much so that I get PTSD flashbacks to third-grade multiplication quizzes.

The fifteen kids rushed to the windows. Sure enough, the grass was pulsing with an enormous nest of snakes making a beeline (snakeline?) right to the front door. The sea of serpents parted to surround the house. One snake raised himself above the rest. "Hear ye, hear ye! King Zilvynas is ready to receive the beautiful Eglė as his bride!"

"Hard pass!" Eglė's father yelled from a window. "As if we'd send our youngest, prettiest daughter to marry a snake!"

Wow! We all suspect our parents have a favorite, but to be so blatant about it is something else. I'll give him the benefit of the doubt and blame his tactlessness on fear.

The herald snake cleared his throat. "If it is a question of dowry, our king isss flexible."

Dad snorted. "I don't care if he offers to pay *me*! No deal!"

"Thisss is awkward," the herald muttered. "Eglė promised herself to King Zilvynas. We have been ordered to leave with Eglė, or to not leave at all!"

Dad closed the window and marched to his daughter's room, suddenly wondering if she'd locked herself there more out of guilt than squeamishness. "Eglė, is this true?"

"I promised under duress!" Eglė protested. "He peeped at us while we were bathing!"

Eglė's parents were in a pickle. Grass snakes were guardians of the home. Pissing one off was a bad idea. But no parent in their right mind would marry their kid off to a snake!

Especially one who sexually harasses their daughter, then sends an army to collect her!

Mom remembered they had a quirky next-door neighbor who might know how to get out of the promise. Dad told the herald that he and his wife needed to conference privately next door. The curtain of snakes parted so the couple could cross the lawn.

Their next-door neighbor was an old lady with a green thumb. She'd taken a break from her garden to watch the snake parade. When the couple arrived, she invited them inside. "What kind of weird magic did you get mixed up in?" she asked.

The couple explained. The old woman considered their options. "Try to trick them," she suggested. "Send them back with a white goose. You said your girl is hiding, right? So they don't know what she looks like."

The couple returned home, making a pit stop in the barn for the waterfowl. Mom fashioned a quick bridal wreath out of weeds and popped it on the bird's head. "Okay, Eglė," she told the goose. "Be good to your husband!"

The family waved goodbye as the snakes escorted the goose-bride down the walk. But the bizarre wedding party only got halfway to the lake before a cuckoo bird sang:

You silly snakes! The family lied!
They sent a goose to be your bride!

Really bold of a cuckoo to tell on them, considering the bird's habit of leaving their eggs in other breeds' nests like changelings. Yeah, cuckoo, that's a goose; but you're no canary, ya big ugly narc!

Murmuring, the serpents set the goose loose and slithered back to Eglė's home. This time, the nest of snakes climbed up the sides of the house, peeking in windows and rattling the shutters.

Eglė's parents asked the snakes for more time to confer, sneaking back to their neighbor's for a fresh idea. "Hmmm," the old lady said. "Try something more human-sized. You got a sheep to spare?"

Did this lady go to school with Donkey-Skin's fairy godmother?

So Eglė's mom made a bigger dandelion wreath and nestled it over the ears of a plush sheep. "Oh, Eglė, we'll miss you!" she said, gesturing for the rest of the family to play along.

"Don't cry, little Eglė!" the brothers shouted over the sheep's bleats.

The snakes escorted the beflowered barn animal back toward the lake. But wouldn't you know it, that feathered snitch was waiting for them.

You silly snakes! They lied to you!
That's not a bride! That is a ewe!
. . . As in e-w-e! Sorry, that was confusing.

Seething, the snakes abandoned the sheep and oscillated back en masse. This time, the snakes covered the house top to bottom, peeping their heads through the thatched roof menacingly. The parents received more lackluster advice from their neighbor **(who had to be trolling them at this point)** and tried to trick the snakes a third time with a cow decked out in evergreens. The cuckoo was having a grand ol' time.

You silly snakes! You're duped, and how!
The family sent a dairy cow!
Maybe ask your king for a physical description of this
*   bitch, yeesh!*

Spitting, the snakes dumped the cow and wriggled back to the house. This time, they fully wormed their way inside.

The creatures herded all seventeen family members into a tight group.

"Sssseee here!" the herald announced. "If you do not send Eglė home with us today, King Zilvynas will curssse your household with a year of famine, drought, and tinnitus!" A thousand snakes simultaneously hissed; the family held their ears at the piercing sibilance. They had no choice but to abandon Eglė to the writhing creatures.

Her sisters tearfully wove her a proper bridal wreath of rue for her strawberry-blond tresses, and her mother loaned her own simple white gown for the sad occasion. Before they departed, the herald wound his way up a post and scrutinized the bride. "Two legs, two arms, two teats, and no feathers. I think we got her, boys!"

If they had any doubts, the cuckoo chimed in:

Hurry up, you den of snakes!
The groom's poor heart for Eglė aches!

The snakes ushered the bride to shore. As the lake came into view, Eglė's teary eyes dried up. No ringed snake waited for her at all. Rather, a lithe, wickedly handsome fellow with bright green eyes stood at the water's edge. His smile was magnetic, and he moved with a fluid grace unlike any man Eglė had ever known. He wore a snakeskin suit and a golden crown perched atop his wild black tresses.

Snake grooms are cross-continental. Anthropologists theorize the tales could have a common root in ancient North Eurasian mythology. India's "Nagray and Himal" features a romance like Eglė's; the Lenape's horned serpent myths echo Eglė's themes of forbidden love and lost memory; sometimes the plots diverge into "Cupid and Psyche" motifs of jealousy and estrangement, like Korea's "The Divine Serpent Scholar."

"Who are you?" Eglė asked.

The king offered her his arm. "I am Zilvynas, your betrothed." He winked, and his pupils morphed into slits for a moment. "I assume you'd prefer to marry me in my human form?"

Eglė blushed. Suddenly this sexy snake's interest was irresistible. "If it's not inconvenient!"

Plenty of mediocre old men have charmed under-aged gals, so how is an impressionable teen supposed to resist a gorgeous, magical hunk? RIP all our defenses in the face of such allure!

The king gestured to a simple rowboat in the shallows. The snake army wove themselves together into a bridge so the bride could board without spoiling her slippers. The herald slid in with them, but the rest waved goodbye with their tails as Zilvynas conjured a foamy current to carry them across the lake.

The boat landed at a small island Eglė had never noticed before. A short hike led to a hill with a round door. Zilvynas tapped it three times and it opened, shedding light on a long winding staircase. A golden glow pulsed deep within the earth. The couple descended for ages. But at last, the staircase opened up to a marvelous amber kingdom, with the king's golden palace scaling high into the cavernous sky. Eglė gasped at its opulence. She'd never dreamed she'd get to see such grandeur, never mind rule it.

They were greeted by a huge party of snake-people, who welcomed Eglė, leading her to the wedding altar.

Grass snakes can lay up to forty eggs, so I assume Eglė's siblings were outnumbered for the first time in her life.

Ushers clad in silver held aloft a white lace canopy; the king's mother exchanged Eglė's wreath for a veiled crown. The bride danced with every groomsman. Each tossed gold coins to the king in exchange for a dance, until the king reclaimed his wife. At last, a little baby in snakeskin was put into Eglė's arms. "To your future children!" the queen mom toasted. The couple was paraded to their marriage bed. Eglė feared being ravished by a reptile, but her husband was gentle and warm. By the time they fell asleep, Eglė had fallen hard for the king.

The merry occasion didn't end there. Feasts lasted three weeks; by the end, not only had Eglė fully embraced her role as the Queen of Serpents, but all memory of her family back home had completely faded from her mind.

※ ※ ※

NINE YEARS PASSED. Eglė grew up fast, expecting her first child soon after her wedding. She found Zilvynas to be an attentive husband, and life at the castle was never lonely, as the king made sure someone was always at his wife's side. Eglė bore three sons named Ąžuolas, Uosis, and Beržas, and one daughter named Drebulė. They'd spend their days exploring the underground kingdom or catching sun on their private island.

Then the king's mother died. The loss of their grandmother inspired curiosity in the children about Eglė's family and life beyond the shore of their isolated kingdom.

Ąžuolas, the eldest son, caught his father grieving one morning. Shaken at the show of vulnerability from his strong, proud father, he sought out Eglė. He found her knitting by the fireplace, her needles percussing softly in the amber hall. "I was wondering . . ." He hesitated, winding some yarn back in a ball. "Do we have a grandmother from your land?" He looked up at her as the rhythm suddenly ceased. "Mama?"

Eglė was staring into the fire. Her mind seemed to click open like a locked chest. "You do," she said softly. Indignantly, she repeated, "You sure as hell do!"

I presume Eglė's husband gaslit her with magic, which makes it even more infuriating that mortal abusers get away with the same behavior. Would it be easier to villainize an abuser that uses enchantment instead of mind games? Or are their victims screwed either way?

> She noticed her son cower. "I'm sorry, honey. I'm not mad at you. Let me tell you about my family." She stumbled through hazy memories of her shared bed with her sisters, of mother teaching her how to bake a mile-high šakotis, of playing circle games with her older brothers. The more she talked, the more she recalled.
> Ąžuolas brightened. "Can we meet them?"

He has a backlog of birthday money to claim!

> Eglė tousled his hair. "I'll ask your father."
> The snake queen wasted no time tracking down Zilvynas, whom she found bookkeeping in his study. "Why have I forgotten about my family until today?" she demanded.
> Her husband paused, working out an excuse. "Your family did not receive the news of our engagement well. I removed your memories of them for your own protection."
> Eglė suddenly remembered how Zilvynas had proposed. "Oh my God! You blackmailed me into marrying you!"
> Zilvynas groaned. "See, this is exactly why I enchanted you to forget all that crap! Will you never let me hear the end of it?"
> "It's the first time I've brought it up! Cuz you *enchanted me to forget.*"

Magic also makes domestic spats a lot more interesting.

> The king cleared a chair and guided Eglė to sit. "I'm sorry for that. Truly." He opted for frankness. "I fear that if I let

you go home, your family will not let you come back." His voice broke.

Eglė softened. She too was adjusting to her husband's vulnerable side. "That's a large assumption to make. My parents disliked several women my brothers married, but they accepted them into the family." She covered his hand with hers, comforted that her own love didn't disappear with the return of her memories.

You call it love, I call it codependency. Tomato, tomahto, potato, potahto, my God, Eglė, call this whole thing off!

"I want the children to meet their grandparents," she continued. Zilvynas shook his head. "I cannot allow that."

Eglė rose. "You couldn't allow it when I had no choice in the matter!" she corrected. "But it is wildly unfair to deny our children a relationship with my kin. How would you feel if our roles were reversed? Our children loved your mother. Don't they deserve a chance to love mine?"

The snake king considered this, pacing the room. "Fine. You may take the children to meet their grandparents. But I have a few things around the house I need you to take care of first."

Eglė clapped her hands. "Excellent! I'll start packing while you put together a to-do list!"

* * *

That afternoon, Eglė received the first of her chores. "Spin this silk into thread."

Eglė measured the fiber in her hands. "I'm not sure why this is such a pressing matter, but all right."

She settled at her spinning wheel. Twenty minutes into her spinning, she still had as much silk as when she'd started. She pulled a hunk of fiber from it, then another, and another. The batch refused to change in size. A frustrating hour later, Eglė was sure the silk was enchanted to never run out.

Two can play at that game! she thought. She took the fiber to a sorceress who lived next door. "What's wrong with this silk?" she asked. "I've spun six skeins of thread and it won't shrink."

The sorceress poked the silk and held it to the light. "Throw it into the fire and you'll eradicate the magic."

Eglė paid her handsomely and took the tufts back home. At the fire, she hesitated. If it just burned up, would her husband consider their deal off? She bit her lip and tossed the silk into the hearth.

"Ugh, I thought it would *never end*," came a whine from the flames. A toad hopped out of the fire, carrying a visibly smaller hunk of silk. "Keep producing more, the king said! Don't stop until she gives up, he said! Does he think I have nothing better to do?" The toad left the fibers at Eglė's feet and hopped off, muttering under his breath.

Eglė took the silk back to the spinning wheel; it ran out after one skein. She brought that and the other half dozen to her husband and dropped them on his desk unceremoniously. "All done. What other magically impossible tasks do you need me to do?"

Zilvynas blushed. "Just a couple more chores."

Eglė leaned in, eye to eye. "No more magic."

The king nodded. "No more, I promise."

The second morning, Eglė woke up to find all of her shoes gone, with one pair of iron loafers in their place. She stared at the king through narrowed eyes.

He kept a straight face. "I need you to wear down those shoes until they have a hole in each sole."

Eglė threw her hands up. "That could take eons!" She huffed, slipped on the shoes, and began walking.

An hour of scraping and stomping later, her feet were blistered and her muscles shook like aspic. She pulled the shoes off her feet and brought them next door. "How do I disenchant these iron shoes to wear them down?"

The sorceress didn't even look at the shoes. "Take them to the blacksmith and have him do it." She smiled. "Sometimes it's the easy solution!"*

Eglė dropped holey metal shoes on her husband's desk that night. Even worn down, the shoes dented the wood. "What else you got?"

The third morning, Žilvinas met Eglė in the kitchen. "You shouldn't visit home without a gift for your folks," he said. "So the last thing I need you to do is make a cake to bring along."

Finally, a task that made sense! Eglė attempted to gather ingredients. But the cupboards were bare. She scrounged up enough to make a simple fruit cake, but then there was the matter of utensils. The king had left her with very few tools, and only a sieve to carry the liquids.

Off to the sorceress she went. "Can you help, or should I go to the baker?" she asked.

The sorceress laughed. "I can help. Do you have a sourdough starter?"

"Yes!"

"Make a leaven dough to stop the holes in the sieve. Then you can gather water and use the sieve as a bowl. You can make a cake without the rest of the tools—it will just be a little messy."

---

*Lithuanian folktales frequently feature a structure that folklorist Alan Dundes called "unsuccessful repetition." This is when the good character completes a set of tasks that wind up rewarding them, but when a bad character tries to repeat the tasks, they fail. Think "Diamonds and Toads." "Eglė" is a fun twist of that motif: the first time around, when Eglė's mother tries to deceive, the lady next door has useless advice. But when Eglė goes to her neighbor seeking the truth, the sorceress proves more helpful.

That night, Eglė plunked a lopsided cherry cake on her husband's desk. "We done here?"

The king sighed. "We're done."

* * *

A WEEK later, Eglė and the children reviewed their luggage to make sure they had all they'd need. "You're sure you don't want to come?" Eglė asked her husband.

"I don't think that's a good idea," he said.

He gathered his wife and kids for some final instructions. "I'll take you across the lake myself. When you're ready to come home—no more than nine days from now—you'll need to summon me with a verse." He looked from each son to his five-year-old daughter to impress the impact of his words. "This is a super-secret password, okay? The only people who know it are the six of us. No one else must learn." He bopped their youngest, Drebulė, on the nose.

She gave him a gap-toothed grin. "I promise, Daddy!"

They recited the verse until they knew it from memory:

Dear Zilvynas, come forth, my king,
If you're alive, white foam you'll bring.
But if you've died, a fate I dread,
The bubbly foam will come back red.

I'd probably go with something more Seuss than Poe, but go off, King.

The boat ride was somber, but the kids' excitement grew once they reached land. The siblings donned their knapsacks and tore off toward the woods. Eglė embraced Zilvynas warmly. Despite their spat, she felt the significance of their first parting. And, magic or no, the guy knew how to kiss a woman.

Ah, that sexy oxytocin is its own kinda spell.

On the way to their grandparents', Eglė told her children how she met their father. Well, some of it. She left out the naked parts and beefed up the cuckoo section. They laughed, and asked a lot of questions about the plants and animals they saw.

Eglė's oldest brother was pruning a tree in the front yard when they arrived. "Eglė? Is that you?"

The adult siblings hooted and grasped each other in hard hugs. The commotion brought Eglė's parents outside. Her mother shed tears and pinched each child's cheek. The men went into town to gather the rest of the family, many married, with children of their own.

Eglė's mother fingered her daughter's velvet gown. "He provides well for you, I see." She grew misty again. "But I'm so glad you've escaped, just the same!"

Eglė shook her head. "No, no! We're just visiting. Zilvynas is peculiar, and controlling, yes. But he's a good father. He cares for me." She blushed, not used to talking about romance with her mother. "And I love him very much."

Her mother frowned. "Eglė, you can't be serious."

Eglė squeezed her mother's shoulders. "I'm not a little girl anymore, Mom. We're heading home in about a week. But I promise I will visit as much as I can!"

Just depends how many iron boots her hubby's hiding.

With over a dozen siblings to catch up with, the first five days of the trip flew by. Eglė did everything she could to assure her family that she was happy and safe. But Zilvynas had told her to be evasive about their home life. So her family was reluctant to believe her.

On the sixth day, Eglė's sisters offered to take her into town for some sightseeing. "Let the men care for the children, for once!" they said, laughing. Eglė was happy to indulge them, unsure of the next time they'd be together.

Unbeknownst to Eglė, her twelve brothers were intent on getting more intel on her husband. They knew the most vulnerable of the family would be the way in. They lured Ąžuolas to the shed to question him. They were nice, at first. But quickly their polite questions became harsh demands. The boy was shocked at the sudden anger from the uncles who had welcomed them so happily just days before.

"Dammit, boy! Tell us where your father lives if you know what's good for you!" they badgered.

The boy remembered his father's words. "I'll never tell you!"

He had guts, for one so young. His uncles finally resorted to violence to force the secrets out of him. But Ąžuolas didn't crack.

Next, the men worked on Uosis, then little Beržas. The boys kept their word to their father, clenching their jaws and squeezing their eyes closed against the tears.

At last, the men pulled Drebulė into the shed. She was already terrified, having witnessed her brothers' pain. She broke quickly, trembling as she revealed their home and recited the verse:

Dear Zilvynas, come forth, my king,
If you're alive, white foam you'll bring.
But if you've died, a fate I dread,
The bubbly foam will come back red.

I can get the uncles going after Zilvynas: Eglė's forced marriage is creepy, and in folk beliefs their marriage violates the natural world. But the use of the kids as pawns is so, so cruel. I don't have a joke for it, I'm just bummed the fuck out!

The twelve uncles, each with a scythe in hand, marched down to the lake. They repeated the verse and stepped forward when a frothy white mass of waves surged, bringing the snake king to shore. Caught off guard and defenseless, Zilvynas was no match for twelve armed men. Eglė's brothers cut off his head and dismembered him, burning his remains to ash.

*　*　*

On the ninth day, Eglė was ready to go home. The trip had soured over the last few days. Her brothers returned to their own families with barely a goodbye. Her children grew closed off and nervous. She figured they missed their father, and she understood. Despite their trust issues, she was eager to hold her husband in her arms again.

Eglė led the children back to the lake, trying to raise their spirits with jokes and games. Once the house was out of sight, the boys lightened up, chasing each other the rest of the way. Drebulė plodded behind, until her mother picked her up. The girl clung to her neck.

When they reached the edge of the forest, the lake a shining expanse, Eglė told them all to hold hands. "Let's say it together! One, two, three..."

Dear Zilvynas, come forth, my king,
If you're alive, white foam you'll bring.
But if you've died, a fate I dread,
The bubbly foam will come back red.

The water rippled, then rose into a single bloody wave. It crashed, staining the shore, before receding to stillness.

The family stared at the water in shock. Then Ąžuolas broke the silence, howling, "Who told? Who told?" The boys started fighting. Drebulė curled up in a tiny ball.

Eglė stumbled into the lake. She repeated the verse a second time, allowing the gruesome current to pull her knee-deep. She chanted it again; the third time, she heard her husband's voice in her mind.

Your brothers slayed me, he told her. *They bullied the children to obtain the verse. But only little Drebulė gave it to them.*

Eglė felt her blood run cold as she pulled herself out of the water. The cries of her children battled with her instinct to fold into her own grief. She took in each of the boys, despairing for them. But as she gazed on Drebulė, a thread of resentment cut through her empathy. It sickened her.

In a trance, she staggered toward the forest. The boys followed, tugging her waterlogged gown and sobbing. "I'm sorry, Mama!" they said through tears. "We didn't tell, we swear!"

Eglė gathered them together and gazed up at the trees.

"Take away my sons' pain!" she moaned. "Silence their mouths; strengthen their spirits! Let the rain wash away their sorrow, and never let them recall this terrible, terrible day!"

The boys pulled away from her; their cries ceased. Eglė saw a mighty oak standing where her eldest had been. An ash grew next to him, bending toward his mother. A birch sprouted next, straight and proud.

Eglė turned back. Her youngest sat by the lake sorrowfully, shaking like a leaf. All Eglė could see was a weak little girl who couldn't keep her promise.

"Take away her pain!" Eglė pleaded. "Erase the guilt, both hers and mine. I cannot bear to look on her, my little girl that buckled and broke and lost us her father!"

The forest rustled. Where Drebulė sat bent a weeping willow, trembling over the lake.

Eglė gazed at the sky, stretching her arms toward it as if she could leap out of her own body. "Take away my pain!" she lamented." I cannot bear this loss! I cannot bear my rage! Harden my heart so I may never mourn him, nor blame my child who betrayed us!"

Eglė's voice was sucked into silence. An enormous spruce reached into the clouds, towering over the others.

The forest was quiet, but for the lapping of the lake. Its waters reflected the blue sky once more. A small ringed snake emerged from the tall grass and wound its way to the spruce. It curled up in a hollow between the trunk and the ground, laying its head on one of her roots.

I dunno about you, but I'm gonna go eat my feelings.

✶ ✶ ✶

SOURCE: Irina Zheleznova, *Tales from the Amber Sea*.

Want to read more Lithuanian folktales? Check out *Folktales of Lithuania: Six Comics Inspired by Traditional Stories* by Donna Druchunas.

BLANCA ROSA, MOTHER OF THIEVES

A Chilean Snow White

Once there lived a young girl named Blanca Rosa, who received a very special gift.* Her mother was dying, but before she departed, she provided comfort to her child in the form of a small enchanted mirror. "If you ever miss my face," Blanca's mother told her, "ask the mirror to summon me, and I will be back by your side. The mirror will tell you whatever your heart most desires to know."

This connection between mother and mirror is so satisfying. Giving the mirror the weight of the mother's legacy lends it a uniquely personal and feminine power. It also makes this Snow White folktale a close cousin of "Cinderella," which is generally more reliant on magic passed from a deceased mother to daughter.

The compact mirror became Blanca Rosa's constant companion. Hardly a day went by when she didn't stop to chat with the mom in the mirror.

---

* *The Grimms' "Snow White" is the only version I've read that opens with the "child as white as snow and red as blood" scene, though Blanca Rosa's name indicates a relationship to the white/red color theme. Commonalities in Snow White tales are usually the jealous caregiver, the hit man savior, the poison-induced sleep, and the princely marriage.*

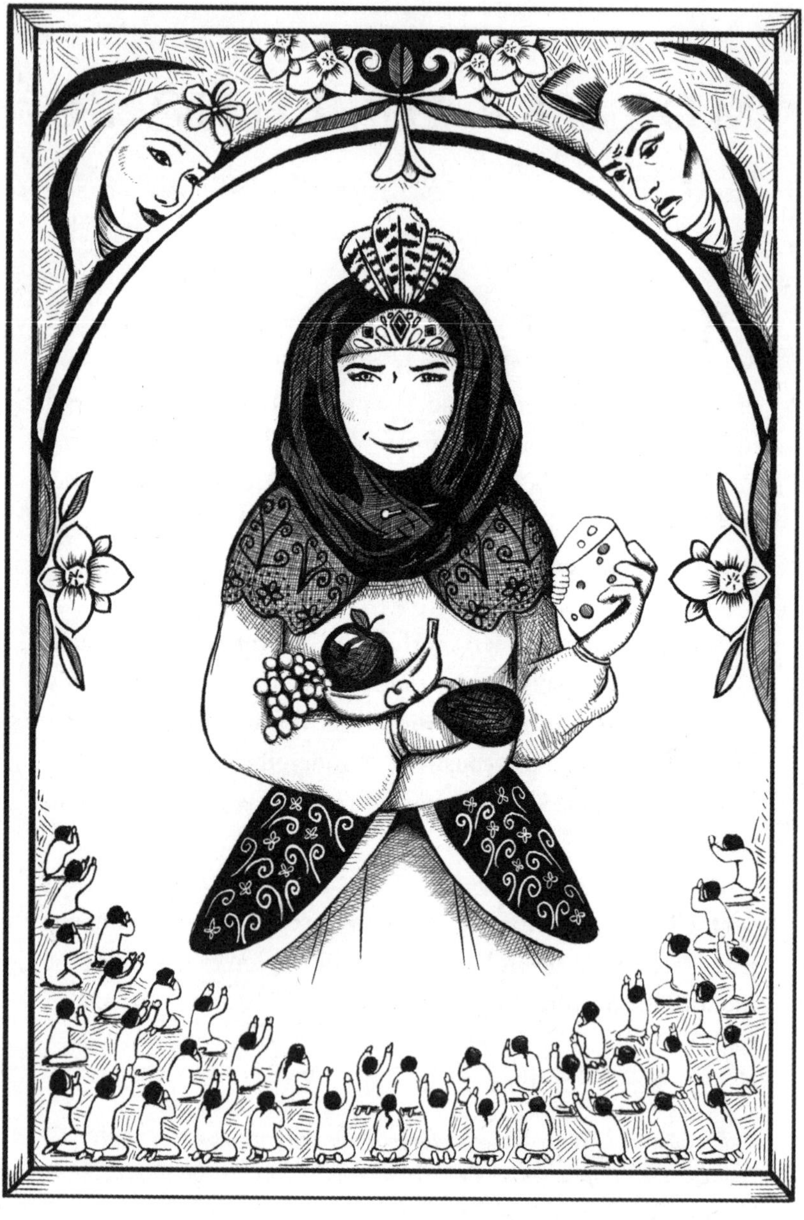

We are not privy to what Blanca Rosa asked of the mirror, but if she was anything like me as a tween, she probably asked questions like, "What is Jonathan Brandis's favorite color?" and "Will NBC visit the Rhode Island Mall to cast Jonathan Brandis's girlfriend on *seaQuest*?" and "Am I gay if I think Jonathan Brandis was cute as a girl in *Ladybugs*?"

The habit followed her into young adulthood, by which time her father had remarried an attractive but vain woman named Martina. When Martina first observed Blanca Rosa confiding in the mirror, it looked like the girl was talking to herself; Blanca Rosa bore a strong resemblance to her mother. But once Martina learned that the mirror was enchanted, she wanted it badly. She demanded that Blanca Rosa hand it over, and the girl meekly obliged.

Martina was proud of her looks. Too proud. She wanted the mirror to confirm that she was the most beautiful woman in the land. "Tell me, mirror, is there a more gorgeous woman than I?" she asked (possibly rhetorically).

The magic mirror didn't mince words. "Your stepdaughter, Blanca Rosa."

Here's where the mother's connection to the mirror really pays off. If it's a vessel for the mother's spirit, the mirror is deliciously catty. It even makes the subjective idea of "the most beautiful woman" better. Of course Blanca Rosa is the most beautiful to her own loving mother.

Martina angrily snapped the mirror shut. Unable to accept second place, she hired a group of hit men to eliminate Blanca Rosa. Unfortunately, she hired softhearted killers. For the men found themselves unable to take the life of a woman so stunning.

They simply abandoned her in the woods. Luckily, Blanca Rosa wasn't left alone for long. As she wandered, wondering which berries were edible and which would kill her, a kind old man found her and took her in.

Martina confidently opened her stolen mirror a few days after the hit men had absconded with Blanca Rosa. "Well, mirror? Who is the fairest woman in the land now?"

The mirror stared back smugly. "It's still Blanca Rosa. She's alive and well, despite your scheming!"

"Shit!" Martina stamped her foot. "Where is she?"

The mirror frowned. "I don't want to tell you that."

"Tough titties, ghost lady. You have to give me my 'heart's desire.' And my 'heart's desire' is to know who is hiding my stepdaughter!"

The mirror begrudgingly revealed her daughter's hiding spot, and Martina marched right over. She knocked, and after a bit of a scuffle, the old man answered. Martina batted her eyes at the guy. "I know you're hiding Blanca Rosa. But hopefully you haven't gotten too attached to her. I want you to kill her."

The old man did his best to object. "Why would I do that?"

"Because I'll have you executed if you don't," Martina declared. "To make sure the job gets done this time, I demand proof. Give me the girl's eyes and tongue."

The old man recoiled. "Jeez, lady. You won't settle for an internal organ? Her heart? Her liver?"

"Hearts and livers all look the same," Martina reasoned. "But no one has eyes as blue as Blanca Rosa's. Plus, it'll really fuck up that pretty face!"

The old man stalled. "Well, what do you need her tongue for?"

Martina had no answer for that, so she ignored him. "You have twenty-four hours."

The old man and Blanca Rosa tried to brainstorm a way out of this situation. "Let me turn myself in," Blanca Rosa insisted. "If she's so intent on killing me, she can do it herself."

The old man patted her hand. "I'm sure there's another way. Perhaps we could trick her." As he racked his brain wondering where he could get his hands on a random set of eyeballs and tongue, he felt a wet nose poke his hand. It was his dog, a beautiful dapple-coated Great Dane. For the first time, the old man noticed how the dog's eyes matched Blanca Rosa's baby blues.

NOOOOOOOOOOOOOOOOOOOOOOOOOOOO!!

So this was how the old man tricked Martina into believing Blanca Rosa was dead. She received the dog's eyes and tongue on a fancy platter. If the tongue smelled of kibble, she didn't notice.

Fearful for the old man's safety, Blanca Rosa left to hide out in the forest. **(If someone killed their dog for me, I'd probably skedaddle too. Family dinners would be way too awkward.)** She survived there for a long time. One morning, nestled in the branches of a tree, and quite the worse for wear, Blanca Rosa saw a band of men making their way through the woods. They were a rough-and-tumble batch of characters. Some were hauling heavy bags behind them. She counted forty men in all. Though Blanca didn't have much tracking experience, she was able to follow the noisy group all the way home. They resided in an underground den carved into a hilly area of the forest. The girl made her way up a nearby tree, and slept there until the following morning, when the forty men hiked out of the cave.

Forty men coordinating their schedules is more unrealistic than a talking mirror. Since when has a large group of adults ever been able to regularly meet? I've had bands, D&D groups, and

book clubs all fall apart due to this problem, with only five or six of us.

Blanca Rosa snuck into the den, hoping to find better food than the roughage she'd been consuming for weeks. What she found was more than she could have dreamed. All the best artisanal meats, cheeses, sweets, and wines in the land awaited her. She also saw a horde of jewels and other valuables. It was clear that this was a den of thieves. So, she did a little thieving of her own, filling her stomach for the first time in ages. Stuffed, she scaled her tree for a proper food coma.

When the men returned that evening, they could tell that something was off. A very fancy Bordeaux they had been saving was almost empty. Their piles of jewels looked as though someone had run their fingers through them. The floor was strewn with dead leaves and pine needles. The leader of the bandits decided they would post a guard the next day to find out who had discovered their den.

After the sun rose and the men left for their daily marauding, the guard watched Blanca Rosa descend from her tree like a weird bird and waltz right past him into the den. Apparently sleeping in trees had not diminished her beauty. The guard found her so enchanting that he didn't believe her to be mortal at all. As Blanca Rosa rapturously ate raspberries from each finger, he fell to his knees and began earnestly praying. He didn't stop until his fellow bandits returned. "What the fuck is going on here?" they asked.

"My friends," the guard announced. "We *have* been found out: by an angel from heaven. We have been visited by the Virgin Mary herself!"*

---

* *Just as pagan traditions were later adopted for Christian holidays, Mary (as well as Jesus and Joseph) often took the place of wise women and other immortals in folktales with Catholic influence.*

His fellow thieves looked at each other incredulously. "Have you already started drinking?"

"No, I swear!" The guard took them through what he'd witnessed. "The Virgin descended from that tree and entered the den. Some time later, she ascended back up to heaven by that same tree, this time with a handful of hazelnuts."

The bandits decided they'd leave five men as lookouts the following day. (They never thought to investigate the tree?) This time, when Blanca Rosa crept down the tree and gnawed on a shank of ham, five thieves fell to their knees, praying for heaven's forgiveness. The leader of the bandits declared he himself would be the watchdog the next day, to figure out this mess once and for all.

The next morning, Blanca Rosa eagerly scurried to her den of goodies. She had scooped a handful of goat cheese halfway to her mouth when she heard a shocked cry. She cursed and turned around to face the man who'd found her. A burly, tattooed bandit knelt at her feet, muttering Hail Marys. "I'm so sorry to break in, señor," Blanca began awkwardly.

"Nonsense, my lady!" the bandit cried. "It is I and my men who owe you an apology. Please, forgive us our sins, Mother of God!"

Blanca Rosa looked around. "Uh, what?"

"I didn't believe the others when they'd told me the Virgin had visited to punish us for our sinful ways." The bandit wept, clinging to Blanca Rosa's tattered skirts. "But I see now what must be done."

"You're mistaken, friend." Blanca Rosa patted the bandit's shoulder, clutching her handful of crumbly cheese. "I am just a lost girl who needed something to eat."

"It is my band of thieves who are lost!" the bandit wailed. "Please let us repent! How can we serve you?"

"I don't require repentance!" Blanca Rosa insisted, laughing. "I could use some shelter, though, if you would provide?"

"Yes!" the bandit rose to his feet hastily, still hunching his bulky shoulders respectfully. "We shall convert the den into a shrine to you, our merciful Mother. We will clothe thee, collect alms in your name, and lay tributes at your feet. What can I do first as your humble servant?"

The girl decided to roll with it. "Do you have any more of this awesome cheese?"

From that day forward, the forty thieves converted their den into a house of worship for their new saintly Mother. Blanca Rosa was dressed in silk and sparkling jewels and sat on a throne of gold. Instead of thieving, the men collected for "the church." Blanca Rosa acted as a caretaker to her swarthy adopted "brothers" and was happy for the first time since her mother had died.

So, of course, her stepmother and a weird prince had to ruin everything!

See, the town was buzzing with the sudden change in behavior of the notorious bandits. These tough guys everyone tried to avoid were humbly collecting donations in the name of God and extolling the virtues of their sacred Mother. One of them, talented with a paintbrush, crafted a portrait of the "Virgin," and everyone who laid eyes on it was stunned at her beauty. They spread the word that the most alluring, angelic woman was guardian of the scariest men in town.

It just goes to show: You can try to get off the grid as much as you can, but the grid will track you down if it grids hard enough.

When Martina heard this, she was furious. "Mirror!" she cried after rushing home in a sulk. "Is it true? Is there a more beautiful woman than me living in the woods?"

The mirror cackled. "Yes, bitch! It's Blanca Rosa! She's alive and worshipped by forty strapping men!"

Martina sighed. "Never hire a man to do women's work!"

She put out an ad for a powerful sorceress. An old witch answered the call.

See, this is secretly a *feminist* story. SUPPORT WOMEN-LED BUSINESS!

The witch disguised herself as a beggar and hunted down the bandits' lair. She begged to see the famous Virgin, and Blanca Rosa was happy to oblige. But when the old woman offered her a basket of fruit, she refused. "We have plenty here. Keep this food for yourself!"

"You are gracious, Mother Mary," the old witch intoned. "Before I take my leave, would you allow a poor old woman one last request?"

"Of course, doña."

"Would you let me stroke your beautiful raven hair?"

Blanca Rosa crouched, and the old woman ran a wrinkled hand through her silken locks. Suddenly Blanca Rosa gasped and fell into a faint. For the old witch had jabbed her with a cursed pin, sending her into an impenetrable sleep.

Here we see the continuation of our feminist screed: Women can be just as bad at killing people as men!

The thieves were beside themselves when they found Blanca Rosa. They tended to her for a short while, but when it was apparent that she would never wake up, they organized a lavish burial. She was adorned in lace with layers of skirts carefully cushioning her. Pearls dotted her folded hands, her tresses, and the tips of her shoes. Her casket was crafted of pure gold and silver and sealed up tight. They buried Blanca Rosa at sea.

Now, a ways down the long Chilean coast lived a young prince named Nicolas. He had a simple life, as far as princes go. His sisters, two old maids, lived with him at home. They were very demanding housemates, so Nicolas would often go fishing to get away. One day, as he was pulling his nets in, he noticed a large hunk of gold lodged against the rocks onshore. With the help of a few other fishermen, he pulled a gleaming metallic casket from the waters and decided to take it home.

I regret to inform you: He brought the casket straight to his bedroom. "Don't bother me!" he barked at his sisters, who glared back suspiciously.

Alone, he puzzled over the fine craftsmanship of the piece. Sure, that's it. He was just a coffin nerd! He realized he wouldn't be able to simply lift open its lid, so he found his toolbox and began tinkering like a fuckin' weirdo.

Nicolas remained shut up in his room for most of a week before he was able to extrude the casket's last rivet and remove the lid. He took one look at Blanca Rosa laid out like a saint and immediately fell for her.

Well, I wish I could tell you Nicolas was a perfectly lovely gentleman who asked around town about the fancy lady in the golden casket to give her a proper burial. But not our prince. As far as he was concerned, he had just found himself in a forensic science experiment. He proceeded to lay Blanca Rosa out on the bed and strip her naked, poring over each piece of jewelry and clothing as if it would offer him clues to her identity. Stumped, he decided the natural next step would be to comb her hair. It didn't take long for his comb to hit a strange bump on the girl's scalp. Parting her hair, he saw the head of a pin sticking out, which he removed with a pair of tweezers.

Awaking Snow White with a kiss is rare. I haven't yet read a folk version where it happens. Disney yoinked this from "Sleeping Beauty." Generally, she wakes when the item that "kills" her is removed, either accidentally when her corpse is mishandled

(thank you, Brothers Grimm) or when someone notices it while dressing the body for burial. So far Nicolas is the only prince I've encountered who made Snow a life-sized Totally Hair Barbie.

Suddenly Blanca Rosa's eyes flew open and she sat up. She took in her unfamiliar surroundings with growing fear and pulled back from the strange man hovering over her with tools. "Where are my brothers?" she cried. She realized she was naked and scrambled for the sheet to cover her. "What the hell are you doing to me?"

"Relax!" Nicolas said. "I am a friend. I found you floating in a casket on the sea—"

"Listen, buddy!" Blanca Rosa snapped, justifiably freaking out. "The last time I was conscious, I was home and fully dressed!" She got up and reached for her gown, trying to keep some semblance of modesty.

Nicolas, like many princes before him, believed he had called dibs and wasn't about to give them up. "Don't leave!" he pleaded, grabbing her arm. "We're just starting to get to know each other!"

Blanca Rosa tried to pull away. "Let. Me. GO!"

Nicolas decided he liked the girl better when she wasn't yelling at him. So he restrained her and pushed the tack back into her scalp. She flopped back onto the bed like a rag doll.

Are you screaming in rage like I did when I read this plot point? Sometimes it's the prince's mother who puts her back to sleep! Don't be like that, Mom!

Nicolas decided to take a walk and figure out what to do with his beautiful but annoyingly self-assured toy. He locked his room up tight. His older sisters stared, having overheard the scuffle. "Don't mess with my things!" he yelled like a teenager. He left for his walk.

His sisters immediately crowded around the keyhole of the door, straining for a glimpse of whatever (or whoever) their brother was hiding. "I see fancy clothes and jewelry," one of them hissed. "But that's all I can get from this angle."

Nicolas arrived back with a plan. Stowed in his room once again, he removed the pin from Blanca Rosa. "Listen, I looked around for your brothers, and they're nowhere to be found," he lied. "But I can provide a lovely life for you, if you'd be willing to stay as my wife. Here. In this room. In secret. Because my sisters just won't get it."

Blanca Rosa fumed, staying silent to avoid his magical roofie. Nicolas shuffled his feet. "Look, it's this or live on the streets!"

What a choice! In the absence of better options, Blanca Rosa decided to stay with Nicolas.

For some time, the two holed up together in the prince's bedroom. Nicolas's sisters let their little brother have his weird charade, though anyone could see he was bringing a lot more food in; and, wait a minute, was that an extra chamber pot? They bided their time until Nicolas left for another fishing trip. One sister used a hairpin to pick the lock, and the nosy ladies broke into his chambers.

Blanca Rosa sat by the window forlornly. She stood wearily when the two strange women busted in.

"So, you're the little tramp who Nicolas is obsessed with!" the sisters declared. They seized the poor girl and yanked off her jewelry, claiming anything Nicolas gave to Blanca Rosa belonged to the family. Not satisfied with that, they tore at her silk gown. After stealing all of her finery and thoroughly humiliating her, they shoved Blanca Rosa out into the street without so much as a doily of clothing.

What the fuck is it with this family and removing everyone's clothes?

Thrust into yet another scary situation for—what is this, the third or fourth time?—Blanca hid out until she could fashion a toga out of a stolen tarp. She ran as far across town as she could, then looked for the first kind face she could find. It belonged to an old cobbler, who was a normal, sympathetic man, thank God! He ushered Blanca Rosa inside and helped her get cleaned up and calmed down. He welcomed her to stay as long as she needed.

When Nicolas discovered his chamber had been ransacked and his pretty prisoner—I mean, common-law wife—had been thrown out, he was devastated. He set out to find Blanca Rosa, but once again proved to be a useless detective. His methods consisted mostly of loafing around town sulking. He had no success until he was lucky enough to learn that a beautiful lady was shacked up with the cobbler. He sprinted to the shop.

I don't know how that oaf managed to convince Blanca Rosa to return with him and properly marry him, but he did. If I were telling this story—

Wait, I am! Ahem:

Nicolas delivered the most incredible apology ever given to a woman in the history of fairy tales. He also agreed to a laundry list of demands from Blanca Rosa: "First, *actually* track down my burglar brothers so that I know who to turn to if shit goes down. Second, get my magic mirror back from my stepmother. Third, evict your maniacal sisters. Finally, you do not get to so much as lay a *finger* on me without permission from my lips. Otherwise, I'll have my brothers break your fucking knees. If you can agree to those terms, in writing, in front of several witnesses, then I deem you cute enough to make my life partner."

Nicolas accepted those terms. Not only did he evict his two sisters, he had them torn to pieces by a pair of wild horses! Yikes! Their blood had barely been rinsed from the pavement before the town celebrated the wedding of the prince and his beautiful bride. The forty thieves were in attendance, and I like to think a couple of them moved in to make sure their beloved Virgin was being taken care of properly. But if what I hear is true (and I hope it is), Blanca Rosa lived happily for the rest of her days.

✳ ✳ ✳

SOURCE: Yolando Pino Saavedra. *Folktales of Chile*.

Want to read more Chilean fairy tales? Check out my source for this tale!

Part 2

SWIPE RIGHT TO YOUR HAPPY ENDING

You have to kiss a few frogs before you find your prince. So many frogs.

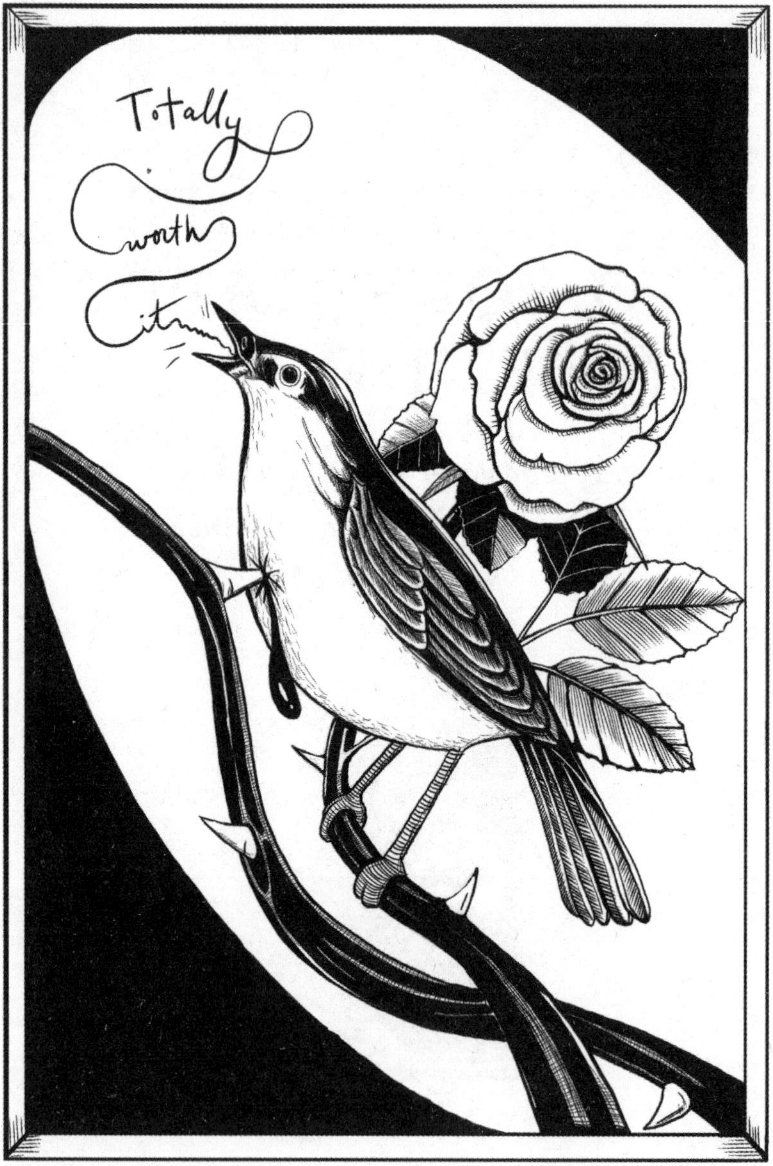
Totally
worth
it

LOVE IS FOR THE BIRDS

Oscar Wilde's "The Nightingale and the Rose"*

In the branches of a holm oak tree lived a nightingale. Like other birds of her breed, the nightingale sang 24/7, belting her face off. She was louder than bagpipes in a small pub on St. Patrick's Day. Louder than a table of theater kids on karaoke night. But, unlike her fellow birds, she sang of a singular subject: She sang about love. Love in all its forms. Love across time and space. Love for love's sake. The nightingale wished above all that she could experience ~True Love~.

I considered changing the sex of Wilde's nightingale, because female nightingales don't sing. But the way the nightingale is treated rings very true to my experience as a person of a marginalized gender, so inaccurate lady bird she stays!

The oak tree stood in the rose garden of a philosophy student. As she sang, the nightingale often watched the young man hunched over books, scribbling notes. But today the student interrupted the nightingale's ditty. He slammed the door, stomped across the garden, and flopped onto a stone bench. "I've been cock blocked by a red rose!"

The nightingale was fascinated by this outburst from the

---

* *This tale does not come from the oral tradition. Oscar Wilde's fairy tales, while referential to folklore, are all original works.*

otherwise studious gentleman. She saw for the first time how handsome he was, with curly, tousled dark hair, a clear ivory complexion, and deliciously pouty lips as red as the rose he scorned. The nightingale's heart raced. She had sung about lovers and yearning for so long, but the lover had no face. Until now.

I relate to the nightingale, because I too was a young person aching for romantic connection, who transferred those feelings onto a cute curly-haired young man mourning lost love: Joey McIntire of New Kids on the Block.

"All the professor's daughter wants in exchange for one dance at tomorrow's ball is a single red rose," the student continued expositionally. "I'm her dad's best student. I run circles around my classmates. But what does it matter, if I can't get her that damn rose!" He stalked the garden, kicking plants just beginning to blossom. "I've got yellow roses, white, and a bunch of stupid daisies, but not one flippin' red rose!" He buried his angelic face in his hands and groaned.

The nightingale hopped out farther onto her branch, inching as close to the cranky student as she dared. *This is the romance I have held in my heart,* she thought, tilting her head toward the boy. *I sing of joyous love, and he grieves for lack of it. Love must surely be the most splendid gift, more valuable than all the gold and diamonds a man can carry.*

"Tomorrow I'll be sitting alone like a loser while a bunch of friggin' posers cozy up on my girl," the student monologued to no one. "The band's love songs will mock me as I slowly die of humiliation. All for a fucking! Red! Rose! UUUUUGH!" The young man sprawled out on the grass, pounding his fists.

"What is the deal with this guy?" asked a little green lizard, scurrying clear of the student's flailing.

"Hell if I know!" a butterfly answered him, only half paying attention.

"Why on earth is he sobbing, and so loudly?" a daisy muttered.

The nightingale sighed dreamily. "He weeps for a red rose."

"A red rose?" The group laughed. But the nightingale understood.

Would she have understood if the student wasn't the Timothée Chalamet of the Victorian Era?

Suddenly the bird was inspired. She flew across the garden to a rose tree by the fountain and alighted on a spray. She gently pecked the tree awake. "Friend, would you give me a red rose in exchange for a song?"

"I'm sorry," the tree replied. "My roses are white: whiter than the ocean's foam; whiter than the snowy Alps; whiter than a lady clapping on the counts of one and three. But check with my brother, the tree that grows by the sundial."

I adore how Wilde's fairy tales riff on Hans Christian Andersen, offering homages and subversions of the original text. Here, we see him mimic Andersen's use of flora and fauna as characters (see "The Fir Tree," "The Snow Queen," and others). Sometimes they operate as a Greek chorus, and other times they're just loquacious time-wasters. (For further reading, see works by Wilde scholars Christopher S. Nassaar and Peter Raby.)

"Thanks for the tip!" the nightingale chirped. She flitted off to the second rose tree. "Would you give me a red rose in exchange for a song?"

"Sorry, nightingale," the tree replied. "My roses are yellow. As yellow as Rapunzel's tresses; as yellow as goldenrod; as yellow as the belly of an anonymous commenter on YouTube."

The tree went on like this, anachronistically mansplaining colors. The nightingale waited.

"But you might ask my brother," the tree continued, "the one who grows under the student's window."

The nightingale soared off to the next rose tree. "Would you give me a red rose in exchange for a song?'

"You're out of luck, bird," the tree replied. "I usually sport loads of red roses. More red plumes than a cardinal in the snow; more red dots than a strawberry farm in June; more red flags than a pickup artist at a bachelorette party. But this winter has been long and harsh, spilling well into spring. I haven't been able to produce a single bud."

"I only need one," the nightingale fretted. "Is it truly an impossible task?"

The tree sighed. "Technically, there is a way. But it's frightful."

"Tell me!" the nightingale insisted.

"To get a rose from my withered form," the tree began, "you must build it with music and moonlight. For it to be a red rose, it must be stained with the blood of the seeker's heart."

"Well, that doesn't sound too bad," the nightingale reasoned. "I frequently sing at night, and I can spare a few drops of blood."

"It's much more grisly!" the tree argued, his bark blanching. "You have to sing while piercing your heart on one of my thorns, transferring your life's blood fully to me."

"Oh." The nightingale hesitated. "The price for a single red rose is death? Seems kinda steep."

Here's another mirror to Andersen: the nightingale devotes herself to the idea of ~True Love~ as fervently as the Little Mermaid worships the idea of being human. They see those passions personified in hot, annoying strangers who toss aside their excruciating sacrifices. It's easy to pity them and forget that we

sorta do the same, but through parasocial relationships and celebrity worship. We keep putting our faves on pedestals until they inevitably cancel themselves.

    She considered it. "I love my life. I love watching the sunset through the trees in the park. I love the sweet taste of birdseed, the sweet scent of the bluebells, and the sweet triumph of defecating on a man's carriage." She regarded a thorn curving out from one of the tree's sprays. "But I've always sung about love *larger* than life. Perhaps a bird's heart is no match for a man's love." She swooned at the student, who was rolling on the lawn, tearing up fistfuls of turf.

    The tree grimaced. "That's the guy?"

    The nightingale returned to the oak tree, perching just above the student's prostrate body. The lad looked up at the sound, noticing her for the first time. "Do not despair!" the nightingale told him. "You will have your red rose! All I ask in return is that you fully devote yourself to love, for love is worth much more than your philosophy books. *C'est la raison d'être!*"

    The oak shed a tear. "Would you sing me one last song, nightingale?" the tree asked. "To remember you by?"

    The nightingale crooned a silvery peal of notes to the oak tree. Her voice was as pure as an eight-year-old choirboy's, with a melismatic range Mariah Carey herself couldn't manage.

    The student puzzled over why some bird was tweeting its ass off at him. "That's not a bad tune! But what could her little ditty offer to me? She's just squawking away with no meaning or purpose." He chuckled. "Never did meet an artist who could keep up with a philosopher. Still, it's pretty. Ya nailed it, birdbrain!"

    Condescending to the bird seemed to lift the student's spirits. He retreated to his house and fell asleep to visions of plowing his sweetheart.

    As the moon rose, the nightingale steeled herself for an operatic all-nighter. She trilled through vocal warm-ups and coated her delicate throat with sugar water from the hummingbird's trough. Ready at last, she alighted on the red rose tree, next to a pointy thorn.

The rose tree called out, "Sing for me!"

The nightingale centered her breast over the thorn and leaned onto its tip. She gasped at the bite of pain. Then she sang.

She sang of emerging love. The love that first blossoms in the heart of boys and girls. Of new affection between crushes. Of a youth's first heartbreak. As she sang, a stem burst forth from the tree, growing past the student's windowsill, and from that, the delicate white petals of a rose bloomed.

"Keep singing!!" the rose tree commanded.

The nightingale leaned in farther to the thorn, her voice catching. She rallied, and sang of passionate, intimate love. She sang of the first touch to flesh, of the cozy morning after. Blood sparkling like garnets slid from her feathers, and the thorn drank it in. The outer petals of the rose became veined with crimson. But the heart of the rose remained as pale as the moon.

"SING!" the rose tree shrieked maniacally. "SING FOR ME!"

The nightingale gritted her beak and pushed with all her might, until her breast met the branch. The thorn pierced into her heart. An anguished cry strained from her throat, but she turned it into song. A song for the sanctity of love promised for a lifetime. For the loyalty of love folded between wrinkled hands. For the power of love to live beyond death.

The rose's petals quivered, then burst fully open as color rushed to its center. The flower perched large and lovely outside the student's window, vibrant in the cool of the night. The moon paused in the sky, reveling in the nightingale's triumph. Her notes traveled beyond the city, to sleeping shepherds in the countryside, whose dreams suddenly burst with the scent of roses and the tang of blood. The whole world stood still.

"You did it!" the rose tree spoke in a hush. "Look at your creation!"

But the only response was the breeze rustling through the leaves. For the nightingale lay dead in the grass, the thorn still hooked tightly to her heart.

The next morning, the student opened his window to air out the stench of dust and depression. His eyes bulged as he saw the glorious red rose waiting for him. "Holy shit! I'm the luckiest man alive!" he cried. Eagerly he grasped it and tore the thing free, cursing as a pricker caught his thumb.

Quickly, he cleaned himself up, grabbed his hat, and dashed out the door with the flower. He ran to his professor's house and waved gaily when he saw his crush sitting prettily on the front lawn. She was winding a skein of blue silk thread and cooing to her lapdog.

"Babe!" the student cried, breathless. "I have it! I have the perfect red rose!" He stopped at the edge of the yard, panting and bracing himself on his knees. He held out the rose limply.

"Run much?" the professor's daughter quipped. The student pushed the blossom in her face and she sneezed, batting it away.

"You told me you'd dance with me if I brought you a red rose," the student reminded her.

The young woman rolled her eyes. "Well, it's no use now. The red will clash with my outfit. Besides, the chamberlain's nephew sent me jewels for his spot on my dance card. What's a cheap rose compared to gold and diamonds?"

The student gaped at her. "The rose is a symbol of my everlasting love!"

The professor's daughter yawned and packed up her sewing basket.

"You're an ungrateful whore!" the student spat.

"You're a deluded prick!" the young woman retorted, scooping up her dog and marching up her drive.

The student turned from the house. "God, I wasted so much time on that bitch! Love is for cucks. I should be putting my energy toward changing the world, not moaning over some stuck-up ho. Fuck this!"

He puffed out his chest and stomped away, casting the rose into the gutter, where it was crushed under a wagon wheel.

Here, of course, is where we see the twist on Andersen's "Nightingale." In the former, the materialism of an emperor and his kingdom are toppled by a rustic bird and her song. In Wilde's world, those who open their hearts (literally) to love, art, and beauty get crushed under society's fickleness. Did Wilde know he was predicting his future?

✳ ✳ ✳

SOURCE: Oscar Wilde, "The Nightingale and the Rose."

Want to read more of Oscar Wilde's fairy tales? I particularly love the comic book versions by P. Craig Russell.

LOVE IS LIKE A TREE

The Xhosa's "Kamiyo of the River," South Africa

Once there lived an old man who owned a full stable but an empty house. He had enormous herds of cattle, making him one of the wealthy men in the village, but all that money couldn't buy anything to fill the silence when he came home. One evening, as he finished up another solo supper of phuthu, he thought, *I'm tired of cooking my own dinner and talking to the walls. I should find a wife.*

Cattle were a main source of wealth for Xhosa tribes. You might say this rich old man is ready for his sugar-daddy era! Though I have some questions about how such a wealthy man stayed single for so long.

The old man took a walk by the river the following morning to plan his romantic pursuits. But where to begin? It was hard to meet new people in a small community. Sure, every generation raised new ladies, but they weren't interested in bedding a village elder.

He sat at the river's edge, dipped his feet in the water, and looked up at the beautiful fruit tree providing shade. Its branches stretched toward the sky like long limbs. The old man had an idea. "I'll carve myself a wife out of the wood of this tree. That way, I can craft the perfect bride."

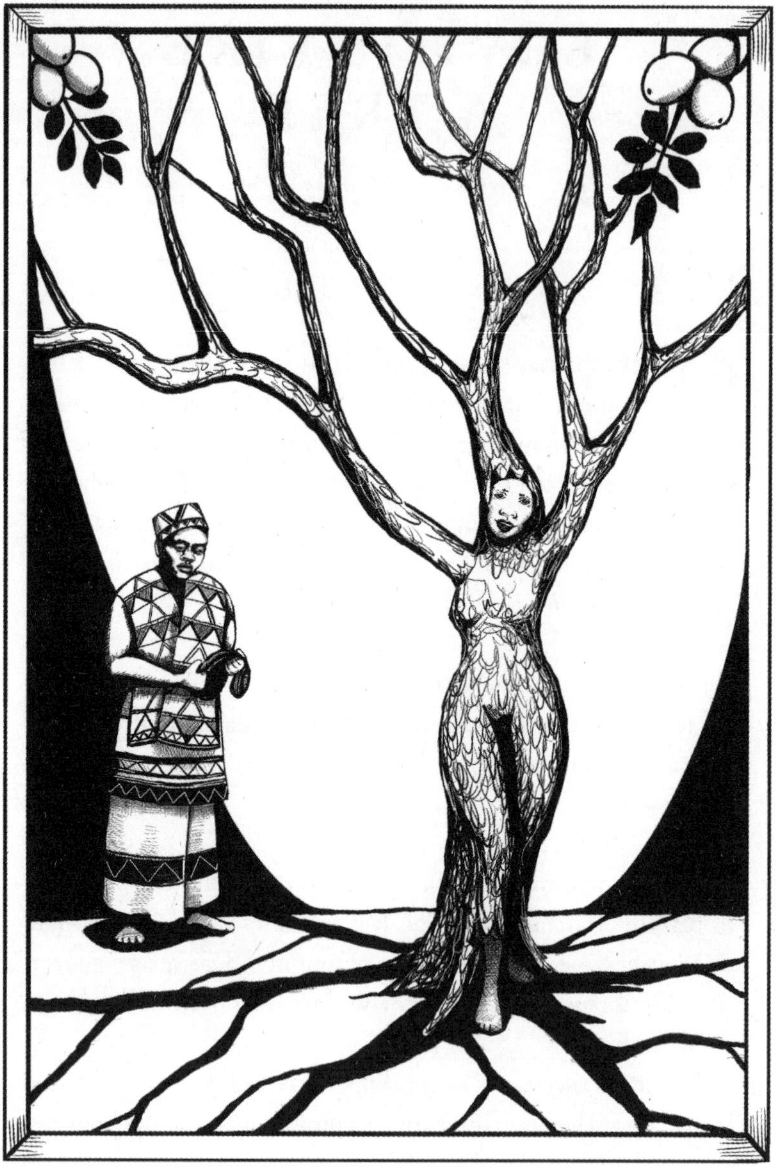

As I began researching this story, the Facebook algorithm offered me a set of AI-generated images depicting Elon Musk getting cozy with a robot girlfriend. There it was, my modern equivalent of a rich man crafting his ideal mate, better than any joke I could come up with. I sighed, witnessing AI taking my job away in real time!

He retrieved an ax and cut down the tree. He brought the wood back to his farm to carve, where he fashioned a lovely young woman from the trunk and branches.

I guess it was too much to hope he'd carve himself a lovely mature woman.

He admired his handiwork. She was so comely, he leaned in and kissed her eyes. When he stepped back, he saw that the wooden woman had transformed into flesh and blood.

Other literal objects of affection in folklore include: "Pygmalion" of course; an Italian boyfriend made of cookie dough; a Nigerian girlfriend made of oil; an Inuit lover made of whale blubber; and, speaking of Wales, a Welshwoman made of flowers.

"You're alive!" the old man cried.
"I am?" the newborn lady replied.
"You are, and you are my wife," the old man said. "I shall call you Marula, after the tree that bore your body."
The old man quickly purchased garments and other necessities for his custom wife: her marital headcloth and apron,* beautiful

---

* *Xhosa women traditionally wore headwear to indicate their marital and social status. Young women wore a plain headband and upgraded to an attention-grabbing hat when they reached marrying age. A conservative*

garments, face paint, and beaded jewelry to highlight her looks, and all the tools a homemaker required. Once he'd taught Marula her chores, he had dinner and a clean house waiting for him every night. He had someone to massage out the knots in his legs from a long day overseeing his farm. Best of all, he had another person to talk at without the pesky obligation to listen back.

DIY Brides are perfect for men of a certain type because they are actual empty vessels. No personality or passions and basically zero vocabulary. It's *The Giving Tree* **meets** *The Stepford Wives.*

The village was surprised that the old man had obtained a wife out of nowhere. Not only that, but the bride was a stunning and demure lady. The young men who passed through seethed with jealousy. How had this old drip landed such a prize?

One day, a cocky young rogue and his entourage decided to make a pass at the most beautiful woman in town. They sauntered up to Marula while she was picking out food from the market. "Pretty lady, tell us your name!" the rogue called.

Marula paused, remembering her husband's advice: *Don't tell anyone about your tree-birth, Marula. People can be pretty weird about sexy dolls coming to life. If anyone asks, tell them you come from the river.*

She smiled innocently. "I am Marula, of the river."

"Well, well, well, Marula of the River." The young man licked his lips. "Why do you waste your delectable fruit on a toothless old man?"

Marula blinked at the boys. "I don't know what you mean."

The group chortled. Their leader closed the space between himself and his mark. "I mean, you deserve a virile, strong fellow

---

head wrap was worn by newly married women, and a voluminous headdress that would be at home at any Easter service was reserved for grand older ladies.

to dote on you. One who could run circles around your ancient husband." He ran a finger down the sharpness of Marula's cheekbone. "Come live with me, Marula of the River."

Marula may have been Born Sexy Yesterday, but she had enough sense to be leery of strange, menacing men. "My home is with my husband," she insisted. Still, when the young man's friends each took one of her arms, she had not the strength nor the wit to resist. They took her up the hill to the home of the thirsty rogue, where they kept her under lock and key.

The old man despaired when he found his home empty. He begged the villagers for information and pieced together why Marula had deserted him. The next morning, he stretched his arm out a window, summoning two pigeons onto the crook of his elbow. "Little birds, fly up the hill and carry a message to my wife," he told them.

The birds flew to the home of the young man. Marula opened her arms, and a bird landed on each of her wrists. They sang to her:

Marula of the River,
Our song comes from your husband.
Marula of the River,
He wants your beaded apron.
Marula, send us home with
Your pretty beaded apron.

The boys laughed at the pigeon's song. "He can have your apron, Marula," their ringleader replied with a smirk. "As long as we have you."

The birds carried Marula's apron back to the shepherd, beating their wings hard to lug the heavy canvas garment across town. The old man laid it out on the table, running his hands over its small glass beads with a sigh, while the pigeons flopped on the ground in exhaustion.

The next day, the old man reached out the window for his little bird messengers to send them after Marula again. "Tell her I want her head wrap." The little birds rolled their eyes, but flew swiftly to the young man's window, where they sang:

> Marula of the River,
> Our song comes from your husband.
> Marula of the River,
> He wants your beaded headband.
> Marula, send us home with
> Your pretty beaded headband.

Once again, the young cad agreed, happy to send Marula's accessories away as long as he had power over her body. The pigeons, thankful that today's luggage was much lighter, dropped the scarf outside the old man's window, where he caught it. He laid it out alongside the beaded apron.

So it went each morning. The old man would summon his United Pigeon Service and send them to gather another belonging of Marula's. The birds retrieved her wristbands, her necklaces, and lastly dragged back her robe. When the old man summoned his messengers the next morning, they happily told him Marula had nothing left to take, assuming they were finally off the hook.

"Then take her life," the old man replied.

Say what? You're really gonna "if I can't have her, nobody will" this situation, my dude? Why don't you use some of that Big Cow money to get your tree woman away from those cretins! And what about you, birds? I thought we were cool!

The pigeons exchanged a look, but set sail to Marula. When they landed, their signature song was in a minor key:

Marula of the River,
Our song comes from your husband.
Marula of the River,
We've come to take your young life.
Marula, raise your eyes up.
We've come to take your young life.

The young men stood up, each ready to swat a bird. But Marula held out her hands to stop them, tilting her head back. The pigeons hovered over her. Each bird kissed one of her eyes, and the men jumped as Marula's body hardened back into polished wood. But her transformation didn't stop there. Her body began to crumble piece by piece. The pieces rolled away from the men, out the door, and down the hill, all the way to the river.

As each wooden chunk fell into the water, the soil by the river burst open. The marula tree sprouted and grew rapidly, her roots grabbing hard and fast onto the earth. Her canopy stretched even higher into the sky than it had before. The old man looked out his window, admiring the beautiful marula tree casting shade over the river once again. That was where she wanted to be, and is where she stands to this day.

In Swahili versions of this tale, the statue-wife transforms into a tree right in her abductor's home. But I like this version, because Marula finds her way home. That feels more like a reclamation. "You can't fire me, husband. I quit!"

✱ ✱ ✱

Source: Nelson Mandela, "Kamiyo of the River."

Want to read more South African folktales? Try *Southern African Folktales*, edited by J. K. Jackson.

LOVE IS A REVOLUTION

A Filipino Myth of Mount Makiling

In 1984, Bonnie Tyler asked, "Where have all the good men gone / and where are all the gods?" Well, Bonnie, the gods got sick of those douchebags and left us to fend for ourselves! At least, that was the case for the Filipino diwata Dayang Makiling.

Makiling lived in the mountain villages of Laguna, where she oversaw the happiness and health of the Tagalog community. Her hut was small, but her powers were enormous; she redirected natural disasters like one of the X-Men; she restored the broken forest if she didn't catch the storm in time; she transformed ginger and other vegetables into gold for those in need; she summoned monsters to chase trophy hunters and greedy loggers from the jungle; and, of course, her beauty was luminous (likely because she was born of moonlight).

You can moisturize all day long, but good celestial genes will buck beauty trends any day.

Life ain't always easy for a ravishing, mighty goddess. Makiling was an intimidating woman to date.

It's easy to feel inadequate when your girlfriend can fend off a typhoon and turn your onions into life savings—or send a salivating beast to eat you if you cheat on her.

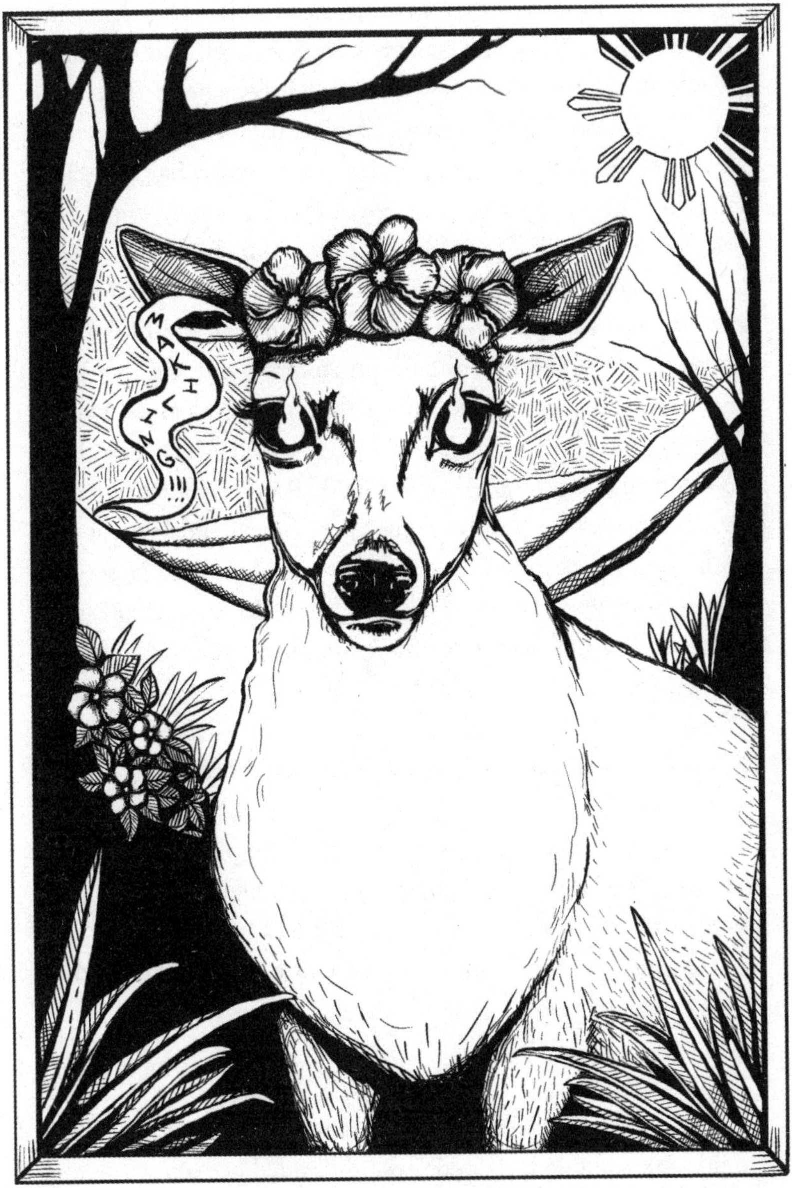
MAKHILING!!!...

But even an immortal woman has needs. Here and there, she crushed on a villager bold enough to love her back. She especially loved crunchy granola types. If a cute birdwatcher or tree hugger crossed her path, she'd reveal herself from the mist, kicking a long leg from the slit of her gauzy white gown like Angelina Jolie. That's all it took to lure a guy back to her hut, where he'd pass the next few weeks or months in romantic bliss.

These guys had commitment issues. (**It's hard to promise everlasting love to a woman literally as old as the hills.**) The birdwatcher turned out to be a philanderer and the tree hugger married a local girl to dodge the draft. Any time Makiling got dumped by a mortal, the entire island felt it; trees bore no fruit, and rivers dried up while Makiling dyed her hair a weird color and ate ube ice cream by the pint. Legend has it that birds consoled her with the tune that would eventually become Olivia Rodrigo's "Drivers License." Then she'd swear off men, transport her hut deep into the mountains, and live alone as a white deer.

I'd do that too if I didn't have to go to work every day!

Being a generous spirit, she knew when to pull herself out of her depressions so no one suffered for long. She truly loved protecting the mountain and those who made it home.

That is, until the Spanish arrived and monumentally fucked everything up.

* * *

MAKILING LEARNED about the new empire in town at a girls' night with some fellow goddesses. She ended her centuries-long exile to catch up with her besties. (**Always a restorative move!**)

"So, who broke your heart this time, girl?" Cacao asked, topping off Makiling's kagatan. "A hunter with a heart of gold?"

"He said I was too emotional," Makiling grumbled. Thunder rumbled in the distance.

Sinukuan tutted. "These modern humans are swine. I should know, I've transformed them into pigs myself! But the new government has made things really strange."

Makiling cocked her head. "What are you talking about? I've been in the mountains for a while; I think I missed a few generations."

The girls brought her up-to-date: Tribal rule had been eradicated; more than seventy-five hundred islands had been lumped together as one territory under the Spanish flag. "And worst of all," Sinukuan said, "the new guys are trying to shove the three of us out of the picture!"

Makiling laughed. "How can mortals manage that?"

Cacao grew somber. "By pushing new gods on our people. Well, one new god. His name is God."

"Speaking of names, they've been renaming us!" Sinukuan spat. "You're *Maria* Makiling, she's *Maria* Cacao, I'm *Maria* Sinukuan. We're all Marias now!"

"This is just a fad," Makiling insisted. "I'll return to the village to suss things out."

The next day (**about fifty years in mortal time**), Makiling moved her hut back down the mountain. She was shocked to see the Catholic churches, the blend of island and Spanish architecture, and swaths of military men ordering locals around. She wandered in a daze, until she heard a wolf whistle. "Hey, long-legs," someone crowed in Spanish, "you got a boyfriend?"

Makiling glared at the offender. Two men ogled her from a construction site. Well, a lot of men ogled her, from all over the place. But these two were a burly Spanish officer with a thick mustache and a fancy, slight mestizo.

"A village girl," the mestizo snarked. "You can tell by the

primitive costume." He waggled his brows. "But you wear it well, senorita."

Makiling rose to her full height. "What the fuck did you just say to me?"

The men laughed. "Hot in more ways than one!" the officer cried.

"Shut up," Makiling snapped. "I am Makiling, the protector of Laguna. I'm here to put an end to this coup."

"Oh, she's one of the Mountain Marias!" the mestizo said as if she weren't there.

"That's not my name," the goddess retorted.

"Maria, Maria, calm down," the officer said, closing in on her. "Such beauty shouldn't risk the frown lines. I am Captain Lara. This is Fernando Gaspar—he is the architect of this beautiful fort we are building. Let us show you around, maybe treat you to a drink? You need to loosen up."

Makiling shook them off. "Get bent!"

She walked away, ignoring their jeers.

The goddess spent the rest of the day healing the plants that were lost from construction, all while observing the locals. She was devastated to see them grovel to their occupiers.

Hey, lady, it's tough to overthrow an empire when you're not all-powerful!

Her grim mood affected the weather; a rainstorm broke out, which halted construction of the fort. By twilight, her anger cooled, and the storm with it. She hiked to one of her favorite waterfalls, breathing deeply of the clear air near the pool at its base.

"It's the best feeling, right? That crispness in the air? The spray of the falls?"

Another man broke her reverie, but less obnoxiously so. A

farmer, by the looks of him, dipping his toes in the lake. He nodded to her but went back to admiring the scenery.

The goddess sat down beside him. "This is the most beautiful spot in Laguna!" she gushed. "I am always happy to meet someone else who appreciates it."

The young man started to introduce himself, then faltered. "You're Dayang Makiling!" He scurried into a bow quickly. "My lady, I . . . How is this happening? How are you talking with me right now?"

Makiling laughed. "It's your lucky day, I guess! Please, sit back down." She gathered her blossom-crowned hair over her shoulder coyly. She liked the guy's kind face (not to mention his puppy-dog eyes).

Look, she has a type!

The man's name was José. He was primarily a farmer, but also a jack-of-all-trades: he sculpted, dabbled in poetry, and volunteered as a translator between locals and Spaniards.

Makiling frowned. "Are you one of the foreigners?"

"No, I grew up in Laguna," José said. "But many of us have had to adopt Spanish names. You've been gone a long time!"

"Ugh," Makiling groaned. "How is it these Spaniards have won everyone over? We used to be made up of many proud nations here."

José considered this. "A lot of folks are just trying to survive. Besides, there's resistance happening on many levels. Some of it is subtle. Look with a closer eye. You'll see."

Makiling and José spent the rest of the night getting to know each other. Legend has it that, as they grew closer, the birds sang a tune that would eventually be covered by Lea Salonga in Disney's *Aladdin*. When they parted, Makiling was smitten.

You can take the goddess out of the village, but you can't take the villager out of the goddess, if she wants said villager inside her.

The goddess settled into a swoony slumber, determined to find the fighters in her beloved Laguna the following day.

The morning brought an unexpected visitor. Makiling answered the door to Captain Lara, gesturing to two men carrying an enormous dead pig.

"Good morning, Maria!" The captain had one red boot perched on a stump, as if posed for a portrait. "I've brought you a gift."

Makiling sputtered, "That pig could feed ten families, at least!"

The captain gave her the ol' finger guns. "And I killed it just for you."

Makiling gawked at the workers, who bowed their heads. She remembered her conversation with José. "Thank you, Captain," she said, forcing a smile. "Why don't you leave your two men to help me butcher it?"

The captain was happy to do so, though he ordered them to hurry. Makiling noticed how the men gave short responses, glowering despite their subservience. After the captain was gone, the goddess leaned in to them conspiratorially. "Bring this pig to the family with the best litsong kawali in town. If they are up for it, spread the word that Dayang Makiling will provide a feast tomorrow!"

The men bowed. "You are forever gracious, my lady!" one said.

At the feast, Makiling and José reunited. "You were right," she told him as they shared a plate of crispy pork and lumpia. "I have been counting the quiet revolutionaries. Those men over there have been dragging their feet on construction for the fort. That woman shared a fable with her children that was obviously about the officers. But those dipshits laughed it off as native nonsense." Her shoulders slumped. "I just wish they would speak out more bluntly."

"The little things add up," José assured her.

Rest assured, José is not encouraging performative activism. Rather, oppressed communities have used subtle methods to push back against colonization. Filipinos specifically earned a reputation of being rude and difficult prior to the Philippine Revolution. But educator Fernando A. Santiago Jr. cataloged records of such behavior and makes a compelling case that this was intentional activism.

The two took a walk, eager for alone time. At the edge of town, as José reached for Makiling's hand, someone shouted, "Maria! Is this man bothering you?" It was Fernando, the smarmy architect.

Makiling crossed her arms. "No. You are!"

Fernando shooed José as if he were a fat housefly. "Leave the woman alone. Don't you have better things to do?"

José turned to Makiling. "Would you like me to stay?" he asked in Tagalog.

Makiling shrugged. "I can handle myself. Take the opportunity to escape this jerk and meet me at the waterfall?" José nodded and took his leave.

"What the hell were you two talking about?" Fernando asked.

Makiling smiled tightly. "Nothing important."

The man scoffed. "My mother insists on speaking the native tongue as well. But you speak Spanish beautifully."

"Actually, I can communicate with anyone who resides in Laguna," Makiling explained. "You're just hearing me in your preferred language. It's a goddess perk." She paused. "If your mother is native, why don't you speak her language too?"

Fernando took Makiling's arm, leading her back into town. She allowed it only for the intel. "My father is Spanish. I am studying in Manila for the year before I settle in Spain. I have no wish to stay in this backward territory longer than I have to." He pulled her in tighter and purred, "I would love to show you my home country someday."

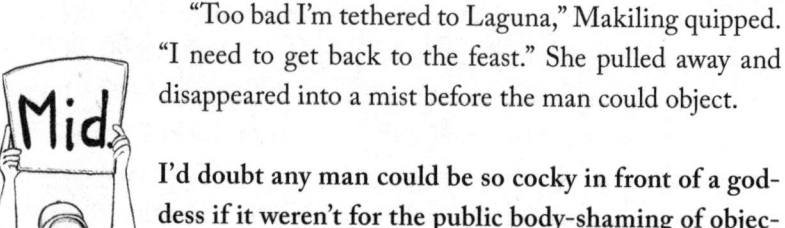

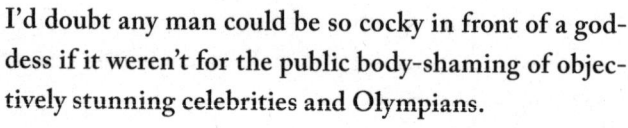

"Too bad I'm tethered to Laguna," Makiling quipped. "I need to get back to the feast." She pulled away and disappeared into a mist before the man could object.

I'd doubt any man could be so cocky in front of a goddess if it weren't for the public body-shaming of objectively stunning celebrities and Olympians.

* * *

FOR THE next few weeks, Makiling could go nowhere without running into the captain or the architect. Captain Lara lovebombed the goddess with gifts—monuments, cornucopias of delicacies, gold and jewels, all at the cost of the flora and fauna. Fernando dragged her to the nearest church to wax about the beauties of the plazas, lecture her on the merits of Catholicism, and bemoan the lack of decent paella. Makiling would summon a thick fog to lose them **(the goddess equivalent of putting in earbuds on the subway)**, then run away in deer form to meet José at the hot springs for a romantic hike.

Makiling thought the unwanted attention couldn't get worse, until Lara and Fernando showed up at her hut together one day. "What now?"

"Maria," the captain said, "the day we met in town, Fernando and I set a little wager."

"We bet on which of us would win you," Fernando continued.

"But neither of us can get the upper hand!" the captain huffed. "We simply won't wait any longer. Who do you choose, Maria?"

Makiling had a wicked idea. "Meet me at Dampalit Falls at midnight for the next full moon. That is when I will reveal my choice."

Now, this is the Bachelorette Rose Ceremony I wanna see!

* * *

THE FALLS glowed beneath a supermoon. So much light touched the jungle, one might forget midnight approached. Makiling sat on a throne of rock cushioned with emerald vine and orchids, overlooking an intimate clearing. Mist shrouded her shoulders like a feather boa and sparkling dewdrops hung from her earlobes. She had never looked sexier (and that's saying something).

José arrived first, jogging across the damp grass. "I got here as soon as I could. Is everything all right?" He registered the goddess's lewk. "Wow! You look incredible. Is this a special occasion? Your birthday? . . . Do you have a birthday?"

Makiling laughed. "No, no! I want to make an impression tonight. Thank you for coming."

"What's this bum doing here?" The captain and the architect arrived. Captain Lara stalked the perimeter of the clearing and Fernando puffed out his chest.

"I invited José," Makiling asserted.

"Makiling . . ." José furrowed his brow. "What's going on?"

The goddess stepped down from her perch, holding a fiery hibiscus. "Three men stand before me, but only one can win my heart tonight." She approached Captain Lara. "Captain, from the way you leered at me in the town square, I learned everything I need to know about you. You mow down jungle to build property in my name, wasting more resources on me in four weeks than I'd seek out in a lifetime. And I am like a thousand years old, dipshit!" She patted his arm condescendingly. "Captain Lara, you will not receive my heart tonight."

The captain's jaw dropped. "But I gave you so much pork!"

"Food you should have used to feed the people," she said. "Like I did!"

Fernando thumbed his nose at Lara. "Haha! Sucker!"

"Not so fast!" Makiling strutted across the clearing to the architect. "Fernando, you're a real piece of work. I am the literal spiritual guardian of this mountain. Yet you have the balls to assume I am dying to get out of this 'sad little backward island'! You're constantly trying to convert me, even though *I am one who is worshipped!* And you demean your ancestors, your kin, as if they are vermin! Get, like, an ounce of a clue, man!" She whirled away so fervently that her hair whipped his face.

She walked up to her actual boyfriend. "José, my love. You are the most thoughtful, intelligent, talented person I've ever met; yet you maintain the sweetest humility. I'll never forget the starlit picnic you planned for us overlooking Laguna de Bay, or the night you nursed a wounded fruit bat back to health. You may not have filled my hut with a dozen barrels of amontillado, and you may not have studied at the best universities, something I know about Fernando because he has told me at least Nine. Thousand. Times! But you showed me the strength of our community in the face of"—she flapped her hand at the other two—"this bullshit! I am yours, José, for as long as you'll have me." She tucked the hibiscus in his buttonhole and pulled him into a showy kiss.

The rejected pair fumed but wasted no more of Makiling's time (for once). They left, conversing in angry whispers.

Makiling stretched her hands to the sky. *"They're finally gone!"*

José was less enthused. "Makiling, I . . . I appreciate your declaration . . ."

Makiling froze. ". . . But you're marrying a village girl."

Legend has it that "Purple Rain" began to fall from the sky . . .

If it feels like I'm overdoing the pop ballads, all I can say is that we Filipinos kill at karaoke. Sometimes literally; google the "My Way Killings."

"No!" José laughed. "I love you. I don't know how I ended up courting Dayang Makiling. I mean—what is my life?" He kissed her hands. "But Captain Lara is a powerful man."

Makiling snorted, then sobered when José stayed silent. "You don't have to worry about him with me around!"

José bit his lip. "I'm sure you're right." He sighed. "I still think we should lie low for a bit. Maybe take a break? Just for a week or so? Flaunting our relationship is a very bad idea." He tipped her chin, though he was a head shorter. "I am not ashamed of it. I just think it's the smart thing to do."

Makiling took a shaky breath. *Don't freak out...* The air thickened as the weather waited for her response.

"Okay," she replied softly. "We'll lie low."

José kissed her cheek. Makiling pulled away, disappearing into the fog. When the clouds parted, a white doe trotted deep into the jungle. José hung his head and walked away, as the wind began to moan.

Remind yourself of this scene the next time someone you adore tells you they're not looking for anything serious. You weren't rejected. You're a *goddess*!

* * *

THE NEXT week was tense, not only for the lovers, but for the entire village. The diwata's climate connection wasn't totally at fault. Construction on the fort was going badly. A mild but pesky illness swept through the village. The vibe was way, way off.

Then the fort was set ablaze.

Any villager associated with construction was imprisoned. Captain Lara forced each man through a grueling round of questioning. José was one of them.

"You say you were home the night of the fire," the captain sneered. "But no one can verify this."

"My family can," José reiterated, bloodied and exhausted.

"How do you explain reports that a man of your description was seen skulking around the property?"

"The gossip I've heard is *that* person looked like a gentleman," José said coolly. "The arsonist must have an intimate knowledge of the building, based on where the fire began." He eyed the captain. "Most would agree that Fernando Gaspar and I could be mistaken for each other in the dark."

The captain shook his head. "Rude and insubordinate, just like your countrymen."

The prisoners were kept late into the night. By dawn, many men pointed to José as the arsonist: Men who had families who needed them. Men who'd been beaten and threatened and humiliated to the point where they barely knew what they were confirming.

The following day, the villagers were summoned to witness the execution of José by firing squad. José held his chin high as he was led onstage at the square. He shook his head when they went to blindfold him, glaring down his executioners.

At the last minute, as muskets were raised, José's eyes filled. He stretched his neck, and shouted, "Makiling!"

The squad fired. José fell forward, dead.

* * *

BACK IN the jungle, the white doe leaned over for a drink at the falls. She shook her head as she straightened her neck and licked the last few drops from her lips. Then she heard it.

"*Makiling!*"

The deer tore off in the direction of the village. She burst through the greenery, flinging herself over hedges. Beyond the jungle, her hooves pounded the road, upsetting the quiet countryside. As she closed in on the square, a crowd of people turned and gasped at the ethereal animal barreling toward them. The villagers parted, the firing squad stumbling with them.

As the doe leapt onto the stage, her form shifted. Makiling knelt by José and scooped him into her arms. She called his name in a strangled voice and pressed her hands to his body, but her healing ability couldn't mend her love's wounds. It was far, far too late.

The diwata turned to the crowd. They flinched at the rage in her eyes. "You should have been brave!" she screamed. Behind her, lightning crackled. "You should have protected him! He would have done so for you!"

The winds picked up and torrents of rain poured from the sky. The village folk clung to each other, terrified but unable to look away from the grieving goddess. Makiling lifted José as if he were no heavier than a child, leaning him over one shoulder. She saw Captain Lara and Fernando cowering on the outskirts of the crowd and advanced. They backed away, pressed up against a wall in terror.

"You will pay," she seethed.

* * *

THE STAGED arson, José's execution, and Makiling's fury sparked a large uprising. Captain Lara and Fernando fled to Manila, far more frightened of the goddess's threat than of the revolt.

Fernando holed up at the university, rarely leaving his rooms. One day he grew sick. Slowly and steadily he became too weak to leave his bed, with no stomach for food, yet an unending thirst. He begged his nurses for more and more water. One night, he groped for the pitcher and pulled it to his lips. Before him, the water pulsed and turned a sickly green. He screamed, just now feeling the poison that had long been coursing through his veins. The nurses found him dead, his face contorted in fright.

The captain was called back to Laguna to quell the uprisings peppering the village. One night, while pursuing a group of rebels, he wound up deep in the jungle. He drove his horse farther up the mountain, tracking the rebels' torches through patches of fog. The cloud cover grew thick, so he couldn't see his hand in front of his face. He abandoned his horse, groping through the dense air. All at once, he felt a cold sharp pain in his chest and buckled to his knees. The villagers discovered him the next day, with a machete buried deep in his heart.

Makiling never again showed herself to the people of Laguna. Once in a while, a hunter would spy a white deer through the trees and get lost trying to track it. Occasionally, a hiker would notice a beauty sitting in the mountain mist and stumble out of the jungle a few days later with no memory of the time that had passed. Here and there, a forager would take more than his fair share and be swarmed by bees.

When these men returned to the village, they'd be reminded: "You must have run into Maria Makiling."

* * *

Sources:
Marlene Aquilar-Pollard, *Myths and Legends of the Philippines.*
Michelle Lanuza, "The Legend of Maria Makiling."
José Rizal, "Mariang Makiling."

José Rizal is regarded as a national hero by many Filipinos, due to his extensive writings, which inspired the Philippine Revolution of the 1890s. The character of José was inspired by him. Interested in more Filipino folklore? Pick up *A Treasury of Philippine Folk Tales*, with volumes by Maria Elena Paterno, Neni S. Romana-Cruz, and Sylvia Mendez Ventura.

LOVE IS A FAMILY AFFAIR

VIETNAM'S "HON VONG PHU"

Long ago in the city of Lạng Sơn lived a young man named Văn and his wife, Quyen. The two provided a happy home to their child, Sang. Văn had established himself as a farmer at a young age, and Quyen came from a wealthy family, so things were easy for them. Văn was handsome, a kind supervisor and a protective father. One might call him a bit overprotective: when his wife was expecting, he'd obsessively babyproofed their home. While other dads enjoyed roughhousing with their kids, he preferred quiet play. And he could be a little wishy-washy, easily swung by others' suggestions or judgments. Quyen, on the other hand, was very easygoing, having been raised by overly protective parents herself. "If he eats the banh nam while it's too hot, he'll learn to blow on it first," she'd remind her husband. Like him, she was good-looking, but she was funny where he was serious. She was loose where he was uptight. And she was headstrong, able to hold her own in a staring contest with a cat or a battle of wills against a toddler who wouldn't eat his veggies. The parents balanced each other nicely.

Have you ever met one of those couples that were so cute and perfect, you salivated for the moment something would tear them apart? Or are you a well-adjusted person?

One evening, Quyen's parents offered to take their grandchild so that the couple could enjoy a night out together. While

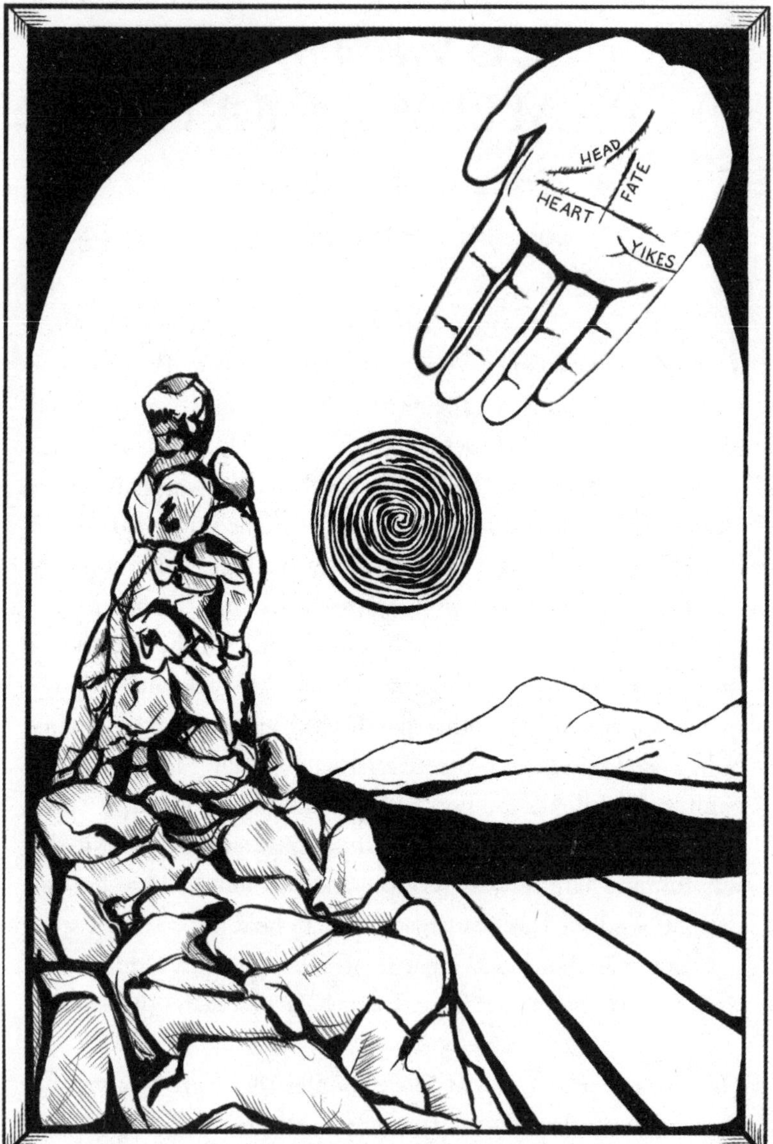
HEAD
FATE
HEART
YIKES

Sang's grandparents gave the kid extra candy and let him destroy the place, the young couple attended a festival downtown. They held hands under the swinging silk lanterns and delighted at the fluid lotus dancers in their luminous costumes. On their way to find a snack, they passed a fortune teller's tent where an old man moved cards around a mat. The fortune teller caught Văn's eye and winked.

Fairy Tale Facts: If a poor stranger shows up at your door, always give them food, shelter, or money; besides the basic kindness, you may be magically rewarded for it. However: if that person turns out to be a psychic, tell them to keep their damn mouth shut!

Quyen's eyes lit up. "Let's have our futures told!" she suggested, and eagerly began pulling her husband toward the shack.

Văn, however, was reluctant. "I'm not really a fan of fortune-telling," he mumbled.

"Really?" Quyen leaned in to tease him. "Afraid of what your future holds?"

Văn forced a laugh. "Something like that. Look, there's an empty table. I'll find us something to eat."

Quyen let the subject drop, reverting to small talk over steaming bowls of bún thang. She contemplated Văn's odd reaction. Twirling the last of her noodles, she revisited the topic. "So: How bad was it?"

"How bad was what?"

"Your fortune."

Văn tried not to choke on his dinner. "Pretty fucking bad!"

There it was again, his short, forced laugh, and now a vulgar turn of phrase. Quyen laid her hand on his arm. "You know I'm not going to let this go, right?"

"You wouldn't be my wife if you were anything less than tenacious." Văn smiled despite his unease. "The orphanage I was raised in was next to a boardinghouse. A fortune teller stayed one night, and us older kids thought it would be fun to have our palms read. Most of what he said was pretty routine, but he got all weird when he looked at my palm and asked to speak alone. And then he told me . . ."

Quyen was so engrossed, it took her a moment to realize her husband had faltered. "Told you what?" she nudged.

Văn hesitated. "He told me I would grow up to marry my sister."

Quyen's mouth dropped open. Then she chortled. "Well, damn!" She covered her mouth as people looked over at their table. "How did you react?"

"I called him a pervert and a liar!" Văn cried. "And he said, 'Deny it all you want, but you can't outrun your fate.' So I told him to outrun his fate right off a cliff, and I left."

With a laugh, Quyen returned to her noodles. "Thank goodness you ended up an only child!"

Văn's brow furrowed. "I didn't. I had a sister. But she died."

Quyen was shocked. "You've never mentioned that. Why didn't you tell me?"

"I don't like to talk about it." Văn cleared his throat and stood. "I think we should go home."

He turned quickly, knocking his seat over. As he leaned down to reset it, he caught the fortune teller staring at him. The old man gave him a sly smile and a wink.

I am obsessed with stories about characters trying to outwit fate, particularly when this narrative intersects with romantic relationships. If I were Văn, I'd probably tell this story very early on in a relationship, no matter how confident I was that I evaded the issue. For one thing, it's a great story. And if I'm destined to boink a relative, I'm gonna make fate work for it! I guess that makes me more of a Quyen.

The conversation put a damper on the rest of the evening. Quyen retired early, and when she awoke, she found that Văn had nodded off in the drawing room. Last night may have been a romantic loss, but Quyen was determined to get something positive out of the rest of her free morning. She indulged in some luxurious alone time with no toddler pulling her skirts. She took a long bath and washed her hair, then reclined on a chair outside, combing her long locks over the back of it to dry while she relaxed.

Văn woke up uncharacteristically late. He helped himself to a cup of tea before he heard his front door open, followed by the babbling of his son. Sang tore into the kitchen ahead of his grandfather. "I've brought lunch," the old man said, setting a paper bag on the table and taking a seat as Văn poured a second cup.

They dined, chatting about some repairs Quyen's father had contracted. "We may travel south to visit family while the work is done," he said. "Perhaps you can join us. They would love to meet the little one."

Văn cocked his head. "I thought your family was from Lạng Sơn."

"We are," his father-in-law confirmed. "But I have a brother who settled in Quy Nhon after his time in the military. I haven't visited him for many years, not since we adopted Quyen."

"Quy Nhon? Quyen is adopted?" Văn croaked. "How was I not aware of that?"

The old man smiled sheepishly. "Ah. She lost most memories from that time of her life due to an injury. I'm not surprised she hasn't brought it up." His eyes grew misty. "My wife and I had a little girl, who died very young. We were visiting Quy Nhon, still grieving, when we had the chance to adopt Quyen. It helped us move forward to raise her in our own child's stead."

By the time Quyen returned from outside, her father had left.

Văn was sitting in front of a cold glass of tea, staring into it as if he could read its leaves. Quyen perched on a stool by a sunny window and lifted her hair. She paused. "Did I drop my scarf?" She looked around. "Oh, I did, it's by the door. Would you grab it for me?"

Her husband retrieved the long black hair wrap. He handed it to Quyen but didn't let go. "You were adopted," he stated. Quyen blinked at him for a moment, trying to place his statement. "Your father told me when he dropped off Sang."

Quyen nodded. "Yes. But I barely remember. My folks are just... my folks!" She slipped the scarf from Văn's grasp and slung it over her lap. "I didn't keep it from you intentionally," she explained as she pulled a comb through her hair, lifting it from her neck.

She felt Văn's hand on her shoulder. "What is that?" he asked. "Pull back your hair again!"

Quyen did so, thrown by his urgency. "What is what?"

Văn ran his thumb along the edge of Quyen's hairline. "This scar," he said, tracing the ridge where it disappeared into Quyen's thick hair.

"Oh." Quyen brushed her hair over it self-consciously. "That's why my parents adopted me." She sighed. "They found me injured in the forest while they were visiting my uncle. I'd been cut by a hatchet. At least they presume so. A blade was lying next to me. I nearly died."

Văn's hand fell from his wife's shoulder. He began to back away, sick to his stomach. "No...!" he breathed. "Why didn't they try to reunite you with your family?"

"They were more concerned with saving my life," Quyen retorted. "I have no recollection of a family before my parents took me in." She shrugged. "If I did have one, they left me for dead."

Văn stumbled into a large planter, knocking it to the floor with a crash. Sang began wailing. Quyen rushed over. She slung the little boy on one hip and held out a hand to her husband. "Văn! What's going on? You've been out-of-sorts ever since we saw that psychic." Văn waved her away and ran outside. He held his head painfully against the memory. One day, as a teen, he had gone into the forests of Quy Nhon to chop firewood. His little sister tagged along, insistent that she could help despite her young age. As he chopped, the hatchet blade had come loose and fallen on his sister's head. She fell to the ground unconscious. There was so much blood, and she was so still. He thought he had killed her. And so he ran.

This version of events is the one shared by Vietnam's government and tourism sites. But some retell the tale with the twist that the brother intentionally tried to kill his sister to escape what, to him, was a mutually horrific fate. Which begs the question: Which is worse, intentionally murdering your sister or accidentally fucking her?

Back in the present, Quyen called after him. The baby wouldn't stop crying. Văn couldn't face either of them. "I have to go," he called. Grabbing his shoes off the deck, he looked down the road. Once again, he ran.

In a world with so much personal data available online, it's harder to marry your sibling. Unless you are one of those "off-the-grid" people we talked about earlier. While I admire your grit, don't come to me for sympathy if you end up in a Luke and Leia situation.

* * *

Văn ended up at a local pagoda, where he prayed for guidance and clarity. He recounted the events that brought him here.

He knew from an early age he was born unlucky. The first fifteen years of his life delivered a parade of misfortune; the death of his parents, that terrible prediction, the presumed death of his sister. After he left home and found happiness with Quyen and her family, he thought he'd reversed that luck. But not only had he been wrong, his son would now bear his curse and its effects.

I love using a fate vs. free will plot to debate blame. Are the Macbeths *that bad* if they are predestined to be traitorous mass murderers? If a prophecy declared a whiny teen wizard would take you down, wouldn't you do your damnedest to stop it? If the Oracle predicted Ross and Rachel's break, would Rachel still be so mad about Chloe?

As he prayed, he sensed another person in the temple. He glanced up and saw an old soldier paying his respects. That gave him an idea.

Long after dark, he finally returned home. He slipped into his bedroom, thankful to see Quyen and his son asleep. He inched to Sang's hammock and gazed down at his son. He swallowed hard past a lump in his throat and assured himself he was doing the right thing.

He crept to their wardrobe and packed a few belongings quickly and quietly, stowing them in a small bag.

"Running away for good this time?"

Quyen was sitting up, watching him. Her tone was measured, her expression impossible to read.

"I am not running away," Văn denied. "I've been drafted."

"Isn't that convenient?" Quyen turned away from him. The moonlight illuminated her profile as she tilted her chin up proudly, cradling a pillow to her chest. "I know you are worried that your fortune came true. But we have a child. Would you abandon him the same way you abandoned me all those years ago?"

Văn was aghast. "You don't seriously believe we can go on as before? It is illegal, it is immoral, it . . ." He covered his face against the implications.

Other incestuous siblings in folklore include the Philippines' "Juan and Maria," King Arthur and Morgause, Russia's Prince Danila Govorila, and a lot of dirty jokes from the Ozarks.

"Running away won't change it!" Quyen argued. "And no one needs to know, outside of us two." She got out of bed. "I understand things will not be the same between us. But you don't need to leave. That would bring its own shame upon me and Sang."

Văn flinched as she reached out to touch his arm. They were silent for a long time. "Look," he finally said, shuddering, "my military assignment is only six months. Let us take that time, and when I return, we will figure out what to do."

Quyen considered this. "Fine," she agreed. "We will be waiting for you."

Usually the wife is ignorant of her sibling relationship to her husband. To me it's more interesting if both parties deal with the information. Am I alone in imagining that Quyen might put her own discomfort aside so that their child will have his father in his life? This isn't exactly *Flowers in the Attic*!

✳ ✳ ✳

VĂN HAD no intention of ever coming back. Once again, he changed his name, determined to leave the sins of his past behind him.

In the meantime, Quyen held out for his return. When six months passed, she bundled up her son and hiked northwest up the mountains, where she would see the troops walking home. She and Sang remained there until sundown, but when the army returned, Văn did not arrive with them.

So the next morning, Quyen rose early, took her son by the hand, and returned to the mountain. Day after day she waited at the rock face. As time passed, her parents argued that Văn was unlikely to come home. Still, Quyen stubbornly showed up.

One night, many months into her dedicated routine, Quyen and Sang did not return to the house. The next day, her father walked out to the perch where the mother and son held their daily watch. The man was surprised to see a new stone outcropping. As he walked around the formation, he realized how its shape mirrored Quyen holding Sang to her chest, gazing out at the land below.

On closer inspection, he saw the resemblance even clearer. Quyen's distinctive, proud gaze was chiseled in limestone, with her son etched in peaceful sleep. The old man touched Quyen's cheek in disbelief, flinching at the cold stone. His daughter, so hardheaded, had transformed herself and her son into a damn rock.

The rock is a real site in Lạng Sơn, though it's been a man-made replica since the 1990s. The east coast of Asia is peppered with mountainsides that resemble yearning women, each with their own legends. Some depict a war widow; others feature star-crossed love between humans and deities. This is the Internet's favorite version. It's easy to see the appeal; we've revisited the fear of "I accidentally dated my cousin" in many sitcoms and Reddit threads.

* * *

Sources:

"Hon Vong Phu—The Mountain of the Woman Who Is Waiting for Her Husband."

"Núi Vọng Phu: Những Thiếu Phụ Choờ Chống Muôn Kiếp."

Want to read more Vietnamese folktales? Try *The Dragon Prince: Stories and Legends from Vietnam* by Thich Nhat Hanh.

LOVE IS DEAD

"The Finger," a Jewish Folktale

Once, in the city of Safed, three young men indulged in a few too many drinks and found themselves carousing in the forest. The eldest of them, Reuven, was to be married the next day, so they were in great spirits. While resting by a stream, one of them noticed a bone sticking out of the ground that looked a lot like a finger. Normally such a discovery would be horrifying, but the boys had a mellow that just couldn't be harshed. They joked that someone should put a ring on the finger, and Reuven stepped up. "I could use the practice," he said, snickering.

I know there wasn't a lot for entertainment back in the old days. But this is some Logan Paul–level bullshit! #CancelReuven

He slipped the ring on the skeletal finger, and counted out the seven blessings as was required by tradition. The boys laughed at the sight of Reuven forging his soul to a bone. Under the chuppah of hawthorn trees, the groom stomped on a glass to great hurrahs. But their cheers caught in their throats when a skeletal hand emerged from the ground. A crack widened around the hand. A decaying woman, more bones than skin, pulled herself up from the earth and shook off the dirt. She was wearing the worm-eaten remnants of a dingy bridal gown. The undead woman looked up at Reuven with empty eye sockets. Her grinning teeth opened, and a surprisingly sweet voice trilled out, "I'm so happy to meet you, my husband!"

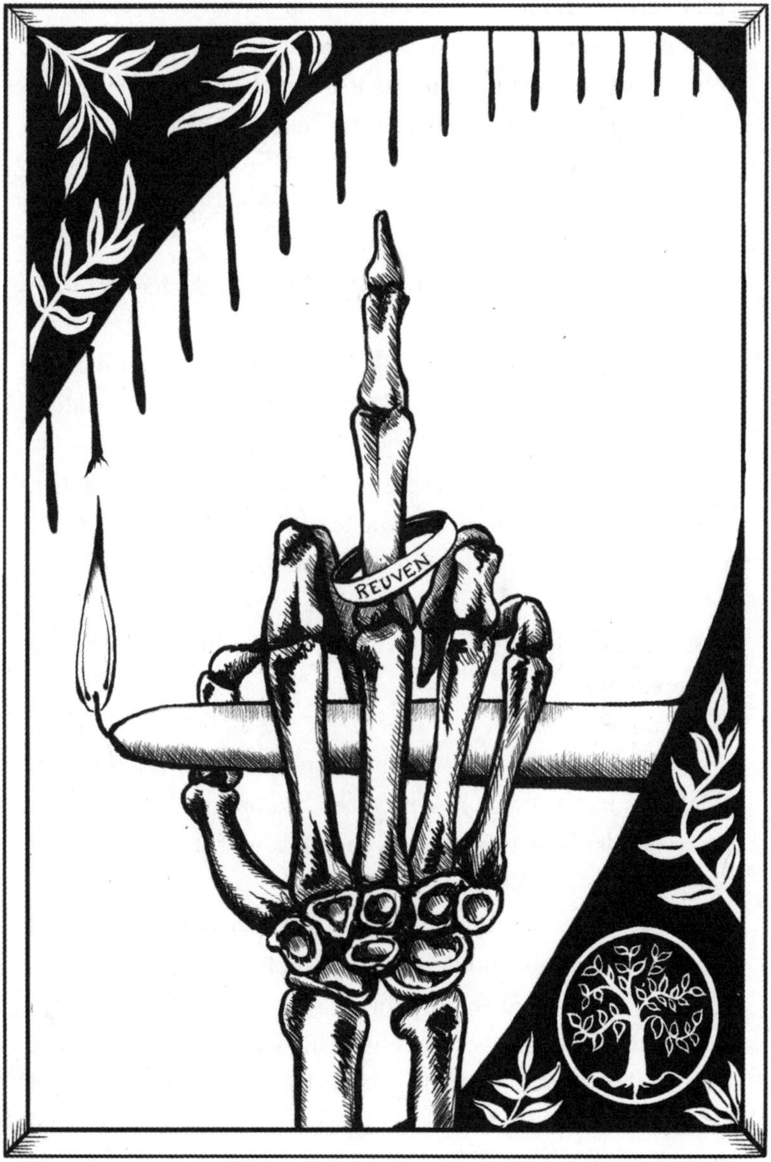
REUVEN

You likely remember this plot from Tim Burton's *Corpse Bride*. Burton's version was inspired by a folktale, though he claims to have forgotten which one. As is often the case, underrepresented folklore was generalized into Victorian melodrama.

Reuven raised his trembling hands. "What are you talking about? Who are you?" he whimpered.

The skeleton stepped closer, and the boys backed away "I am your bride, Eliana!"

Reuven shook his head wildly. "You are not my bride! My bride is named Meira, and she is getting ready for our wedding with her family right now."

The skeleton held up her hand and tapped her ring finger. "Nuh-uh! You just consecrated me to you!"

"You're crazy!" Reuven cried. "I did nothing of the sort!"

Men will cry, "Bitches are crazy!" after promising themselves to a finger bone.

"Then what do you call this ring on my finger?" Eliana smirked, which was impressive considering she had no lips. "What about the seven blessings you recited? The glass is shattered, Reuven! Now, don't be shy! Kiss me!"

That sent the men into hysterics. They screamed and shoved and sloshed straight through the stream, barreling off the trail. Branches caught their soggy pants as they tripped over logs. But they didn't stop, for the whole way home they could hear the wails of the rejected undead woman. By the time they reached Reuven's home, the guys were haggard and exhausted **(the usual aftereffects of a raging bachelor party)**. They bolted the door behind them.

The next morning, before the wedding, Reuven swore his friends to silence about the night before. "We disrespected the dead, ran away like a bunch of babies, and (most importantly) unleashed a zombie. We're taking this secret to the grave!"

What Reuven left out of this conversation was that Eliana had followed him home that night. She spent the wee hours banging on his window, trying to convince him to sleep with her.

"Reuven!" she hissed. "We can finally be alone together! Don't be shy! I'll be gentle!" Neither dead bride nor groom slept that night, and not in a fun way.

The yichud is the period when the bride and groom get time alone together between the ceremony and the reception. Ages past, this was when the relationship would be consummated. These days, couples simply enjoy the quiet break together. Though I wouldn't blame any couple who wanted to revive an old tradition!

Both Reuven and his betrothed came from wealthy, important families, and the wedding was a large affair. Just before the ceremony was to begin, the well-dressed crowd heard a frightful shriek and saw Eliana rattling down the aisle. Terror seized the guests. They knocked over chairs and each other, emptying the courtyard as fast as possible. Only Reuven, Meira, and the rabbi remained. Reuven was frozen, with Meira clinging to him, but the rabbi was curious and composed.

"Miss, would you tell me a little about yourself?" the rabbi asked gently.

Eliana folded her hands politely but held her jaw high. "My name is Eliana. In my life, I was supposed to be married. But I was killed minutes before my ceremony could take place."

Meira's fear melted. "How awful," she uttered.

The rabbi stepped forward and offered his arm to Eliana, gingerly leading her to a seat. "Awful, indeed. Still, why have you left your resting place to crash this wedding?"

"Resting place? As if you could call it that!" Eliana adjusted her gown. "I'm here because that man is my husband!" She extended her skinny finger at Reuven, whose knees quaked once more.

Meira looked from her fiancé to the dead woman. "You must be mistaken." Then she clocked Reuven's guilty expression. "Is this true?"

Reuven scratched his head, knocking his kippah at an awkward angle. "Uh . . . some parts?"

The rabbi raised an eyebrow at him. "Which parts? Did you put your ring on her finger?"

Reuven patted his breast pocket. He had forgotten about the ring! He hesitated, but Eliana held up her hand to show off the band, engraved with Reuven's name. Meira gasped, and Reuven gulped. "I did," he admitted.

"Did you pronounce the seven blessings?"

Reuven's face shifted from white to deep pink. "Yes."

"Was it done in the presence of witnesses?" the rabbi asked incredulously.

"He had two friends with him," Eliana piped up from her seat when Reuven waffled.

The rabbi sighed. "Well. I have never dealt with this situation before. I'll need to meditate on it. We may need to consult the rabbinic court."

Meira began to cry, and Reuven whined, "Why?"

"Because, young man," the rabbi said, "by the laws of our faith you have married this poor dead lady!"

In *Lilith's Cave*, Howard Schwartz collects over a dozen Jewish folktales recounting demonic or undead partners. Sometimes a man is tricked into the marriage, and sometimes the bride is cursed or abducted by a demon. Schwartz notes that the stressful nature of weddings is a natural setting for the *super*natural.

Anyone who's talked down a bride having a meltdown over her seating chart would agree.

* * *

ON THE day the court convened, the rabbi summoned both Reuven and Eliana, as well as Meira and both sets of parents. He began his questioning with the undead bride, who verified the ceremony in the woods.

"Considering the unusual circumstances," the rabbi broached, "would you consider giving up your claim for Reuven's hand?"

"No," Eliana declared. "I was cruelly denied a happy wedding day, not to mention the joy of my yichud! Don't make me die a virgin, Reuven!"

"You *did* die a virgin!" Reuven groaned. The families murmured among themselves. "Besides, I already told you, there is no way I am going through with *that*!"

"If you didn't like it, you shouldn't have put a ring on it!" Eliana snapped, waving her jeweled hand for all to see.

After interviewing Eliana, the rabbinic court had Reuven and his family testify. Reuven admitted his actions but protested his intent. "It was a joke! Can we really be married if I didn't mean it?"

If I were Meira, I'd be questioning my own future with Reuven. The way a partner talks about their ex is very indicative of how they will treat you!

Inspired, he jumped. "Also, Eliana never performed the seven circles!"

"I did too!" Eliana objected, then explained, "I was underground."

Reuven's parents raised two new points. "Reuven and Meira have been intended for each other long before he went bonkers and married a finger bone," his mother testified. "In fact, their betrothal was established before either of them were even born. Meira's mother and I grew up together and always dreamed we might be family. So my husband and Meira's father agreed that if one of our families bore a son and the other a daughter, the two children would wed and secure our families together."

Eliana scoffed. "Reuven is clearly rebelling, like any kid would! If it helps," she added, "there's a nice dead guy up the road. I'm sure he and Meira would get along great."

Meira's mother spoke up. "Plus, the ketubah has already been signed!" She produced the document.

Eliana threw her hands up. "Forgive me for being *murdered* and unable to hold a pen due to the decay of my muscles!"

This raises some interesting questions about disability justice for zombies.

With all statements recorded, the rabbinic court began to debate. Some argued there was enough reason to make Reuven follow through with his commitment to Eliana. Others pointed out that important traditions had not been followed to truly make the marriage legitimate. Still others pointed out that one vow could not be made to negate another—but could the families' vow be considered the initial one?

Demonic and undead folktales likely developed out of the lore that Lilith, queen of demons, was a great seductress. Because of this, sleeping with a demon is not considered adultery. Talk about demonizing the other woman!

At last, the men came to a decision, which Reuven's rabbi announced to a tense audience. "Reuven's vows to Eliana are valid in the eyes of this court," he began. Eliana pumped her bony fist. "However, the informal and formal agreement between his family and Meira's cannot be denied, and it cannot be reversed by Reuven's vows in the forest. That, combined with the fact that Reuven's intention was not true, as well as there being zero precedent for a corpse laying claim to a living spouse, leads me to declare that the marriage of Reuven to Eliana is null and void."

"No!" Eliana keened. The buzzing of the court fell silent as the dead woman wept.

Then Meira suddenly stood. "Wait!"

Reuven looked at her. "Meira, what are you doing?"

Meira approached the skeletal bride cautiously. "It's unfair that this poor woman should have to grieve the loss of her life, and what she dreamed it would be, all over again." She stretched out her hands to the undead bride's. "If it would ease your pain, Eliana, I offer to share my husband with you."

"WHAT?" Reuven yelped.

"Be quiet!" Meira admonished him. She cleared a cobweb from Eliana's cheek. "We can make sure you are properly buried. Reuven can visit you each night. His company can't make up for what you've been through, but at least you will have the comfort of family again." She gave Reuven a *look*. "Right, Reuven?"

Reuven rushed to her side. "Y-yes, I would be happy to," he agreed. Then he sighed and addressed Eliana sincerely. "I'm so sorry, miss."

Eliana nodded to the couple. With a shudder, the life dropped from her old bones. She swayed, and Reuven caught her body before she could fall.

Reuven and his family arranged a speedy funeral for Eliana, burying her with the ring he'd promised. For the next seven years, Reuven visited Eliana's grave for an hour each evening at sunset, where he would tell her about his day. One night when Reuven arrived at Eliana's stone, he found his old wedding band resting on top of it, as if to release him from their agreement. Reuven put it in his pocket and bade his corpse bride one final goodbye.

* * *

SOURCES: Howard Schwartz, "The Finger" and "The Demon in the Tree."

Want to read more Jewish folktales? My favorite collections are by the aforementioned Howard Schwartz, Jane Yolen, and Josepha Sherman.

Part 3

SO . . . YOU MARRIED AN ANIMAL

Actually, the frog wasn't so bad.

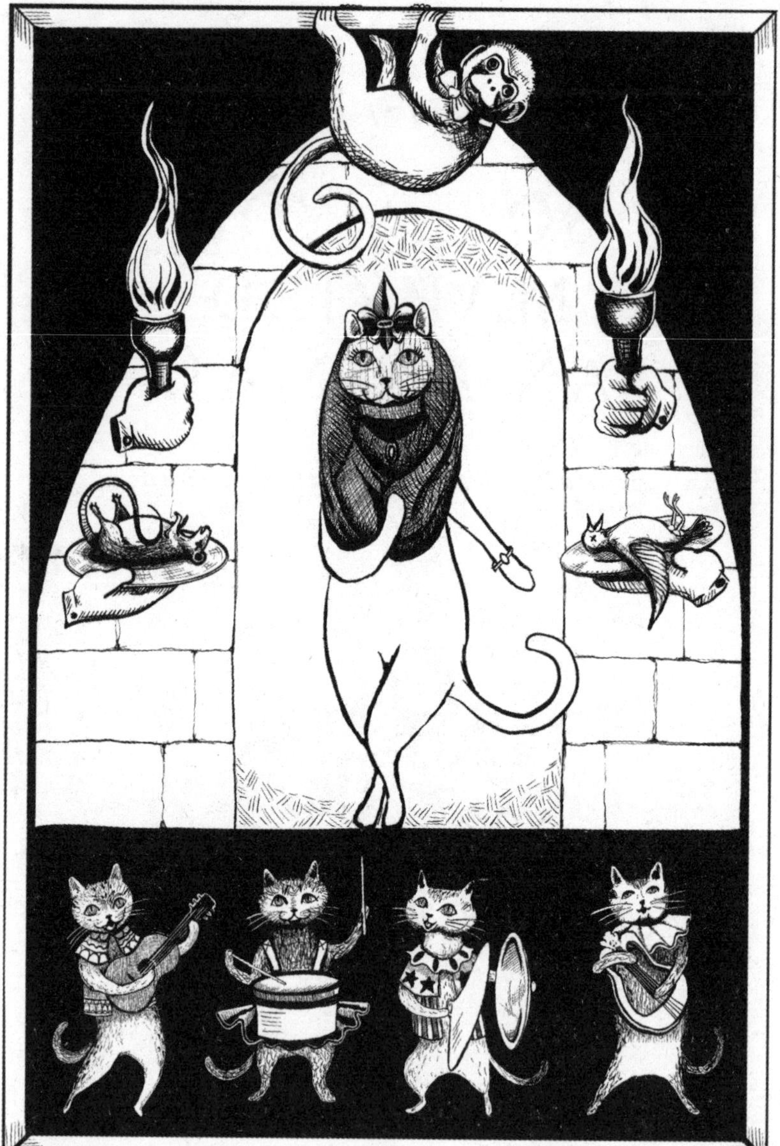

TILL THERE WAS MEW

Madame d'Aulnoy's "The White Cat"*

Long, long ago, there lived a king who was in no rush to abdicate the throne. Sure, he was closer to eighty than seventy. Sure, a recent hip injury made it difficult to physically ascend the throne. Sure, he had three stand-up sons, any of whom could run the country in his stead; in fact, his counselors advised such. But the guy loved being the king! He loved the attention, the ceremony, and he really loved the *power*.

So he stalled. First he gathered his three sons to discuss the terms of succession. "While I'm happy to hand off my kingly responsibilities," he lied, "I want to spice up the inheritance routine. Any of you would make a fantastic ruler. So, rather than hand the crown to the eldest, I challenge you to a competition: whichever of you brings me the prettiest, smartest, and most loyal little dog shall win the kingship."

The eldest son swallowed his disappointment.

For this is what we eldest children do. Why put up a fight when you can clench your jaw so hard you require a night guard?

"What does finding a dog have to do with the ability to rule?" the prince countered.

---

* Madame d'Aulnoy is largely credited with first using the term *"fairy tale"*—contes de fées, in her native tongue.

"Consider it your first administrative act; an animal companion is one of my retirement benefits," the king told him. "We shall host the Puppy Pageant exactly one year from today!"

The two younger brothers jumped at the chance to yoink the crown from the elder's hands. However, the men pledged that they wouldn't let the competition ruin their camaraderie. They threw a big ol' party to kick off the search and established some rules: each brother would work alone, but they'd present themselves as a team on the day of the pageant to support each other (and avoid any backstabbing). The boys embarked the following morning, each using a secret identity.

Madame d'Aulnoy and her peers developed fairy tales with storytelling competitions. This competitive aspect led to overdramatic plot points, such as concocting an alter ego to go dog-shopping.

The adventures of each gentleman could fill its own book, but our only concern is with the sibling 99.9 percent of fairy tales focus on: the youngest. **(I swallow my disappointment.)** The prince, whom we shall name Denis, was a protagonist of the highest caliber: handsome, athletic, artistic, funny, and sweet. In fact, he had only one flaw: a complete inability to pick a dog.

"The floppy ears of this basset hound hang low (and wobble to and fro), but that's what makes him the Perfect Puppy-Wuppy!" he declared on the first day. An hour later, he met a chestnut dachshund whose "wonderfully wacky pup-portions" won his heart. Shortly after, the dachshund was traded for the "fantastic fluffy flamboyance" of a Maltese, who was rehomed to make room for a "curly-wurly little girly" labradoodle. On and on this went, until the puppy parade had reached forty thousand contestants, and Denis had to admit he might not be a discerning judge.

This fairy tale has something for everyone. Dog people, cat people—there's even something in it for bird people, a pet owner largely neglected by the media despite arguably being the most devoted.

"I need to clear my mind," he decided. He returned the latest dog (a shar-pei he deemed Mister McSmooshy WrinkleButt III) and took a day off to hike. The walk was refreshing, but a sudden thunderstorm left him drenched. Worse, he lost his way when he sprinted off-path for shelter. The prince stumbled in the darkening woods until he found a road. The road wound into a clearing, revealing an ornate golden gate decorated with fiery garnets. Denis jogged up the driveway, eager to see more.

The drive ended at a lavish castle with porcelain walls. Delicately painted murals depicted every French fairy tale known to man: the titular Donkey-Skin threw off her robe on the west wing. Princess Laidronette discovered her serpent lover on the east. One turret pictured Clever Finette grasping the bloody head of an ogre, while Prince Aimé transformed into a sprawling orange tree on a second. Gracieuse and Percinet pined for each other on either side of the front entrance, while Sleeping Beauty drooled on the garden wall.

Other than "Donkey-Skin" and "Sleeping Beauty," these characters all come from tales penned by Madame d'Aulnoy herself. As we see in modern fandom, the conteuse was establishing her own extended universe!

The castle featured details made of precious gems. Denis reached for the diamond doorbell chain and tugged. An angelic chime sounded as the sapphire doorknobs turned of their own accord. Crystal doors opened to reveal the blinding light of a dozen torches held by disembodied hands.

Classic movie buffs will remember the hands from Jean Cocteau's *La Belle et la Bête* (an early "Beauty and the Beast" movie). That imagery directly references this fairy tale, which preceded the defining version of "Beauty and the Beast" by over forty years.

Denis grasped his sword warily, but a harmonic chorus assured him he would find no danger here, "unless you fear Love itself!" Denis sensed the hands winking at him. The prince relaxed, and allowed these odd servants to carry him forward, as if he were crowd-surfing in a serene mosh pit.

The castle interiors were a maximalist's dream: walls of rose quartz and lapis lazuli glittered from the light of a dozen prismatic girandoles. The ceilings were bordered with intricate coral molding and vaulted into the stratosphere. The upholstery was cushy velvet and slippery satin.

We get it, mysterious homeowner, you're rich!

Farther inside, the walls were crowded with fine art. These paintings continued the fairy tale theme, but narrower in focus, depicting great cat heroes. Not just Puss in Boots either; Tom Tildrum; the kitties of La Fontaine's fables; uh . . . more cats than T. S. Eliot (or this narrator) could name! Before Denis could register the specificity of that gallery, he was whisked to another room, and then another—he eventually lost count. At last, he was plopped down in a large dressing chamber. A snazzy golden suit with emerald buttons was laid out. A pair of white-gloved valet hands helped him change; not only that, Denis received a full makeover from curly head to manicured toe.

Bedazzled, bothered, and bewildered, the prince was shown to a table set for two in the cat gallery. Here, more servants entered: an orchestra of live cats! The whiskered musicians picked at guitars with their claws and sang in an indiscernible language. It sounded terrible. Denis politely plugged his ears and tried not to laugh, for other than the clowder of kittens in starched collars, the procession was dignified.

The music crescendoed into a fanfare. A series of cat guards with swords held aloft ushered in a tiny figure, a black crepe veil masking her. She pranced up to Denis and lifted her veil. Before him stood the loveliest little white cat he had ever seen. The cat curtseyed low, and from her snoot a youthful voice emerged, tinged with sadness. "Welcome to my hidden home, sweet prince. I am Queen Caterina and am so pleased to make your acquaintance."

Madame does not name her title character, which is unusual for her. I hope she'd appreciate the pun.

Denis found himself blushing under the gaze of the cat's wide green eyes. He stammered through an introduction. "Pardon my astonishment. I've never encountered such a magnificent estate and hostess!"

"Oh, stop," the white cat said, pawing the air dismissively. "I'm just an ordinary girl." She slowly winked, then hissed at the orchestra. "Cut the music! This man has no idea what the hell you're singing!" She bowed her head apologetically. "We're a bizarre group, but rest assured, you're surrounded by talent of the highest caliber."

A silver dining set was wheeled in by the bodiless servants, who waited on the pair hand and paw. As their meal arrived, Denis noticed the cat wore an exquisite golden bracelet with a framed miniature at its center. "May I see whose portrait you wear on your paw?" he asked, and the cat slipped the piece into his hand with an affirmative chirp. Inspecting it closely, Denis was surprised to see that the portrait showed a man who could be his doppelgänger. He began to comment on this, but the white cat was suddenly melancholic. So he changed the subject, bringing her up-to-date on current affairs as they dined on a roast squab (for him) and a mouse casserole (for her). (Mouserole?) Caterina was well versed in local politics and gossip. The two soon chatted like old friends.

A flurry of fantastic days and nights at the white cat's castle followed. Caterina was an entertainer like no other. The prince stayed in a bedroom covered with a kaleidoscope of fluttering butterfly wings. The next morning, Caterina took the prince on a hunt. They wore matching uniforms; he rode a sentient wooden horse while she rode a monkey. Her howling hunting party, five-hundred-strong, obliterated the local birds and rodents. Over the next few months, the prince was treated to a theater troupe of cats and monkeys, as well as other zoological ballets and operas. Of course, cats will be cats. Domestic squabbles were settled with literal catfights; an occasional hairball ended up in Denis's slipper; a hundred lint-rollers could not control the sheen of cat hair on all the furnishings. But Denis didn't care. Every day he woke up eager to pass the time with Queen Caterina. He'd never met anyone who made him so happy.

"The White Cat" has a lot in common with "Beauty and the Beast," right down to the monkey theater troupe and invisible servants. But in Madame's version, the prince is no captive and the couple's mutual love is given time to grow. Madame's subversion is likely due to her own arranged marriage at age fifteen, to a man thirty years her senior, a man she despised so much, she framed him for treason.

"You know," Denis told Caterina one evening after a couple bottles of Bordeaux, "sometimes I wish that I could become a cat, or you could become a woman, and we could make this thing legit!"

Caterina's whiskers twitched sadly. "If only!"

"No, really!" Denis scratched a finger under Caterina's chin. "No other cat exists such as you. How is it you came to be so ladylike? Is there more than meets the eye?"

The white cat pulled away, knocking his wineglass off the table disapprovingly. "That is none of your business. Besides, you're due home in just a few days for the Puppy Pageant."

Denis slapped his forehead. "Good Lord! I forgot about that. Has it been a year already?" He groaned. "I'll never find a dog in time. Even if I could, it will take me a week to find my way home!"

Caterina clapped her paws, and the nearest butler scampered up carrying a velvet cushion. "No fear, sweet prince. You may have forgotten your purpose, but I've got you covered." She gestured to the cushion, where a small acorn perched. "Inside this nut is the prettiest little dog in the universe. My wooden horse can traverse five hundred leagues in half a day, so you'll be home in time and win the crown with no trouble."

Denis held the acorn to his ear. Sure enough, he heard a teeny "woof"! Caterina cautioned him not to open the acorn until the big day, for the dog's safety and for an impressive show.

The prince took the white cat's paw gently. "This has been the happiest year of my life," he told her. "I cannot imagine my world without you in it. Would you accompany me back home?"

Caterina tearfully refused. "You have your duties abroad, and mine keep me here." Still, she bumped her forehead tenderly to his. "You are welcome back anytime."

The wooden horse galloped Denis back home as fast as a hurricane. In fact, he arrived early and played a little trick on his brothers. He borrowed a dog from the palace kitchen, a sad little turnspit singed at the ears.* Denis held the ragged puppy under one arm and waved as his brothers arrived, each leading a perfect Pomeranian, the dogs indistinguishable in their beauty. His eldest brother wrinkled his nose at the turnspit. "That mongrel is the most beautiful dog you could find?"

"That is for Father to decide," Denis replied coyly. Before he could be questioned further, the three brothers were summoned to the throne room.

The king hemmed and hawed between the two Pomeranians, trying to decide if one was a prettier shade of blond or which had brighter eyes. Denis interrupted him just before he made a decision. "Perhaps, Father, you might consider this dog." He plucked the acorn he'd stowed in his breast pocket, and carefully cracked it open on the arm of the king's throne.

A minuscule terrier of a thousand colors shook itself off and greeted the sovereign with a bell-like yip. The court gasped as the dog turned a few flips and jumped through the king's wedding band. They giggled when the dog pulled out castanets and danced the flamenco. They cooed when the animal sneezed and applauded as it bayed the national anthem.

The king smiled as he announced Denis the clear winner of the Puppy Pageant. But inside, the old man quaked. He still wasn't ready to hand off the kingship! He quickly improvised another stall: "I am so pleased with all three of you that I wonder if my task was too easy?"

The elder brothers' sulks transformed into smiles. "A rematch, perhaps?"

"Yes!" The king clapped his hands. "A year from today, I want

---

* *A turnspit was a dog used in the kitchens to turn the spit of roasting meat by way of a wheel. Ugh, I know. The happy ending here is that this practice led to the establishment of the ASPCA.*

you boys to bring me a length of cloth so fine, it can pass through the eye of the smallest needle!"

Denis wasn't disappointed to see his victory overturned. Rather, he swung that wooden horse around and galloped off to get more pussy. Upon his arrival, the floating hands rolled him into Caterina's sitting room. The kitty queen was back in her mourning blacks, caterwauling sadly. But when her nose picked up Denis's familiar scent, she threw back her veil and leapt into his arms. "Oh, my sweet prince!" she intoned between purrs, rubbing her cheek to his. "I couldn't let myself hope you'd return, but I am so glad you have!"

Denis told the queen of his triumph at the pageant, as well as his father's new decree. Caterina assured him that she had exemplary spinners on staff. "I've only had to fire a few for losing their mittens."

In the meantime, she had a million diversions to share: fishing on her crystal-clear lake, jousting matches between her accomplished tomcats, a public pardoning of prisoners that led to a fireworks show!

I cannot overstate how much detail d'Aulnoy and her female contemporaries put into their stories, an aspect I am merely hinting at. Once again, it comes across as a side effect of storytelling competitions. I imagine each lady one-upping the others with creative side-plots or egging each other on for more flowery details.

Of course, there were quieter moments: nights of tummy rubs, afternoons of bird-watching, and long conversations about life and the universe over catnip and edibles. Denis and his pet could hardly believe when their year of bliss had passed and he was facing another journey home.

"I have your cloth ready—four hundred yards of it!" Caterina divulged. "Not only that, we'll send you home in style. Your father cannot deny you the crown if you show up with an entourage that outranks his own!"

Male beasts are violent or lascivious louts, but female beasts like Caterina and Russia's "The Frog Tsarina" must prove their worth a hundred times over.

The wooden horse was swapped for a gilded carriage drawn by twenty white mares. Denis had an escort of a thousand bodyguards and noblemen, each gussied up in lacey livery, bearing cameos of the white cat herself. **(Wait, are they still just hands? This is the problem with writing in a salon sans editor.)**

Before Denis and Caterina parted ways, she batted a walnut shell at him, instructing him to crack it open only when it was his turn to reveal his bounty.

"You put four hundred yards of fabric in this?" Denis questioned.

Caterina scratched his hand, well, cattily. "Do not doubt me, sweet prince!"

But Denis was merely delaying their goodbye. "You've done so much for me, Caterina. I no longer desire my father's kingdom. I'd much prefer to spend my days here, if you'll have me."

Caterina affectionately twisted through his legs a few times but refused. "What good is a cat to a king but to catch mice?" she insisted.

"You know you are not a mere housecat!" Denis protested. He crouched on one knee. "If you told me you were an enchanted princess, it would not surprise me. Hint, hint!"

A growl stirred low in Caterina's belly. Denis backed off. "I'm sorry. Let's not part on angry terms." With a kiss to her head, Denis returned home.

The prince's immediate devotion to the cat is another great subversion. Usually a stunning girl learns to love a beast, or a stunning girl learns to "fix" him. Madame asks, what if women were offered the same chance as beastly men; and what if men felt open to love them despite their imperfections?

This time, Denis arrived late to the proceedings. His older brothers found impressively delicate muslin. Their yardage passed through the eye of a needle, but only a large darning one. The king used this as an excuse to delay his decision, bickering with his exasperated sons. Amid this, Denis spoke up. "There's still my fabric, Father."

He produced the walnut shell from a box encrusted with rubies. The court, remembering the wonder of the tiny acorn dog the year before, hushed as the prince opened the walnut shell. But he found no fabric: just another shell, this of a hazelnut. Denis laughed, and cracked that open, revealing a cherry stone.

At this, the king and the court began to titter. Denis blushed and pried open the cherry stone, which revealed a corn kernel, and in that a grain of wheat. When Denis reached a millet seed, he wondered if Caterina had tricked him. At the thought, he yelped in pain, for once again he felt the white cat swipe at his hand as if she were beside him!

Being an accomplished hunter, an exemplary hostess, and a wealthy, benevolent ruler is not enough: our feline must also astral-project.

Denis quickly cracked open the seed, and out tumbled an endless length of the airiest toile, printed with a menagerie of mythical beasts. The king's seamstress picked up a corner, and, sure enough, the fabric passed through not only the eye of the darning needle, but through the tiniest beading needle she could produce, without a single snarl.

The king's throat began to close as the courts cheered Denis's triumph. He scrambled for a way to put off the end of the competition. His gaze fell upon a couple observing the ceremony arm in arm. "That's it!" he shouted, clearing his throat as the room silenced. "Uh, what I mean to say is, that's *not* it at *all*! Despite Denis's impressive feat, I cannot hand the crown to any of my sons, for none have secured themselves a bride. What is a king without his queen? A year from today, whoever brings home the most enchanting fiancée shall be crowned king on his wedding day. No take-backsies."

Denis sailed out of the throne room with a whoop, thrilled to get another year with his furry girlfriend. This time, Caterina anticipated his return. The driveway was lined with lilacs and a heady scent of jasmine thickened the air. Denis found the cat queen sprawled across a Persian carpet, blinking at him with bedroom eyes that would put Cleopatra to shame. "What does the king ask of you this time?" she purred.

"A beautiful princess!" Denis laughed. "It's obvious my father is not ready to relinquish the throne. And I no longer care to have it."

"Why not?"

"A kingdom without you is worthless." Denis paced. "Caterina, I cannot go another day without knowing your story. Are you a fairy? A sorceress? Do you take on human form overnight, or out of my sight?"

The prince repeatedly grills the cat about her past, but Beauty passively (and rather densely) accepts the Beast's odd persona despite a lot of hints to the contrary. Maybe this is less of a statement on gender and more the prince justifying his romantic love for the mascot of Fancy Feast.

"What you see is what you get!" Caterina evaded. "Stop interrogating me! I must find you a superior *human* princess." She sat up and thumped her tail with annoyance. "Get some rest. Tomorrow is the annual naval showdown between my army and the rats! You won't want to sleep through that."

Another blissful year passed, filled with chess matches, boat rides, and lots of short naps. Caterina didn't bring up his quest again. Denis was happy to put off his inevitable nuptials. In the final weeks, he couldn't hide the gloom he felt counting down his time with the cat queen. On the contrary, Caterina was growing more and more excited. She often made herself scarce, claiming to be wedding planning. "Chin up, sweet prince!" she'd assure him. "I've the ideal match in mind."

The night before Denis's departure, he was summoned to meet his bride-to-be. The handsy valet dressed him in full regalia, shining his epaulets and positioning his sword just so. At last, the butler led him to the sitting room, where Caterina sat awash in the glow of a roaring fire.

"Well?" Denis asked, shuffling from foot to foot. "Where is she?"

Caterina self-consciously cleaned her face. "She will arrive soon. But before we part, I must ask a favor."

Denis swallowed past the lump in his throat. "Anything, my pet."

The white cat trotted to his feet. She circled the floor a few times, before stretching out on her side, neck out and tail straight. "I need you to cut off my head and tail."

Denis stumbled back. "What? How could you ask that of me?"

"I wouldn't ask if it weren't necessary."

"I don't understand," Denis protested, turning away. "This is so perverse! Are you punishing me for leaving?"

"Nonsense!" Caterina scampered after him. "It is not a matter of punishment or a matter of despair. Rather, it is my destiny!" She padded up his calf, pawing at his stocking gingerly. "Please,

Denis. As long as I stand on these four paws, you cannot meet your princess. And she has been waiting for so long."

Denis broke down, but even tears could not dissuade the queen of her gory request. She stretched herself out in front of the fire again. At last, with a heavy heart and hand, Denis did as she asked.

No sooner had the prince's blade cut through Caterina's tail than her body began to transform. She swelled and stretched, animorphing into a beautiful young maiden with flaxen hair and wide chartreuse eyes. She held a white catskin in her hands, which she held out to Denis. "This is what I couldn't tell you," she said.

The doors of the sitting room burst open. Dozens of courtiers swarmed in, each carrying a catskin of their own. They surged to their queen Caterina, abuzz at her transformation as well as their own. Caterina greeted each of her subjects graciously but finally asked them to leave. "I owe Denis the full story."

The most astonishing part of this tale is the amount of backstory dropped at this climactic moment. Madame used seven thousand words up to this point, then takes *another* seven thousand to tell the white cat's convoluted backstory. I've summarized as briefly as possible!

"My story opens like so many princesses' do," Caterina began. "With my mother's intense pregnancy cravings for forbidden food."

Caterina joins the ranks of other French Rapunzels such as "Persinette" and "Parsilette," but Madame was likely riffing off Giambattista Basile's "Petrosinella." The mothers in *those* tales crave parsley, a food no one should lose a baby over.

"She and my father ruled over six kingdoms, so they rarely wanted for anything. Bored with mortal delicacies, my mother traveled to Fairyland in pursuit of the legendary fruit they cultivated. Their orchards were enclosed by a fence that grew of its own accord if threatened by invasion. Most of my mother's attendants died vaulting it on her command. When it looked as though she wouldn't get to taste the, well, fruits of their labor, as it were"—she laughed at her joke—"my mother fell deathly ill. The fairies took pity on her and agreed to allow her a taste if she promised them her unborn daughter. They assured her that I would want for nothing, but that she could not reunite with me until my wedding. She agreed to the bargain."

Denis interrupted her. "Your mother gave you away for fruit?"

"For *fairy* fruit," Caterina corrected him. "It's really good stuff! Anyway, my father was enraged. He imprisoned Mother in a tower. When I was born, he refused to hand me over to the fairies. So they sent a dragon to wreak havoc on the kingdom. The beast polluted the air, devoured every citizen he could set his fangs on, and ravaged our forests and cities. My father had to give me away to stop the carnage."

"Wow." Denis didn't really know what to say. Luckily for him, Caterina was just getting started.

"Anyway, the fairies sent a pearl chariot driven by seahorses to take me away—"

"You lived underwater?"

"No, no, the seahorses traversed the land."

"What?"

"Just listen. They put me up in my own doorless tower, though it was a much nicer prison than my mother's. Thousands of rooms, with every diversion I could ask for. They bewitched a parrot and a dog to speak so I had some friends. **(Bird people, your time has come!)** But you can only imagine my reaction the first time I saw a man in the flesh! I was sixteen, I think? And he was about thirty . . . stories below me. But even from that height I could tell he was a looker. He courted me from the bottom of the tower for some time, shouting poetry through a megaphone and whipping jewelry at me with a trebuchet. My parrot took pity on us and became my wingman. Ha ha! Wingman, isn't that funny?"

In a daze, Denis agreed.

"Eventually, my beau and I concocted an escape plan, for my fairy mothers absolutely despised mortal men and would never allow our marriage. I crafted a silken ladder. We had to rush, because the fairies wanted me to marry a horrid fairy king! Plus, my relationship with my fairy moms was deteriorating quickly. Every night I'd throw a tantrum, and they'd threaten to burn me alive. But I couldn't help acting out. Can you imagine how miserable I was, with no one but a dog and a parrot for companionship?"

"Actually, that's the one thing I can relate to in this story," Denis offered, "having spent the last three years with a castle full of cat-people. Sorry, could we get back to that whole burning-alive part? How are you handling this so well?"

"Oh, that's all in the past!" Caterina got to her feet to pantomime her story. "Once I finished the ladder, my beloved ascended to my room. As fortune would have it, he was just as handsome and charming as I'd hoped, considering I'd been squinting at him for the last six months. We made our vows to each other with my dog and parrot bearing witness. But alas, that was as far as fate would allow our star-crossed romance. The fairies got suspicious after I refused to marry their horrible suitor. When they discovered me and my husband together, they sent their dragon to devour my love right in front of my eyes."

"Holy shit!" Denis sputtered.

"Oh yes, that was a very bad day. I attempted to throw *myself* into the dragon's jaws, but the fairies had other plans."

Between her negligent, abusive parents and her tyrannical abusive abductors, the princess seems remarkably well adjusted. Perhaps she had a cat therapist on retainer?

"As punishment for my betrayal, they transformed me into a cat and banished me to this castle. They also turned the entire court into cats. Anyone who ranked lower than a baron they magicked into floating hands."

Being turned into a cat generally seems preferable to being eaten by a dragon, but the flip side is you have to clean your butthole with your tongue.

Caterina paused to take a sip of water. "Where was I?"

"The hand thing!" Denis chimed in.

"Oh yes. The fairies promised to release me if I won the love of a man who looked exactly like my pulverized husband. So you can imagine how thrilled I was when you showed up at my door! You could be my beloved's twin! All I had to do now was seduce you with my charm and riches. Which was surprisingly easy. You really like cats, don't you?"

"It was a shock to me as well." Denis grasped at an appropriate response to Caterina's horrifying story. "Wow! All of that over some fruit."

"*Fairy* fruit," Caterina corrected.

If Denis was alarmed at the traumatic baggage Caterina was bringing to this relationship, he didn't show it. The couple swiftly prepared for the Fiancé Face-Off. Just as they'd done with the puppy and the fabric-so-fine, they arranged a showy send-up. She hid inside an amethyst egg set on a curtained palanquin carried by four sexy strong men. Denis's brothers had already arrived with princesses on their arms. The king received the first two ladies graciously, impressed by their beauty and elegance. Then he turned to Denis. "Have you arrived alone, my boy?"

Denis milked the moment, sighing dramatically. "I'm afraid I couldn't find a princess who captured my heart as much as . . . well, as a little white cat."

The court broke out into murmurs, which the king hushed with a tap of his staff. "A white cat, you say?"

"Yes. She is so charming, so impressive, and such a beauty. I couldn't imagine anyone else worthy of my companionship. Would you like to meet her?" He gestured to his handsome attendants, who opened the curtains, revealing the crystal egg.

The king stepped forward to inspect the odd container. Suddenly the egg exploded in a shower of glitter and light! Queen Caterina revealed herself with a perfect pirouette, her gauzy gown floating on air, her platinum ringlets tumbling all the way to the floor under a crown of lilies. She curtsied low as the room burst into applause.

The king helped her up. "You have outdone yourself, my dear! I am enraptured!" His smile dissolved into tears. "And devastated!"

Denis and Caterina caught the king's arms. "Father, what is wrong?"

"I have loved being king," the old man blubbered. "But I made a promise, and I won't go back on my word again. Take my crown, Denis."

Caterina broke the mood with a bright laugh. "Why, there is no need for you to abdicate, my lord! I am heiress to six entire kingdoms, which is far too many for one couple to manage. Why don't you take a small one? That way you can enjoy the title as well as your retirement." She danced over to Denis's brothers and their girlfriends. "Each of these fine princes can take one as well. That leaves Denis and me with three kingdoms, well, four if you count this one. Wow, I just gave away half my wealth and I still got wealthier! Someone should do something about that!"

The family was so ecstatic, they threw a triple wedding, with festivities carrying on for several months across all seven kingdoms. Each couple flourished as rulers and as romantics, but none so much as Denis and his queen, a truly purrfect pair.

* * *

SOURCE: James Robinson Planché, translator. "The White Cat" from *Fairy Tales by Madame d'Aulnoy*.

Want to read more of Madame d'Aulnoy's fairy tales? I like *The Island of Happiness: Tales of Madame d'Aulnoy*, edited by Natalie Frank and translated by Jack Zipes.

WHEN A BIRD LOVES A WOMAN

THE TZOTZIL MAYAN'S "THE BUZZARD HUSBAND," MEXICO

Once there lived a peasant who was the laziest bastard you could ever imagine.

Bold choice, to open my one Mexican folktale with the "lazy Mexican" stereotype! Rest assured, dear reader, this man is the exception, not the rule.

Every day he'd ask his wife to make him a basket of tortillas to keep him fed through his workday. He'd set off into the forest, where he was supposed to slash trees and clear the land for farming along with his hardworking neighbors. As soon as he arrived, he'd stack his wife's homemade tortillas into a soft pillow, lie down, pull his sarape up to his chin like a blanket, and watch the birds overhead.

"If only I could be a bird!" he'd whine. He'd spy the turkey vultures soaring with their enormous wings stretched and cry out to God, "Diosito! If only I could swap places with a buzzard! I'd never have to work again. I wouldn't have to fly; the wind would carry me. I wouldn't even have to hunt, since others would kill my food for me." He complained about work a lot, for a man who barely did anything!

Vultures play varied roles in Latin American folklore. They've saved humans from the great flood; they've been the keepers of

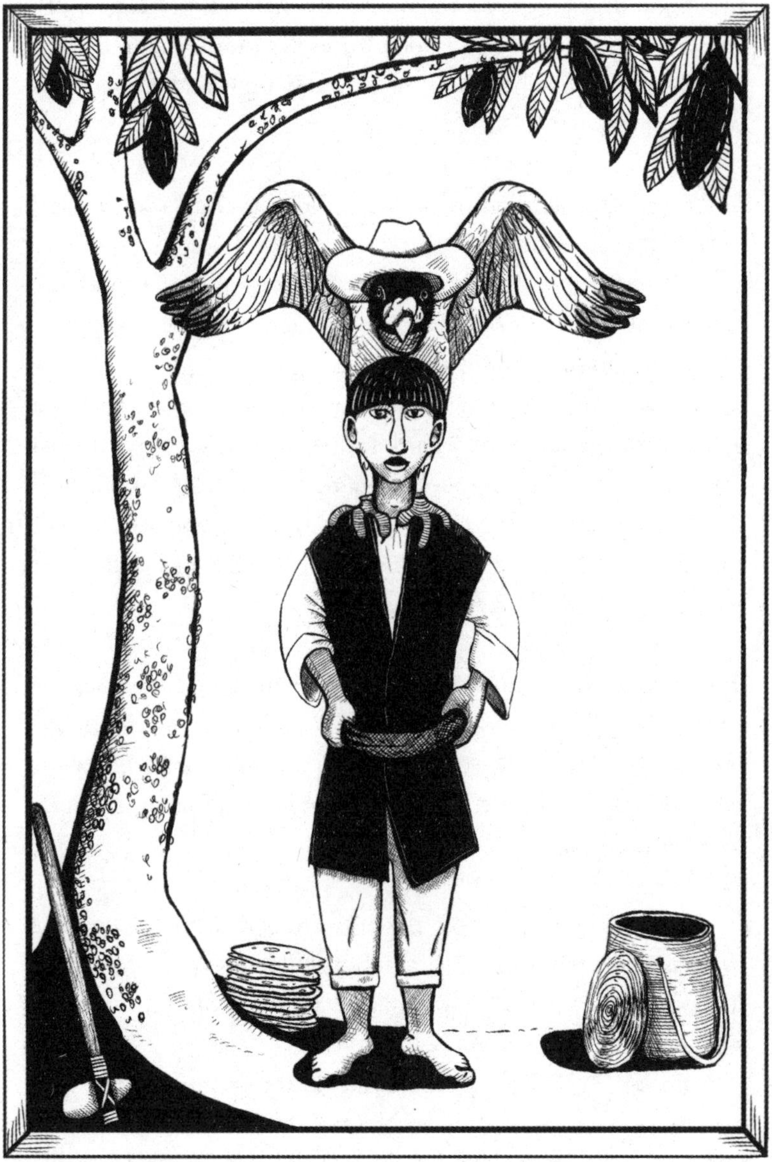

fire. Sometimes they're antagonists: the Mbyá folk have a myth where humans are turned into vultures as a punishment for cannibalism. I am a huge fan of the adorably fugly and ecologically vital animal!

At twilight, he'd return home. "Did you clear a lot of land today?" his wife would ask.

"The process is never-ending!" the lazy peasant would fib. "Every day I clear trees, and when I return to where I left off, it is as if the damn trees grow back overnight!"

His wife, an observant woman, knew that her husband was a loafer. He claimed to work hard during the day, but *somehow* lost the will to do anything once he came home. "Fall is upon us," she'd remind him. "The other men keep asking why you haven't shown up at the cornfields to harvest!" But her husband didn't hear. For he was already sleeping off his dinner.

Tzotzil Mayan women learned embroidery and weaving as young girls to contribute to the family economy. You can imagine how frustrating it would be to do all that work while your husband naps, full of the food you cooked and using the leftovers as pillows.

This routine went on for the entire first year of the couple's marriage. The wife was impatient but couldn't do anything about it. Someone else was growing tired of the guy's attitude too, someone who had a lot more leverage.

"Diosito! Why do you make me suffer so much?" the lazy peasant complained. "You let the vultures explore your wide, wondrous sky all day long! But not me." He stumbled to his feet and picked up his smallest ax. He swung it into the skinniest tree he could find. He cried out from the exertion. "Look at these fingers, Lord!" The peasant held his hands to the sky.

They were flawless. "You make me work them to the bone! The bone, Diosito!"

Up in his heavenly estate, God's head was pounding. "If I have to listen to this asshole beg to be a buzzard one more time," he said to Saint Peter, "I swear to Me, I'll turn him into salt."

St. Peter shrugged. "Why turn him into salt when you could turn him into a buzzard?"

God cackled. "See, that's why I keep you around, Pete! Hmmm . . . Only that wouldn't solve the wife's problem. She doesn't deserve to be widowed." He snapped his fingers. "I've got it. Summon one of those buzzards, Pete!"

A lot of public storytelling in Mexico takes place around death rituals. Wakes as well as Día de Muertos celebrations are honored with shared stories. Each of the Latin American tales I feature in this book touch on death in some way.

The following day, when the lazy peasant woke up from his lunchtime nap, he found a large turkey vulture standing by his head. "Buzz off, bird!" he mumbled, tipping his hat over his face.

The vulture spoke up. "I thought you wanted to trade places with me."

The peasant peeked out from under his hat. "That's a real option?"

The vulture nodded his fleshy face. "The Lord offered me a chance to be a human, if you really want to trade places. He said we could give it a trial period. Live each other's lives for a few days, then meet back up and see how it's going."

The peasant hesitated. "I'm not so sure my wife would like to be married to a bird."

"Oh, she won't know," the vulture assured him. "Once you put on my feathers and I put on your clothes, you'll look just like a turkey vulture, and I'll look just like you."

Both man and bird have no problems with tricking their wife, I see. I take back all those nice things I said about vultures!

The lazy peasant agreed. He dropped his clothes into a pile and the vulture dropped his feathers into another. The two swapped places. The vulture sprouted human legs and stepped into the peasant's pants. The peasant put handfuls of feathers onto his body, which grafted into his skin. He shrank down, while the vulture elongated in size. Once the transformation finished, and they admired God's handiwork.

"So, is there anything I should know about being human?" the vulture-husband asked.

"Every day for work, you need to clear a plot of trees," the lazy-buzzard told him. "At home, my wife takes care of most chores, but you are responsible for the yardwork and some of the heavy lifting on the farm. She'll tell you what to do."

The vulture-husband nodded. "I can handle that. How do humans stay cool while working in the sun all day? Do you shit and piss on your legs? That's what I do."

The lazy-buzzard shook his head. "Definitely don't do that. Now: What do I need to know about being a vulture?"

"We find our food by sniffing out fumes of a dead animal," the vulture-husband explained. "If you smell faint fumes, it's likely a small animal. Strong fumes indicate a large animal, and if you're overwhelmed by the pungency, you've found a feast! Also, if you get hot, poop on your legs. Trust me, you'll feel much better."

The lazy-buzzard was skeptical. "Won't the other birds laugh at me?"

The vulture-husband shook his head. "Embarrassment is a human problem."

The two agreed to meet at the same spot in three days, then parted ways.

* * *

THREE DAYS later, the lazy-buzzard reported back. He looked around. A large area was completely cleared of trees. "Wow," he said when the vulture-husband arrived. "You got a lot more done than I ever did."

The vulture-husband was surprised. "Really? Once I figured out how to use these gangly limbs, it wasn't too bad. Hard work, for sure. I shadowed one of the other men in the village on the first day. Since I helped him, he came and helped me. Not much different from vultures, to be honest. The predators kill the animals and get first dibs, next we get our share, and eventually even the little maggots get theirs. Community is key."

"That may be how you operate," the lazy-vulture said. "But I've been shaking things up a bit!"

The vulture-husband tutted. "Be careful. There's a natural order to things."

The lazy-buzzard waved him off with a wing, falling over in the process. He hopped back up and changed the subject. "How are you getting along with my wife?"

The vulture-husband smiled. "She's lovely! But suspicious. She keeps saying I stink. I told her it was from working all day. I'm bringing her with me tomorrow to convince her."

"So are we committing to this bit?" the lazy-buzzard asked. "I'll stay a bird, and you stay a man?"

The vulture-husband nodded. "I'm happy if you're happy!"

They parted ways for good.

* * *

THE NEXT day, the lazy-buzzard soared through the sky, looking for the biggest cut of roadkill he could find. *Maybe I'll find a bobcat today,* he thought. *Or an anteater. Or a wolf!*

"Hey!" A group of yellow-headed vultures flagged him down. "We just smelled some fumes downwind; we think it might be a possum! You want in?"

The lazy-buzzard considered this. Then he caught the scent of large billowing smoke in the other direction. "Hell, no! Look at that! It smells like a herd of dead bison!"

"I don't think so, man!" The yellow-headed birds replied. "Those aren't the right kind of fumes!"

The lazy-buzzard laughed at them. "Go enjoy your mealy roadkill. I'm gonna gorge myself on that buffet!" He flew off.

The yellow-headed vultures watched him, shaking their bare heads. "Unbelievable."

※ ※ ※

"So, you can see why I smell so bad," the vulture-husband explained to his wife, back in the forest.

She looked around. Her husband and his fellow loggers had created a large fire lane down to the soil. Then they lit fires to clear portions between those lanes. Plumes of black smoke wafted through the remaining trees as they burned off the brush.

Vultures are associated with fire and rain in Mayan culture because the birds are attracted by the cultural burns used for farming. The fires drive out (or take down) small animals that the vultures scavenge. Those fire seasons take place just before the rainy seasons. Maybe our vulture character picked up the work easily from observing these slash-and-burns year after year.

"You've been working very hard," she admitted. "I'm sorry I thought otherwise."

"Oh, don't apologize," the vulture-husband replied. "You were right about me. I was a lazy sonofabitch. But I had a change of heart."

The couple sat down together to share lunch. Well, Mrs. Vulture-Husband did. The man-bird caught sight of a dead gopher and stopped to sniff it.

"Your lunch is over here!" his wife said, raising her eyebrows. It was not the first time he'd been caught making quesadilla out of roadkill.

As they ate and chatted, they saw a buzzard awkwardly flying toward the black smoke. "Oh dear," the vulture-husband muttered.

The bird nosedived right into the thick soot. Then it realized its mistake. It beat its wings furiously to turn around. But the smoke was too dense, and it plummeted to the ground.

"Useless bird," the wife scoffed, watching her husband out of her peripheral vision. "Vultures are revolting animals."

"Hey, now!" the vulture-husband countered. "That bird wasn't behaving properly. Vultures are resourceful creatures! They break down carcasses and prevent disease!"

His wife raised her eyebrows. "Seems like you're a big vulture fan!"

Her husband averted his gaze. "We shouldn't judge creatures we don't know much about."

His wife put down her lunch and stood, her hands on her hips. "I was testing you!" she said. "I know why you smell like death all the time. It's not the smell of soot or sweat. You *are* a vulture!"

The vulture-husband blushed nearly as red as his buzzard face used to be. "I don't know what you're talking about!"

"You're a terrible liar. Besides," his wife insisted, "our neighbor saw you and my husband switch places! Plus: you keep eating roadkill! And the other night when that man at the bar threatened you, you vomited in his face and ran away. That's vulture behavior!"

"I refuse to waste perfectly good meat!" the vulture-husband retorted.

"Humans can't eat roadkill!" His wife shouted back. "Why do you think you puked on that guy?"

They stared at each other. Then the wife broke into a broad grin. "Look: I don't really care. You've been a better provider and more attentive husband in the last week than I've had all year. Keep it up, and I'll happily remain a vulture's wife."

And so he did.

While European folktales tend to end on a marital happily ever after, indigenous America more often explores the conflicts of married couples or the rejection of marriage outright. The desire for romantic narratives beyond the wedding day can be found in folklore. You just have to dig a little, and maybe get out of Western Europe, to find it.

* * *

SOURCE: John Bierhorst, "The Buzzard Husband."

Want to read more folklore from indigenous Latin America? Try *The Sea-Ringed World: Sacred Stories of the Americas* by Maria Garcia Esperon.

MULE BE IN MY HEART

Tunisia's "The Donkey's Head"

Once there lived an old widow named Sahar who worked as a weaver. Despite breaking her back to craft luxury fabrics for the city elite, Sahar and her fellow craftswomen were dreadfully underpaid. Her earnings barely covered rent and meager meals.

Has anyone used fairy tale evidence to lobby for universal basic income? Shouldn't we be concerned that a widow in 2024 is flipping burgers for minimum wage, just like poor Sahar here in ancient Tunisia?

As if poverty weren't stressful enough, conflicts between her kingdom and a neighboring one led many in the city to tighten their wallets. The guild laid off half of its employees, including Sahar, with no notice. The widow found herself homeless, with only a loaf of bread and a jar of olives. She walked the city to find work but was turned away at every door. That night, Sahar slept on a bench just outside the square.

The next day was no better. Sahar was back at her bench by dusk, nursing sore feet and a bruised ego, when the town crier began the evening's announcements: "The old spice shop is once again open to thrill-seekers interested in removing the malevolent spirit that inhabits it," he recited from a scroll. The fatigue in his voice suggested he'd read these words many times before. "Should a citizen survive the night, they will inherit ownership of the

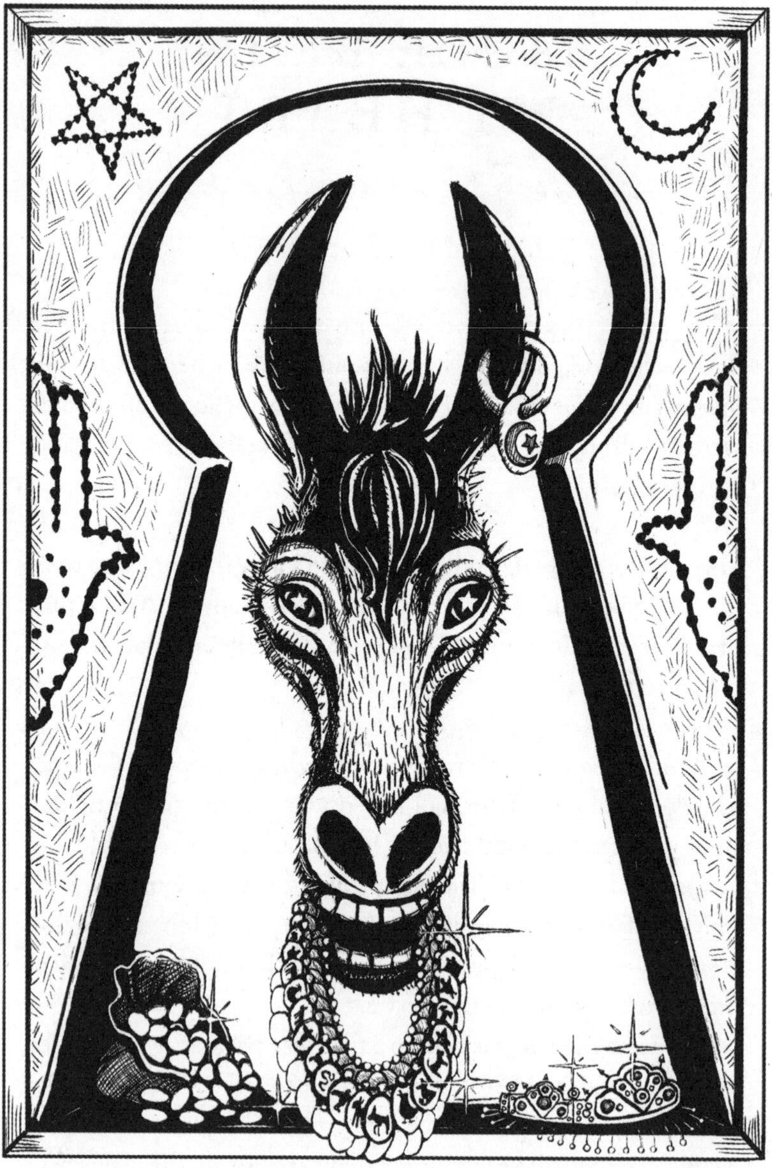

property immediately. Should this same citizen perish, we will bury them at no cost to their family, in thanks for your attempt to eradicate the haunt. Yadda, yadda, yadda, you know the drill."

This fairy tale has a half dozen variants in Tunisia alone, and each has fun little quirks. I love how this setup crosses over with the Grimms' "Boy Who Went Forth to Learn Fear" and other haunted house challenges.

Sahar was aware of the notorious "murder house" located in a ritzy neighborhood not far from the sultan's palace. The year before, the shopkeeper was found dead, and every night after, the surrounding residents heard terrible moans coming from within. The shopkeeper's family attempted to exorcise the demon, or ghoul (or whatever was squatting), but when several clerics were lost to the mysterious monster, they abandoned the place. The neighbors, exhausted from sleepless nights and frayed nerves **(not to mention a severe dip in property values)**, lobbied the city to find a solution. That's when this ill-fated challenge was announced. As time passed, only the most desperate citizens attempted to silence the spirit, for no one who walked through the shop door ever walked out again.

What have I got to lose? Sahar thought, stretching her cramped muscles. *Half a loaf of bread and a couple of olives? At the very least, I'll gain a proper burial.* She straightened her back and walked to the shop.

A neighbor directed her to a coffeehouse across the street for a ring of keys, a candle, a tinderbox, and a lot of waivers to sign. Before long, she was settled in the dismal remnants of the spice shop. Bloodstains stretched across moldy carpets and cushions; walls were cracked from past scuffles. A previous inhabitant had boarded the windows, cutting off any comforting street sounds. The scent of death still clung to the tattered tapestries.

Even Spirit Halloween was too afraid to move in.

The main room had several doors, at least one on each wall. The one farthest from the exit looked like it had been repeatedly repaired, with reinforced hinges and three large padlocks. "So that's where you're hiding," Sahar observed. She shuddered for a moment, then decided to look on the bright side. "Never thought I'd spend a night in this part of town before!" She pressed herself into a corner of the shop, where she had a full view of the menacing door. As the hours wore on, nothing disturbed her, so she dozed off.

Sahar woke just before midnight with a gurgling stomach. She lit her candle and took out her jar of olives, grimacing at the ratio of fruit to juice. She'd just opened it when the padlocked door across the shop shook with a hard thud. Sahar froze.

The door shook again with a second pound, and a third, and a fourth. Someone—*something*—was trying to barge in. Sahar figured she could wait until the fright on the other side broke through, or she could get things over with and confront it. Gritting her teeth, she fumbled for the keys and rushed the door before she could change her mind.

The padlocks rattled as the creature repeatedly hurtled against them. It shouted, a strangled baying that sent goose bumps down Sahar's spine. "Calm down!" she snapped. "You can batter yourself bloody, or I can let you in like a civilized creature!"

The thudding and wailing stopped. Sahar paused, unsure if this was a good sign. She thrust a key at the bottom lock, cursing as she dropped it with shaking fingers. Eventually all three padlocks were wrenched off. Sahar bit back her queasiness and opened the door, hiding between it and the wall.

A rush of air passed through as the creature entered. Then there was stillness. Sahar peered around the door. Something floated in the middle of the shop, staring back at her. But it was hard to make out its shape with only the single candle and slivers of lamplight glowing through the boarded windows. Cautiously, Sahar stepped out from behind the door, hugging the wall. Inch by inch, she crab-walked around the border of the room toward the candle in the corner. The creature stayed away, though it bobbed around to keep its own eyes on her. At last, Sahar reached her belongings. "I just want to get a good look at you, that's all," she said slowly. She bent down to grasp the candle and illuminated the monster.

"Oh my!" Sahar exclaimed. She'd never seen anything so bizarre in her life. The creature was not fully a creature at all, but merely a floating head. An enormous head. The head of a wild-eyed, haggard donkey.

"Donkey" is a common insult in Arab culture, used to call someone an ignoramus. The animal is severely miscast in many cultures' fairy tales as dull and undesirable, even though it's smart, sweet, and a mainstay of global farming. You know who I wouldn't want to run into in an abandoned building? A giant jellyfish. Honestly? Not even a small one.

The two stared at each other for a long moment. Then Sahar broke the silence. "You want something to eat?"

She sat cross-legged, setting her candle down between them, and tossed a hunk of bread to the animal. It snatched the morsel from the air, scarfing it down quickly. (Though where the bread went after it passed the animal's throat, Sahar didn't know.)

The two munched in silence. Sahar tossed the last olives to her strange companion and kept the briny liquid for herself. When their meal was done, the donkey spoke with a soft tenor. "Thank you."

"Boy, you're full of surprises, aren't you?" Sahar said. "If I couldn't see you with my own eyes, I'd think a fine gentleman sat across from me."

The donkey chuckled with her. "I was a gentleman once. Ages ago, it feels like." He told her his story.

His name was Nasim. He was a prince from a faraway land, and he'd fallen in love with Princess Zara, the daughter of Sahar's sultan. "I courted her for a time, but Zara's elder sister had not yet married, so we waited our turn. One night, back in my own country, I was attacked by a ghoul. I managed to strike it with the first stab of my sword, but in my anger, I stabbed it a second time, like a damn fool.* It rose back more powerful than before and took me hostage. The ghoul had a daughter he wanted to marry off to the kingdom's heir. I refused, protesting that I was already betrothed. So he cursed me into the form you see now."

I imagine the ghoul crying, "I curse you into a donkey," and Nasim snarking, "Well, at least I'll get that huge donkey dick." But the ghoul is suddenly inspired. "I DON'T THINK SO, BUDDY!"

Sahar whistled through her teeth. "Did he give you an out? You usually get an 'out' in these situations."

"If I convince my beloved to marry me with no knowledge that I am a prince, my curse will be nearly broken. But even then, I must continue to live like this for another month." Nasim floated to a window, peering through the boarded slats. "Worse, he trapped me here, close enough to see the palace through these shop windows, with no way of contacting her, in a form no woman could love."

---

* *In Arab folklore, if you strike a ghoul twice, the second stroke will negate the first, and the being will rise again. The rationale of this belief is that evil must be regarded with caution, and the repeated act of stabbing is considered reckless.*

Right about now, I'm regretting using up all my donkey puns in "Daddy's Little Donkey-Skin."

"I see." Sahar tapped her chin. "What you need is someone to appeal to the girl on your behalf. You'd have better luck with that if you stopped killing everyone who showed up at your door."

The donkey scoffed. "Easy for you to say. Everyone who shows up at my door comes ready to kill me first!"

Sahar conceded the point. "Humph. Let's sleep on it. We'll think better in the morning."

At daybreak, Sahar's mind was sharper, and her purse was heavier. A small pouch of gold coins had appeared next to her overnight, with a note bearing a royal insignia and short, messy signature: *Thank you. —N.* She smiled, then walked to the café across the street.

The coffeehouse manager was flabbergasted to see her alive. "I don't think you'll be bothered by that old ghost anymore," Sahar told him. "I'll take a bag of beans as thanks, though."

Tunisia is sometimes cited as home to the oldest public café, El Mrabet, dating back to 1628. I don't know that women had much of a role in these early cafés, but I like to think ridding the block of a ghost earns one certain privileges.

* * *

NEWS OF Sahar's triumph spread. People swarmed to her door with gifts and dozens of questions. She evaded those questions by saying that the haunt would return if she revealed her secrets. That first night, she treated herself and Nasim to a rich supper and downy velvet bedding. For each night of kindness the old woman showed Nasim, she received another pouchful of gold. By the week's end, Sahar had enough to hire a team to fix up the place. After week two, Sahar purchased the apartment on the second floor. By the end of the month, she had renovated the entire building and made herself a lovely little home.

Exorcising a ghost is still the only way a single woman can afford homeownership.

One night, Nasim pitched a plan. "Now that you've established a good reputation in town, what do you think of appealing to the sultan for Zara's hand?"

Sahar bit her lip. "I can't tell him the whole story, right? I have to convince his daughter to marry a disembodied donkey head?"

"Yup!" Nasim flared his lips in an unconvincing smile.

Sahar paced. "I suppose some of that gold you pay me could sweeten the deal."

Nasim's ears perked up. "I actually have something else you could offer. But you have to turn around and close your eyes while I get it." Sahar made a skeptical face but complied.

She heard an odd scraping noise and sensed a glow through her eyelids. Presently, Nasim returned, announcing through closed teeth, "You can look now!"

A layered golden necklace jingling with coins hung from Nasim's lips. Sahar took the piece and peered closer. She breathed in awe; the necklace was enchanted. Engraved animals on the coins pranced and scurried around, a living picture.

"Bring this to the princess," Nasim said. "Perhaps the precious metals will soften her heart."

Arab marriage customs included frequent gifts of jewelry from the groom leading up to the wedding. On the day of, the bride wears all of the bling her fiancé has bought. Interestingly, in the modern U.S., we ask for a single ring that costs more than all of those gifts combined.

Sahar presented herself at court, using her credentials as the local ghost whisperer to win face time with the sultan and Princess Zara. The sultan was impressed by the necklace but revolted to learn they came from a bodiless barnyard monster. For the widow's impertinence, he ordered a sound lashing. Sahar arrived back home limping and surly.

Nasim felt terrible. His daily offerings of gold doubled in recompense, and he produced an oil that healed Sahar's wounds. After a short time, he sheepishly (**Ass-ishly?**) dropped a gold diadem in her lap. A rainbow of gemstones dangled from the piece. When Sahar tilted it, the stones changed color ten times over.

Nasim hesitated. "Will you try again?"

Reluctantly, Sahar agreed to go back. This time, the sultan was almost swayed by the splendid gift, but Princess Zara refused. "What does a pretty crown matter if my husband is an animal?" she cried. "Not even a whole one. Am I not worth a whole donkey for a husband?"

"Princess, you should consider it," Sahar chimed in with a wink. "There's no-*body* else like him!" Once again, the widow was turned away with a beating. (**It wasn't *that* bad a joke.**)

This time, Nasim waited as long as he could before he asked Sahar to visit again. "I do not like to see you hurt," he pleaded, "but I don't have much time, and no one else to ask."

Sahar groaned. She had come to love Nasim as a son, and his stakes almost felt like her own after all these months together. "Fine. But I need you to pull out all the stops with this gift."

This time, the old widow wheeled a golden chicken coop right up to the feet of the Sultan. Inside, three hens tended to a dozen chicks. Their litter was chunky gold pebbles and their feed was delicate pearls. When the sultan stroked a hen's feathers, more pearls fell from her coat.

The sultan appealed to Zara, but she was still resistant. He sighed. "I cannot send my daughter to marry this creature, no matter how wealthy and magical he appears to be."

Sahar stood resolute. "And I will not stop asking until your daughter agrees to marry my son." *Or I die trying.*

"Fine." The sultan tried a new tactic to keep her away. "If your son can produce five hundred camels dressed in gold, with five hundred handmaids, each bearing a box of five hundred gemstones, *and* if the beast can build me an ivory castle with five hundred rooms, each richer than the other, then and only then will my daughter marry the donkey's head. If you cannot, and if you dare to show your face again, you will leave this palace in a funeral shroud."

Sahar returned with the bad news. But Nasim was thrilled. "I can do that!" he said.

"You can?" Sahar grumbled. "You've really been holding out on me!"

Like other animal bride/groom tales, the beast provides flashy goodies to make up for his appearance. But how? Is it a side effect of the curse? Is the prince owed some favors from a jinni or parī (an Arab creature similar to fairies)? Is he a sorcerer himself?

The sultan celebrated when a mob of camels and ladies walked to the palace the next morning, dragging riches with them. **(Insert me singing the entirety of "Prince Ali" here.)** Hundreds of carpenters also showed up with supplies and blueprints for the palace renovation. Zara begged her father to reconsider, and her elder sister Mariem even offered to be married in her stead. But Sahar was resolute. "It must be Princess Zara."

That night, the princess was brought to the widow's home in a discreet carriage, with her sister to bear witness. Sahar let the women in but turned away their attendants. Zara wore the jewelry Nasim had given her over a dress sewn with pearls hatched by the magical chickens. Sahar offered the princesses food and drink, trying to keep the conversation light. But Zara was inconsolable, and Mariem smoldered with resentment.

Sahar saw the curious palace staff peeking in the windows and closed the shutters. Once the building was secure, Nasim floated through the back door. Sahar had dressed him in a golden circlet and braided his gray mane, but it was like putting lipstick on a . . . well, on a donkey. Zara sobbed through the ceremony, barely able to make her vows, and hardly paying attention to Nasim's.

When the wedding concluded, Nasim ordered Mariem away. Sahar put a pot of tea on the fire, while Zara sank to the floor. She was all cried out.

The donkey's head nuzzled her, but she cringed. "It will be all right, Zara," he assured her.

The princess looked at the donkey in disbelief, registering his familiar voice. "Nasim? Is that you?"

The donkey's head nodded. Then the animal's bones shuddered under its hide. The women gasped at the alarming sight. Nasim's eyes rolled back into his head, and he fell. When he hit the floor, he was nothing more than a pile of skins; a pile of skins at the feet of a handsome youth, wearing green robes studded with emeralds. His eyes shone. "My love!"

Zara rushed into Nasim's arms, and he twirled her around. Sahar clapped and danced, overjoyed at the turn of events. Nasim embraced his adopted mother as well. Pressing a hand to the wall, he invited the women to his apartments. A panel opened with a scrape. Golden light spilled into the shop, revealing a hidden passage.

Nasim led the women up steps alternating in gold, coral, and silver. The staircase led to a stately suite with sumptuous decor, carpeted in scarlet and aubergine, with sparkling mosaics of topaz and mother-of-pearl. Despite the fancy furnishings, it was a goddamn mess. Nasim apologized. "I haven't had hands for quite some time. I haven't even had hooves!"

Sahar got her own section of the house, down the hall from the couple's chamber. Her eyes twinkled, and she bade them good night.

Zara and Nasim spent the night making love and catching up. He told her about the ghoul, his time haunting the spice shop, and how Sahar had helped save him. Zara apologized for not trusting the widow sooner, and Nasim assured her she was blameless. The princess nestled her face in the crook of her husband's neck. "Well, at least the curse is broken," she cooed. She was met with silence. Her dark eyes widened. "The curse is broken, right?"

Nasim kissed her head. "Please don't worry about it tonight," was all he said. And so, she didn't.

When the sun rose the following morning, Zara found herself embracing the donkey's head. She was less averse to him, knowing her beloved was somewhere inside the beast. She wrapped her arms around his muzzle, and he whuffled into her hair. The new wife spent the next day cleaning up the apartments. She cooked a meal for Nasim and her mother-in-law, overjoyed when at midnight the prince once again shed his donkey skins for his human form.

In some animal bridegroom tales, the wife chooses if her husband is an animal during the day and a man at night, or vice versa. The choice comes down to whether you care more about your reputation (having to show up at important events with a hedgehog on your arm) or your sex life (having to . . . you get it).

Things continued in this fashion for some time. Zara had a lot of questions, but for now she was happy to be reunited with the prince in whatever manner she could have him. Her days were spent keeping house and refusing visitors, for she wasn't sure what the hell to tell people about her odd situation. Eventually Sahar advised Zara to allow her sister to call, if only to assure the royal family that she was alive. But Nasim had some reservations.

"You cannot speak a word of my enchantment," he begged her. "You can tell them you are happy; you can tell them you are miserable. Either way, they must believe you are married to a monster, for just a few more days!"

Zara promised to keep her husband's secret and arranged a visit with her sister the following morning. Mariem was thirty minutes early, anxious to know how her sister's peculiar marriage was working out. The widow made a breakfast of shakshuka and toast, then gave the women some privacy.

Mariem inspected her sister. "You look well enough," she said, holding Zara by the chin.

"Stop! I am fine." Zara waved Mariem away. "Tell me all the news from back home."

"The news?" Mariem was a tough woman to bullshit. "The news is that my sister married the head of a donkey a month ago and no one has heard from her since!"

The sisters bickered for much of their visit, as Mariem kept pressing for details. "What does a floating head do all day?"

"I don't know. We only see each other after midnight."

"So you're telling me he ignores you. Is he merely negligent, or cruel as well?"

"No, no! He is as sweet as any domesticated beast."

"If he is so sweet, then why haven't you been home?"

"I've been busy. Even just a donkey's head leaves a mess behind him."

You may recognize this argument about the husband's identity from "Cupid and Psyche" and "East of the Sun, West of the

Moon." I hate how often the wife spills the beans to her sisters. If my beloved was cursed to be an animal for twelve hours a day, I could hold out. Luckily, Monia Hejaiej collected a version from a storyteller who thought like me.

Mariem eventually dropped the subject, but later she paid an attendant to distract Sahar, enabling her to sneak back inside, where she hid behind some old barrels in the pantry. That night, she watched through a keyhole as Sahar and Zara locked up, drew the shutters, and conversed by the light of the fireplace until midnight. Her hand flew to her mouth as she witnessed Nasim's transformation and the magical passage to the hidden suites. She busted out of the pantry as the passage door shut, running right into Sahar. "Was that Prince Nasim?" Mariem barked.

Sahar gasped. "How did you get in there?"

"Who cares how I got in there—how did my sister's suitor become a floating donkey head, is what I want to know!" Mariem planted her feet firmly. Sahar couldn't get her to budge.

"Look," the widow whispered. "I can't get into details, but it's a curse, and it will end—but it requires patience, which your sister has been good enough to honor."

"Perhaps Zara should be more creative!" Mariem saw Nasim's donkey-skin lying by the wall. She ran and scooped it into her arms. Sahar tried to stop her, but Mariem dashed past and threw the donkey-skin on the fire.

"What are you doing?" Sahar squealed.

"I'm trying to help!" Mariem said. "If he doesn't have the skin, he stays human, right?"

Wrong. A bloodcurdling scream sounded from the room above. Sahar and Mariem ran upstairs, skidding to a stop when they found Zara sprawled out in Sahar's parlor wearing her nightclothes. "He's gone!" she cried. "He and the house, they just disappeared!"

* * *

Having lost her love a second time, Zara withdrew to her bed with no intention of leaving it. Sahar tended to her as best she could, but suggested the princess be moved back to the palace, in hopes that the sultan could arrange better care for her. Zara refused any doctors or healers. She also banished Mariem from her side.

In hopes of making amends, Mariem told her father everything and offered to organize a search for the missing Prince Nasim.

Aforementioned "Cupid and Psyche" fans are asking, "Wait, doesn't Zara go on a series of quests to earn back her hubby?" Sometimes! Other variants outsource this job to another character. After working on a glut of fairy tales where the prince swoons till the end, I opted to let my princess take the long nap in this one.

The story of the enchanted prince spread far and wide. News of the steep reward for locating the prince spread even farther. But no trace of the man was found, and Zara grew weaker.

Then one day a peasant woman came to Mariem with a very strange story: "Two nights ago, my mother sent me to the baker for bread. On my way home, a gust of wind took the loaf right out of my hands. I chased after it, and when I finally got hold of the thing, I saw an unbelievable sight. A camel stood at a fountain washing dishes. When it finished, it flew away. I returned to the fountain at the same time the following two nights, and the camel came back." The peasant shrugged. "I don't know if it has anything to do with the missing prince, but it seems as strange as a donkey head haunting a spice shop."

Mariem thanked her and promised the woman a reward if

her information proved helpful. That night, she sought out the fountain. Sure enough, when the moon was high a camel flew in from the south carrying a basket of dishes, and washed them, whistling a working song. Mariem tiptoed up to the animal as he finished his chores. Before he could fly off, Mariem grabbed the camel's tail. The animal started, and took off into the sky, with Mariem in tow.

The camel swiftly flew across dozens of kingdoms, all the way to a vast desert. They made their descent when a large manor came into view. The camel flew to the front door—thank goodness for Mariem it was a gentle landing. The door opened and Mariem hurried in after the beast.

Inside the manor, the camel spoke. "Listen, guys, I know this is technically a prison, but does it have to look so shabby? We're getting ready to celebrate a wedding, after all." He poked his head out a window and called, "Could I get a little help straightening up?"

Mariem ducked as a great gust of wind blew into the house, picking up the scattered laundry, litter, and leftovers. The wind replaced books onto shelves and swept out the dust bunnies. Once the wind dissipated, a passing rain shower followed, polishing the floors and other hard surfaces (and conveniently avoiding the soft ones).

As Mariem marveled at the self-cleaning house, she heard men's voices approaching. She slipped into the next room, watching from the seam of its double doors.

Three men entered and sat around the table. One of them was young and handsome, in robes of green studded with emeralds. Mariem recognized him as Nasim. She watched as the camel laid out a fine meal, but she stayed quiet for fear of ruining another enchantment.

Nasim plucked an apple from a bowl of fruit and cut it into four pieces. He placed one quarter before each of his tablemates, one before himself, and set the fourth at an empty seat. "This slice is for the one absent from the table, but permanently lodged in my heart."

One of his tablemates spoke up. "Nasim, every night you leave an apple slice for your beloved. Why this symbolic gesture?"

"If my love eats a single bite of fruit from the ghoul's orchard, her health will return and my curse will be broken," Nasim replied. "But in three days, I'll be forced to marry the ghoul's daughter, and a dozen apples won't save me." He buried his face in his hands and wailed. "The very walls of this house should weep for the love I've lost!"

The walls were empathetic. They quaked for a moment, then ran with salty tears.

I haven't yet read a lot of fairy tales with this enchanted house motif. Naturally, it makes me think of *Encanto*. Did Disney find a cool folklore thing before I did? I begrudgingly commend them!

When the men finished their meal, they shook hands and departed from whence they came. The camel refilled his basket with this batch of dishes. Mariem eyed the slice of apple dedicated to Zara among the leftovers. She racked her brain for a way to swipe the thing off the table without the camel noticing. *Maybe I'm overthinking it,* she thought. *He didn't notice me hanging from his tail the whole way here—maybe he won't notice me pocketing the apple.*

She spied a stone paperweight on the table beside her, and decided a distraction was in order. When the camel leaned down to drop some platters in the basket, Mariem said a quick prayer and threw the stone in the direction of the kitchen. It hit a pair of hanging copper pans, which fell to the floor with a clatter. The camel trotted over to inspect the disturbance. Amid the kerfuffle,

Mariem slipped the apple off the table and into her purse, then positioned herself at the door, waiting to grab the camel's tail and stow away back home.

Back at the fountain, Mariem was in such a hurry she didn't even wait for the camel to land before she let go of its tail. She hit the street roughly and limped back to the palace.

"Wake up Zara!" she cried as she burst through the door. "I've found her husband!"

She ran through the palace, ignoring questions and pushing past attendants. She banged on Zara's door until the maids let her in, whereupon she crouched at her sister's side. "Zara, you must eat this!" she insisted, thrusting the apple, now brown and mushy, to the princess's lips.

Zara moaned and turned her head away. Mariem coaxed, then bargained, then nagged, until her little sister took a nibble of the old fruit. Mariem steeled her shoulders for a shimmer of light or a rush of music, something to indicate that the curse had lifted.

At first there was nothing. Then Zara's eyes fluttered open. Color returned to her skin for the first time in weeks. Next, a gasp sounded from outside the bedroom, followed by giggles.

Zara rolled over, pulling the blankets over her head. "Am I delirious, or do the very walls laugh at my heartbreak?"

The door opened, and there stood Nasim. Upon finding himself in the palace, he had laughed in exhausted relief. Seeing his love, he now laughed for joy. He knelt beside the bed and kissed the tears from her cheeks. "Never cry again, my love; the curse is finally broken."

* * *

SOURCES:
A. Fermé, "Contes Recueillis a Tunis—IV."
Monia Hejaiej, "Women's Oral Narratives in Tunis."
Sonia Koskas, *Contes des Juifs de Tunisie. Aux origines du monde.*
Pinḥas Sadeh and Hillel Halkin, *Jewish Folktales.*

Want to read more Arab fairy tales? Try *Abu Jmeel's Daughter and Other Stories: Arab Folk Tales from Palestine and Lebanon*, collected by Jamāl Salīm Nuwayhiḍ.

MY CARP WILL GO ON

Haiti's "Tezen"

Haitian folk have a communal method of beginning a story. The teller asks the audience for permission with the phrase, "Kric?" The audience affirms by answering, "Krac!" Since you are roughly halfway through my book, I'm gonna assume we're good to go.

Long ago on the island of Ayiti[*] lived a couple with two children: Noemi, their teenage daughter, and Jean, their ten-year-old son. Each morning, Papa would go harvest fruit or sell his wares at the market, while Maman and the children kept house. As soon as breakfast was cleared, Maman would call, "Noemi! Jean! The water won't fetch itself!" Noemi would quickly tie her braids into a bun and retrieve two buckets from the kitchen, and the siblings would walk down to the river.

One day, the two got a late start. Noemi found her little brother swaying on their rope swing. "Stop messing around, Jean! We're having a guest for dinner."

Jean groaned. "Another one?" He ran around, hunting for his sandals. "What was wrong with the last guy?"

"I don't want to talk about it." Noemi pointed out Jean's shoes, which were lying under the swing the whole time. "Let's go."

The siblings set off toward the river, a short walk from their

---

[*] *Haiti's original name, Taino origin.*

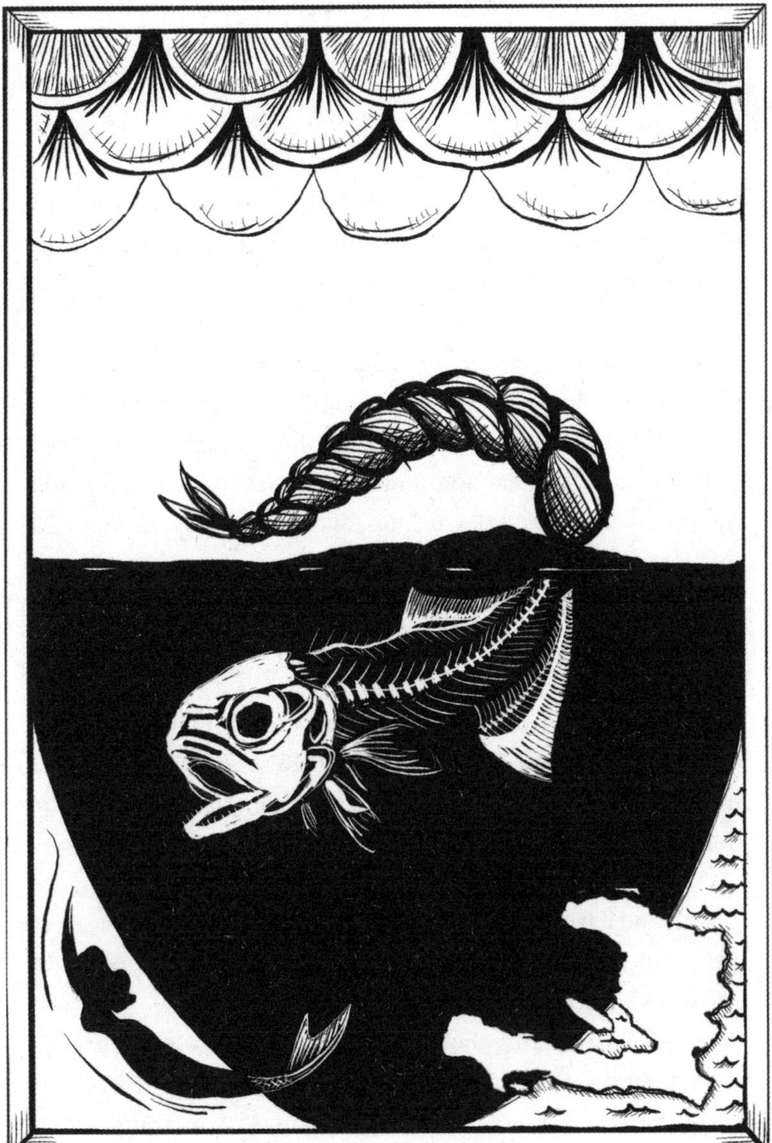

thatched hut. Jean continued to poke fun at his sister. "I don't think Maman is being picky about your suitors. I think they just take one look at your face and head for the door." He stuck out his tongue and ran off.

I suppose it's silly to want realism in fairy tales, but I like how these kids are acting like kids. Saintly little girls and boys get so boring sometimes!

Noemi sighed. For months her family had been rejecting young men. Most boys were kind and hardworking, which was Noemi's only requirement. But according to her parents, none of them were good enough. Frantz was unserious, and Ricardo was a downer. Anel was stuck-up, and Evens was a suck-up. At this rate, Noemi feared they'd reject every man on the island! But maybe her family was pretending to be choosy to protect her pride. Maybe no man wanted her.

How many of us felt this way as teens, only to look back at our old photos in middle age and think, *OMG, look how fuckin' cute I was! What was I thinking?* **Noemi! I yell through the page, you're so fuckin' cute!**

Jean and a friend were cannonballing giant rocks into the river when Noemi caught up. She set her brother back on task and knelt by the river's edge to dip her own bucket in the water. She removed the silver ring she wore, a treasured gift from her grand-mère, to stow safely in her bodice. But the ring fell from her grasp into the river. "Oh no!" she cried, running downstream, trying to catch up with it. She jogged all the way to a shady glen, the bucket rattling against her legs, before she gave up.

"Pardon me, miss. Did you lose this?"

Noemi looked up, pleasantly surprised to see a young man

wading waist-deep, holding her ring in his palm. She thanked him, then smiled. The guy was a dreamboat. He had the lean body of a swimmer. Long dreads framed a face with full lashes and sharp cheekbones. *Too skinny, too unkempt,* her mother would say. But Noemi liked what she saw. "This ring is very important to me," she told him. "I'm lucky you were here to catch it!"

The young man introduced himself as Tezen. He outstretched his arms for the bucket. "Let me retrieve the water, so you don't ruin your dress," he offered. Noemi was happy to be waited on.

Women love a man who'll take the initiative and do our chores!

Tezen walked deeper into the river and dipped one hand in the water, which was yellow with sand and silt. The current formed a gentle whirlpool around his fingers. Noemi couldn't believe her eyes. As the water swirled, the clearer it became. Tezen waited until the water reflected the blue sky before he dipped the bucket in.

Noemi cupped a handful of water from the supply Tezen brought back and lifted it to her lips. It was the purest, most refreshing drink she'd ever had. "How did you do that?" she asked in awe.

Tezen shrugged. "The river is my home. I take care of it, it takes care of me." He had a quiet confidence that Noemi found irresistible.

The two perched on a rocky ledge and got to know each other. Tezen was a traveler, Noemi learned. She asked where he was traveling to, and he said, "Wherever the river takes me." She pressed him for specifics, and he laughed. "I'm not trying to be mysterious. My only family is the fish, so I enjoy the freedom to come and go as I please. I guess you could say I'm a hopeless bachelor."

Noemi chuckled. "I'm becoming an old maid myself, but I

don't think I'll get the freedom you enjoy." She vented to Tezen about her parents' high standards. He was a very good listener.

"Do you love any of these men?" he asked her, trying to play it cool.

"No," Noemi assured him, thrilled at how obviously he was into her. "I don't necessarily need a great romance. But it's a little embarrassing that no one has desired me enough to call again. Maybe my parents scare them off. Or maybe I'm the village hag," she half joked.

I find it fascinating how our parents influence our dating. Even if they aren't directly matchmaking, our subconscious often seeks the parental figure we lack or is drawn to mates who model our caregivers. In a way we are all in subconsciously arranged marriages.

Tezen laughed in disbelief. "That's not what I see." He leaned toward the pool and stirred his hand around the depths. The water cleared, and Noemi saw her reflection as Tezen did. She looked radiant, even in her faded headscarf. But more than her own reflection, she loved how Tezen looked next to her.

The two chatted for so long, Jean had to shout for Noemi from up the river. Noemi gathered up the tiered skirts of her sundress. "I've gotta go. Maybe we'll run into each other again?"

Tezen grinned. "Just come to the river and sing my name. I'll find you!"

∗ ∗ ∗

OVER THE next few weeks, Noemi took every opportunity to meet Tezen. She began sending Jean home early so she and her beau could enjoy extra time together. With romance to look forward to, she met each day with renewed vigor, singing through her morning chores, and finding beauty in the sunny alder flowers along her daily route. She no longer worried about her parents scrutinizing every local boy. They could take forever, as far as she was concerned.

At first her parents didn't notice the change in her behavior. But Maman did observe that the water Noemi collected was much cleaner than Jean's. Initially, she chalked this up to the boy's immaturity. "Jean," she snarked one day after the siblings arrived home, "do you love your family?"

"Yes, Maman."

"And you are *my* son, yes?"

"Yes, Maman."

"Well, I'd never know it from the mud you bring home." She plopped his bucket in front of him, tossing him a rag when some sloshed over the side. "Your sister manages to find clean water! Tag along with her. Noemi, don't forget to help your little brother."

Similar to "Snakes That Cannot Shed Their Kin," this tale explores the disruption of the natural world. But further, Tezen and Noemi's relationship upsets the collective needs of Haitian life, distracting Noemi from her duties. Between hormones and adolescent egocentrism, it's a wonder we don't all end up in a Romeo/Juliet situation at age fourteen!

At first Noemi was annoyed. So, she skirted this hiccup by cleverly offering to fill her brother's bucket too, leaving Jean free to play while she snuck off with her love. But sometimes Jean had to pull water on his own, like when Noemi visited their grand-mère. "Find a calm part of the river," Noemi instructed him on those mornings. "Wait for the sand and debris to settle before filling the buckets." Jean wasn't as practiced at finding the quiet spots, and he could tell his mother wasn't impressed with his solo efforts. He began to resent Noemi a little. This chore was just another thing he always did wrong and she always did right. Noemi, his perfect sister.

It's refreshing to encounter a sibling rivalry that isn't a jealous sister plot or a fight over inheritance. But boy, do siblings fuck things up for each other in fairy tales. If fighting with siblings IRL brought on curses, my sister and I would both be suffering; but we never once fought over a man.

Jean wondered if she was sneaking off to a different water supply entirely. So one day, when Noemi offered to take both buckets, he circled back discreetly to follow her. His interest was stoked when he saw Noemi lean over the river and sing:

My love, Tezen, is deep as the sea.
Oh, Tezen, rise up to me!
Tezen, your love is calling.
Oh, rise up, Tezen, come to me!

Tezen emerged from a thicket by the river, and the two teens walked downstream together. Once they were out of sight of the village, the lovebirds clasped hands. They walked all the way to a misty lagoon. Jean hid behind a large rock to spy. He gagged as the two began to fool around, then tapped his foot while they argued over who loved the other more.

His ears perked up when he heard Noemi sigh and say, "I should get home. Would you get the water for me?"

Jean wrinkled his nose indignantly when he saw Tezen doing his sister's chore. She got all the credit, and she didn't even do anything! Then he saw the water magically swirl around Tezen's hand. "Whoa!" Jean breathed softly as the young man drew perfectly clear water into the bucket.

He kept still and quiet as the lovers departed, then ran to their spot, swirling the water and cupping it in his palms. But Tezen's spell didn't work for him. He stomped home, and before his mother could berate him, he pointed at his sister. "Noemi has a boyfriend!"

Noemi eyed daggers at Jean as Maman turned on her. "Is this true? Who are you seeing?"

Noemi tried to choose her words carefully. Jean took advantage of her hesitation. "He's a bum, and a tricky devil, by the looks of it." Noemi lunged at her brother, but Jean dodged, skipping out the door. "Oh-oh!" he sang. "Noemi's in trouble!"

Maman caught Noemi before the girl could run after Jean. "What do you think you're doing? You've become your own matchmaker now?" Noemi was surprised to see both hurt and anger in her mother's eyes.

Do you remember the gut-wrenching moment you realized your parents were also human beings with their own feelings, affected just as much by your actions as you by theirs? That's the true coming of age.

"Noemi," her mother prodded, "why haven't you brought this boy home to meet us?"

Noemi bit her lip. "Because you'll shoot him down, like every other boy!"

"Your father and I work hard to make sure you'll be happy after we are gone. And you thank me by sneaking around and talking back?" Maman studied her daughter sadly. "Is it true, what your brother says? This boy is a beggar? A vagrant? And what did he mean by tricky?" She shook her head when Noemi didn't answer. "Your silence is all I need to hear. You may see this boy one more time: to end it."

✷ ✷ ✷

THE NEXT DAY, Noemi's mother sent her out alone to break it off with Tezen. They met at the lagoon, and the girl pretended all was fine so she could be happy for a little while longer. But as they spooned by the water's edge, her body shook with sobs.

"Noemi, what's wrong?"

She told Tezen about her mother's demands. He didn't know what to say, so he simply held her tighter. His own eyes welled up. As the two cried, their tears mixed with the river.

The lagoon began to churn. Noemi looked up at Tezen to see if it was his doing, but he was surprised too. The trees began to pulse with music, the wind sounding through hollows like a vaksin, and branches brushing against bark like a graj. As the rhythm reached a fury, the water sprayed apart, and an actual goddamn sea goddess crested to the surface! She wore a golden comb threaded into her shining blond hair. She pulled herself up onto the shore with toned brown arms. The lovers saw that her stomach merged into a bright salmon-colored fishtail, with golden and blush-colored diamonds dancing among her scales.

"Lasirenn!" Noemi breathed.

Lasirenn is a Haitian water deity in close relation to Mami Wata of African mythology. She is the loa of the sea, beauty, love (including queer love), music, and wealth in Haitian Vodou. Imagine moping by the river and mermaid Beyoncé dives out. Same vibe!

The goddess took in the couple and burst into singsong laughter. "Why, you two are practically children!" The teens heard her musical voice in their heads. She plucked her comb from her hair and primped while she chatted with them telepathically. "From the powerful love that summoned me, I expected two devoted old folks, not a couple of skinny teenagers."

The sweethearts understood that meeting an actual deity was a pivotal moment for their relationship and pled their case. Lasirenn listened to their story, an enigmatic smile twitching at her lips. Once Noemi finished, the mistress of the waters took each of their hands.

"I can offer your love some protection," she told them. She cooled their excitement with a hard squeeze of their fingers. "But even under my watch, you need to be careful." She dipped her hand into the lagoon and pulled up two golden rings. "First, you'll need to be married."

"Of course!" Noemi replied. She blushed at her eagerness, but Tezen was nodding too.

Lasirenn turned her magnetic gaze to the young man. "And you, Tezen, will need to hide." She considered the options. "Since you make the river your home, I suggest we hide you in the body of a fish."

The two teens gaped for a moment. "Why a fish?" Tezen finally asked.

Lasirenn narrowed her eyes. "Do you have a problem with fish?"

Tezen waved his hands. "No, no! Fish are great! Fish are fantastic!"

Noemi figured out a tactful way to address their concerns. "I think what Tezen is trying to say is: a girl can't marry a fish!"

Lasirenn chucked her chin. "He will be human for you. As long as you're willing to swim!"

Other oceanic folk romances include: "Chichinguane" of Mozambique, India's "The Fish Prince," Japan's "The Fish Wife," and Indonesia's "Mankarikadi." Pink dolphins shapeshift into predatory men in the Amazon, but in the Pacific islands, you might fall in love with a playful dolphin girl.

* * *

The goddess instructed the lovers to return to the lagoon the following night, after the village was sleeping. They snagged three seashells and a cut of lace as payment for Lasirenn's gift. Noemi wore her best dress and set out an hour after her parents went to bed, saying a prayer she'd make it to the lagoon and back without rousing her family or neighbors.

When she arrived, Tezen and Lasirenn were waiting. The distant music of whale song provided a mysterious soundtrack. Their ceremony began with a parade of aquatic couples; dolphins, rays, manatees, even the crotchety crocodiles paired up to usher in the couple's union. The two exchanged vows in the pool, Noemi's skirts floating around her ethereally.

Lasirenn is apparently also the loa of wedding planning.

The party receded so the couple could spend time alone together. Lasirenn had some words of warning before she left them: "Now it's up to you to protect your secret. Should harm come to one of you, I can send a warning. But by then it may be too late."

Lasirenn conjured a downy field of moss and magnolias to act as the sweethearts' marriage bed. They lay in each other's arms as long as they dared. When they parted, Tezen slipped into the water. A flash of light illuminated the lagoon, and a spray of seafoam misted the air. When Tezen popped back up, he was a large iridescent red fish. Noemi dipped her hand under the water, and Tezen nuzzled her palm. He carefully pulled the gold ring off her finger and swallowed it for safekeeping. Noemi returned home, holding her secret close to her heart.

* * *

The couple moved their meeting spot to a new location in the woods, in a dark cavern under a bubbling waterfall. When Noemi arrived, she would sing Tezen's song to alert him. He'd swim to the surface, and she'd drop her dress and don a bonnet before slipping into the water. Tezen had her wedding band waiting for her. In a way, Noemi liked wearing it exclusively while they were together. It felt like they got married all over again every time she slipped on the ring. They decided to stay submerged while they met, in case someone caught them and Tezen needed to transform quickly. Noemi found the underwater tête-à-têtes very sexy.

Doug Jones's fish suit in *The Shape of Water* awakened things in a lot of people. I hope.

The two thought they took every precaution. But teens are only so sly. Maman and Papa noticed a change in Noemi. She was more reserved around them, and she wasn't eating as much, especially if seafood was on the menu. Maman assumed she was still depressed over the loss of her secret boyfriend. But she also noticed that Noemi changed her hair, opting for two twists pulled close to her scalp instead of her usual intricate microbraids. Most damning of all, Tezen kept sending Noemi home with clean water, for they didn't know this habit had betrayed them the first time.

One day, Maman reminded Jean of this. "You're still bringing home buckets of scum. Did you never find out where your sister pulls water from?"

Jean remembered Tezen filtering the river with his bare hands. He didn't think Maman would believe him. He decided to spy again and make sure. Besides, if Noemi was still seeing that weirdo with the magic touch, he'd have something to lord over her.

It took some time, but eventually Jean figured out his sister's new canoodling spot. He followed her once again, where he saw her sing that little love song:

My love, Tezen, is deep as the sea.
Oh, Tezen, rise up to me!

Tezen, your love is calling.
Oh, rise up, Tezen, come to me!

The kid was befuddled when a fish jumped out of the water in excited arcs. He covered his eyes when his sister dropped her garments, and peeked through his fingers just in time to see Noemi put a golden ring on her finger, followed by a burst of light and seafoam. Tezen now treaded water where the fish had been. The couple was too entranced to notice the boy run out of the woods, his heart beating as fast as his feet pounded the forest floor.

Jean found his mother hanging laundry. "Maman!" he sputtered through gasps. "Maman, the boy—Noemi's boyfriend. He—he's a fish!"

His mother pinned some sheets to the line, not in the mood for a runaround. "Don't tell lies. Your sister promised she wouldn't see that boy. Now you say he's a fish? Ridiculous."

"Maman, it's not a lie. That's how Noemi's water is so clean!" Jean pulled back the sheet his mother had just pinned, looking up at her. She stopped short at the fear in his eyes. "It's her boyfriend who cleans it. He's a lougarou! Noemi sings him a song, and he changes from a fish to a boy! He cleans the water with his hands, just for Noemi."

Maman still looked skeptical. Jean jumped up and down. "I can show you!"

Jean led his mother there the next day. At first Maman seemed frightened at the magical transformation she witnessed. Then she silently fumed as the two cavorted like a married couple.

"You won't believe what I witnessed today," she relayed to her husband late that night. "A fish, turning into a man, and back! Worse, our daughter was all cozied up on him, with her goods hanging out! My God!" She squeezed her eyes shut to dispel the image.

Her husband was shocked. "I'll go talk to her."

"I don't think talking will help," his wife fretted. "She has lied to us so much; I don't even recognize her."

Noemi's father nodded. "Do you think it is his doing? The fish-man, I mean."

"I have to believe so. He is clearly a demon, shape-shifting like that." Maman paced. "We need to break the spell he has over Noemi before she is lost to us entirely."

Her husband considered their options. "Well, a fish is no match for a man. And I am a very good fisherman."

The next day, Maman pulled her son aside. "Jean, I want you to follow your sister for a few days and practice the song she uses to summon the fish-man. Once you have memorized it, I will send Noemi to your grand-mère. On that day, you will take your father to the fish-man and summon him yourself. And we will get rid of this shady boy once and for all."

* * *

NOEMI USUALLY loved seeing her grandmother. But ever since she had married Tezen, she hated to be separated from him. Still, Noemi trekked across the village to pick fruit from Grand-mère's garden and prepare meals for the week. The two plucked a basketful of oranges, shelled peas, and cooked a large batch of plantains. As they finished, Grand-mère gestured at Noemi's apron. "You hurt yourself, chère!"

Noemi frowned and glanced down. She saw a small spot of blood over her heart. Before her eyes, a second spot of red appeared. Then a third. A wave of nausea hit her as Lasirenn's voice echoed in her head. *Should harm come to one of you, I can send a warning. But by then it may be too late.*

"I have to go!" she blurted, and ran, leaving her perplexed grandmother behind.

* * *

THE FOREST was eerily quiet, but for the patter of the waterfall. Noemi sang Tezen's song, but he did not appear. She sang again, then a third time, fear hitching her voice higher with every attempt. But the waters remained still.

With a pit in her stomach as heavy as iron, Noemi walked home. Jean sat tensely outside the hut. When he saw Noemi, he ducked his head with guilt.

Noemi heard her parents talking in a hush behind the house. She approached them with lead feet. Papa sorted firewood by their small oven while Maman finished dinner. "Get your brother, Noemi, it's almost ready."

"I'm here, Maman," Jean said, appearing at Noemi's side. He reached out and took his sister's hand like he had as a much younger boy. She looked at him questioningly, but he couldn't meet her eyes.

The family gathered at the table. Maman opened the lid on a steaming platter of fish braised in tomato broth. She divided the dish into four, dropping a portion over rice. "Eat up!" she said.

Noemi stared down at her plate. A flash of gold caught her eye from under the fish. She pulled at it. The meat fell apart to reveal a pair of golden wedding bands. A hair-raising scream emerged from her throat. She shoved her chair back.

Papa and Maman exchanged glances. Her father sighed. "Noemi," he said, kind but serious. "Listen to me. It had to be done."

"Please, Noemi!" Maman said. "You need to eat the fish to break the magic!"

In a haze, Noemi ignored them. She stumbled away, clutching the rings in her fingers. At the far end of the yard, she staggered to her knees. The world blurred as tears filled her eyes. She rocked back and forth slowly, singing Tezen's song in a trembling voice.

My love, Tezen, is deep as the sea.
Oh, Tezen, rise up to me!

Tezen, your love is calling.
Oh, rise up, Tezen, come to me!

As Noemi sang, the trees began to pulse with the rhythm and music of Lasirenn. The earth grew damp around the grieving girl. Water seeped up, forming mud that drew her slowly into the ground.

"Noemi!" Jean cried, sprinting toward her, their parents hot on his heels. The little boy reached out and grasped his sister's arms as she was pulled down to her waist. But the earth held her fast, nearly dragging Jean down too. His father quickly pulled him away and tried himself. But even his strong arms were no match for the magic below.

The three watched, helpless, as the mud roiled and strained and sucked their daughter down. Noemi did not seem to notice. She sang for Tezen as long as she could, her soprano becoming a wail as the earth crept over her tear-stained face.

At last, the earth stilled. One of Noemi's long twisted braids coiled out of the ground. Maman and Papa frantically dug at the earth around it. But when Papa pulled the hair loose, nothing else remained of Noemi but three drops of crimson blood pooling at the edge of the braid.

* * *

SOURCES: Suzanne Comhaire-Sylvain, "Creole Tales from Haiti" and "Thézin."

Want to read more Haitian folktales? Try *When Night Falls, Kric! Krac!: Haitian Folktales* by Liliane Louis.

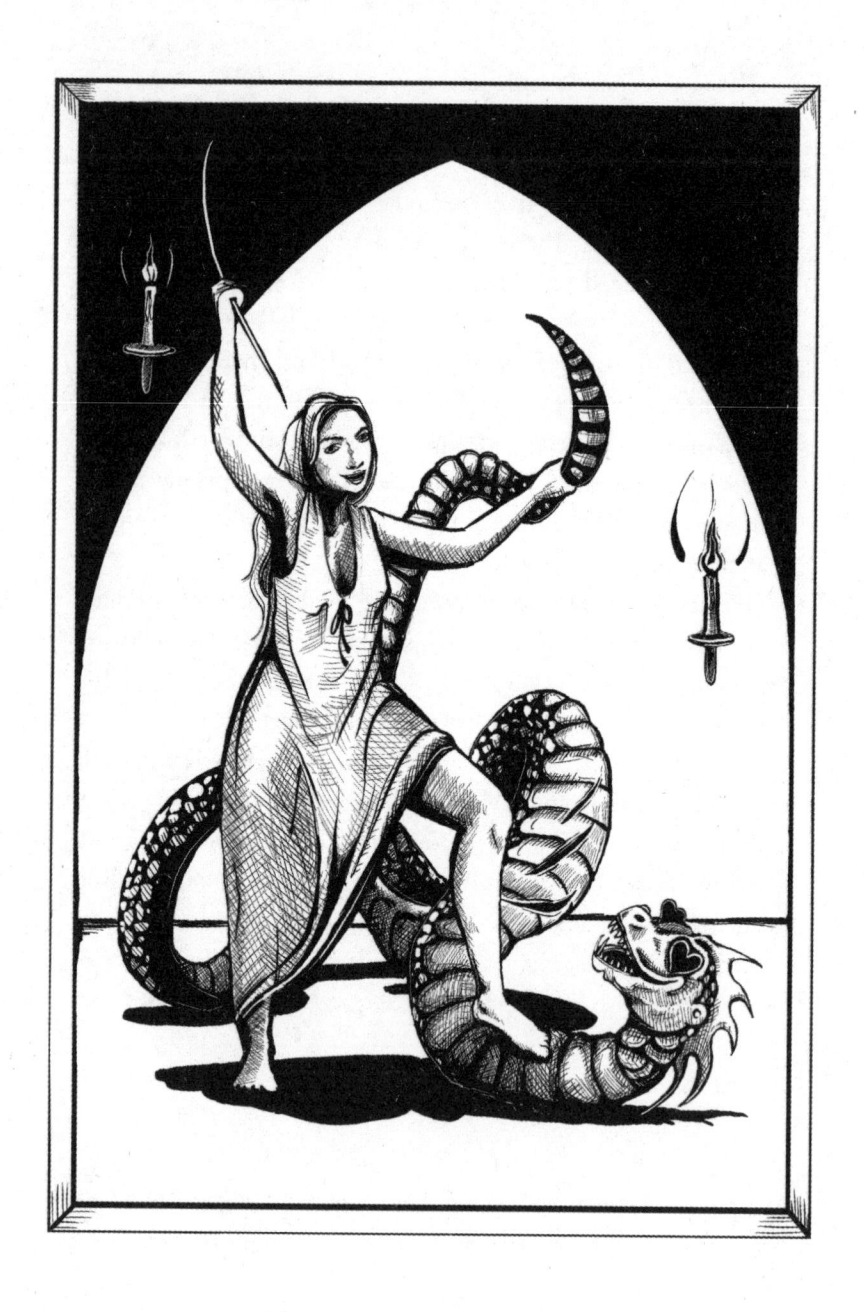

MASTER AND SERPENT

Denmark's "King Lindworm"

Once upon a time, there was a king and queen who received a terrible wedding gift. When the couple woke up the morning after the ceremony, a glowing scroll of script magically unfurled on their headboard declaring they'd bear no children. Was it a cruel trick? Or a prophecy? No matter which, the situation was upsetting. Either they'd have no heirs, or someone stowed away on their honeymoon just to troll them!

Not to mention the fact that this gift was clearly not on the registry.

As time passed, the words proved true; the queen bore no children. When her husband was called abroad, she was doubly lonely and depressed. The court was full of judgy nobles who stared at her in pity, for the royals were too humiliated to reveal their wedding night prophecy. One day, the queen took herself for a walk in the woods seeking peace and quiet. Instead, she met a nosy old lady, colorfully dressed in a red skirt and blue apron.

"My, my, I've never seen a sadder woman than you, and I've lived a long life!" the old woman observed. "You want to unload some of those heavy thoughts?"

The queen brushed her off. "What use would that be? You can't change my situation."

The old lady winked. "You'll never know what I can or can't do if you don't tell me."

The queen took a seat on a stump and told the old woman about the bizarre prophecy that appeared on the headboard of the king's king-sized bed. As sometimes happens when one reveals a deep secret, the queen lost all composure; she finished her story in sobs, leaning into the kind old woman's comforting embrace. **(I apologize to the entire staff of the Crate & Barrel in Salem, New Hampshire, for my Meltdown of 2015.)**

"As it happens, I know a lot about getting pregnant," the old lady said. "My version is much less invasive, too!"

Modern medicine is frequently catching up with fairy tales.

The woman briefly summarized the charm the queen should attempt. Excited, the queen thanked the woman and rushed off.

"Wait!" the old woman yelled. "I need to clarify a few things!"

"It's fine, I've got it!" the queen replied, tearing off to the royal gardens.

Poor communication between characters is regarded as a cheap plot trope. In media, I find it annoying; but I also wonder if we keep revisiting it because poor communication continues to have costly consequences in our actual relationships.

The queen set a glazed pot upside down in the northwest corner of the garden and left it alone until sunup the following day. *The next morning you will find a red rose and a white rose growing underneath the pot*, the old woman had said. Sure enough, the flowers were waiting. The queen picked both and fingered the velvety petals as she considered the next step. *You must pick one of the roses and eat it. If you want a little boy, eat the red rose. If you want a little girl, eat the white. But don't eat them both. That will make your situation a whole lot more complicated!*

The queen lifted the red rose. She knew the king would

love to have a boy. "But if I have a son," she rationalized, "he'll likely have to travel a lot like my husband. I'll be as lonely as I am now."

She lifted the white rose. "Now, a girl would be wonderful company. Even when she marries and bears her own children, she'll need a mother's guidance. Plus, we'll gain a second kingdom through her union." With that in mind, she daintily ate the white flower.

The flower was surprisingly delicious. So delicious, the queen found herself tempted to eat the red flower too, despite the old woman's warning. "I suppose bearing twins *would* be more complicated," the queen considered. "But women do it all the time!" She gobbled up the red rose without a second thought.

The king was still abroad when the queen realized that the spell had worked. She was pregnant! She wrote to the king with the good news, and he was thrilled to receive it. Unfortunately, he was away so long, he had not returned for the birth of their child. In hindsight, he'd be happy about that. For the queen gave birth to a lindworm.

Lindworms are portrayed as either legless serpents or with two little legs. The legged dragon was used mostly on royal insignia, whereas the legless predominates common circles. I picked legless for our working-class hero. Also for penis reasons.

The midwife screamed. The queen screamed. The serpent screamed! Then he wriggled out of the midwife's arms and busted a hole under the bed. He thrashed around in there until he had created a sizable den. There, he finally settled.

Later that night, the queen crept out of bed, holding a lantern over the den. The lindworm slept peacefully, a little snot bubble inflating from his nostril. "Aw, he's kinda cute," the queen admitted. "I'll name him Aleksander."

Aleksander began his life no more monstrous than any infant who cannot use his words. His mother would serve him stewed peas, which he'd slap across the room for fun. What baby wouldn't do the same? But then his mother would merely retrieve the jar and bring it back. The event would repeat itself until the lindworm got what he really wanted (a whole chicken). He quickly applied this manipulative tactic in other facets of childhood: destroying the playroom if his favorite toy was taken away; screaming and baring his fangs at bathtime; winding himself around pillars tight to avoid bedtime. His mother would laugh, shrug, and do little to teach better manners.

This unfortunate family dynamic continued into Aleksander's teen years—which came about only six months later. Based on his sudden stink and the constellation of zits across his face, his mother estimated one month was about two lindworm years. She decided it was time to stop nursing him.

The lindworm became friendly with a group of lecherous lords who wanted to get "in" with the royals. He picked up their habits: lurking under the stairs for upskirt peeps, cracking rude jokes about their bodies, worm-spreading so they'd have to brush up against him to get by. When the staff complained, his mother said, "Well, monsters will be monsters."

By the time the king arrived home a year later, Aleksander was a full-grown terror of a man-serpent. Besides being a sex pest, the prince was a bully. He'd observed that honey didn't get him as many flies as threatening to bash someone's face did. He ignored his mother's feeble and rare attempts to discipline him.

He was very excited to meet his father, the king of the land, the ultimate alpha. At least, that's what he assumed. As the king's carriage rode through the gate, Aleksander, now the length and width of three people, emerged from his hidey-hole and slithered up to the passenger-side window. "Welcome home, Dad!" he roared.

The king stopped shitting himself long enough to register the greeting. "Did you just call me 'Dad'?"

"I did! I'm your son and heir to the throne!" Aleksander said. He realized the king wasn't exactly excited to see him. He pivoted to his usual move. "And you'd better not disown me! If you do, I'm gonna split both you and this castle in two!"

"Split me in two?" the king cried. "What the fuck does that mean?"

The lindworm leaned in, nose-to-nose with the monarch. "You don't want to find out."

The king's throat went dry. "Welcome to the family!"

* * *

LATER, THE queen explained her magical conception. The king was shocked, but what was there to do? The queen loved the monster she bore. He also didn't seem too worried about Aleksander's bullish ways. Most dragon-types hoarded treasure and ate a virgin a day to make the sovereign obey. Routine debauchery was a relief.

Three days later, the queen threw a big "Welcome Back" party for her husband. Every nobleman, every officer, and all of their fancy wives were in attendance. So a huge crowd witnessed Aleksander drill through the ballroom ceiling, taking down a chandelier with a crash. "Dad, it's time for me to get married!"

The king was confused. "You're barely a year old!"

"Yeah, in *people* years! In lindworm years, I'm a bachelor in my prime!" The serpent eyed the unmarried ladies, whose step back was so in sync it could have been mistaken for an early Electric Slide.

The king approached his son begrudgingly. "Listen," he whispered. "I don't want to hurt your feelings, but where in the world am I supposed to find a girl who'd have you?"

Aleksander bristled, his scales shedding shards of Swarovski.

"Hey, now, I'm not picky! I'll take any type of woman!" He drew himself up to his full height. "But I demand a wife. Because if you don't find one for me, I'll split you and this castle in two!"

"What the fuck does that mean?" a noblewoman stage-whispered.

"We don't want to find out," the king hastily answered. "I'll get right on it, son."

* * *

THE KING sent out a peculiar summons to unmarried princesses. The memo specified that the princess who accepted a proposal would not see Aleksander until the marriage ceremony. Despite this ominous condition, they found a willing woman. (**More likely they found a willing dad.**) The wedding was arranged quickly, lest the bride discover her husband was more reptile than human. Bless this poor princess, for even when her frightening fiancé was revealed, she went through with it. She exchanged rings (well, she put on her own ring), made promises she wasn't sure how to keep, and tried not to pull back when her husband's tongue darted out for a kiss.

The couple was ushered to their bridal chamber. The king and queen waited a few doors down for confirmation that the marriage had been consummated. (How that would happen, they had no idea.) Confirmation came in the form of an ear-piercing shriek. The king and queen ran to the bridal chamber, where several spooked ladies-in-waiting pointed at a puddle of blood oozing out from under the door.

The king steeled himself and walked inside to assess the situation. Almost immediately, he ran back out and threw up in a planter.

"What happened?" his wife cried.

The king cleared his throat. "I now know what split in two means."

JESUS FUCKING CHRIST! How am I supposed to make the lindworm a romantic figure after all this?

* * *

The king and his wife tried to make up for the vicious death of the princess. They paid for all the funeral expenses and made public apologies about as sensitive as a Notes screencap posted to Insta. They offered to name a wing of the palace after her. They did *not* punish Aleksander in any way. The late princess's family couldn't be appeased. They threatened war. Aleksander offered to secure the borders, but the queen thought that would be in poor taste.

At last, the tensions ended, albeit with a very tenuous treaty, and the royal couple attempted to live normal lives. The king's birthday was coming up. They hosted a public festival for the occasion, in hopes of reestablishing themselves as benevolent rulers.

The royal baker wheeled out the king's beautiful six-tiered cake just as Aleksander tunneled through the ceiling once again, bringing the newly replaced chandelier with him. The partygoers, having heard all sorts of rumors about the king's terrible son, fled the scene.

When the chaos died down, the king weakly attempted to reprimand the prince. "What do you think you're doing, young man?"

"It's time for me to get remarried!" Aleksander roared.

"Now, now, dear," the queen said, wagging her finger at the monster. "It was hard enough getting you a wife the first time. Who would marry you after you tenderized that poor girl?"

Aleksander groaned. "I already told you, that was an accident! No one ever taught me how to sex a lady!"

PSA: Please don't skip "the talk" with your children. Especially the giant monster ones.

The king paled. "Don't blame me! I just assumed you'd picked something up from those boys you hang out with!" He switched tactics. "What if we found you a nice wyvern to settle down with?" **(Wife-vern?)**

"*No!*" Aleksander coiled himself around his father menacingly. "I want a human bride! 'Human' is my only qualifier! If you refuse, I'll split you and this castle in two!"

The king left to change his pants again.

✳ ✳ ✳

I wish I could tell you wedding number two went better than the first. But you weren't born yesterday! You know how these stories go! We gotta go number two before we go number three! **(I definitely could have phrased that better.)**

Another ill-fated princess was betrothed to the king's son, under the same terms. They sought this princess from the other side of the globe, because those closer knew the sordid story of the lindworm's first wife. This time the king sat down with his son and tried to give him some tips for the wedding night.

On the big day, our new lady loyally vowed to love and cherish Aleksander. She bravely took him to bed. She died horribly.

Most old versions of "King Lindworm" are very gory. The first two princesses are eaten alive in Kay Nielsen's and "torn to pieces" in Andrew Lang's. But my main source, translated by Thomas Pettitt, ups the ante by maintaining the original storyteller's phrase "split apart," implying sexual violence. Pettitt analyzes this as a "grotesque and sadistic parody" of the tradition of checking a bed for blood to prove the bride was a virgin. It's "the first time might hurt a little" directed by Sam Raimi.

"How could this happen again?" the king asked his son after the carnage had been cleared.

"I don't know!" the lindworm blustered back. "I did what you told me to!"

The queen tapped her husband's shoulder. "What exactly did you tell him, dear?"

The king reeled at her accusatory tone. "I told him what my father told me! Be confident. Women like a man who's rugged and commanding. Sex is like a sport. Show the girl who's in charge. She's just an innocent flower. When you're erect, enter her maidenhead. You may encounter some resistance."

The queen nodded. "This explains a lot," she said to herself, and sighed. "I think we're in over our heads."

Let's pour one out for the many nameless princesses fridged in fairy tales.

War was once again threatened against the king and his wife. The first grieving kingdom allied with the second out of solidarity. The royal couple called in every favor they had, quashed the conflict, and wondered why they were no longer invited to parties.

When the queen's birthday came around, the royal family hosted a second public festival. Unsurprisingly, it was not as well attended as the last one. Even less surprisingly, Aleksander crashed the party (and a third chandelier) yet again.

"Time to find my third wife!" he roared.

"*Come on!* We can't afford this charade!" the king whined "When you inevitably shish-kebab another princess, we'll have three kingdoms united against us. We will not survive that!"

The queen nodded and said, "Also, killing people is bad!"

Aleksander growled. "I've already told you; I don't care if she's a princess! I just want a wife! And if I don't get one—"

"Yeah, yeah, yeah, you'll split us in two!" the king interrupted. "At this point, I'd welcome it!"

His wife had a thought. "You know, we never considered a poor woman. If we'd done that from the beginning, we'd merely be quelling a peasant rebellion and not a full-out war."

Look, the book's called *F*cked Up Fairy Tales* for a reason!

* * *

THE KING decided to look for Aleksander's third bride closer to home. His secretary forwarded a list of the palace underlings with eligible daughters. He began with the poorest of the lot: their shepherd, an old widower with one child, a young woman named Thora.

The king pitched the proposal to the family as if he were doing them a huge fucking favor. The old man objected. "My daughter is the only family I have. If your son has laid waste to two princesses, how could Thora stand a chance of survival?"

"Eh, I'm sure he just hasn't met the right gal yet," the king replied.

But the shepherd held firm, taking his daughter's hand. "We are not interested."

The king squared his shoulders. "I'm afraid I gave you the impression this was optional. You have three days to say goodbye. I mean, to prepare for the wedding. She'll marry the prince on Sunday."

* * *

AFTER THE king left, Thora and her father considered their few options. They could run away, but the shepherd couldn't manage the rough journey, and Thora couldn't bear leaving him to incur punishment for her actions. They opted to appeal the decision. Spirits were low as the sun set that evening. Thora grabbed a basket and told her dad she needed to gather produce, an excuse to take a walk with her thoughts.

Thora half-heartedly filled her basket with blueberries, then sat under a beech tree to rest. She stared ahead, numb to the fact that she would likely be gored to death in three days. Well, not that numb. She was stress-eating her berry haul.

"You know, you should really wash those first." An old woman in a smart red skirt and blue apron stood over her with a wry smile.

Not this bitch again!

Thora looked down at her hands, stained purple with berry juice. She laughed humorlessly. "It doesn't matter," she droned. "Nothing matters anymore."

"My, my." The old lady clucked her tongue. "Such a sad statement from one so young. You want to unload those dour thoughts?"

Thora picked herself up. "No use burdening you with my problems. Nothing can be done."

The old woman winked. "I'm surprisingly resourceful." She patted a stump next to her.

Thora took a seat and explained her situation. Voicing her dark fate snapped her out of the numbness. Her fear and anger rushed forth and she bawled into the old woman's handkerchief. **(I apologize to the hostess of that sushi restaurant in Cranston, Rhode Island, for my Meltdown of 2012.)**

The old woman hugged the girl tight. "Oh, my dear," she bemoaned. "Every generation ends up fixing their ancestors' fuckery. When we're young, we see how unfair that is; but we rarely remember once we're the elders." She patted the girl's knee. "So I want to help. Luckily, I happen to know a thing or two about handling a beast."

Thora felt the tiniest glimmer of hope. "Really?"

"Oh yes," the old woman said. "He'll be wrapped around your

little finger by morning. Just follow my directions to the letter, and you'll come out of this on the other side."

* * *

THORA'S WEDDING to Aleksander was much different than the previous two. Since the bride knew exactly what she was walking into, the air in the castle was very somber. The king tripped over himself to make Thora and her father as happy as possible for a pre-funeral. Thora took advantage of this. She requested an embroidered satin gown and a tiara of diamonds so at least she'd die in style. She demanded a hefty retirement gift for her father, including a small house in town for him to spend his last days comfortably. Then there was her list of supplies for the wedding night: "I want ten cotton chemises, a bucket of vinegar, a bathtub of your creamiest milk, and as many birch switches as your valet can carry."

The king's staff tittered at these requests. "What in the old wives' tale?" one of them scoffed, and everyone laughed louder.

"Silence!" the king shouted. "This woman may be sacrificing her life to keep peace in this castle. She'll get whatever she wants, and you'll give her the utmost respect."

The ceremony was quick. Thora forced herself to stay calm, though her heart leapt into her throat as the lindworm prince slid up to her side. When the monster leaned in for his kiss, she boldly pulled back. Aleksander sputtered. The court murmured among themselves. Thora hastily exited the altar with her head held high.

Two hours later, she awaited her husband in the bridal chamber. She stood steadfastly at the foot of the bed in ten layers of chemises, overdressed in all senses of the word. The switches and the basins of vinegar and milk sat to one side.

One of the reasons I love this objectively appalling tale is how rich it is for analysis and reinterpretation. Scholars have dis-

cussed themes like the lindworm's curse as rebirth, uncomfortable ideas of how motherhood and wifehood intersect, persuading young women that marrying an abusive oaf ain't so bad, and riffs on purity culture. However, I've yet to come across a scholar who reads the story with the most obvious theme: kink!

There was a knock at the door. Thora closed her eyes and drew a deep breath. "Come in."

A lady's maid opened the door and curtsied, avoiding Thora's eyes. Aleksander entered, undulating slowly up to the bed. When the door clicked closed, he looked around at Thora's supplies. "What's all this?" he growled.

Thora wasn't certain herself. "It's what I require for my wedding night," she finally explained. Which wasn't a lie! Still, she bit her lip, anticipating a swift devouring.

Aleksander inspected everything. He didn't argue, though. He leaned toward Thora, taking a slow whiff of her. She shivered when his hot breath hit her neck. The prince grunted, seeming satisfied. "Take off your shift," he said.

"No." Thora's voice quaked just a tad. But she reminded herself of the old lady's instructions. *Make it a bargain; a one-for-one trade. And be clear about what you want.* "I will remove my shift, but only after you shed a skin."

Aleksander cocked his head curiously. "No one has dared speak like that to me."

Thora forced herself to hold his gaze. "I do. Now do as I command," she slowly reiterated.

The lindworm grunted again. But he moved to a corner of the room and rubbed his cheeks against the stone wall. A layer of scaly skin sloughed off. Aleksander inched his body out of the shell, breathing heavily at the effort. When he was done, he nudged the long coil toward her.

"Good," Thora said simply. She took her time unbuttoning her top chemise, then laid it over the lindworm's discarded skin.

Aleksander made a strange noise. Thora realized he was chuckling at her many layers. "What is this game?" he said. "Remove your gowns!"

"No!" This time, Thora's voice was strong. The prince's acquiescence eked out her confidence. "You shed a skin for me, I shed a shift for you."

Aleksander paced a little. But once again, he nuzzled the wall and inched out of a second layer of skin. He flopped the carcass onto the first. Thora shimmied out of her second shift and laid it out before him.

This time, Aleksander bowed his head. "Will you take off another one?" he asked.

Thora lifted her chin and smiled, thrilled at his humility. "You haven't yet earned it, Prince."

The lindworm and his wife performed their little burlesque for one another, with seven more sheds and seven more shifts. Each round, Aleksander struggled and panted, but he became more and more vulnerable and eager to please. By the time Thora was down to her last chemise, the beast lay at her feet.

* * *

DOWN THE HALL, the king and queen paced. Time passed, and no one summoned them to the telltale blood under the door. The queen glanced at the clock. "Should we check on them?"

The couple crept to the chamber. Everything was quiet. The maid on guard shrugged.

The royals crouched by the door and listened. "What's happening?" the king whispered.

The queen frowned. "I can hear talking and . . . oh! Um, moaning, I think?"

"Well, that's promising? Right?"

The queen hesitated. "I don't know. It could be fine. It could be terrible!"

The king put a cup to his ear. "Let's keep listening."

※ ※ ※

INSIDE, ALEKSANDER tenderly curled his tail around Thora's ankle. She hissed. "I didn't say you could touch me yet."

The lindworm apologized, and lay still, intently watching Thora as she walked over to the basket of switches. The first round had energized her. She soaked the switches in the bucket of vinegar like the old woman had told her, brought them over to Aleksander, and dropped them by his side. They scattered like pick-up sticks.

Thora grasped one and stood over the prince. "You have been a little terror since you arrived, haven't you?" she asked, wondering where she'd suddenly gotten this swagger.

The serpent picked up what she was putting down. He hung his head. "Yes, I have," he answered.

"Yes, *Princess*."

"Yes, Princess!"

"And after all you've done, you haven't once been disciplined, have you?" Thora fingered the switch in her hand, stalking around the prince in a wide circle.

Aleksander stretched himself out. "No, I haven't, Princess."

As she walked, Thora teased his pale pink body with the tip of the switch. "Are you ready for your punishment, Aleksander?"

The prince gasped. "I crave it, Princess!"

Thora performed the second part of the old woman's instructions. She tentatively struck the lindworm with a vinegar-coated switch. He leaned into it, so she struck him harder.

Now, you mustn't strike him to pieces, the old woman had cautioned. *Show him you'll respect his boundaries, just as you taught him to respect your own.* Thora checked in. "Have you had enough?"

"No, Princess. More. I need more!"

Aleksander's body radiated with heat, and blood began to seep from his wounds. But still he begged for more attention from Thora's ardent hand.

The floor was littered with shredded branches, as one switch after another broke apart. At last, the prince pulled away and cried, "Stop!"

Thora dropped the last switch to the floor.

* * *

OUTSIDE, THE royal couple hastened away from the door as the newlyweds' saucy exchange crescendoed. The maid stifled giggles, clocking all the amazing tea she'd spill tomorrow.

The queen blushed. "You know, I think we should give them some privacy."

"Oh, thank God," the king sighed. With crossed fingers for a happy morning, the couple retired for the night.

* * *

WHEN THE monster is subdued, show him tenderness.

Thora gently carried Aleksander to the basin of milk and bathed him clean. As he relaxed, she pulled her cotton shifts from the pile and laid them out. She bandaged the prince up tight in the garments. Carefully, she pulled him into the bed. He curled up against her.

Thora hesitated. Last night, she'd been dreading this final moment, when the old woman told her to show love for whatever gory mess was left of the lindworm. But after the intimacy they'd shared, it felt natural to hold him close. She pulled the slithery prince tight to her, circling her arms around him. Aleksander cooed sweetly, and the pair fell into a deep sleep.

(I apologize to my parents for making them read my Furry smut of 2025.)

* * *

THE NEXT morning, the king and queen were unsure how to proceed. The staff was too nervous to enter the bedchamber. Sure, it got around that the shepherd's daughter had a Mommy Domme streak. But had it saved her, or merely delayed her bloody end?

It was well past breakfast when the king took matters into his own hands. He knocked on the chamber door. "Ah . . . good morning! Is—is everyone okay in there? Hello?"

* * *

THORA SNUGGLED deeper into the warm sheets. She heard knocking and turned away from the noise toward her bedmate. She hummed as someone kissed her forehead and pulled her in tight.

But something was off. As her grogginess faded, she registered an extra set of limbs woven with hers. Her forehead brushed against a scratchy jaw.

She sat up in a daze. Next to her slumbered a statuesque young man, half-wrapped in her bloodstained shifts. No sign of the lindworm remained, but for a pattern of scars up the man's legs and back. Thora traced them lightly with one finger.

Her bedmate's eyes blinked open. He craned his neck and sleepily stretched his arms. Then he realized he had arms. "Well, this is new."

They were interrupted by louder knocking. "Son!" the king shouted from the other side of the door. "Stop keeping us in suspense!"

Thora started laughing, and Aleksander joined her. They laughed themselves into a breathless fit. Only a third round of frantic knocking brought the pair out of their hysterics. "Come in!" Thora called. "Everyone is fine!"

The king peered in, then threw the door fully open when he saw two humans in one piece. He whooped and called the queen, who cried with relief.

The king called for champagne. They toasted to Thora's triumph, to Aleksander's transformation, to the old woman who had helped get them into and out of their mess. At some point, the royals noticed the state of the room: bloodstained, covered with dead snakeskin and branches, and stinking of sour milk and vinegar. The king balked. "What the fuck happened in here?"

Thora and the prince exchanged a secretive look. "I split him apart," Thora deadpanned. The couple collapsed in giggles again.

The king and queen changed the subject. "Let's get these kids to a clean room," the king ordered. "Plus, fresh clothes and a hearty meal and whatever my daughter-in-law wants, now and forever. She saved my son! She saved this kingdom!"

I find it fascinating how this fairy tale opens with problems in the bedroom and is solved with solutions in the bedroom. Praise be to the horny storytellers of Denmark just trying to figure their shit out!

From that day on, Thora and Aleksander lived happily. Oh sure, there was that whole thing where Aleksander went abroad, and a treacherous knight tricked him into thinking Thora gave birth to puppies, forcing her to hide out in the woods where she breastfed a couple of birds who *also* happened to be enchanted princes . . . But other than *that*, they lived happily ever after.

Yes, "King Lindworm" has a part two. But I'm stopping here . . . unless you're willing to beg for it!

* * *

SOURCES:
Svend Grundtvig, *Kong Lindorm.*
Pettitt Thomas, translator. "King Serpent (Kong Lindorm)."

Want to read more Danish folktales? Look up *Folk and Fairy Tales from Denmark*, Volumes I and II, by Stephen Badman.

Part 4

WHAT'S YOUR BODY COUNT?

. . . *Not THAT one.*

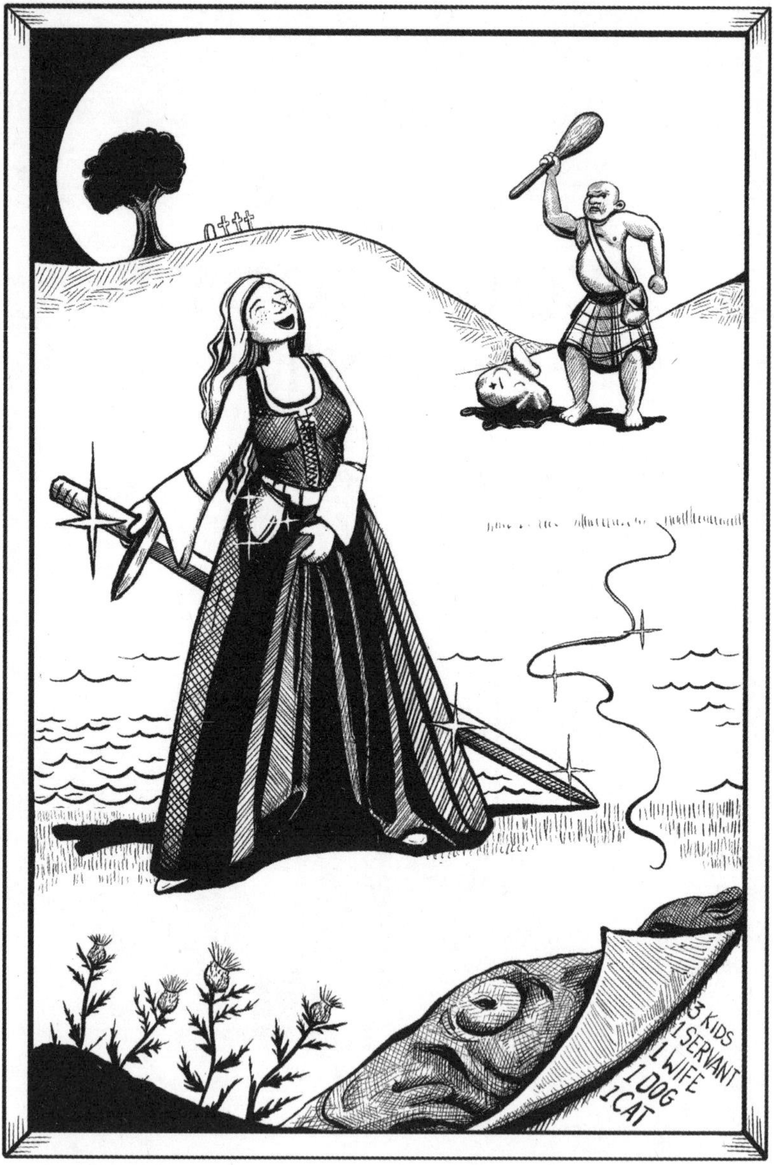
3 KIDS
1 SERVANT
1 WIFE
1 DOG
1 CAT

THE X-TREME SPORT OF GIANT KILLING

Scotland's "Molly Whuppie"

Once, three lovely lassies longed for adventure outside the walls of their childhood home. They packed their bags while their mother baked bread to feed them along the way. When Mom presented each daughter with her portion, she gave them a choice: "Would you like the larger loaf with my curse, or the smaller loaf with my blessing?" The two older sisters took a gamble and asked for the larger loaf with their mother's curse.

If a mother's love is powerful enough to drop ball gowns from trees and save wizard babies from Voldemort, a mother's curse must be terrifying!

The youngest, called Molly Whuppie, was the smartest girl of the lot. "I'll take the smaller loaf with your blessing, Mother," she replied. Her mother smiled, and not only gave her the blessing, but gave her both loaves!

Perhaps this favoritism made Molly loathsome to her older sisters, or maybe it was because she wasn't much to look at.* Whatever the reason, they tried to ditch her on their journey. First

---

* *Molly's Gaelic name, Maol a Chliobain, roughly translates to "bald simpleton." Likely one of those mean Cinderella names, cuz Molly is a smart cookie.*

they tied her to a rock. This was where Mother's blessing came through: it freed her, enabling Molly to catch up with her sisters, carrying that same rock on her shoulders.

I love the pettiness of this. The competitive sibling relationship shines (alongside the tall-tale implication that Molly can lift ten times her body weight).

Next, they tied her to a sack of peat, then to a tree, but no knots could hold her. She merely wriggled a little, and the ropes fell free.

The sisters traveled all day, then spent most of the night looking for a family to board them. They knocked at the first house they saw with a light on. A rough, large woman answered, and rubbed her eyes wearily when the sisters asked to stay the night.

"This is the last place you want to stay, ladies," she told them, "My husband is an ogre and his favorite meal is lost little girls. Skedaddle, and thank the Lord I answered and not him."

Molly argued, "Ma'am, we are so cold and hungry. Could you just warm us up and give us a bite? We can leave before your husband gets home."

The ogre's wife relented, impatiently ushering the girls inside. She sat them next to the fire with blankets and supplied them with milk and bread to fill their bellies. Alas, the ogre had gotten off work early that day (. . . **from guarding a bridge and bullying goats, I presume**) and walked through the front door before the girls finished supper. He sniffed the air, as an ogre is wont to do. "Are we having children for dinner?" he asked eagerly. He was excited; his wife never indulged his taste for kidflesh!

"NO," the woman replied firmly. "Molly Whuppie and her sisters are my guests. We'll bunk them with our own girls. Don't you touch them!"

I'm so intrigued by the wife's reluctance to eat the girls. Is she herself a human, merely cursed to marry an ogre? (It's happened in folktales before.) Is she an ogre with an ethical stance against eating humans? A vegan ogre?

The ogre begrudgingly allowed his wife to put Molly and her sisters up in the kids' room. But not before he tied a crude length of hemp around each of their necks. Molly made note of this. (And wouldn't you? What a strange thing to do.) As she and her sisters were shown to their bunks, she observed the ogre's three daughters, who lay sleeping with a shining gold amulet around each of their own necks.

As soon as the ogre's wife had closed the door behind her, Molly sat up and shushed her sisters. "Listen here!" she hissed. "That ogre is planning to kill and eat us tonight. See how his daughters have gold on their necks while we have hemp? I'm gonna switch ours with the gold ones. If anyone enters, pretend you're asleep. Hopefully Mam's blessing keeps working so we'll be spared!"

Molly knew what she was doing. Sure enough, the ogre summoned his servant. "I crave a Bloody Mary with the blood of those humans," he told his servant. "Kill them. Hang the meat to dry but bring me that blood fresh!"

"The human girls are sleeping in the same room as your three daughters," the servant pointed out. "How will I know who is who in the dark without waking them?"

The ogre told him to feel for the girls' necklaces to distinguish them. But since Molly swapped the necklaces, the servant believed the ogre's own children were the humans. That's how Molly Whuppie tricked the ogre into putting a hit out on his own kids and drinking a cocktail of their blood.

At this point in the story, perhaps you are thinking, *Was the killing of these innocent ogre children necessary? If Molly Whuppie is clever enough to see the danger coming, couldn't the girls just sneak away without the gratuitous bloodshed?* **Probably! But the general folktale opinion is that the only good ogre is a dead one.**

After the servant killed the last ogre girl, Molly gathered her sisters to escape. She noticed their guest bed had a luxurious golden throw blanket. She snatched it up.

"WARNING! WARNING!" the blanket cried. It was bewitched! "I HAVE BEEN STOLEN. I REPEAT, I HAVE BEEN STOLEN."

"Fuck you, ya wee clipe!"* Molly cried. She crouched down. "Up on my shoulders!" she ordered, and her two sisters hopped into a double-piggyback. Then Molly ran like hell.

The ogre, alerted by his home-security linens, dashed after them. Molly and her sisters had a good head start, but the girls' escape was thwarted when they came to a broad river. Molly plucked a hair from her head and threw it across the water. As it soared from the riverbank, the hair lengthened, creating a delicate copper bridge that she and her sisters dashed across. When the ogre reached the river, he stomped his foot.**

"Molly Whuppie!" the ogre roared. "You killed my children!"

Molly plopped her sisters down, put her hands on her hips, and screamed right back, "I see you're a master of the obvious!"

"Well, I'd better not see you again!" the ogre demanded. **(Despite what Shrek taught us, ogres aren't known for their comebacks.)**

Molly spat at him. "I'll come back whenever I damn well please, ya howlin' scabby scrote!"

The sisters ran until they reached a beautiful mansion. It was the home of the king, who took the girls in. Molly regaled him

---

* *The first recorded use of the f-word is from sixteenth century Scotland!*
** *In Scottish lore, supernatural creatures cannot cross fresh water.*

with stories about the ogre and their riveting, if violent, escape. This intrigued the ruler.

"Molly Whuppie, what do you think of returning to the ogre on my behalf? He has a magnificent pair of combs; one of silver and one of gold. Do you think you could bring them back to me?"

The young woman considered the request. "It's very dangerous, but I can try. How will I be rewarded for my efforts?"

The king gestured to his family portrait, featuring his three handsome sons. "If you bring me the sword, your eldest sister may marry my eldest son."

Molly shook on it. "Done!"

At this point in the story, perhaps you are thinking, *Why would Molly commit such a dangerous deed to secure a marriage for the sister who tied her to a rock and left her for dead?* **Based on the evidence, I think Molly was in it more for the story than for the reward. She was the Evel Knievel of early Scotland, the Johnny Knoxville of fairy-tale folk, a little lady with a taste for big thrills.**

The courageous lass snuck back to the ogre's home the following night. She snatched the fancy combs, but they too made an alarming racket. The ogre chased after her. She plucked out another hair and threw it. Once again she easily crossed the lithe bridge while the ogre was stuck sulking on the other side.

"Molly Whuppie!" he yelled. "You killed my children!"

Molly snorted. "I was merely an accessory to the murder, at most!"

The ogre grumbled. "Now you've stolen my fine combs!"

Molly held the combs up to the moonlight. "And what good are they to an ugly troll!"

The ogre stomped his foot. "I'd better not see you 'round these parts again!"

Molly flipped him off. "I do what I want, ya smeggy fucknugget!" She ran to the palace.

This tale has variants within Scotland depending on the community. Doric speakers call her "Mally," and that version opens with the "Hansel and Gretel" abandonment motif. Further, the giant's treasure includes a ring Mally must steal right off the ogre's finger.

The king was delighted to have the fancy combs in his possession. Wedding plans for the eldest prince and the eldest sister began.

But the king wasn't satisfied. He summoned Molly again. "Molly, the ogre has the Sword of Light in his possession. Such a weapon shouldn't be left in the hands of monsters. What do you say I offer my middle child's hand to your middle sister if you get me that sword?"

Molly was already sprinting away. "I'm on it!"

She waited until dark again, camping in a tree by the ogre's well. The ogre's servant approached to gather water, using the Sword of Light for visibility. When he put the sword down to pull up the bucket, Molly pounced from the tree and shoved the servant into the well, where he drowned. Molly no longer had to trick someone else to do her homicide. She was a cold-blooded killer!

Molly snatched the Sword of Light and ran away. The sword wailed and flashed like a siren, so the ogre chased her once more. Molly plucked a third hair, crafting a third slim bridge. (**I'm starting to see why Molly is balding.**)

"Hey, Molly Whuppie! You killed my children!"

"Tell me something I don't know, ya gamey dobber!"

"You stole my finest combs!"

"I did, and I'd do it again!"

"You killed my servant!"

"Had to be done, ya warbling tube!"

"Then you stole my Sword of Light?"

"You mean the *king's* Sword of Light?"

"I'd better not see you 'round these parts again!" The ogre shook his finger.

Molly grabbed her crotch defiantly and yelled, "Bite me bawsack, ye vacant codpiece!" Then she ran the sword back to the king.

The king hung the item where he could admire it. Invitations were issued for the middle prince's wedding to Molly's middle sister. But the king *still* wasn't satisfied. He spoke with Molly once more. "Molly Whuppie, the ogre has a coin purse that would fund fantastic projects for the kingdom."

Molly rubbed her hands together gleefully, but the king said there was a catch: "The ogre keeps it under his pillow when he sleeps at night."

The redhead salivated at the risk. "What do I get when I steal it?"

The king smiled. "My youngest son, for you, the youngest sister?"

As she ran off, Molly called over her shoulder, "My wedding colors are blush and bashful!"

After British folks emigrated to the American South, the Jack the Giant Killer tales took on a distinctive regional flavor. So I stand by my *Steel Magnolias* reference.

The ogre's household—what was left of it, anyway—was fast asleep when Molly arrived. She slipped inside, prowling through the house like a cat burglar. When she made it to the ogre's bedroom, she found him snoring. She slipped to his bedside, took a deep breath, and slid her hand under his pillow. Her fingers closed around the velvet purse, and she pulled it toward her.

Suddenly a massive hand closed around her wrist. The ogre was wide awake and glaring at her. He rolled out of bed and stood, dangling Molly before him by an arm. The coin purse fell to the floor with a jingle.

"I've finally caught the great Molly Whuppie," the ogre

drawled. "Now I just have to pick the perfect punishment." He paced the house, dragging Molly behind him while he scratched his chin. "What is the right retribution for a woman who killed my children, my servant, and robbed me of house and home?"

"I know what I would do if our roles were switched!" Molly piped up.

The ogre pulled her up so they were eye to eye. "Oh yeah? How would you punish yourself, Molly Whuppie?"

Women crafting their own violent punishment is a common trope in fairy tales (see the Grimms' "The Goose Girl" or "Strawberries in the Snow"). It speaks to a long history of invisible labor. Women care for the kids, we clean the home, we concoct our own executions. It's exhausting!

Molly considered this. "Well, first I'd throw me in a sack with your dog, your cat, and a sewing kit. Then I'd get the biggest stick I could carry and beat the pulp out of me right there in the sack."

The ogre narrowed his eyes. "Seems like a lot of work when I could just beat you with a stick right now."

"But if you do it my way, the cleanup will be much easier."

The girl had a point. The ogre scooped up the family pets, the wife's sewing kit, and Molly, and tumbled them all in a big sack. Then he went to the backyard to find the perfect club.

When Molly heard the door shut, she began yelling from inside the sack, "Fuck me sideways, I can't believe my eyes! God Almighty, nobody would believe me if I told them the sights you could see in this hairy sack!"

The ogre's wife was intrigued. She approached the sack. "What do you see in there?"

"Incredible sights!" Molly continued. "Oh, if only you were here, ma'am!"

The ogre's wife begged Molly to tell her more. "Let me in so I can see!"

The wife's laughable gullibility is evidence that she is an ogre herself. Or perhaps, having just brutally lost her three kids, she needed a win. What grieving mother wouldn't want to be cheered by the mysteries of her husband's giant sack?

Molly took the shears from the sewing kit and cut a hole in the bag. She slipped out, holding the gash open for the ogre's wife. "After you!" she said. Once the woman slipped inside the bag, Molly sewed the hole up with quick, sturdy stitches. Then she grabbed the ogre's coin purse and bolted.

Alas for the ogre's wife (and the animals), the ogre returned soon with the biggest stick in the yard. Elated, the foolish creature beat the sack, thinking he was destroying his adversary. His wife cried out from the bag, but he couldn't hear her over the tortured shrieks of the animals.

At this point in the story, you may be thinking, *Holy hell, is Molly Whuppie the actual villain of this piece? Why kill that nice old lady who tried to save them? Why bring the pets into it?* **I'll be frank: I don't fuckin' know, and I don't fuckin' like it either!**

Eventually the ogre realized the grotesque trick Molly had played. Once more he pursued her to the river. Molly stood waiting at the other side, haloed by sinister lightning, the wind whipping her hair and carrying her maniacal laughter across the water.

"Molly Whuppie! You killed my children!"

"Technically, yer eejit servant did!"

"You stole my finest combs!"

"Yeah, they look real good on me too!"

"You killed my servant!"

Molly sighed. "Can we move this whole thing along? I get that we repeat stuff a lot in these stories, but I'm a busy woman."

"Then you stole my Sword of Light!"

Molly prodded, "And then I killed your wife, your dog, and your cat."

"And then you killed my wife, my dog, and my cat!" The ogre tore at his hair.

Molly cackled. "Well, you can tongue my fartbox, ya fucking walloper!"

She turned on her heel to go. But the ogre surprised her with one more shout. "Molly Whuppie! If I were you, and you were me, what would you do to cross this river and catch the villain who destroyed my family?"

"Seriously?" Molly couldn't believe her ears. That blessing was working overtime. "I'd stick my face in the river and drink the whole thing dry so I could walk across easy-peasy."

The ogre stuck his face in the river and drank until he exploded.

Covered in ogre guts, Molly Whuppie returned to the palace. The king met her there with his youngest son. "So, Molly, what do you say we get this marriage contract drawn up?"

Molly looked the prince up and down. "You can keep your contract. I've got greater things waiting for me than marrying some pampered inbred weakling. No offense." She patted the prince's shoulder. "I'm gonna see what else this great big world has in store."

Thus ends the tale of Molly Whuppie, monster killer, animal abuser, and royal heartbreaker.*

* * *

---

* *J. F. Campbell recorded several variants of this tale. In many, Molly marries the prince. But in one, told by a young nursemaid in Inverary, she stays unmarried. I think this ending suits Molly best.*

SOURCES:

J. F. Campbell, *Popular Tales of the West Highlands, Volume 1.*
Joseph Jacobs, *English Fairy Tales.*

Want to read more Scottish fairy tales? Try *Scottish Folk & Fairy Tales: Fables, Folklore & Ancient Stories*, edited by J. K. Jackson.

HOW TO TRICK FRIENDS AND EXECUTE PEOPLE

Hans Christian Andersen's "Little Claus and Big Claus"

In a little Danish village lived a couple of psychopaths, both named Claus. One was poor, with only a single pony to his name, and one was rich, with four whole horses. So the town called the poor one Little Claus and the rich one Big Claus. One day, they wouldn't need to differentiate them at all. This is the true story—

(ahem)

This is the *story* of how Little Claus became Big Claus.

Little Claus worked for Big Claus, plowing his fields six days a week with his lone pony. **(I guess Big's four horses were just for show.)** In exchange, Big Claus allowed Little to take his four horses out for a spin every Sunday. This was Little Claus's favorite day of the week. He'd hitch his pony up in front of Big Claus's foursome, and ride around town pretending he was a fancy sonofabitch. The majestic team made quite a sight, and Little Claus loved the attention. When churchgoers gawked at his carriage being pulled by what looked like a stampeding herd, Little Claus would cry, "Giddyup! See my five fine horses?"

Word of Little Claus's shenanigans got back to Big, and he didn't like people confusing which Claus was "big" and which

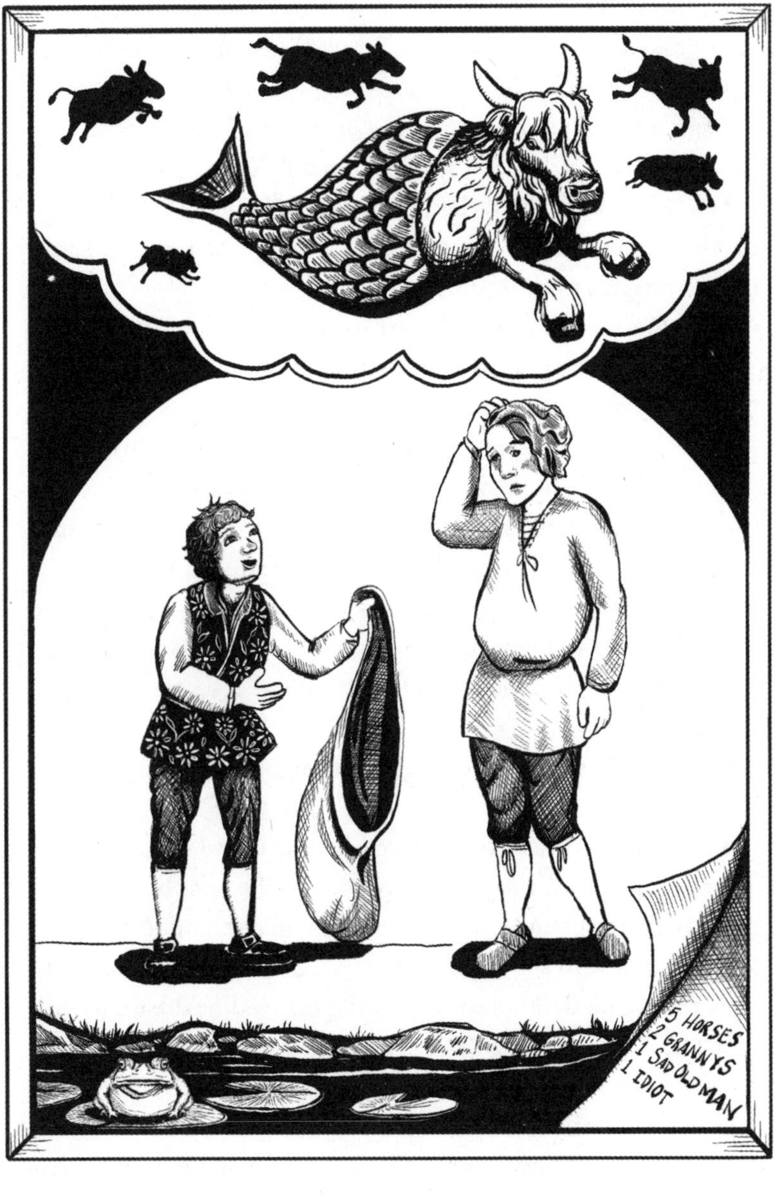
5 HORSES
2 GRANNYS
1 SAD OLD MAN
1 IDIOT

was "little." He pulled Little aside one day and said, "Stop lording around town with my four horses, pretending they're your own, you hear me?"

Little Claus nodded and "yes-sirred" his boss. But back in town on Sunday, he couldn't help himself. As he approached the church he gleefully cracked his whip and shouted, "Giddyup! Y'all see my five fine horses?" People oohed and aahed. Little Claus preened as they admired him.

"Listen, you little creep," Big warned Little again, "if you don't stop claiming horses that ain't yours, I'll clobber your one horse and you'll be S.O.L., ya hear me?"

"Yes, sir, no problem, sir. It won't happen again!" Little Claus swore. Then, on Sunday, a pretty lady peeped over her glasses at the handsome herd and Little Claus called, "Giddyup! March forth, my five fine horses!" Everyone cheered!

Big Claus was so mad, he took a mallet and cracked Little Claus's pony on the noggin so hard it fell down dead. "Giddyup your five fine horses now, you fuckin' phony!"

Andersen, coming out of the gates strong with equine-icide!

Little Claus cried, for he loved his pony, and on top of that he now had no way to make a living. But the poor dead animal still had some value. Little Claus skinned it and stuffed the skin in a sack to sell in the next town over. It was a long journey through a dark forest, and Little realized he'd have to find shelter. At the first sign of civilization, he knocked on a farmhouse door. The farmer's wife cracked it open a sliver, her eyes similarly narrowed.

Little Claus tipped his hat. "Evening, ma'am. Do you have an extra bed that a fellow could—"

"No!" the farmer's wife barked. She slammed the door in his face.

Little Claus shrugged. "Guess I'm sleeping under the stars tonight!" He spied a group of hay bales leading up to a thatched shed and decided that would work for him. He made himself comfortable on the roof, rolling onto his belly and almost kicking a nesting stork.

When Little Claus rested his chin on his hands, he realized he could see into the farmhouse. The windows were shuttered, but the shutters didn't completely cover the panes. Little watched as the farmer's wife poured a glass of wine for a sexton.* The two shared a lavish, intimate meal of roast beef, fried fish, and a rhubarb cake. Little Claus's stomach growled.

Next, he saw the farmer riding home. The farmer's wife heard the cart pass the house. She ushered the sexton into a large trunk. Then she hid the meal, stowing the wine in a wardrobe and shoving dinner and dessert back in the oven. "That's a damn shame," Claus muttered.

The farmer, walking past the shed, overheard him. He peered up. "Who are you, and what the hell are you doing on my roof?"

Little Claus explained that he was looking for a place to stay overnight, and the farmer invited him in. Little Claus happily hopped down from the roof, toting his sack of dried horse skin. When the man introduced Claus to his wife, the woman acted as though she'd never laid her narrowed eyes on him. She graciously invited them in and served the men a big bowl of bland porridge. The farmer dug in, but Claus couldn't stop thinking about the beef, wine, and cake. He decided a ruse was in order.

He laid his foot upon his sack, which he'd placed under the table for the meal. When he stepped on the dried skins, they made a loud squeaking noise. "Oh, be quiet, you," he said to the sack, apologizing to his hosts.

---

* *A sexton was the groundskeeper of a church, who sometimes acted as the bell ringer and/or gravedigger.*

Does leather squeak, Hans? How do you know this? What the fuck are you up to when you're not writing?

"What have you got in there?" asked the farmer.

"A little wizard man!" Little Claus claimed. "He told me there's no need to choke down this plain porridge. He's conjured up a feast of roast beef, fried fish, and rhubarb cake! He left it in the oven!"

The farmer's wife scoffed, but the farmer ordered her to check. She glared at Claus, then feigned surprise when she opened the oven to the meal she'd cooked. She served the men and sat back down.

Just as her butt hit the cushion, Claus stepped on the sack again for another squeak. "What's that you say?" He conferred with the sack. "He said he left some wine for us in the wardrobe."

The farmer's wife glowered, but she retrieved the wine.

The farmer got super sauced over dinner. Claus learned that the guy really hated sextons.

Okay, obviously the farmer's wife and the sexton are fucking. In folk versions of this tale, that plot point is made clear. My friends Drs. Brittany Warman and Sara Cleto theorize that Andersen, emphasizing Christian values, skips a blatant affair and invents another reason the farmer would be angry to find the sexton in his home.

As Claus poured wine and kept the farmer talking, the wife stole fretful glances over her shoulder at their large trunk. Over the last bites of cake, the farmer pressed Claus for details on the wizard in the bag. "Can he conjure anything for you? Could he conjure the devil himself?"

Claus conferred with the sack. "Oh, he can summon the devil.

But you won't like it. The devil will appear to you as your worst enemy. He'll look just like that old sexton you loathe so much."

The farmer slapped his knee with laughter. "Oooh, he must be one ugly bastard! Go ahead, I won't mind, as long as he doesn't get too close."

Claus listened to the sack, dropping some "Mm-hmms" and "Oh, fascinatings" while he did. "All right, if you pop open that old trunk, you'll find the devil waiting for you there," he told the drunk farmer. "But when you look inside, only open it a crack. And hold the lid firmly so he can't escape!"

The two men peeped inside and chortled at the sight of the frightened sexton. The farmer snapped the lid shut and cranked the latch tight. "Listen, you gotta sell me that sack of wizard," he begged.

Little Claus hesitated. "I wasn't planning to sell. But you can have him for a bushel of silver, full to the brim."

The farmer whistled. "A steep price. I'll pay it if you dispose of that big trunk and the devil inside."

I wonder if Hans was riffing on a "Town of Fools" motif of folktales. He satirizes high society in "The Emperor's New Clothes" and "The Nightingale." Perhaps this was his send-up of common folk, such as we see in stories like "The Wise Men of Chelm."

Little Claus was so pleased with his con, he didn't bother staying the night. He headed straight home with a wheelbarrow carting his bushel of money and the sexton in the trunk. Along the way, he managed to blackmail the sexton out of a second bushel of money by threatening his life. Things were really turning around for Little Claus!

Once home, Little Claus made sure that Big Claus found out about his riches. When Big Claus questioned his former plowman about it, Little told him he'd earned the bushel by selling the hide of his horse. Flush with inspiration and avarice, Big Claus immediately returned home and bludgeoned all four of his horses to death.

He set off to town the next day with the four horse skins. "Hides fer sale!" he called out.

He immediately had interest from shoemakers and tanners alike. But when he revealed the price—a full bushel of silver a pop—those same parties pushed back. "Ridiculous! We don't have bushels of money to spend on skin!"

"That's too bad for you," Big Claus jeered. "A bushel's the going rate these days."

These townies were so angry, they ganged up on Big Claus and beat the snot out of him. Big arrived back home with four horse hides, no money, a lot of bruises, and a thirst for homicidal revenge. He marched to Little Claus's house in the middle of the night and crept into his bedroom with an ax. There, he sank the thing into the sleeping man's head. He left without even cleaning the blade.

This is an early story written for Andersen's first collection *Fairy Tales, Told for Children*. I see it as a violent goof à la "Tom and Jerry." But according to translators Diana Crone Frank and her husband, Jeffrey, Andersen wrote for adults *and* children, and only chose that title for this collection to get critics off his back, as the literary elite of Denmark didn't like his narrative style. Seems like more of a self-own than a work-around.

Here's the thing: The person in bed was not Little Claus at all. While Big was off getting his own hide tanned, Little Claus was preparing a funeral. His grandmother had passed away, and, while she was an ornery old crank, he was sorry to see her go. He wondered if tucking her into a nice warm bed would bring her back to life.

I can't tell if this is (a) another sign that literally everyone in this town is a dimwit, *including* our con man, or (b) Andersen's profound fear of being buried alive making its way onto the page.

He moved her into his own bed and slept in his chair in the den. That's how he witnessed Big Claus's midnight assault. *What a jerk!* Little Claus thought. *He could have killed me! He could have killed my gran-gran, if she weren't already dead!*

Now, Little Claus had some experience turning a dead body into a small fortune. Why let another go to waste? He dressed his grandmother's corpse in her best Sunday clothes, tied her bonnet around her head to bind the ax wound, and propped her body in his cart as if she were enjoying an afternoon ride. Little Claus drove her to an inn, whose owner was notoriously wealthy and short-tempered.

"See here, innkeeper," Little Claus said, summoning him over. "I'm driving my gran-gran to town, and she'd like a glass of mead. But she's refusing to come in. Would you be a good man and bring it out to her? Mind you, she's almost deaf, so you may need to shout."

The innkeeper brought a hefty glass to the carriage and held it out to the deathly still old woman. "Your grandson sent this for you," he said loudly.

He got no response. "You hear me, old woman? Your grandson has sent you this glass of mead!" he shouted. He repeated himself again and again, louder and louder. He thought that the old lady was ignoring him. It infuriated him so much that he threw the heavy glass of mead right at her face.

Business owners got away with so much before access to Yelp.

The impact nudged the old lady off balance, and the corpse tumbled out of the cart. Her bonnet flopped off and her head cracked fully in two.

"You monster!" Little Claus pointed at the innkeeper. He ran forward and wrapped his hands around the guy's throat. "You killed my gran-gran! You've cleaved her in two!"

The innkeeper wriggled out of Little's grasp and fell to his knees. "Please forgive me! It was an accident—my temper...!" He trailed off, panting and palming sweat from his brow. "Listen, the court will have my head for this, no matter what plea I give them. What do you say I give you a bushel of silver and bury the poor woman as beautifully as I would my own grandmother? If I did that, could you to keep this to yourself?"

He could indeed! Little Claus happily left his grandmother's corpse behind and toted away another bushel of riches.

Big Claus was bewildered. "How the hell did you get all this money?" he demanded. "How are you alive?"

"Ah, well, you killed my gran-gran, not me," Little Claus replied matter-of-factly. "So I sold her body for a bushel of silver."

Big Claus rubbed his chin. "That is a good sum for an old lady," he mused. So: even though he'd been conned by Little Claus the first time, he promptly went home and axed his own very much alive grandmother.

I feel that if the Little Mermaid had seen *these* humans, she wouldn't have been so eager to give up her tail, ya know?

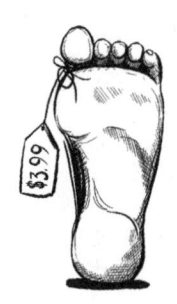

Big Claus brought her body to the apothecary, who was polishing the counter, and pitched, "How'd you like to buy a cadaver?"

Apothecaries occasionally used bone, tissue, and fluids of the dead as medicine. One of many reasons I have no interest in time travel.

The apothecary didn't look up from his task. "I need more information than that."

"It's like this," Big Claus said. "I killed my granny so I could sell her for a bushel of silver."

The apothecary stared at him for a long moment. Then he pointed to the door. "Get out."

"You'd pass up a perfectly good body?" Big Claus insisted.

"Let me summarize." The apothecary folded his arms. "You walk into my shop, confessing to your grandmother's murder, a crime punishable by execution, and you want me to turn my head the other way so you can earn a few bucks from it."

Big Claus grew pale. "I think I forgot something in my corpse—I mean carriage." He ran from the shop and rode off in a cloud of dust.

"I gotta get a new trade," the apothecary muttered.

Yes, the man who buys dead people is the most rational person in this tale.

Now Big Claus was furious. He dropped off his carriage and grabbed the largest sack he owned. He took that to Little Claus's home, kicked open the door, and pulled the man up by his collar. "First you tricked me into killing my horses! Then you tricked me into killing my grandmother! But I won't be played a fool again, you sneaky piece of shit! You won't live long enough to even *plan* another prank!"

He stuffed Little Claus into the sack and tied it up tight. "I'm dropping you in the river, and, *man*, do I hope you drown slowly!"

Hefting a grown man in a sack is not easy work. Big Claus had a long walk ahead of him. About halfway to the river was a church, and Big Claus could hear they were in the middle of a service. The music was good, there were sure to be snacks, and the only people around were sitting in the pews. So Big Claus dropped the sack by the church door and sauntered in for a rest.

Little Claus flopped around inside the sack, trying to rip a seam or loosen the knots. The only thing he succeeded at was rolling the sack into the middle of the street. Exhausted, he lay there, unsure of his next move.

A lot of people in fairy tales end up in sacks. I didn't even know they made sacks that big.

An old cattle driver turned the corner, leading his bovine charges. They ambled toward Little Claus. When the old man reached the sack, he prodded it with his cane. From inside came a muffled voice. "Oh, to be so young and just outside the Pearly Gates!"

The old man leaned on his staff. "Well, how about me? So very old, and yet the Lord won't do the right thing and let me die already!"

There was a pause. Then Little Claus spoke up. "Wanna switch places?"

The old man teared up. "At last! Goodbye, cruel world!"

Wow. Deus Ex Euthanasia. You don't see that every day.

He untied the sack, and Little Claus scrambled out, shaking himself off. The old man creakily pulled the large bag around himself. He paused. "Sonny, you'll take care of my cows, won't you?"

"Hell, yes!" Little Claus cried. Not only would he get to live, but he got a dozen cows too? What a day! He tied the old man up tight and drove the cattle back toward his place.

When Big Claus left church and lifted his sack, he noticed how much lighter it was. "Ah," he said, pointing a finger to the heavens. "This is what a good Christian earns by paying a visit to church. The Lord carries your burden. Now: off to drown my nemesis!"

In no time, Big Claus arrived at the bridge and hucked the old man into the deepest part of the river. He danced past the church singing, "I'm free!" He danced past the apothecary and the inn. "I'm free!" He danced right into Little Claus driving his newfound cattle. "I'm— *What the fucking fuck?*"

"Oh, hi, Claus," Little Claus said calmly. "Would you believe I found all these cows at the bottom of the river?"

"*No*," Big Claus said.

Little Claus smiled beatifically. "It was so beautiful, down in the depths. I was terrified, you know, when you chucked me in. But I landed on the softest, downiest grass. Then I heard beautiful music. Someone opened the sack; it was a sexy little mermaid all in white, with seaweed in her hair! She crooned, 'Handsome Claus, we've been waiting for you. Just up the road is a herd of mer-cattle. They're all yours, if you'll have them.' She swam me down the winding river, the highway of the mer-people. The place was incredible! Exotic flowers, lush greenery, hell, even the people were hotter than anyone up here!" He patted a distinctly dry cow on the rump. "And sure enough, there they were! These majestic sea-cows!" He walked right up to Big Claus, nose to nose. "To think, if you hadn't thrown me in that river, I'd never have found them. And now I am even richer than before. Richer even than you!"

Big Claus scrunched up his face, trying to read the other. "If it was so great down there, why did you come back? I wouldn't leave a magical underwater land full of sexy mer-people wearing white clothes underwater, leaving nothing to the imagination." He gestured wildly to the cows' rear ends. "And where are their fish tails?"

"Oh, I'm just taking a shortcut back," Little Claus explained. "The cows shed their tails on land."

Big Claus considered this. "Do you think there are any sea-cattle left for me?"

"I'm sure of it. Your best bet is to drop off the same bridge as I did. Maybe you'll run into that sweet little piece of fish, if ya know what I'm saying." Little Claus winked, then snapped his fingers with sudden disappointment. "Crap! There's no way I'd be able to carry you all that way. Hmmm. You wouldn't consider meeting me there? We can put you in the sack at that point."

"That's a good idea," Big Claus confirmed. "But just so you know, if you're lying to me and there aren't any sea-cows down there, I'm coming back to put my foot in your ass."

"That makes sense," Little Claus said. "So, I'll see you there?"

Big Claus was waist-deep in his own sack when Little got to the bridge. He even suggested Little toss a big stone in the sack to get him to the bottom faster. Little Claus triple-knotted the bag and pushed the big oaf to his watery death.

Gazing down the river, the lone Claus chuckled. "Sea-cows? What a blockhead!"

* * *

SOURCE: "Little Claus and Big Claus," a translation of "Lille Claus og Store Claus" by Jean Hersholt.

Want to deep-dive into all things Andersen? I love Maria Tatar's *The Annotated Hans Christian Andersen*.

NEVER CROSS A CINDERELLA

Korea's "Kongjwi and Patjwi"

Once, very long ago in the kingdom of Joseon, lived a young woman named Kongjwi. She was the picture-perfect fairy-tale maiden: kind, beautiful, talented, hardworking, blah, blah, blah, blah, BLAH.

My kingdom for a Cinderella with even one imperfection!

How Kongjwi ended up so saintly is a goddamn miracle, considering her very sad and sorry upbringing. She never knew her mother, who died just before her family could celebrate her hundred-day birthday. Her father remarried when she was fourteen, but picked one of those evil stepmother types, a sour-faced widow named Bae. The widow had a daughter named Patjwi, who, despite their similar names, was Kongjwi's opposite: She was cruel, graceless, and lazy. She could have been quite a beauty if she dropped the attitude once in a while.

Scholars debate the origins of Kongjwi and Patjwi's names. Kyung Chul Joo argues that Kongjwi is named for the bean field where her mother prayed for a child. (*Kong* means bean and *jwi da* means to grab.) In Hwan Gu writes that the names indicate their status. *Pat* means red bean, considered more of a delicacy. Both names are still better than Greasy Matty (Denmark) and Slut-Sweeps-the-Oven (Belgium).

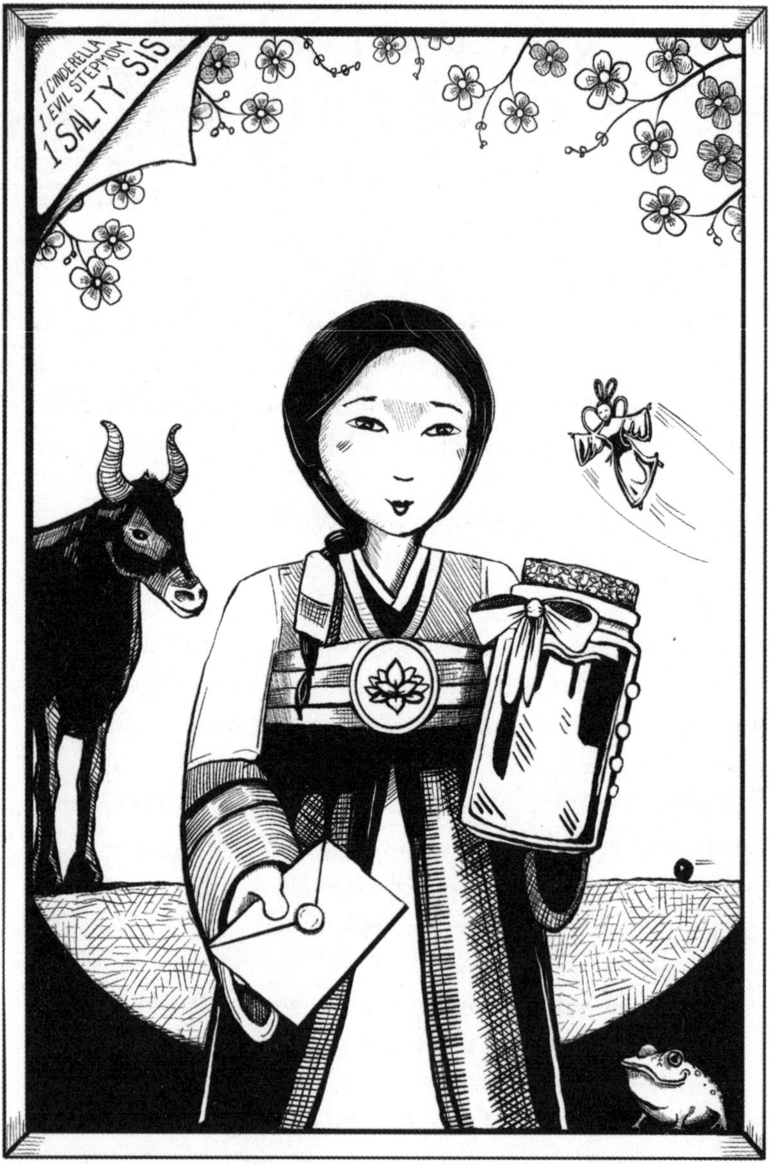
1 CINDERELLA
1 EVIL STEPMOM
1 SALTY SIS

Bae quickly took charge of the household, putting both her daughter and stepdaughter to work. Kongjwi was a natural housekeeper, eager to help and quick to finish her chores. On the contrary, Patjwi would bitch and moan if she was asked to brush a single hair off the counter, and it took her a whole fuckin' day to darn a stocking. Despite this, Patjwi was never admonished for her shortcomings, while Kongjwi couldn't please Bae if she brought her the moon on a jade platter. In fact, Bae began to find creative ways for Kongjwi to fail.

Women in the latter half of the Joseon Dynasty could only remarry if they had not borne a son. This context adds nuance to the stepmother, who would have been subservient to Patjwi if she'd been born a boy. I don't usually root for patriarchy, but this might have made Kongjwi's life a lot easier.

For example, one day Bae sent her daughters out to weed the yard. She handed Patjwi a sturdy metal hoe and ordered her to the front of the lawn where the soil was soft and the weeds were few. But Kongjwi received a fragile wooden hoe and was sent far off to the borders of the property where the weeds were as plentiful as the gravel. Kongjwi barely got three digs in when her hoe broke apart. The poor girl's dignity broke with it. She fell to the hard ground and wept.

Fairy Tale Facts: If you make a drinking game out of any fairy tale book, do NOT to take a shot every time the fairy tale heroine is found crying. That's a short road to alcohol poisoning.

An unfamiliar voice spoke. "Kongjwi! Your savior is here!"
Kongjwi's eyes widened as a majestic black ox floated down from the sky. She reached out to scratch his ears, as a kind gesture and to verify that this talking, flying animal was real. He

nuzzled her back. When he pulled away, he dropped a metal hoe into Kongjwi's hands.

"That'll work much better," the ox said. "And since you're such a dedicated and responsible young lady, I'll help you finish the job." The ox went to town on the weeds. With his help, Kongjwi was done before Patjwi could break a sweat. Of course, Bae accused Kongjwi of stealing the hoe and beat her with the instrument, so in the end, was the ox really that helpful?

Then Bae gave Kongjwi a jug with a giant hole in it and told her to fill it with water. Naturally, Kongjwi couldn't get the damn jug to stay full! **(Look, this fairy tale encourages virtue and femininity, not crafty problem-solving.)** The poor girl sat down by the river and sobbed. **(Drink!)**

"Oh, hunny," she heard a stranger sigh. "Ya gotta think outside the box!" It was a fat electric-green frog, who jumped into Kongjwi's lap. "Rather, ya gotta think 'inside the jug.' Why don't I hop in and snug my belly up on that hole? Then you can fill it with no problem."*

Kongjwi kissed the frog and helped him gently into the jug. Once he was splayed out at the bottom, she filled the container easily. Bae yelped when she saw the frog and cracked Kongjwi on the head for bringing home vermin.

It's feeling like these heavenly animals care more about Kongjwi's homemaking and less about her welfare.

Kongjwi's miserable days passed much the same way, until Chuseok arrived. Bae's parents invited her and the kids to a banquet to celebrate the harvest. The ladies got excited think-

---

* *"The Green Frog" is a popular Korean folktale that cemented the frog as a mischievous figure, so much so, sometimes parents will call their naughty children little green frogs.*

ing about the games they'd play and the sweet hangwa they'd indulge in for dessert. Of course, Bae said Kongjwi could only attend if she finished a sadistic to-do list.

Assigning hard jobs to keep the heroine from the ball is a classic Cinderella motif. Part of me wants these evil stepmothers to commit to the fuckin' bit and just forbid her to go! Though passive-aggression is its own kind of torture.

"First, spin this pile of hemp and weave it into bolts of the smoothest fabric. Then dehull these two humongous bags of rice. If you finish that, and if you can find something *suitable* to wear"—Bae eyed Kongjwi's ragged robe—"then you can join us at the banquet."
Not only did Kongwi's family leave her a day full of chores, but she had to delay those chores further to help them get ready. She pinned up Bae's hair and steamed the wrinkles from her sister's hanbok. She adjusted her father's coat and gazed up at him forlornly.

Weird how the dad just disappears and reappears, right? While dads are often killed off in modern versions of "Cinderella," in many folk variants dads are merely absent, neglectful, or naive. I understand why we would soften this nowadays. Us artists are constantly trying to fix our daddy issues.

He smiled back at her blandly, but, as usual, he deferred to Bae's parenting. The family left Kongjwi weeping over bundles of hemp. (Drink!)
Luckily, that magical black ox returned, poking his head through an open window. A couple of sparrows perched on his horns. "All right, birds, you pound that rice, and I'll take care of the spinning."
Kongjwi moved the hemp outside as a flock of birds joined

the sparrows dehulling and sorting the rice. The ox bent over and chomped up some greens. Kongjwi shifted from foot to foot. "With all due respect, sir"—she hesitated—"if you eat the hemp, there won't be any left to spin."

"Trust the process," the ox told her.

As the ox chewed and swallowed, a line of yarn began spiraling out of his butt.

You might call him Rump-elstiltskin!

As the fiber piled up, Kongjwi gingerly wound the fine thread around embroidery cards, making a mental note to wash the yarn (and her hands) at least twelve times when they were done.

"Oh, I'll take care of that!" An airy voice entered the mix. "You'll never weave it fast enough." An ethereal fairy floated down from the sky. She removed her winged robe, tucking it safely under a bench,* and carried a batch of yarn to the loom inside. "But before I get to work, let's freshen you up. What are you wearing?"

Kongjwi showed the fairy to her chest of clothes, pulling out a serviceable dress. The fairy tutted. "No, that won't do." She took the garment by the shoulders and shook it with a hard *snap!* The gown transformed into a lavender brocade jeogori and a matching periwinkle skirt. Her straw sandals became red leather slippers, decorated with scrolling silver embroidery and a stitched lotus on each toe. The fairy pulled a comb through Kongjwi's hair and kissed each of her cheeks. Now the girl's locks were plaited and pinned up with a silver daenggi, and her dewy skin was highlighted with pink blush and red lip stain. She looked like a princess!

---

* *The winged robe is a reference to another popular Korean fairy tale, "The Woodcutter and the Fairy," in which a fairy takes off her wings to bathe and is forced to marry a mortal after he steals her winged clothes. I love the idea that a fairy can remove her wings for a quick dip!*

"Now shuffle along. We have a lot of work to do while you're gone!" The fairy shooed Kongjwi out the door.

Kongjwi peered back over her shoulder. Through the windows, she saw the fairy weaving three times as fast as any mortal could. "Thank you, my weird and wonderful friends!" she called.

Kongjwi hurried up the road toward the banquet, upstream of the river. Halfway there, she saw a procession. It was the new governor, carried on a gilded palanquin by four state officials in smart uniforms. Governor Kim was a young widower and very handsome. He caught Kongjwi's eye as the procession passed, gazing at her with admiration. She blushed and bowed low. When she straightened back up, one of her red slippers fell off and tumbled into the river. Kongjwi yelped and chased after it. But the current carried the shoe far out of her reach.

Kongjwi limped the rest of the way to the banquet, a little embarrassed to show up with one bare foot. But her stepmother's parents were kinder than their offspring. They were surprised to meet a personable, polite young woman in Kongjwi, quite the opposite of the wretched stepdaughter Bae had described. The couple took Kongjwi on a tour of their mansion, introducing her to the party's VIPs.

Patjwi fumed when she saw Kongjwi's shining silk ensemble and grew even more jealous as her relatives fell over themselves to please her annoying stepsister. But Kongjwi's triumph was only just beginning. Shortly after her arrival, it was announced that a surprise guest was approaching—Governor Kim and his procession!

Bae and Patjwi had been sulking on the veranda as the governor's party approached the house. They watched the attendant march up the walkway, carrying a red slipper. The governor had seen a young woman running after the slipper along the banks of the river, the attendant said. His Excellency had instructed his men to scoop it from the water and find the stunning woman.

"That's my daughter's shoe," Bae quickly fibbed. "Go on, Patjwi, put it on and show the man."

Patjwi bowed, and quickly stepped out of one of her own shoes, keeping it hidden under her skirt. "I'm so grateful the governor found it, sir," she yelled, batting her eyes in Kim's direction. "It's my favorite pair!" She shoved her foot into the slipper as the attendant held it out.

The shoe did not fit. It wasn't even close. "This is clearly not the girl," the attendant sniffed.

Korean flower shoes, named for their petal shape, conform to the wearer's foot over time. While Kongjwi's shoes are magical, I like the idea that even an unenchanted shoe might fit her best.

"Of course not," another man said, amused. It was the governor himself, who stepped out of the palanquin, eager to meet the slipper's owner. "I believe it belongs to the young woman in purple." He gestured past the veranda, to where Kongjwi stood filling her family's teacups. The governor reached out, and the attendant handed him the shoe.

Modern women are mocked for obsessing over shoes, but we were led to believe a really great one could land a king, so who's to blame here?

Bae and Patjwi gaped as the governor introduced himself to Kongjwi. They gasped as Kongjwi demurely lifted her skirts to show the matching red slipper. They squawked as the governor bowed low to Kongjwi and offered her his arm. By the end of the banquet, the governor was asking Kongjwi's father for permission to marry her.

Kongjwi and Governor Kim celebrated their wedding the following spring. The entire kingdom agreed that they made a lovely couple. Well, all but one cranky stepfamily. Bae and Patjwi were never more miserable. They waited for the fervor of the royal wedding to die down. Then they plotted a way to eliminate Kongjwi and move Patjwi into the governor's palace—and his arms.

Opportunity arose when Governor Kim was called away for business about a month into his new marriage. Bae and Patjwi arranged to call on Kongjwi when they knew she'd be alone. They sent her a thoughtfully written letter, full of apologies and pleas for forgiveness. Kongjwi, perpetually hopeful that she and her stepfamily could come to love one another, was happy to receive them.

She treated the two women to a tour of the grounds. They settled in the garden in the shade of the cherry trees, looking out over a large pond bordered by lotus flowers, with an elegant platter of gimbap to munch on. Bae poured generous rounds of rice wine, refilling Kongjwi's glass often. When Kongjwi's cheeks were flushed from the booze, Patjwi spoke up. "Do you think we could take a dip in that gorgeous pool, Kongjwi?"

"What a marvelous idea!" Kongjwi jumped up, swaying a bit. "You'll come too, won't you, Stepmother?"

"Oh, I'm too old to frolic, but you girls have fun."

Patjwi discreetly gestured to the servants standing nearby. "Sister, might we bathe alone? Without these people watching?" She acted shyly, and thanked Kongjwi as she dismissed the staff. Bae helped the ladies strip down to their slips, neatly laying out their garments as the sisters jumped in the pond.

Patjwi did not have to wait long to catch her stepsister off guard. Kongjwi was blinking sleepily at a dragonfly when Patjwi pushed her under the water. With her reflexes dulled from the wine, Kongjwi struggled weakly. Strengthened with rage and resentment, Patjwi straddled her stepsister and pushed her shoulders and head beneath the water. She glared down at Kongjwi icily, until her body was still.

Quietly, Patjwi and Bae tied a heavy stone into Kongjwi's skirts. Patjwi pulled the girl's body to the deep end of the pool, watching with satisfaction as the stone dragged her down to the bottom. Patjwi dried off, and her mother helped her dress in Kongjwi's garments. Patjwi steeled herself as her mother picked up the empty platter from the table and struck her across the face.

"Dammit, Mother!" she gasped, spitting out a tooth. "If I didn't know any better, I'd think you've been waiting to do that my whole life!"

Bae shrugged and inspected her daughter's swollen face. "It will have to do."

That night, Governor Kim arrived home to learn that his wife had taken a bad fall down the stairs. He found Patwji reclining on a settee, the room dark.

"Please don't put a lamp on," Patjwi spoke in a strangled voice. "I have such a headache."

Kim gawked down at the woman he assumed was Kongjwi. Her eye was swollen shut and the whole side of her face was black-and-blue. "My God!" He didn't want to be rude, but she looked unrecognizable, even on her uninjured side. He summoned his staff and made sure they treated her with extra care. Patjwi smiled to herself. It was almost too easy!

You're telling me! This soap-operatic motif of Cinderella's sister taking on her identity pops up in versions from Korea to Ireland. While it may be hard to believe a man could accept an entirely different woman as his wife, remember that in this world, cows can spin hemp with their butts.

Patjwi had tricked the governor and his staff with her busted face, but she couldn't hide her personality. Kim and his servants grew confused as the lady of the house lost her charm and grace. They wondered if her change had been caused by the head injury, or if this was just the inevitable end of the "honeymoon period."

The governor began to take his meals alone, and rarely visited his wife's rooms overnight.

The governor spent hours walking in the gardens, saddened by "Kongjwi's" changed personality. Patjwi wondered how she might tempt the governor back to the bedchamber, but he had developed a new fascination: a uniquely beautiful lotus that grew in the garden pond. It appeared in the deep end one day, growing a head above the other flowers. It had double the petals of most lotuses, and its color was a unique blend of lavender and blue. Governor Kim spied the flower one day on a walk, and had his staff pull it up to decorate his office. He spent long hours there, enraptured by the stunning plant.

Patjwi began to feel neglected. Once, she snuck into the office when Kim had left for the day, rummaging through his paperwork and tchotchkes. When she brushed past the large lotus flower, she felt a sharp pinch on her arm. "Ow!!" She whirled around, but she was alone.

Another day, she brushed past the flower and felt a hard tug at her hair. She bit back a curse, but still there was no one there. Then she noticed strands of her hair caught in the lotus petals. She ogled it. "Kongjwi?"

The flower was still. Patwji reached for the blossom. Invisible teeth closed around her finger. She pulled away with a yelp. The bite drew blood. Hurriedly, Patjwi summoned a servant and ordered them to toss the lotus in the fire.

It's giving *Little Shop of Kongjwi.*

That night, Kim and Patjwi had a visitor. Their next-door neighbor, an elderly woman who had befriended Kim's first wife, occasionally dropped by for assistance. Today she needed a light for her fire. When she opened the stove, she found the fire had already burned out. But shining from the ashes was a multicolored jade marble. The old woman plucked it out and stowed it in her pocket. At home, she placed the marble on a cushion in a closet for safekeeping.*

Later, while the old woman puzzled over her needlework, she heard a woman's voice in the closet. "Hello? Could someone open the door? It's pitch-black in here!"

The old woman found Kongjwi, drenched and blue-faced, sitting on the cushion that housed the marble. "Can I help you?" she asked, bewildered.

"Lord, I hope so!" Kongjwi wrung out her slip dress. Water fell from its folds and passed eerily through the floor. "I've been trying to tell my husband that my sister drowned me."

"You're Governor Kim's wife." The old woman frowned. "And you're a marble?"

"Yes!" Kongjwi clapped her hands. "Oh, I'm so glad you get it! My sister keeps obstructing my efforts. Do you think you can get my husband over here? I need to tell him the truth, but not before I torture him a little for thinking my sister is me."

The old woman was very excited to help Kongjwi out with her revenge plot. She threw herself a fake birthday dinner, extending an invitation to Governor Kim and his impostor wife. Patjwi made it plain she had no interest in some old fart's party, so Kim attended alone. When he arrived, he found he was the only guest. Out of politeness, he stayed.

The old woman sat him at the table and laid out his place setting. When dinner was served, Kim picked up his chopsticks. But he couldn't eat the spicy cucumber salad because the uten-

---

* *The Korean Ministry of Culture, Sports and Tourism explains in their article on "Kongjwi and Patjwi" that both the lotus and the marble pop up repeatedly in Korean literature. The ancient religion of shamanism in Korea decreed that spirits could imbue everyday objects, especially if the person was the victim of murder or died with unfinished business.*

sils were different sizes. "Ma'am, it appears you've given me two different chopsticks."

A familiar voice jeered at him. "So, you can tell the difference between two wooden sticks, but two different women look the same to you?" Kim paled as Kongjwi revealed herself from behind a bamboo screen. She squelched over to him, planting herself in an adjoining seat.

The governor stuttered, "Kongjwi? What happened to you?"

"What happened is my stepfamily murdered me while you were traveling last month! Since then, Patjwi's been wearing my outfits and sleeping with my husband!" Kongjwi scrutinized him. "Are you face-blind, or something?"

The governor retraced the last few weeks. He realized she was right. "Wow. This is embarrassing."

"Good!" Kongjwi gestured to the old woman, who brought the jade marble to Governor Kim. "Take this marble and fish me out of the bottom of the pond. My corpse has been sitting there, held down by a big rock. I don't even want to think about what I look like right now."

When Kim's staff dredged the pool for Kongjwi's body, they were all shocked at how well preserved she was. Then they were further astonished when the body suddenly spit up pond water and sucked in much-needed air. Kim, who had fainted at the sight of his dead wife, snapped awake. "You're alive!"

"I am," Kongjwi confirmed. "And so is Patjwi. For now."

Kongjwi's reincarnations and resurrection are sometimes regarded as the character's true coming of age. She is now an adult. She's seen some shit.

The governor had Patjwi quietly executed, and the couple served revenge to Bae with a side of her own barbarity. See, ever since her stepdaughter's death, Bae had enjoyed the benefits of placing her own daughter at the governor's side, mostly in the form of fine jewelry, clothing, and delicacies from the gubernatorial palace. One day, a new gift arrived: a big jar of jeotgal. Excitedly, she sampled the fermented seafood. It was unlike any she'd ever tasted before.

A card came with the gift. Bae spooned more of the sauce over noodles and settled in with the bowl and her letter. It was more of a governmental decree than a greeting card: *Citizens who plot the violent death of another shall be slaughtered, salted, and jarred. Those who assist such schemes shall dine on the killer's flesh.*

Bae looked closer at the jar beside her. She gave it a tentative swirl and an eyeball floated to the top of the jar. Realizing she'd imbibed a pickled Patjwi, Bae screamed, and screamed, and screamed some more. She didn't stop screaming until her heart gave out, and she fell over dead.

* * *

SOURCE: "Kongjwi and Patjwi" from *Encyclopedia of Korean Folk Literature*.

Want to read more Korean folktales? Try *Tales of Korea: 53 Enchanting Stories of Ghosts, Goblins, Princes, Fairies and More!* by Im Bang.

SKIN-DEEP

Giambattista Basile's "The Flayed Old Woman"

Long ago in the city of Roccaforte, two old sisters lived in a small apartment nestled below the king's palace. An intimate garden sat underneath a palace window, shaded by a sprawling Aleppo pine. One day, the sisters (we'll call them Lorena and Sofia) settled themselves under the tree to rest.

They had chosen the pine because it hid them from view. You see, in the eyes of their cruel world, the sisters had not aged gracefully. (Also in the eyes of our cruel world, though, as I write this, old crones like Strega Nona and Baba Yaga are dominating mood boards.) They had every feature you'd bestow upon the most heinous old witch: thick unruly brows, more hair on their chins and bodies than on their heads, complexions marred by spots, skin folding with age. They could not be bothered to hold their toots. Plus, hygiene was not very advanced in those days. Most would call them smelly old crones. Me? I'd call them Boss Ass Biddies.

The ladies were happy to have a hidden nook to chat, away from the neighborhood's judgment. Their main mode of small talk was one-upping each other with their various ailments. A flower fell on Lorena's head, and she cried out as if she'd been hit by a log. Sofia met that with a series of coughs, blaming the dandelion fluff. Her sister rallied back, claiming the coo of a pigeon gave her a migraine.

All the while, the king himself eavesdropped from his window with great interest. For in those days, the It Girl possessed

ONE JELLY MEATSUIT

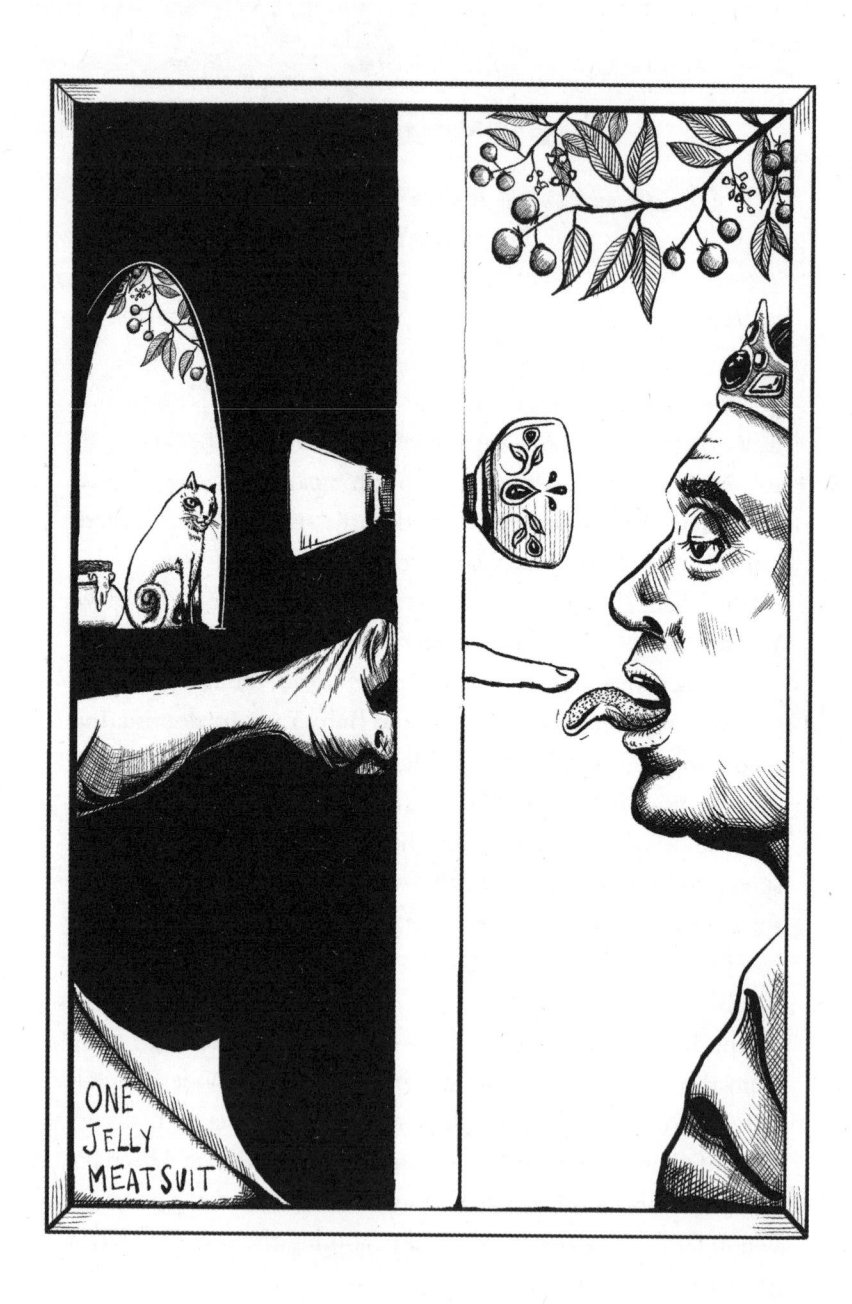

an overly sensitive nature. You were nothing if you weren't a beautiful, virginal, easily bruised princess!

Cosmo headlines of the day would read, "Princess of the Pea spills her sensitivity secrets; PLUS—how to ride him so hard you fall off all 20 mattresses!"

Hearing their exaggerated moans, the king fantasized about the beauty and virginality of the women lamenting so delicately below. Boy, did he let his imagination run wild! The longer he listened to the soft whispers of the women, the faster his motor ran. He peered out the window, but his dream girls were obscured by the tree canopy.

He called out, "My dear ladies, why so shy? Your chatter is as melodious as birdsong. Your breath carries through the air like the welcome touch of a spring breeze. Please show yourselves, and let a yearning man bask in the glow of your beauty!"

Lorena and Sofia exchanged a bewildered look. "Is that the king?" Sofia whispered.

Lorena smiled mischievously, and called back, "Oh, we could never, Your Grace. The summer sun would be far too harsh on our smooth white complexions."

Sofia gasped. "Sister, what are you doing?"

Lorena shrugged. "Having a bit of fun. Come on, play along!"

The king, meanwhile, had groaned audibly, imagining the deliciously pale skin of his beloveds.

A man once called me "deliciously pale" during a Hinge chat. I take my trauma, and transform it into ~Art.~

"Even the whitest lily craves a bit of sun now and then," he protested. "Let your king admire the jewels of his kingdom!"

Sophia shushed her sister, but Lorena would have none of it.

"Not today, Your Majesty!" she lilted. "You've caught us by surprise! We'd prefer to primp and pamper for your gaze!"

The two engaged in more repartee, with Lorena teasing the king and declining his requests to gaze upon their beauty, while Sophia wrung her hands with fear. The king came back to the window the next day, as did the sisters. He was persistent, and even trepidatious Sophia had to admit she enjoyed the attention. So they kept it up! They'd sneak under the tree before the sun could rise, and the king would lean out to laud them with saccharine compliments and beg for a look at their faces. Lorena would respond with a tittering voice and bashful rebuffs. It should have been harmless fun.

As the ruse went on, however, Sophia grew sick with worry. "We are playing with fire, sister!" she pressed. "What if he finds out? He'll have us imprisoned, at the very least!"

"He's the one who started this," Lorena breezed. "We haven't done anything wrong. He's making a lot of assumptions!"

Lorena wanted to keep the king hooked as long as possible. So she thought up a way to allow him a tiny glimpse at their bodies. The following day, when the king once again begged for an audience, she said, "At this time, the most we can offer you is the sight of a single finger. Come to our door in eight days' time and wait by the keyhole."

The king found this development exciting. He saw himself as a soldier encroaching on an enemy camp. First he'd take the finger; then he'd conquer the lips; then, at long last, savor the sweet victory of, um, planting his flag. While the king was strategizing sexy times, the old women launched a campaign of extreme finger beautification: They moisturized and oiled and sucked on their fingers to smooth them out. Lorena insisted that whoever had the most youthful-looking finger in eight days would present it to the amorous king.

At the end of the week, they compared digits. "I think it's got to be you," Lorena stated.

Sofia gasped. "Lorena, you got us into this mess! It should be your body on the line!"

"Oh, relax!" Lorena giggled. "I'll do all the talking!"

The king arrived promptly, extremely eager for his, um, fingering. Sofia lubed up her pointer one more time, then pressed her finger through the keyhole. She might as well have gone straight for the prostate; the king was overwhelmed with the hotness of Sofia's pampered extremity. It was the greatest catfish since Anne of Cleves airbrushed her portrait for Henry VIII.

The problem was the pretty little finger only made him crave more. He frenched Sofia's knuckle, coming up for air to cry, "Mesmerizing maiden, cease this unending game of hard-to-get! Do you have no pity for me? Why hole up in this miserable little flat, when you could stretch your languid limbs in the plush sheets of a king?"

You ever sleep with someone whose dirty talk was definitely more for them than for you? Oh sorry, he's not finished yet—

"Venus has turned the tables, making a sovereign beg on one knee at the throne of a young girl's beauty! Talk is proving cheap! Let me put my mouth to better work!"

Sofia and Lorena leaned in for a hushed conference. "What now?" Sofia hissed. "I'm kinda horny myself, but he's gonna be angry when he sees how low these tits hang!"

Lorena chewed a nail, no longer worried about her own manicure. "He talks as if we have a choice. But you and I both know that a king's request may as well be a command. I think you have to let him have his way."

This story is no doubt a cruel cautionary tale against vanity. But it's interesting that the tale's author, Giambattista Basile, points out the unbalanced power dynamic. The guy's got a talent for simultaneously victimizing and victim-blaming his characters.

"Me?" Sophia cried. "You are the one he's been flirting with! You show yourself!"

"He's already seen your finger. Besides," Lorena admitted, "you were always the greater beauty."

She pushed her sister from the door to speak through the keyhole. "Oh, Your Grace, you have been so good to lower yourself from the grandeur of your court to our modest hovel. How could I keep refusing you? I am willing to let you have your way with me, but I pride myself on my virtue. If I were to grant you access to the well of my womanhood, would you grant me the modesty of scheduling our visit for the dark of night? While I tremble at the thought of your hands upon me, I recoil at the idea of you taking in my nakedness under a harsh light." She tongued the keyhole for emphasis.

The king hastily agreed, and both the leader and his lady began preparing themselves for lovemaking. Sofia had a much greater effort. All the king did was douse himself in Ye Olde Drakkar Noir. But Sofia, with her sister's help, tugged and clamped the loose parts of her flesh to her back in order to lift her bosom and buttocks and everything else they could lift. They plucked and shaved every inch of flesh and teased the thin locks on top of her head. Then, late in the evening, Sofia donned a veiled cloak and knocked at the palace door.

The king's valet ushered the trussed old woman into the king's bedroom. The lights were put out, and Sofia was left alone. She disrobed and groped her way to the bed, slipping beneath the covers and lying on her back to conceal her DIY nip-and-tuck. She shivered as she heard the door click open and shut. The king's soft footsteps approached the bed. For luck, Sofia crossed her very sexy fingers.

As hard as the sisters had worked, it didn't take long for the king to realize he wasn't in bed with the supple youth he'd been expecting. His cologne overpowered Sofia's stench, but taste and touch betrayed her. She displayed a curious ratio of gum to teeth. Skin felt dry and delicate where it should feel lustrous and firm.

Not to mention whatever the fuck was happening on this lady's backside.

But the king made his bed, and now he had to lie with the woman in it. So he fantasized that he was schtupping the girl of his dreams. Once he'd finished, both lovers rolled over. The man soon heard loud snores next to him. He slipped out from under the sheets and lit an oil lamp. Like Psyche before him, he held it over his bedmate to reveal his sleeping lover.

Unfortunately for him, Sofia was no Cupid. The king recoiled with a cry, waking the old woman. He summoned his staff and flung a finger at Sofia, who pulled the sheets up frantically as guards poured into the bedchamber. "See what vile trickery has occurred tonight!" he cried. "I was led to believe I was taking a coy and winsome babe to bed. But all the while, an ancient, lascivious crone lay waiting to sink her claws into me. Give her the punishment she deserves: throw the old bitch out the window!"

Giambattista Basile is regarded as one of the first writers to popularize fairy tales as a literary form. He's a real hit-or-miss for me; his madcap plots loop around like a roller coaster, and his dialogue is vulgar and snappy. But the cost is his violent kings. His version of "Sleeping Beauty" is notorious for the rape of its title character.

Sofia channeled her sister's feistiness. She fought back, kicking, spitting, and even biting the men who lifted her out of the bed. "You made me come here!" she cried. "How could I refuse the king?" When that didn't work, she tried another tactic. "Besides, you wouldn't have had as much fun with a younger broad, sonny! I am ten times the lover I was when I was your age. You could learn a thing or two from me!"

Despite her fierce fight, the king's men thrust Sofia from the palace window. It was by pure luck that she didn't hit the ground. Her hair halted her fall, entangling her painfully in the canopy of the tree below. **(She must share DNA with Rapunzel!)**

As Sofia swayed in the breeze, a group of fairies passed through the garden. The sprites were sulking over a disagreement that this narrator is not privy to. **(And how I wish I was! French fairy tale writers are better at providing an elaborate fae backstory.)** As they rounded the corner and saw the pitiful old woman (now rotating slowly like a rotisserie chicken), the party fell into gales of laughter. Their melancholy was broken, so the fairies thanked Sofia for the lark with a bevy of gifts worthy of a princess's christening: They gave her youth, beauty, riches, and rank. They declared all would love her and great fortune would embrace her.

Sofia's evening had turned on its head. She no longer hung neglected from a tree like an out-of-season wind sock, but sat upon a velvet, fringed throne surrounded by servants and guards. A maid held a mirror to her face, and Sofia gasped. She looked every inch what the king believed he'd been wooing: a youthful maiden with dewy skin and thick, soft hair curling around her smooth shoulders. Her old rags were now damask and lace that pushed up her décolletage and snatched her enviable waistline. Jewels sparkled along her fine hands. "What the fuck just happened?" she cried. The curse tingled from her throat as sweetly as a bell.

Suddenly the king was before her in his pajamas. He threw himself at her feet. "My lady! I looked out my window to see what befell a dame who cruelly deceived me, when what should I see instead but your heavenly form gracing my humble avenue!"

Classic "neg the ex to flatter the new girl" tactics. (Plus, he's simultaneously negging the new girl too. He was ahead of his time in the worst way.)

"Pity me, my shining porcelain doll, my dove, triumph of Aphrodite herself! If your beguiling eyes see and your delicate ears hear, witness the lovesickness that has befallen this once-powerful and brutish king! Your auburn locks have wrapped around my heart like an iron chain; your penetrating eyes cut through me like a knife; your delectable rosy lips have pierced me with their thorns! If you have it in your heart to acknowledge a man far below your station, if you can find in yourself the mercy to relinquish your torturous hold on me, won't you unburden this prostrate fool by allowing me the glorious song of a single word from those plush lips?"

Sofia piped up, "Sure!" before the monarch launched into another weird and wordy sonnet. The king put on such a show, Sofia almost forgot that only thirty minutes before, the man had attempted to murder her. Then she remembered, and quickly agreed to be his wife, lest rejection trigger his temper.

Meanwhile, as far as Lorena knew, her sister had disappeared after walking through the king's door. She feared that they'd been found out, though no word of an execution reached their door. She stewed in guilt.

One day, she received an invitation. "*You're cordially invited to the wedding of the king and the coronation of his beautiful bride, the Queen Sofia?*" she read aloud in disbelief. It couldn't be! She hastily RSVP'd yes.

When she arrived at the wedding, Lorena was given a favored seat next to the new queen. She couldn't believe her eyes. She was looking at a version of her sister she hadn't seen in fifty years. Envy coursed through Lorena's varicose veins. The reception blurred into the background as she fixated on Sofia's young physique. The queen also could not get over her own appearance. She watched herself in any reflection that she could find, lifting her plate to smooth an eyebrow and run her tongue over her full lips.

"How could this be, Sofia?" Lorena asked as the first course was served. "How have you managed to turn back the clock?"

Sofia shushed her sister. "Now is not the time," she whispered. She wasn't so willing to let her sibling in on her secret. Besides, she hadn't forgotten that Lorena's machinations had nearly gotten her killed.

The king was intrigued by their conversation. Sophia told her husband that her sister was merely asking for some sauce. The king obliged with a flight of condiments. "Eat!" Sofia insisted.

But Lorena was consumed by curiosity. What was the source of Sofia's luck? She pushed food around on her plate. She kept tugging at Sofia's sleeve. "Tell me, girl! What did you do? I'm your sister! Don't I deserve to benefit from a similar makeover?"

Once again, Sofia shut her sister down. Her heart was hammering. "We. Will. Have. Time. To. Catch. Up. Later!" she said through her teeth. She smiled at the king as he tried to nose in again. "My sister is simply craving something sweet!" she explained. The king obliged with a tower of torte.

Tension continued to rise between the sisters, as Lorena's resentment grew and Sofia's nerves frayed. "I will not rest until you tell me how you managed this transformation!" Lorena hissed.

Sofia scrambled for an explanation that Lorena wouldn't dare try. "I skinned myself!" she replied acidly.

Lorena looked aghast. "All right, then," she muttered after a moment. "If that's what I must do, then that's what I must do. I'm not about to let you get all the glory. I'll find my own fortune. Now, if you'll excuse me," she added primly, "I need to take a dump."

Always the perfect excuse. No one asks follow-up questions; they've already received too much information.

Lorena scurried away from the table and out of the palace. Wasting no time, she traveled straight to the barber.

In Basile's day, barbers performed medical procedures like tooth-pulling and enemas in addition to haircuts. Truly top-to-bottom service.

Waving a bag of coins in his face, she barked, "I need you to skin me!"

The barber raised an eyebrow. "Sure, Grandma, let's get you to bed."

Lorena snapped, "I have my wits about me, you pipsqueak!" She shook her coins again. "There's fifty ducats here, so sharpen that razor and skin me!"

The barber poked his head out the door. "Does this old woman belong to anyone?" he called, looking both ways.

Lorena shoved the barber back and slammed the door shut behind her. "You listen to me, young man," she said. "I know what I want, and I speak my own mind. If you refuse me, you'll deny yourself the opportunity to serve a queen. Release me from this dusty skin sack, and I'll make you a barber to kings. A phoenix is waiting to rise from this pile of ash!"

The barber tried his best to get out of this squeamish service, but Lorena refused to leave until she'd gotten what she wanted. And so the barber acquiesced. He peeled the shriveled skin from Lorena's body like a bloody cucumber. Lorena gritted her teeth and bit back her cries. She was delirious with pain, but clung tightly to the vision of Sofia, assuring herself over and over, "Beauty requires pain. Beauty requires torture. It will be worth it to be young again."

By the time the barber reached her navel, the old woman's body could take it no longer. She expired right on the barber's bench, where, adding insult to her grievous injury, her last words were a long, fetid fart.

Morbid Moral: Envy will eat away at you, right down to the bone.

* * *

SOURCE: Giambattista Basile, "The Old Woman Discovered."

Check out Nancy Canepa's translation of *Tale of Tales*, as well as the work of Italo Calvino, for more fun (and less traumatizing) Italian fairy tales!

NO SMALL PEAT

Germany's "The Maid of Wildenloh"

The Clasen farmhouse was bustling with excitement; a cousin was getting married. The wedding was a short ride from their home in Wildenloh,* but Herr Clasen decided it was a good opportunity for a holiday. "Give the hands the day off, but have Johanna mind the house and animals," he told his wife.

Johanna was a relatively new hire at the farm, having joined the staff a few months before from her prior work on a nearby peat mine. She hoped to get her chores done with time to relax. First, she stacked some fresh peat by the oven for the following days' work.

Peat was a main source of fuel back when Lower Saxony was mostly bogland. Bogs all over Europe were rich with superstition and folklore, likely due to how dangerous they were to navigate, and how easily they preserved a body!

Next, she swept and mopped the floors and hearth, fed and milked the cows, and bolted the doors and windows shut. With-

---

* *Wildenloh is the setting of a few colorful legends: the land was created by a spiteful devil; a ghostly maiden wanders the bog; and the forest acts as a prison for sinners cast out by local clergy. "The Maid of Wildenloh" is associated with a real Wildenloh farmhouse, according to the version recorded in 1867 by Ludwig Strackerjan.*

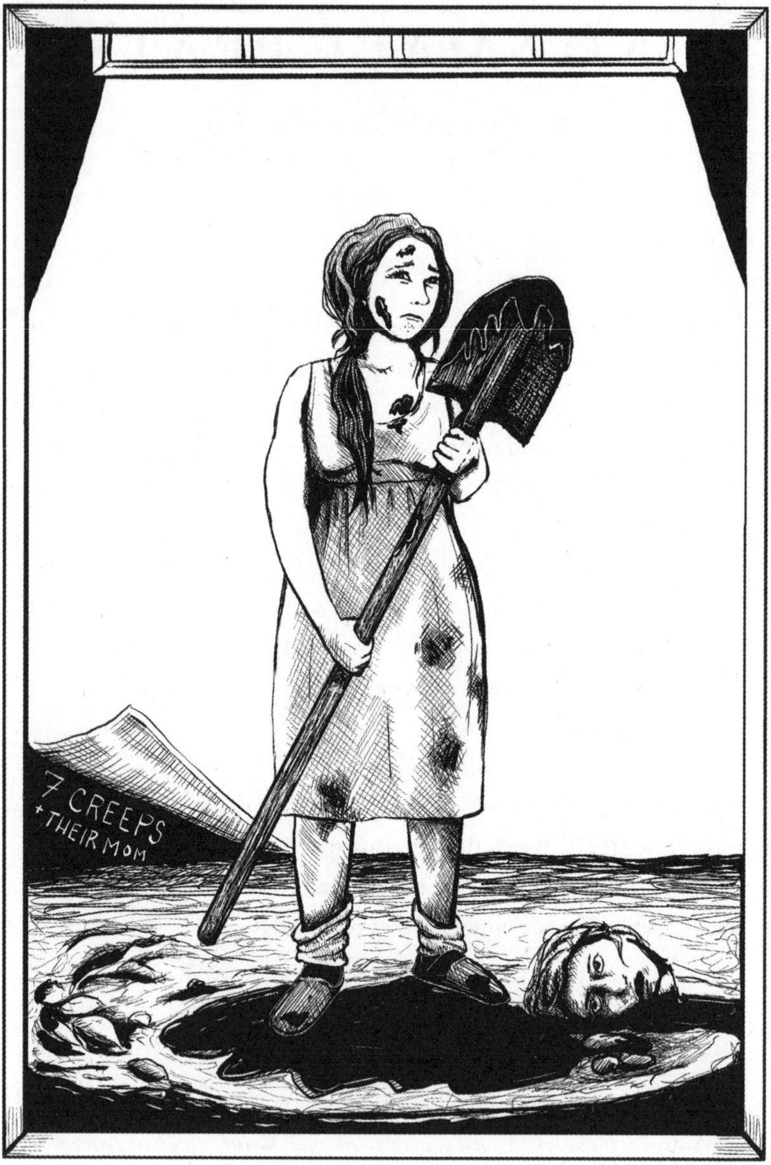
7 CREEPS
+ THEIR MOM

out food prep or childcare to worry about, she now had a couple hours to play Master of the House. She plucked the zither, tried on her mistress's dresses and jewelry for funsies, and, when it got too dark for anything else, planted her butt in their best chair, where she kicked up her feet and enjoyed a nip of the boss's brandy.

Late that night, Johanna lit a lantern and retired to her quarters in the barn attached to the back of the house. She'd only just hung up her wool dress when she heard a scuffle outside. The doors shook with a bang, as if someone had kicked them hard. The noise woke up the horses and sent the barn tabby racing past her door.

Johanna peered out of her room cautiously. The animals settled themselves, but the maid was on high alert. Presently, she heard a group of men softly speaking outside her own window. She jumped as the shutters rattled. The men were trying to break in.

Johanna heard the invaders try to force the kitchen window, then, failing that, move on to the next room. Frantically, she mentally traced her footsteps. She was sure she'd secured every point. Would that be enough to discourage the burglars? She hoped so. If they got in and she let them ransack the house, her employers might accuse her of being their accomplice.

She edged around the perimeter of the house, tracking the men. At one point, they split up. The house was large and low, with many entry points to cover. Johanna tracked the invaders by their voices and the torchlight flashing through the shutters. At last, when each vulnerable point had been tested, the lights and the voices converged back by the kitchen. Johanna leaned her ear as close as she dared to the window slat.

"It's locked tight," a voice said. "We'll have to force our way in."

"This is an old house," another man said, with an air of command. "We can dig under the foundation and worm in that way."

"I saw a light in one of the windows," another said.

"I've been watching the place all week," the leader said. "The family and all the men have left. If there is anyone home, it's only the maid. I think seven of us can handle her."

Johanna's pulse quickened. Seven men?

"What do we do if we find her?" a man asked.

There was a pause. "Whatever you fucking want," the leader said. The men laughed.

Johanna sucked in a terrified breath. But she set her jaw. *Not if I have anything to say about it.*

The most reproduced fairy tales cling to a prince saving the day, even though fairy tales have always featured self-sufficient women. "East of the Sun, West of the Moon" comes to mind. The Grimms write of self-saving women: in "The Robber Bridegroom" and "The Seven Ravens," among others. Most folks have never heard of those, though.

The group decided to dig under the opposite side of the barn. Johanna wagered they'd end up by the feed room. She jogged in that direction, stopping by the stables on her way. On one wall hung a row of tools. She assessed the lot quickly, settling on the one she'd be most confident handling: a sharp peat spade. Then she walked the wall of the house until she heard the scrape of a shovel against the stone foundation. There, she pressed herself against the wall, tightly clutching the spade's handle.

The barn was dark, but for moonlight beaming through the high windows above the main gate. It was always cool in the large space, but tonight was unusually chilly. Johanna, clothed only in her short shift, felt goose bumps up and down her bare flesh. But she kept her eyes steady on the floor next to her. Outside, the men took turns digging. It was a torturously slow process.

By a lucky twist of fate, four beams of moonlight shone through the window almost directly where the dirt floor began crumbling. Little by little, the ground gave way, until the metal of the men's shovel poked through. When a modest space was cleared, the men talked through a plan for once they got inside. Then one poked his head and torso through the hole, for a quick look around. He turned to the left, and saw Johanna's short, scuffed boots. They were the last things he saw before the maid brought the blade of the peat spade down hard on his neck.

Johanna flinched at the hot splatter of blood across her face. Then she got back to work. The blade had not cut cleanly, but a second quick, hard strike did the job. Johanna lifted the man's head out of the hole and batted it away. She dropped the shovel, and hurriedly scooped the corpse from his armpits, dragging him the rest of the way through the hole and then some. She dropped him a few yards away, before scurrying back to her post.

Eastern Europe is particularly rich with lady slayers: warrior queen Maria Morevna, Azerbaijan's Lady Nardan and Lady Nergiz, and "The Pirate Princess" make mincemeat of their enemies.

"Are you in, Karl?" came the voice of the leader.

Johanna dipped her voice as low into her chest as she could, and she muttered a short affirmative.

"Where should we meet you? That front door?"

Johanna prayed she was a better actor than she felt. "Just come in the way I did, it's faster."

There was a pause, but the leader said, "All right, what are the rest of you waiting for?"

The second man slid in and lost his head the same as the first. Johanna made short work of the third and fourth thieves too. By the time the fifth man got in, her muscles ached. The blade was slick with blood, and the hole began to pool with it as well. The sixth man registered the sticky mess, but not in time to save himself. Johanna rolled him onto the pile of bodies, his head dragging along by a length of sinew.

Hand-cutting peat is hard work. Even people who strength-train have commented on the body-breaking task. The turf is tough, and the cut pieces are heavy, requiring core strength and balance to move them without breakage. Johanna is much better prepared to massacre six men in a row than many of us.

Johanna waited tensely for the seventh man, who didn't appear as fast as the others. "Everyone okay in there?" he asked tersely. It was the leader of the band.

Exhausted, Johanna grunted a yes.

After what felt like a lifetime, the seventh man emerged from the hole headfirst. His pale blond hair flashed bright in the moonbeams. He cursed, spying the literal bloodbath he was crawling into, and quickly pulled back. Johanna nearly missed him, but for a piece of his scalp caught by the spade. The man howled but escaped with his head mostly intact.

When Herr Clasen and his family arrived home the next afternoon, they found Johanna pacing by the gate, waiting to bring the horses inside. Up close, the family took in her haggard face, shaking hands, and bloodstained shoes.

She greeted the farmer quickly. "I can explain!"

* * *

A YEAR LATER, the Clasens were celebrating another wedding. But this time, it was Johanna's.

The maid became a bit of a local celebrity, after word got out that she single-handedly defended her lord's home from half a dozen bandits with just a shovel and a lot of muscle. Her employer ordered her a couple of new dresses, gave her a bigger room in the house proper, as well as her own horse in the stables. The ruling prince even commended her bravery. Some effort was made to track down the seventh bandit, but there was only one story that corroborated his whereabouts. Strangely enough, it was at the same wedding the Clasens had attended. Late that night, after the cousin and his bride had retired to their chambers, and only the late-partying guests remained around the fire, a blond man had shown up with a bandage on his head. The man seemed to be drunk on arrival, but he drank another three tankards of ale, the whole time singing to himself:

Heigh-ho,
The Maid of Wildenloh,
Now she waits for the seventh man!

It rhymes better in German.

By the time authorities put two and two together, the man had skipped town.

The Clasen family was grateful to Johanna for her heroism, but she felt far from triumphant. She had been set to marry a cobbler's son, but his fiancée's brute strength unnerved him, and he called off the engagement. Many of her friends and peers were intimidated by her—or perversely fascinated, which was sometimes worse. She grew withdrawn and nervous. With one of the bandits still on the loose, she found herself fearful of leaving the house. She refused to guard the property alone again.

If friends thought her story was a little much, they never heard the folktale of a maid from the Upper Hartz who defended herself against a dozen men with a butcher knife! She was similarly shunned. Me? I would love a wife who could slaughter a football team in one fell swoop.

It wasn't just that others looked at her strangely now. Johanna herself found that when she was around other people, she couldn't control her moods and was quick to anger or bouts of melancholy. The only person who understood was her employer. Herr Clasen had served in the military as a younger man, and he recognized her trauma in his own. He made it plain that Johanna had a home there as long as she'd like, and she assumed she'd spend her spinster days working his fields.

It wasn't until the Clasens befriended a man named Herr Lechner that Johanna saw the chance for a life outside the Clasens' employ. The man was a wealthy trader from the city, who came to hunt and play cards with the family. When he learned the maid's famed story, he became enraptured with her. One night, a month or so into their new social routine, Herr Lechner asked to sit down with Johanna and her employers. "I wish to marry Johanna," he began bluntly.

Frau Clasen clapped her hands, excited for a happy turn of events. But Johanna was shocked. At one time, she would have loved to skip a few rungs on the social ladder. But trust was harder these days, and the man was a complete stranger.

Seeing her hesitance, Herr Clasen spoke up. "What a lovely surprise," he said. "I assume you've brought us some references?"

Dating apps never killed romance. We've always taken an administrative approach!

The trader passed the farmer a small bundle of paperwork. He turned to Johanna. Herr Lechner was a tall and burly man, with a perpetually amused look to him. His eyes twinkled as he took in Johanna's flushed cheeks. "I fear it's not looking good for me," he joked.

Silence stretched among the group, until Johanna realized they were waiting for her to speak. "I'm sorry. I'm just so taken aback."

Herr Clasen stacked the papers up neatly. "Everything here looks good to me, but I'm sure you'll understand if we take the evening to consider your proposal." They rose, and the farmer gestured to his wife. "Darling, why don't you take Johanna for a walk while I show Herr Lechner out?"

The farmer's wife and the maid took a stroll to the chicken coop. The two scattered feed for a bit, until Frau Clasen broke the silence. "Most young women would be jump for a chance at this match. Do you not like Herr Lechner?"

"I do not *know* Herr Lechner," Johanna said softly. "It's not that I am ungrateful. I just don't understand his interest in me."

Frau Clasen took her arm. "Not all men are silly little boys like those around here. I expect Herr Lechner sees the value in having such a hardworking, loyal spouse. He has no need for money, so your lack of dowry isn't a problem. He is well connected, he has spoken fondly of his mother, which I consider a good sign. He's handsome, you cannot deny that. I think this is a wise move, Johanna. Besides," she went on candidly, "he may be your only option."

That hit a nerve. Johanna nodded. "All right, then. I'll accept."

This is a pretty progressive folktale, but if you expect any old story to pass the Bechdel test, I have bad news.

The wedding took place on the Clasens' farm. Johanna had no family to speak of, and neither did Herr Lechner; just his mother, who was too infirm to travel. Frau Clasen commissioned a blue brocade kirtle and gown and styled Johanna's dusky hair in coils under a silk veil. Johanna didn't recognize herself. The whole situation felt unreal.

Despite the horrific memory this house held, Johanna was reluctant to leave it. The ceremony flew by, and before long she sat next to this strange man she was to call her husband, in a modest carriage pulled by two stunning red Hessian horses. The ride was quiet. Johanna didn't have much to say, and Herr Lechner wasn't talkative himself. The cart was so still, the breeze from the window so cool, and the rhythm of the horses so steady, that Johanna nodded off against the cushioned seat.

When Johanna woke up, twilight had fallen. She had no idea how long they had been riding. All around them was marshland, with no property that she could see. She stole a glance at Herr Lechner, who'd taken off his hat and unbuttoned his jerkin. He was studying her with a small smile on his face. "You were dreaming," he told her.

Johanna wondered what she'd been muttering. She considered herself lucky when she couldn't recall the visions of her sleep. "I'm sorry," she said, blushing. "It was an exciting day."

"No matter." Herr Lechner patted her knee. She stiffened, and he laughed. "Too bold?"

Johanna tried to relax. "Not at all." She felt silly pushing him away. When they reached the house, she'd get to know him more intimately than she'd known any other man. Perhaps she should ease into her new role as Frau Lechner. She slid an inch closer to her husband and offered her hand. He took it, studying its lines and fingering the calluses on her palm. Once again, Johanna wondered why such a man wanted a workingwoman to call his wife.

The coach grew dark as the sun disappeared behind the tree line. Johanna lost feeling in her fingers, but Herr Lechner held tight to her hand. She spoke up. "Herr Lechner—I mean, um, Georg... how much longer? I was under the impression you didn't live far. But we've been riding for hours."

"We're a little farther out," he answered vaguely. "You might relax, you know." He slid an arm around her waist and pulled her even closer. "How is this?"

Johanna stiffened. "Come, now," Herr Lechner cajoled. "Don't be shy. I'd love my wife to run her fingers through my hair. Would you do that for me, Johanna?"

A cloud allowed a sliver of moonlight into the carriage. It flashed off of Herr Lechner's pale hair. Johanna tucked a strand behind his ear, then combed through his locks more thoroughly. He leaned his head to hers, and as he did, her fingers brushed over a bald indentation in his skull.

Johanna felt a horrible recognition in her gut and pulled back. But Herr Lechner slid with her, cornering her between his bulky frame and the carriage wall.

"You've found my injury, I see," he murmured into her ear. "A few years back, a maid clipped me there as I ducked into her master's house to nick his horses. I never forgot her. How could I, when the woman killed my six brothers as ruthlessly and thoroughly as my butcher preps the poultry?"

In an Italian variant of this tale, a princess cuts off a home invader's hand, later revealing his stump when she pulls off his glove. In Greece's "The Robber Captain," the heroine kills thirty-nine out of forty thieves! In Russia, she dismembers one robber, bags up his pieces, and tosses them to the rest of the bandits, claiming it's their booty! Hot damn, where is my slasher/historical fiction epic of this, Hollywood?

Johanna stilled as Lechner slid his large hand around her throat. Where she expected a squeeze, he caressed. She shuddered. "If you're going to kill me, just do it already!"

Lechner was charmed by her spirit. "I could, of course. But I am not the only one avenging my brothers. Besides . . ." He pressed his thumb into the hollow of her throat. "I want to watch you go the same way my brothers did. A neck for a neck."

They rode tensely for another half an hour. Lechner kept his air of amusement, even as he held Johanna in his vise-like grip. Here and there, he sang to himself.

Heigh-ho,
The Maid of Wildenloh,
Now she's met the seventh man.

A large manor house finally appeared over a hill. It was mostly dark, but firelight flickered in the downstairs windows. The coachman drove them right up to the front door. Lechner pulled Johanna out of the carriage, twisting her arm behind her painfully. He threw a purse at the coachman. "Tie up the horses, then begone," he commanded.

He led her inside, to a large open kitchen. A matron tended the fire. "So, this is the famous Maid of Wildenloh," she greeted Johanna snidely. "Welcome to the family, dear. A pity we won't get to know each other better."

"Hello, Mother." Lechner pushed Johanna toward a dingy butcher block. A freshly sharpened hatchet gleamed from the top of it.

Nineties girl group TLC mocked men who live with their mothers, but I'd argue the prevalence of serial-killing mama's boys did more damage to male caretakers' love lives than "No Scrubs."

Johanna took in the room. "What's that?" she asked sharply, noticing a large iron cauldron over the fire, bubbling with oil.

"To cook you in," the matron said plainly.

Johanna's fight response kicked in. She stomped hard on Lechner's foot. He yelped and released her arm but caught her dress before she could run. They struggled. He grabbed her by the hair. "It will be quicker if you accept your fate, my dear," Lechner hissed.

Johanna choked back a sob. But she went limp and allowed herself to be pushed down to her knees before the block. "Wait!" she cried. She looked up at Lechner pleadingly. "Won't you let me remove my gown? My mistress had it made specially for me. I'd hate to see it soiled."

He snorted and pushed her head down. But his mother spoke up. "We could sell it!"

"Fine," Lechner said. "I guess it wouldn't be a proper wedding night if I didn't get to undress my wife."

Back on her feet, Johanna steadied herself with calming breaths as Lechner unlaced her outer gown. He pulled it over her head and draped it on one arm as she stepped out of her skirt. His gaze lingered over the curves exposed by her light smock. Johanna breathed deeply into her chest, the swell of it straining against the neckline. Lechner was momentarily distracted by her form—and Johanna took advantage.

She threw her skirt at Lechner's head. He cursed as the voluminous fabric entangled him. Johanna heaved the hatchet out of the block. When Lechner surfaced from the silk, his furious eyes caught Johanna's before she sank the blade in his throat.

"No!" the matron wailed as her seventh son fell. The woman rushed Johanna, who dodged her, running across the kitchen. The two women tussled, until the hatchet blade caught the matron's side. When she bent over painfully, Johanna shoved her away, horrified as the bandits' mother toppled into the boiling oil, upending the cauldron.

Johanna ran from the house as the fire caught the spilled oil and spread through the kitchen. The horses were hitched to the fence. Johanna sliced through the ties with the hatchet and flung the weapon aside. She mounted the driver's seat hastily and snapped the reins. The horses took off with a whinny, leaving the manor house to burn.

As the wind whipped through her curls, Johanna felt lighter than she had in ages. She drove the animals hard, promising them bushels of oats and apples if they got her safely home. Soon she recognized the lay of the land and eased the reins.

Hours later, as she rounded the road onto Herr Clasen's property, she stood and waved. The farmer was in a rocking chair outside with his evening pipe. He stopped puffing and rose in awe.

Johanna stood in the driver's seat in a blood-spattered petticoat, hair as unruly as the horses. She waved again and sang out:

Heigh-ho,
The Maid of Wildenloh!
She finally got the seventh man!

* * *

SOURCE: Jürgen Hubert, *Sunken Castles, Evil Poodles: Commentaries on German Folklore.*

For more German folklore beyond the Grimms, check out my source listed above, as well as Hubert's anthology *Lurkers at the Threshold: 100 Ghost Tales from German Folklore.*

Part 5

CRAPPILY EVER AFTER

*Shit happens!
Even in fairy tales.*

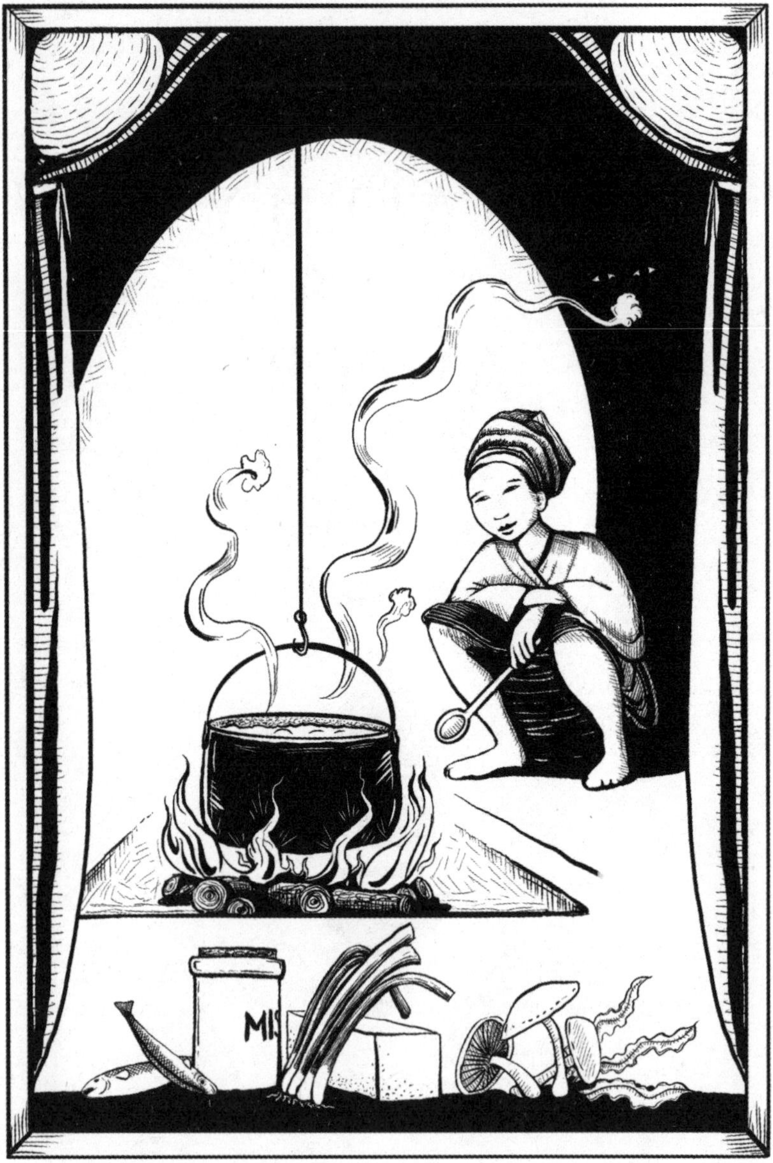
MIS

GOOD SOUP

A Japanese Folktale

Long ago, there lived a lonely peasant named Minakata. Minakata was a hard worker and a kind man, but poor, a little homely, and not much of a conversationalist.

Just an average guy who, like many sitcom men after him, will somehow end up with Miss Universe.

Rather than pursuits of love, which seemed beyond his reach, Minakata pursued the simple things in life: honest work, and caring for the land and the people he shared it with.

He worked at a bait shop by the sea, where he spent the time between customers keeping the coast clean and protecting its creatures. He never fed off the sea more than he needed and wasn't wasteful. He helped the timid seagulls get food when the more aggressive birds bullied them. He taught the local children how to respect animals and shooed away the little jerks who destroyed the flora and harassed the fauna.* The locals found it amusing that their neighbor seemed closer to marine life than to another human being. "Maybe he'll settle down with a nice crab someday," they'd whisper, chuckling beneath their caps.

One day, a dickish kid dug up all the clams in the cove below Minakata's bait shop and threw them all over the beach, see-

---

* *The Japanese philosophy of mottainai is the practice of avoiding wasteful use of resources. This can include respecting the earth and its creatures, in addition to our modern idea of "reduce, reuse, recycle!"*

ing how far he could make the shellfish curve across the sand. Minakata retrieved each one and placed them back in their habitat. This was such an ordinary thing for Minakata to do that he hardly remembered it by the time he ate his evening soup.

But the next morning, he found a surprise awaiting him. A beautiful woman stood at his door. She wore a silvery robe over a pale pink shift, and she smiled broadly when Minakata set eyes on her.

"Can I help you?" he asked in confusion.

The woman blushed sweetly. "I've come to be your wife, if you'll have me."

Minakata looked over his shoulder. *She couldn't be talking to me*, he thought. But he was the only man in the house. "Is this a joke?"

"Not at all," the woman assured him. "My name is Asa. You are always so kind to the creatures of the sea. You deserve a good wife, so I offer myself! What do you think?"

Minakata smiled back. "I think it's my lucky day!"

Japan has a varied category of folktales that feature the hero showing kindness to an animal, which leads to romance. In one, the peasant rehabilitates a stork. In another, the peasant offers shelter to a frog. Ladies love an animal ally!

He invited Asa inside, and immediately she began bustling around as if she'd lived there for years. She gathered supplies for a fire, depositing them in the sunken irori, and picked up a kettle to get some tea started. "Do you keep your miso inside or out?" she asked. "I'd like to have dinner ready when you get home."

Minakata gestured to one side of the hut. "I keep it outside, in the shady corner."

Asa thanked him and reorganized his food stocks. "Don't worry about me!" she said, shooing him away. "Have a good day at the shop!"

That night when Minakata arrived home, he almost walked right in as usual. Then he remembered: he was married now! He greeted Asa from the doorstep and waited for her to allow him inside. When she pulled back the noren, the tantalizing scent of home cooking wafted through. Minakata eagerly sat down by the hearth for dinner. He was surprised when Asa served him a bowl of miso soup, much like the basic stock he made for himself. He took a sip, and almost rolled his eyes at how delicious it was. "You made this out of what I had on hand?"

Asa bowed her head. "I had everything I needed."

"It's so good!" Minakata had to avoid guzzling it too quickly. It was soup to be savored. "How do you make it? You must do something differently than me."

Asa tutted and waved a finger at him. "I've just arrived, and already you want me to give away my family's recipes!"

Minakata blushed. He realized he was being invasive. "Thank you for this delicious meal, Asa!"

Despite their quickie marriage, the young couple got along well. For the next week, life was steady and quiet as before, but Minakata now had Asa's companionship to look forward to at the end of the day. Not to mention that things had leveled up in the meal department.

But Minakata couldn't get the bizarre conversation about the soup out of his mind.

Dude, this babe literally showed up at your doorstep and makes you yummy dinner. Never look a gift-wife in the mouth!

He pressed her again the following week. "I don't understand how you were able to make something so delicious out of so little. Is it a cooking technique?"

Asa shook her head pleasantly. "I'd prefer not to discuss it."

The third week, he tried to let the meal go by without pestering her. But as she cleaned up, he attempted a sneakier tactic. "What if tomorrow we made dinner together? Then you could show me how you make it."

Asa's smile vanished. "That is not necessary. Leave me to my work, please, as I leave you to yours. No more questions!"

Another common plot in this tale type: The wife asks for privacy in completing a curious task. In the stork version, she produces a rare, valuable fabric. In the frog version, she forbids him from meeting her family. This tale teaches listeners to respect women's boundaries, especially in the domestic sphere. The side effect of isolating domesticity to women, of course, is male refrigerator blindness.

Minakata realized the only way he'd get answers was to sleuth. The following day, he gave Asa a kiss goodbye and left for the bait shop. But he came home earlier than usual, hiding himself in a small cluster of trees within view of the hut.

He watched as Asa came outside to scoop miso out of their underground pot. She plucked green onions from a nearby clearing, dropping those and fresh mushrooms into her apron. The process seemed mundane, from where he was watching. When Asa reentered the hut, Minakata waited until he smelled the charcoal of the fire. He tiptoed as close to the hut's door as he dared, peering through the slit in the noren.

Asa was squatting by the hearth, adding ingredients to the pot and stoking the fire. Then he saw her lift the pot off its hook and place it on the dirt floor. She straddled the pot and lifted her skirt. Minakata gasped as his wife straight-up pissed in the pot of soup.

In Fanny Hagin Mayer's translation of this tale, folklorist Yanagita Kunio writes, "[The wife] climbed onto the edge of the bowl

and did something dirty in it." It's fun to be a folklore detective in such cases, brainstorming which body fluid would make the most sense here, and/or be the grossest.

Asa replaced the pot over the fire and stirred. Then she took a sip and nodded.

This was too much for Minakata. He burst inside, accidentally pulling the curtained door off its hanger. "What do you think you're doing? Have you been feeding me your piss every night since you've been here?"

Asa flushed. "You should be at work!" she cried.

"What kind of answer is that?" Minakata thought about the soup and gagged. He gulped water from the bucket.

"You shouldn't require an explanation at all!" Asa fretted. "This is unlike you, Minakata. I thought you'd honor your wife with the same respect you show your work and the island."

Her husband laughed caustically. "How can I respect a woman who urinates in my dinner?"

Asa's nostrils flared. "Do I come to the bait shop and critique your work?"

"That is different!" Minakata scoffed.

"No, it isn't!" Asa tried to keep calm by cleaning up.

"No more of this," Minakata ordered. He took the pot out of her hand and tossed the soup into the weeds. Asa gaped at him. He gestured to the doorway. "I want you to leave, right now!"

Asa held her ground. "Minakata, I've been a good wife. You're jumping to conclusions—about a situation you know nothing about."

Her husband was firm. "Gather your things and go!"

Asa drew in a trembling breath but squared her shoulders. She arrived with nothing, so she simply headed for the door. As she crossed the threshold, she turned back. "It's clam juice," she said bitterly.

"*What* is clam juice?" Minakata responded in bewilderment.

"Clam juice is what makes the soup so flavorful," Asa explained.

Then, in front of Minakata's eyes, the woman's form began to morph. She shrank, smaller and smaller, until she was no longer human. She'd transformed into a clam.

Clam as a euphemism for lady parts is an international tradition. Japan goes so far as to use several varieties of clam to describe a woman's parts, depending on her age or her, um, color. I appreciate the specificity.

With as much dignity as a mollusk could muster, she dragged herself away, grumbling softly inside her shell.

✳ ✳ ✳

SOURCE: *The Yanagita Kunio Guide to the Japanese Folk Tale*, translated and edited by Fanny Hagin Mayer.

Want more Japanese fairy tales? Check out my source above, as well as *Japanese Tales of Lafcadio Hearn* from the Oddly Modern Fairy Tales series.

THE STENCH OF EMBARRASSMENT

A Tale from Arabian Nights*

Three hundred and fifty-three nights. Or was it three hundred and fifty-four? Either way, it made up roughly one year of stories. That number was far less than the number of women killed in revenge by the kingdom's cuckolded ruler. But at least it granted one year of desperately needed respite to a kingdom in perpetual mourning for its executed women.

1001 Nights is an aspirational number; no original documents contain that many stories, nor a conclusion to the frame tale. Some translators attempted to "complete" the collection by stuffing whatever area folklore they could find into the piece. This is one of those tales.

Shahrazad had lost track of how many tales she'd told to stall her own death, and those of future brides. At first she kept careful records. She had to, as the web of stories she wove became larger and more entangled. Yes, she'd finished the story of the ill-

---

* 1001 Nights, *or* Arabian Nights, *is broadly assembled from Persian, Indian, and Arab cultures and has a sprawling, complicated history. The most popular collections in the West today were mostly developed in Syria and Egypt. No adaptation includes the same set of stories (except for a few crossovers). The anthology and individual stories have been revised, reorganized, censored, and uncensored again and again by both Arab and non-Arab collectors.*

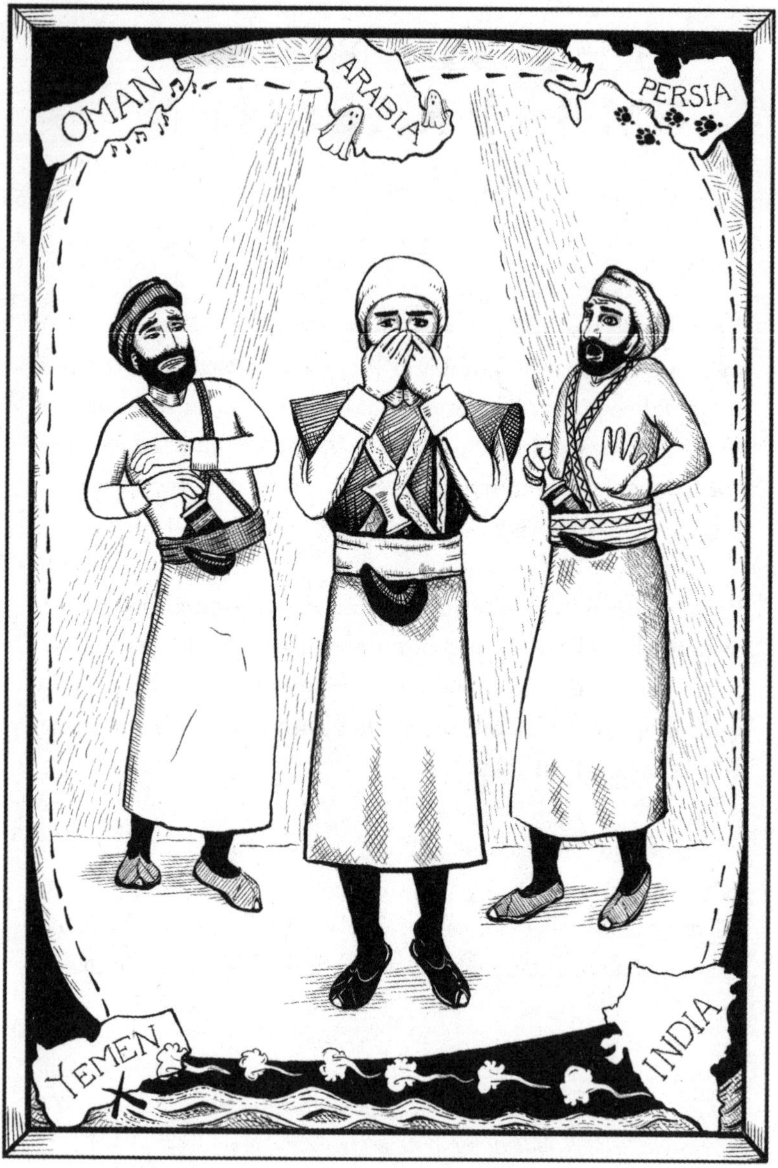
OMAN
ARABIA
PERSIA
YEMEN
INDIA

fated parrot, but where did she stand with the fisherman's narrative she began three nights before? She finished two of the three sisters' tales last week, but perhaps she should stretch out the third sister's story with an amusing fable . . .

This nesting doll of stories is a master class in literary edging.

When she became pregnant, Shahrazad considered taking a break from her nightly tale-telling. The heir would surely provide a stay of execution—at least through the child's early years.* Still, she couldn't trust that a child alone would protect her or the women she worked to save. So she kept the stories coming.

Her husband didn't seem pressed about it. Sometimes she wondered if she'd finally cracked open his hard heart. But until he repealed his decree to kill every woman he wed, this wasn't a risk she was willing to take. So here she was, nearly a year in, readying to spin number . . . three hundred and fifty-six?

"If you aren't too weary, will you pick up the story you began last night? The one about the wedding of Abu Hasan?" Dunyazad asked that evening. Her patient, loyal sister visited every night, in case it was her sister's last. The three developed a routine: the king took his pleasure from Shahrazad, then Dunyazad would join them for storytime.

In many portrayals, poor Dunyazad is literally chilling at the foot of the bed while her sister gets boinked. Her loyalty knew no bounds.

Dunyazad had taken over as secretary of the stories after the king's doctors had recommended bedrest for the final trimester. As the queen changed into her nightgown and primped for her

---

* *The Quran recommends breastfeeding children for two years.*

husband, Dunyazad would remind her sister where she'd left off the night before. In some ways, their evenings together reflected their time as children, sharing stories long after they were supposed to be in bed. Though they never imagined back then that these stories would be the only thing keeping them alive.

I think we'd all like to go back to a time before we knew our siblings have sex.

"I'm happy to continue Abu Hasan's tale," Shahrazad said. "Where did I leave off?"

Her husband spoke up. "We left the merchant on the final night of his wedding, about to enjoy the feast." His eagerness reminded her of a schoolboy, so different from the tyrant she met. "You said, 'One brief moment would make this wedding the event of the century.'"

"Ah yes!" Shahrazad's eyes twinkled as she began tonight's tale . . .

* * *

Let us return to Abu Hasan's homeland of Yemen, and join him for the delectable wedding feast . . .

The groomsmen, over a thousand of them, gathered in Abu Hasan's great hall.* They lounged on carpets and cushions around the expansive spread of meat and delicacies. The hall was stuffed from end to end with people and food. Enormous bowls of maraq and saltah steamed aromatically, punctuated by mile-high piles of mandi. The sheep population was nearly extinct after the occasion, such was the generosity and bounty of the host. An entire

---

* *Traditional Yemeni wedding celebrations are segregated by gender and robustly attended. Even your enemies forgive you for a day to celebrate your wedding.*

grove's worth of olives threatened to tumble from their platters, and columns of lahoh mimicked the tall columns of the hall. You'd think the leftovers would overwhelm, but no—not a bite was wasted on this momentous night.

After the feast, the men retired to the veranda to drink tea and chew qat under the stars. The kingdom's best poets recited romantic verses, and the men danced joyfully to the melody of a dozen lute players. At long last, the music stilled, as the time arrived for Abu Hasan to retire to the side of his beautiful bride.

Abu Hasan, sprawled out on a velvet chaise, laid a hand over his heart. "Before I depart, please allow me a word, my beloved family." He smoothed out his embroidered thobe and stood, raising his hands magnanimously. He opened his mouth to speak, but his bowels had other plans. The hush of the crowd was broken when his body released an extended, trumpeting fart.

The entire company gawked as the never-ending squelch echoed across the veranda. The noise went on so long, one could have recited the Al-Baqara a dozen times over, and still the groom's behind would be groaning. At last, the noxious noise ceased, but his humiliation was far from over. For now the odor permeated the party. Its pungency hit the company in waves, raising an army of white handkerchiefs to noses as each man surrendered to the smell.

Abu Hasan stared off into the distance, avoiding two thousand wide eyes blinking at him. A few coughs punctuated the silence. Then the giggles started, though where they originated was impossible to decipher. The laughter spread and grew into guffaws. The groom cleared his throat, and the crowd quieted. But he couldn't remember a single thing he was going to say. He blurted out, "Excuse me, I need to relieve myself!"

Uproarious laughter followed. He ran from the people's mirth, cringing not only for the fart itself but for the obviously fake excuse too. His attendants tried to intercede, but he waved them off, unable to look even his servants in the eye. He hurried from the patio into the banquet hall, and then sped to the outhouses beyond. But he didn't stop there. Rather, he continued to the stable. There, he saddled his mare and galloped away in a cloud of dust and humiliation.

"Fartlore," a term likely coined by Mary and Herbert Knapp in 1976, has a long lineage. In Ireland and Germany, stories flourish about men tricking the devil with their farts; in Korea, a fellow called General Pumpkin saves a monastery with his powerful toot and another young woman uses her sonic blast to knock fruit out of trees. The Innu of Canada have a god who speaks to us through our farts (if only we could understand him).

He did not stop until he reached the harbor. He drove his animal so hard, I have to assume the poor thing expired on arrival! At the docks, Abu Hasan boarded a boat to India, only relaxing once the coastline of Yemen disappeared.

I need a rebuttal to this story from the jilted bride's POV! What if, simultaneously, she emitted a monumental burp, and fled from her own humiliation? What a tragedy that would be, never knowing they were kindred spirits.

Abu Hasan made a new life for himself in Calicut, where he befriended Arabs with connections to the king. The ruler took to him so well that he was promoted to the King's Guard. Abu Hasan threw himself into the role, protecting the king happily for ten years.

But he grew homesick. He missed the colorful cities jutting out of the Haraz Mountains and fishing in the turquoise waters of Aden's beaches. He longed to eat a meal from the street carts of Shibam and wet his feet in the green reservoirs of Shabwah. And then there was the beautiful wife he'd left behind! His longing frequently brought him to tears. Surely the last decade had erased the memory of his disastrous wedding?

Abu Hasan decided it was safe to return to his homeland. Of course, it's much harder to face your past sins than it is to run away from them. So, he took his time, distracting himself along the way with adventures. He faced man-hungry lions in Persia and soul-thirsty ghouls in Arabia; he fell in love with an enslaved singer in Oman, where he became the protector of a magical amulet; finally, he landed in Kawkaban, the city he'd called home. He disguised himself in the cloth of a beggar, hiding in villages to gather information. What had he missed in the years he was gone? Did he see any familiar faces in town? Most importantly, did anyone remember his stinky exit?

Abu Hasan wandered the city undercover for about a week. No one mentioned the incident. Perhaps they had moved on. He comforted himself by imagining that they'd never held any contempt for him in the first place! Then, one night as he sat outside a modest hut by the marketplace, two adolescent girls emerged from a nearby alley, and ran past him into the hut. Hasan heard them chatting excitedly. "Mama!" one called out. "My friend wants to read my fortune, but she needs to know more about the night of my birth. Can you tell the story?"

"Of course, my child!" a woman replied. "You were born on a memorable night indeed. For the same night you arrived was the night Abu Hasan farted!" The two children burst into laughter, and the mother went on to tell the story with juicy sound effects.

Men of fairy tales are most afraid of women laughing at them; women in fairy tales are most afraid of getting their limbs

chopped off, their eyes gouged out, or being cooked in cauldrons. Must be nice, Abu Hasan!

At those words, Abu Hasan rose and walked away. He walked out of the market, walked past the city limits, and walked all the way to the west coast, where he boarded a ship to Egypt. He vowed never to return to Yemen, where they not only recalled his humiliation with clarity, it had been elevated to a national holiday.

Folklorist Gershon Legman tracked the evolution of this tale in classic literature as well as colloquial humor. Mark Twain adapted it for *1601*, setting it in the court of Queen Elizabeth I. In the old-time joke book *Country Tom's Complete Jester*, the humiliated lover becomes the bride, though the stink she makes on the dance floor works out much better for her than it does for poor Abu Hasan.

* * *

THE KING laughed until tears ran from his eyes. "You are an impeccable narrator, my dear. One day, our child will love that one." He stopped short, as if he'd said too much.

Shahrazad felt a glimmer of hope. Still, she laid her trap to ensure another night's survival. "If only he knew the foolishness he would fall into in Cairo, perhaps he would not be so quick to leave." She stifled a modest yawn. "But that story will have to unravel another day."

As the king began to nod off, Dunyazad took Shahrazad's hand. "You did it again, dear sister. Another delightful story, how I wish they would never end!"

The sisters quietly bade each other good night. As the storytelling queen slipped off to sleep, she sent a small prayer of thanks to Abu Hasan, who cut the cheese and saved a life.

* * *

SOURCE: *The Book of the Thousand Nights and a Night: A Plain and Literal Translation of the Arabian Nights Entertainments*, translated by Richard Burton.

Interested in *Arabian Nights*? While I love this story, I do not recommend its source due to Burton's overt-exoticism and fetishization of Arab life. Instead, try the anthologies edited by Mushin Mahdi or Paulo Lemos Horta.

IT SNOT WHAT YOU THINK

KOREA'S "ORIGIN OF THE COMMON COLD"

Once upon a time, there was a prince born with two dicks.

The penis frequently thrusts itself into folklore to amplify masculinity and explore anxieties around it. In the medieval satire "Das Nonnenturnier," a nunnery brawls over who gets to keep a loose penis that appears at their door. In an Ashanti folktale, Anansi brags that his schlong is longer than "77 poles fastened together" (only to claim it's out for repair when his companion wants to see it in action). Dirty jokes from *Arabian Nights* to Appalachia feature men wishing for bigger bulges but accidentally wishing them gone; and that's just the tip! Of the iceberg, that is.

While some folks may fantasize about doubling their pleasure, the prince found his two tools to be more of a curse than a blessing. As he grew into adulthood, he hoped beyond hope that he had a soulmate out there just for him. When his parents reached out to matchmakers, the prince had one specific qualifier: he wished to marry a woman with two vaginas. I suppose you could say he wasn't looking for a soulmate so much as he was looking for a hole-mate.

Wait, don't go! You've gotten this far, why abandon my book now because of one vaginal pun? (Technically a two-vaginal pun.)

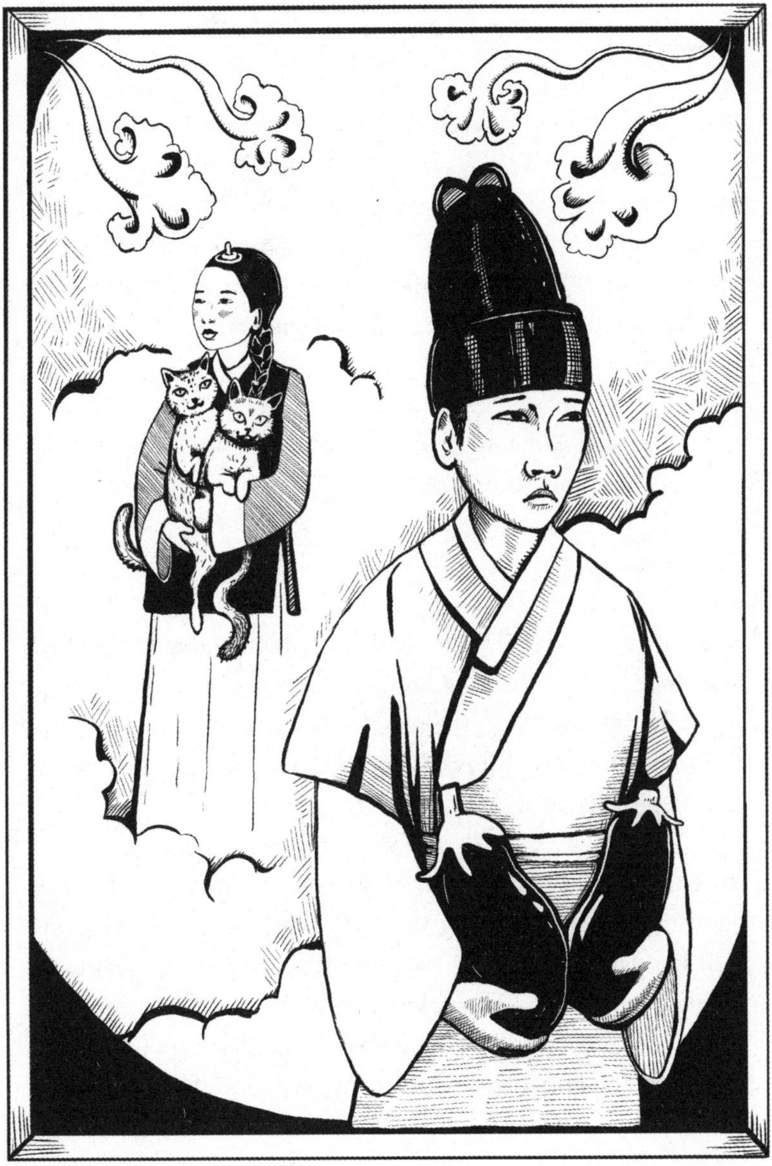

"Are you sure?" his father asked. "It may be very difficult to find such a woman."

She exists! But she's taken. Another Korean folktale features a woman with two vajayays who meets a double-dicked man. He was not born that way; rather, he finds a disembodied peen floating down a river, which he compares to his own member. It magically attaches to him, and the two lovers get a happy ending. So, get thee down to the river, transmasc friends; a new bottom surgery just dropped!

"I must find such a woman, Father," the prince confirmed. "It is what I need, to feel whole."

To feel *two* holes.

So the royal family spread the word: if a double-sheathed woman existed in the kingdom, she had the marriage opportunity of a lifetime! Alas, the search turned up no such lady. The prince lived a lonely life, and died without meeting his personal puzzle-piece of a gal.

This tale would make a fun crossover with "Cinderella." I'm envisioning women trying inventive ways to fake extra genitalia the same way they've tortured their feet and fingers to fit slippers and rings. You could wrap in the motif of detachable privates (see trickster Coyote, Hawaiian deity Kapo, and a lot of medieval German art). Cinderella drops one of her pussies on the steps of the palace! The prince must find the match!

Unable to realize his life's most precious wish (specifically, to blow two loads simultaneously in a woman who resembled an upside-down bowling ball), the dead prince found his spirit unable to rest. He haunted the kingdom forlornly as his remaining family desperately attempted to find this woman—even the ghost of one! For the prince's only hope of ascending to heaven was to marry his dream girl postmortem.

Korea has an exorcism specifically for the ghosts of virgins. A wedding is performed for the two deceased singletons, in hopes their unity will earn them a place in the afterlife. This is the only type of wedding I wish to attend from now on.

As time went on, and hope dimmed, the search for this singular (**two-bular?**) woman was abandoned. The prince's ghost circled the globe himself, hopeful of executing his own exorcism. One day, though, he had an idea. It was a shocking idea. But once he had thought it, he couldn't unthink it. A double-holed princess was not so rare after all. In fact, double-holed princesses were *everywhere*.

The prince selected a poor unsuspecting mortal and positioned his double shafts above the thing we all have that seems sorta kinda like a side-by-side vagina: their nose. It was a perfect fit!

This plot point, objectively shocking and funny, sometimes brings up an unfortunate reaction: The assumption is that our ghost has had nostril-sized genitalia this whole time. That's important to unpack here, as body-shaming is never cool, and East Asian men in particular have carried this size stereotype for ages. Applying such assumptions to this particular tale is a travesty of creative thinking. We don't know how a ghost's body works! Maybe he shrank his whole self so his junk was comparably sized. Maybe he's not even human-shaped at all! There's no way the noncorporeal body faces the same limits as ours. If there is anything to be criticized about this nose fuckery, it's the fact that ghost sexual education appears to lack conversations about consent.

He gleefully pumped the proboscis and came with a gratified "BooOOooOOooooOOooOO!" Thanks to ghost physics, the poor victim felt and perceived nothing. But for the prince it was one of the greatest orgasms in history; the ecstasy literally sent him to heaven.

Unfortunately, the resulting ectoplasmic ejaculation from the prince's nose-humping has had long-lasting consequences: It evolved into the common cold. What began as one person's postcoital nose spooge became a collective orgy of germs. With every cough and sneeze, we all get fucked by the double-dicked prince. He thought he was stuffing one nose, but he ended up stuffing them all.

* * *

SOURCE: *Encyclopedia of Korean Folk Literature.*

Want to read even *more* Korean folktales? Try *Korean Folktales: Classic Stories from Korea's Enchanted Past* by Kim So-Un.

KALENDRIN, THE PARTY PRINCESS

A Muria Period Piece, India

An orphaned prince named Viraj and his adopted father, the diwan of his kingdom, stopped by a Muria village on their way home from a disappointing journey. The men had been searching for a bride for Viraj. This was their second such trip, and the second time they'd given up on finding a girl. Home was a long way off, so they stayed in a ghotul for the evening.

That night, the prince dreamed of a magnetic young woman picking flowers off mahua trees.* A large house stood in the distance, where others dried swaths of buds for fermentation. The woman was draped in a brilliant purple sari embroidered with gold birds. Her face was bejeweled with a piercing on each nostril and her hair shone with golden combs. She stood over a stack of pewter distilling pots, stoking the fire. When she caught sight of Viraj, she plucked a dainty white plumeria blossom, walked up to him, and tucked it behind his ear. "My name is Kalendrin. I'm the one you've been searching for, my dear Viraj." They leaned in for a steamy embrace.

Viraj woke, annoyed that the dream had ended just as it was getting sexy. The murmur of couples getting busy in the next

---

* *In* The Muria and Their Ghotul, *anthropologist Verrier Elwin documents the importance of dreams to the tribe, as well as the prophetic meanings behind them. "The [soul] leaves the body in sleep, goes here and there and what it sees during its adventures is the dream."*

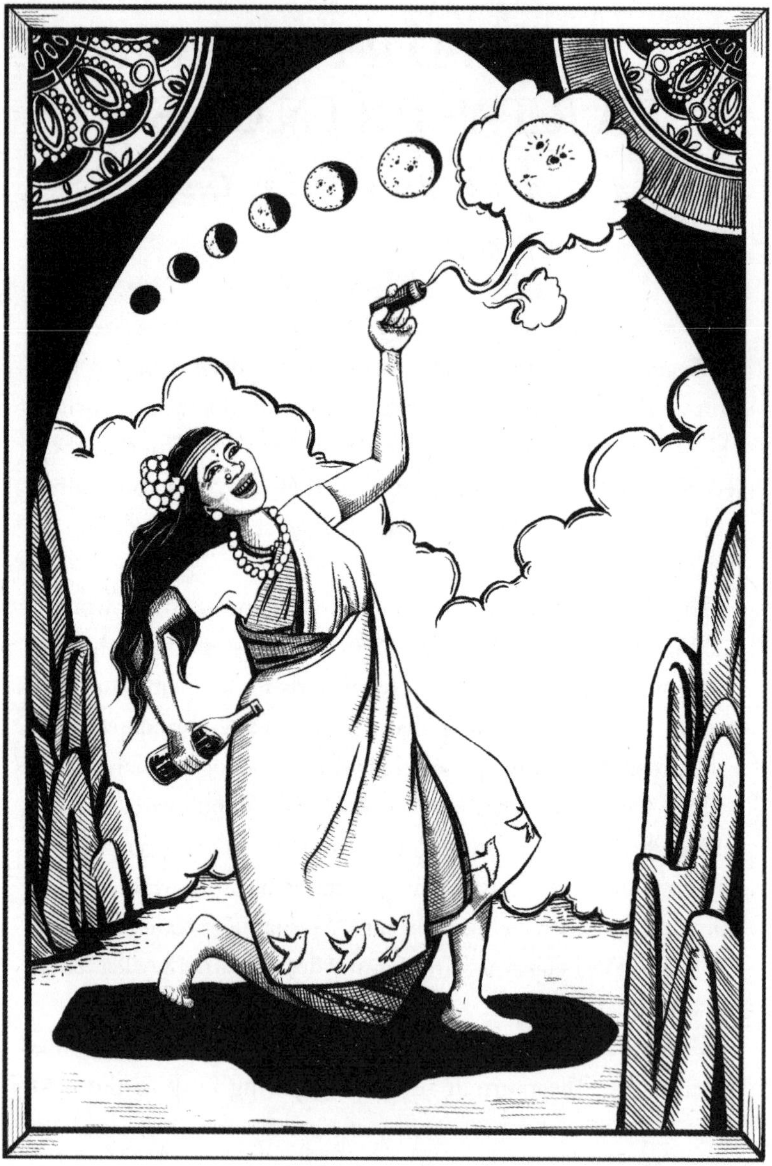

house left him even hotter and more bothered. He nestled his head in his arms and pored over the details of the dream again and again. Viraj was still ruminating on the beautiful Kalendrin as the sun rose over the ghotul.

The Muria encourage young adults to explore their sexuality at ghotuls (co-ed dormitories where youth learn life skills and find a spouse). While the prince doesn't appear to be Muria (their tribes rule by council, not monarchy), it's sweet that he discovers his partner in a setting where the storyteller likely found theirs.

The diwan noticed the bags under Viraj's eyes that morning. "Rough night?" he asked over their poha-jalebi.

Viraj relayed his dream to the diwan with starry eyes. "I think I'm supposed to find Kalendrin," he concluded. "Why don't you continue home? You can manage the kingdom while I search."

Viraj's journey took two months. When he stumbled into a kingdom thriving off mahua crops, his deja vu flared. Each household had their own small distillery, so Viraj began asking around about the beautiful girl in the purple robes. He recalled her jewelry and the full folds of her skirt, and realized he should look for a rich family. "Who sells the most exclusive spirits?" he asked the locals.

Everyone pointed him toward the edge of the forest, to a family famous for their superior mahua. "The cheapest bottles will cost you twenty rupees a pop," an old man told him. "But it's well worth the expense!"

The prince hurried on until he saw a large house overlooking a line of tall teak trees. He felt certain this was the place, but faltered at the door, wondering if the girl of his dreams was watching from a window. He straightened his turban and tentatively knocked.

A fatherly gentleman answered. Viraj briefly bowed and introduced himself. "I've been told this is where I can find the kingdom's best wine."

The gentleman, thrilled to be patronized by royalty, ushered the prince inside. "Yes, yes. We offer bottles starting at twenty rupees. I would be happy to offer you a sample."

He poured a small serving of the crystal-clear drink. The prince thanked him and took a sip, which turned into a full gulp. The mahua was smooth and sweet and went down a little too easily. He decided he needed another round for the courage to ask about Kalendrin. "I'll take your finest bottle!"

* * *

UPSTAIRS, A mother and daughter sorted linens. Mother paused when they heard an unfamiliar voice chatting with her husband. "Kalendrin, I don't recognize this man. Prepare some refreshments for him. Any new customer may become a regular!"

Kalendrin straightened her sari and set off to the kitchen to put together a plate. On her way, she paused outside the door of the den, peering through the small window. She saw a young man in traveling clothes finer than anything her wealthy family owned. She could tell from his sparse beard that he was her age. She was charmed by his youth and quiet manner. She realized she knew him but puzzled over where they'd met. Then her eyes flew open wide.

A few years before, she'd dreamt of opening the door to a young prince. He was wearing wedding attire, with pearls draped off his turban, a necklace of purple orchids, and bright blue and orange robes. He had a thin beard and a kind smile. The dream became a frequent one, drifting into her sleep whenever she began contemplating marriage. Her parents questioned her holding out for a literal dream guy, but Kalendrin had always been a believer in the mystic.

Prophetic dreams would be useful, but I'm gonna have to initiate some uncomfortable conversations if my sex dreams become reality. Too much information? Tell that to my fucking brain!

Seeing Viraj merrily chatting with her father, she knew waiting had paid off. "He is finally here!" she breathed.

He was also very drunk. He laughed too loudly at her father's jokes and slurred his way through complimenting the booze. Kalendrin figured he was just a couple rounds away from falling asleep at the table. She turned right around, dashing upstairs to hiss, "Mother, it's the prince I told you about! The one from my dreams!"

Her mother rushed to join her, and the two crouched at the door, shouldering each other out of the way to spy on the menfolk. "He's a very cute man," her mother commented. "And very rich. But are you sure this is him?"

Viraj passed out on the table. Father patted his cheek to revive him as Kalendrin pushed through the door. "Yes! This adorable lightweight is my husband-to-be!"

Her father raised his eyebrows. "That's why he asked if I had any daughters. Well, before he fell over," he said. He exchanged a measured glance with his wife as Kalendrin lifted Viraj's arm over her shoulders and hoisted him up. "Do you know this man?"

"Yes!" Kalendrin coaxed the mumbling, stumbling prince toward the stairs. "I'm going to put him to sleep in my bed."

Her father opened his mouth and pointed after her, ready to object. But his wife silenced him. "This is the boy she's been holding out for! The boy she keeps dreaming about!"

The parents heard Kalendrin call from the next room. "Mother, can you bring a pot? He's sure to be sick later and I'd rather him not be covered in vomit when we are formally introduced."

This situation reminds me of my friends' collegiate couplings. They met chugging forties at a "Golf Pros and Tennis Hoes" frat party. Twelve years later, they're hanging Paw Patrol decorations for their kid's birthday, praying that photo of Mom sucking a putter in a mini-skort won't surface on social media. Sound familiar?

* * *

THE FIRST thing Viraj saw the next morning was Kalendrin beaming down at him. "I found you!" he cried. He sat up, and immediately regretted it. "Oh God, I have such a headache." It was a very hungover meet-cute.

The marriage of Viraj and Kalendrin was arranged quickly. The diwan paid six measures of rice as a bride-price. The prince gave his kingdom to the diwan in thanks for raising him. "But where will you go?" the minister asked Viraj and his wife.

"I'm gonna try my hand at that cursed kingdom," the prince replied.

The diwan frowned. "The one where every raja dies after only twelve hours on the throne?"

"That's the one!"

The diwan slid his eyes to Kalendrin. "And you have no objections to this?"

Kalendrin shrugged. "I've been reading up on curse-breaking."

The couple packed light for their trip, planning to send for their goods once settled in their new kingdom. They each rode a horse saddled with money, clothes, and nourishment. Kalendrin packed a few bottles of her family's spirits as well as a potent strain of ganja they'd been cultivating.

India is one of the oldest societies to farm marijuana. Some scholars believe India is also the source of many famous folktales. COINCIDENCE? Well, probably.

Their families tearfully bade them goodbye. They were charmed by Viraj and Kalendrin's prophetic meeting, and the kids seemed so happy together. But they were unsure why the couple would walk straight into a death trap.

The two traveled most of the day, until they reached a fork in the road. They stopped for a bathroom break, then discussed which road they should follow.

"Maybe we should split up," Kalendrin suggested. "Whoever makes it to the cursed kingdom can send out a messenger and wait for the other."

Viraj hesitated. "I'll worry about you alone out there."

Kalendrin rummaged through his bags. "I'll dress up as a man!" She exchanged some of her girlish garb for his clothes, wrapping her long hair underneath a turban and removing her piercings. She presented herself, trying to square her jaw.

The prince laughed. His wife's round figure was hard to disguise. "No one will believe it."

"I can take care of myself!" she promised. "Our dreams led us to each other. Why would fate go that far, only to give us a tragic end?"

The lovers parted ways. Despite her bravado, Kalendrin was as nervous as her husband. She traveled discreetly, pulling over for the night in the first kingdom she encountered. She sought shelter from the palace, hopeful her princely disguise would get her in with few questions. She was granted room and board, but her husband was right: most suspected she was a woman.

The six sons of the raja were a group of predatory lowlifes, who eyed Kalendrin when the household came together to dine. One brother elbowed another and pointed. "Ten rupees says our quiet visitor is hiding a healthy pair of melons under that kurta," he whispered. They guffawed, making eyes at Kalendrin. She blushed, hoping her pink cheeks could be explained by the steamy lentil soup.

The brothers cornered her after dinner, pestering her with questions. At last, one reached out and snatched her turban, unraveling the long length of silk. The boys laughed as Kalendrin's hair unraveled with it. She hopped to snatch the wrap back, but the boys played monkey-in-the-middle, until the eldest lassoed her with the fabric, pulling her close.

"A runaway princess!" he jeered. "How do we decide who gets to claim her?"

"I get a say in that!" Kalendrin spat.

The boys passed her around like a toy. "She's a picky princess!"

Kalendrin gritted her teeth and tried to kick their shins. "Put me down, and we can settle this!" she bargained.

They agreed but surrounded her. She paced the circle of boys with her chin high. "I challenge you to a drinking contest."

The boys howled. "You? Such a little thing?" the youngest brother said. "You think you can best six strong men?"

"No!" Kalendrin laughed. "I challenge you against each other! Whichever man can hold his liquor gets to hold *me* tonight." She uncorked a bottle of her father's mahua. "Round one!"

The men took on the game excitedly, especially once they'd sampled the delicious drink. Kalendrin pretended to join them here and there, but let the liquor fall past her lips and down her neck. She fanned herself and pretended she was merely perspiring through her tunic as the liquor pooled at her chest. One by one, the men incapacitated themselves. When the sixth brother fell, Kalendrin tucked her hair back in her husband's turban and left the palace in a hurry.

She rode beyond the kingdom for over an hour before pulling over to rest. This time she stopped at a temple, hoping for a safer sanctuary. She tethered her horse around back, said a brief prayer, then curled up against an outside wall, hidden in the shadows cast between it and a large anthill.

Anthills in Indian folklore are actually termite mounds, considered sacred in some Vedic and Hindu sects. In folklore, they fre-

quently house deities or connect to the underworld. Next time you require pest control, ask the exterminator if these are sacred termites or haunted ones.

The crunch of soft footsteps woke her a few hours later. She lay still, pretending to be asleep, but peering out in the dark. A pale white figure stood before the anthill in flowing yellow robes. Kalendrin sucked in a tense breath. Was it a spirit? A demon?

As the figure stepped fully into the moonlight, Kalendrin relaxed a bit and sat up. The ghostly figure was more spiritual than spirit; a rishi, caked in white funerary ash from his tall manbun to his bare feet. He winked at her, and drawled, "The sleeping beauty is awake!"

A rishi is a person who dedicates their life to study of their faith. In Hinduism, rishis are highly respected. But India's indigenous tribes often portrayed such holy figures as lecherous due to their commitment to single life. The Muria in particular found this habit untrustworthy. Haven't many of us used folklore to work out our conflicted feelings about organized religion and its practitioners? How else did we get so many priests, pastors, and rabbis walking into bars?

The princess was momentarily stunned by the yogi's flirting. "Pardon me, sir," she said, standing quickly. "I'll, uh, leave you to your scriptures." She hurried toward her horse.

"Hey, not so fast!" The rishi padded closer, ash clouding with each footfall. "It's late. You're exhausted. Stay until it's light, and we can get to know each other." He made kissy faces.

Kalendrin retreated backward. "I'm in a hurry."

"Nonsense! The road is much too dangerous for a luscious little lady." The rishi waved one hand in the air, calling forth the sounds of a magical, sultry sitar.

Kalendrin groaned and turned away. She bumped into her horse, eager to get out of this "Baby, It's Cold Outside" situation. She pulled its reins, but the horse wouldn't budge. Its eyes were wide with fear and its body was entranced into stillness. The princess sighed. "Please release my horse from your spell and allow me to leave."

The rishi brushed off her request. Instead, he stretched out on the ground, leaning his head on his elbow and propping one foot up to display his glorious hard-on. "I can see you are in need of spiritual healing."

Oh, so that's what they're calling it these days.

He patted the ground in front of him. "I will free your horse of its spell if you free your mind and mediate. Meditate on my mantra."

Kalendrin planted her hands on her hips. "And what mantra is that?"

"Om, om, om," the rishi moaned, stretching out the consonant. He punctuated each syllable with a jerk of his hips. "Om-Mama!" It was offensive on every level.

Kalendrin steadied herself with a hand on her bag. Then she remembered its contents. She switched gears, batting her eyelashes and biting her lip. "Your mantra is *so* big," she breathed in a voice that would put Marilyn Monroe to shame. "I don't know if I can contemplate such a *big mantra*. Not without a little help." She pulled a pipe and her stash from the bag, holding them up as she sauntered over.

"Aha!" the rishi cried. "I knew you were a believer."*

Kalendrin packed the pipe, which the rishi lit with a flame conjured from his thumb. They passed the pipe between

---

* *Marijuana is illegal in India, but many authorities turn their heads due to its religious significance for followers of Shiva.*

them, the rishi drawing deep pulls and Kalendrin faking it. Smoke billowed from their hands, adding to the rishi's ghostly appearance.

As the sage's high settled in, he grew less licentious and more conversational. "I don't know, man, I just feel like we're all tiny ants endlessly marching around the anthill of life, ya know?" he mused, leaning on her shoulder. Eventually, he got too high to maintain his enchantment (or his erection). Kalendrin's horse sputtered and pawed the ground as it was released. The princess hit the road for the third time in a single evening.

Thankfully, the next place the princess landed was the very destination she and Viraj had set out to find: the cursed kingdom. She found shelter with a kind old couple, finally sleeping through the night (and most of the next day). As soon as she felt refreshed, she returned to her own clothes and asked the couple to lead her to the palace. "My husband is aiming to be the next raja," she told them.

The old couple grimaced. "Do you not know our kingdom's sad story? A ghoul enacted a curse on the palace: Every raja we crown dies twelve hours from coronation! One had a fatal fall down the stairs; another was trampled by a stampede of wild elephants; the next choked on his vindaloo. At least a dozen kings have perished!"

Final Destination: 12 Kings coming to a streaming channel near you!

Kalendrin insisted on taking residence in the palace. The staff accepted her as their eventual queen, figuring it would only last for a day or two.

Seems to me that if they crowned Kalendrin or demolished the monarchy entirely, they might solve their dead king problem!

Kalendrin gave specific instructions for her husband's arrival. "A bunch of d-bags may show up at my door. If any ask for the cross-dressing woman who got them drunk, imprison them! If a horny rishi asks for the luscious lady with the dank grass, put him in chains too. But if a man asks for Kalendrin, the woman of his dreams, he is my true husband—show him to me at once!"

Sure enough, all of Kalendrin's admirers pursued her to the cursed kingdom. The six slimy princes were imprisoned, alongside the salacious sage.

At last, Viraj stumbled into town. He and Kalendrin tearfully reunited at the palace. But Viraj's happy tears quickly turned into stressed sobs. "Oh, my dear wife, what was I thinking? As soon as they crown me raja, I'll only have twelve hours with you!"

"Don't worry!" Kalendrin assured him. "I discovered the charm to keep you safe. We just have to ask the council to postpone the coronation for a couple of weeks!"

Viraj lived as a commoner with the elderly couple while she prepared the charm. The magic required her to be on her period.* One night, she dreamed of the local river overflowing its banks; that meant she was due any day now.

Man, my dreams are not only awkward, they're also useless as fuck. Which is too bad; it's less easy for the government to track dreams than an ovulation app.

---

* *While many Indian cultures, including the Muria, seclude menstruating women and consider them unclean, the Muria attitude seems somewhat less ashamed of the process. Both sexes speak casually of the cycle without pearl-clutching. They regard periods with some reverence too: After their periods, women are treated with extra care by their male partners. The power of the period is also connected to supernatural beliefs. Verrier Elwin notes that when disposing of her menstrual rag, a Muria woman "has to be very careful where she puts it to dry for fear a witch should steal it."*

The following Sunday, she took her used menstrual rag and tied it up using her pubes in a discreet nook above the palace door.

Did she have really long pubes? Did she spin them into thread or felt them into woolly strips? THE PEOPLE NEED TO KNOW.

With the absorbent amulet in place, the council proceeded with the coronation of Viraj, and the couple spent the next twelve hours on pins and needles.

The charm worked! Not only did Viraj survive the night, but the amulet protected the couple against all other future troubles. The rishi found a new paramour! The six smug brothers were banished! Most importantly, Viraj and Kalendrin rehabilitated the trauma-laden kingdom and enjoyed a long and peaceful reign.

✳ ✳ ✳

Source: Verrier Elwin, "The Story of Kalendrin."

For even *more* Indian folktales, pick up *Folktales from India* by A. K. Ramanujan.

THE PONGO'S PROPHECY

THE QUECHUA'S POOPY PARABLE, PERU

Anku was the pongo of a large hacienda in Cuzco. He was a tiny man, quiet, old, and sickly. Everyone at the estate, even the other laborers, regarded him as pitiful. He did his best to get his work done quickly, to take care of the people who worked under him, but above all he tried to avoid notice.

Unfortunately, the most powerful man in the hacienda took a keen interest in him: the misti himself. From the minute the landowner observed Anku, he delighted in humiliating him.

A hacienda was a semi-feudal system of land ownership established by Spanish colonists. A pongo was an Indigenous laborer in charge of the mines that a hacienda was built around—a sort of middle manager, but one subject to the same abuse suffered by the laborers. The misti owned the hacienda, and was often a mestizo. I break this down because we often think of folktales as clear-cut: good vs. bad and right vs wrong. But, of course, the reality and relationships between all of these people trying to live under a divisive, oppressive system is so complicated.

"What the hell am I looking at?" the misti bellowed the first time he met Anku. "Are you a man or a mouse?"

Anku stared at his feet, terrified to be addressed by the Big Boss.

"A mouse!" the misti surmised. "Well, little rodent, take your tiny pink hands and put them to work."

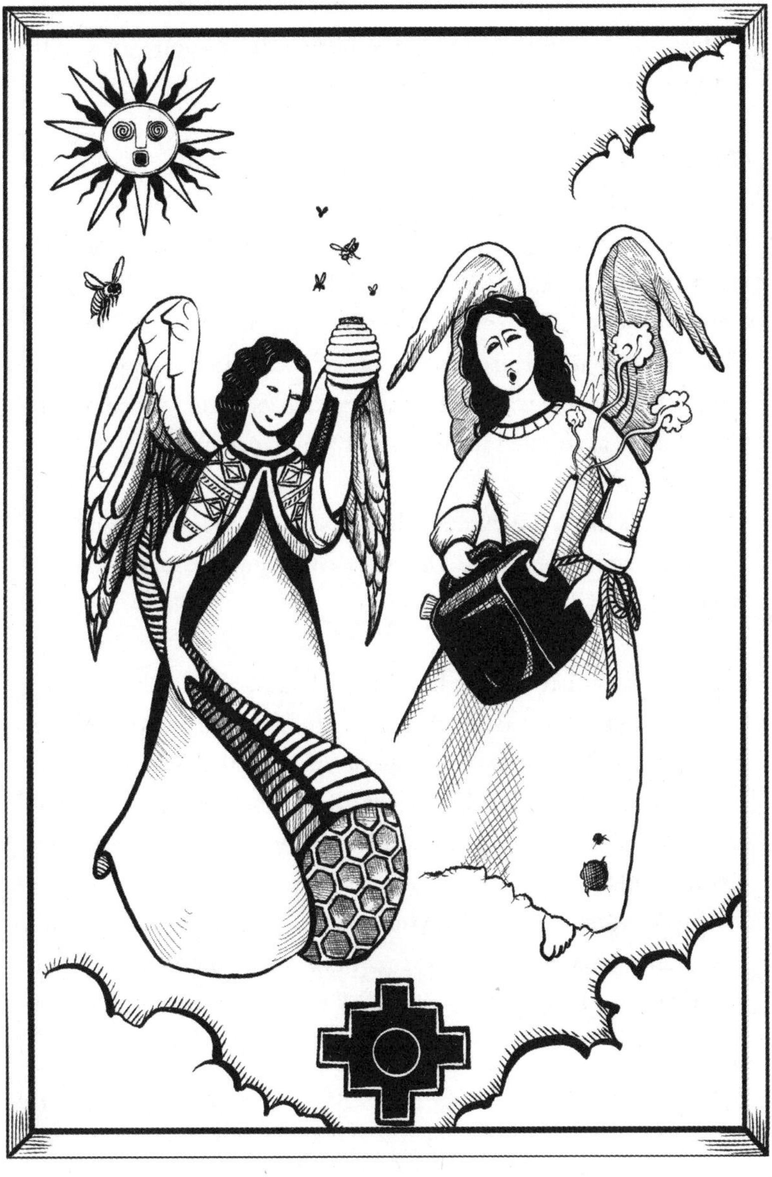

People like to tweet comparisons between the modern rental system and feudalism, but at least our landlords don't generally stand around telling us what shitheads we are.

The misti still had living relatives who were once laborers on the hacienda. But when he was granted ownership of the property, he did his best to separate himself from that past. Picking on Anku was an easy way to establish his dominance. He knew Anku was liked, but he also knew he could play the man's supervisory edge against the other workers. So he always made sure his abuse of the fellow was highly public, such as during sunset when the laborers assembled in the hall of the mansion to pray.

Ugh, this is like a much more abusive version of your boss crashing after-work cocktails. This isn't your space, you tyrannical party-pooper!

Here the misti would humiliate Anku sadistically, forcing him to kneel and walk on all fours. He smacked him around and ordered him to mimic a menagerie of animals. Anku obeyed, for what else could he do? He hardly blamed the other native workers when they laughed at him. They had even less power than he did.*

"Shake your tail like a 'wittle wabbit'!" the misti would command, and poor Anku would squat and shake his bottom. "Get down on your belly, you slimy snake!" the misti would order, and

---

* *This folktale was told to novelist José María Arguedas by a laborer in Cuzco. Arguedas was a vocal ally of the Quechuan peoples. While we tend to think of folktales as stories of the far past, it's worth noting that the storyteller was still embedded in its setting, as the hacienda system was present in Peru up until the 1960s.*

Anku would lie flat and pull himself across the floor. "Repeat after me, parrot: 'I am nothing but a turd.'" The mockery usually ended thus. If the misti wasn't calling Anku an animal, he was dismissing him as excrement.

Quechuan folktale face-offs between the mighty and the lowly feature witty reversals of fortune, elevating storytelling to a powerful act of resistance. Consider yourself foreshadowed!

One such evening, after the workers filed into the great hall at twilight, Anku surprised the entire household. He spoke up before prayers could begin. "May I have permission to address you, my lord?" he asked.

A hush settled over the large room. The natives were terrified on Anku's behalf, even as they sorta wanted to see someone stand up to the landowner. As for that guy, he was so astonished he was momentarily struck speechless. ". . . I have never seen a turd talk!"

"I mean no offense, my lord." Anku's knees shook, and his downcast eyes were wide with fear. But his voice was clear, filling the hall. "If you will allow it, I'd like to tell you about a dream I had last night."

The misti accepted Anku's request, hopeful for more fodder to humiliate him. "By all means, tell me what a turd dreams!" He received a short titter of laughter at his joke, but the room quickly quieted to hear what Anku had to say.

Similar to the Muria, indigenous Andean cultures regard dreams as links between our world and the spiritual one, providing prophetic communication to individuals or communities. This seems comforting for colonized peoples seeking reparation. It's less comforting if you keep having that dream where your teeth fall out.

The pongo took a short breath to gather his words and courage. He'd never had such a rapt audience. "In my dream, both you and I had died, and found ourselves together, naked in front of Saint Francis, awaiting judgment." He paused, unsure if the lord would allow him to finish.

Of the several Saints Francis, this is likely Francis of Assisi, due to his commitment to the impoverished. Scholar Cecilia Castillo Gil points out that José María Arguedas elevates Francis to a godly position to accentuate how the Spaniard's Catholic God, whom Indigenous communities were forced to worship, had failed those people. A biblical coup! Epic!

The big boss itched with curiosity. "Go on, little turd!"

"Saint Francis took us in, weighing the lives we had lived on earth, as well as the contents of our hearts. You gazed back at him with confidence, certain of your might even under God's gaze."

"And you?" the misti prompted.

"Oh, I could never judge my own worth," Anku answered humbly.

The mestizo rolled his eyes. "Boring! Get to the good stuff."

"Saint Francis nodded to himself and called, 'Summon the two most beautiful angels in heaven. The second-most beautiful should bring a pot of the purest, sweetest honey.'" Anku paused, but the boss waved him on. "As soon as Saint Francis ordered it, the angels appeared. Their beauty was unfathomable. The first carried himself as shining and massive as the sun. The lesser angel was as delicate and lovely as the flowers of earth. He carried a golden cup."

"And then?" The misti was at the edge of his seat. "What did these sexy angels do?"

"Saint Francis ordered that the Most Beautiful Angel massage the honey onto your body with his lightest touch. The angel coated your naked form, slicking back your hair with the sweet liquid, and working it down to the tips of your fingers and toes. You looked like you were made of gold. Your face shone with pride as gloriously as your honey-gilded form!"

The misti smirked. "This comes as no surprise. And what of you, little turd?"

"As you reflected the beauty of the angels themselves," Anku replied, "Saint Francis summoned the eldest, ugliest, lowliest of angels. He ordered that this creature carry forth an old gasoline can filled with . . . well, pardon my words, my lord: a can filled with waste."

"With what?" the misti asked.

"With excrement, my lord."

The misti giggled. "Tell me one more time, and slowly."

"With the smelliest shit and dankest piss, my lord."

Other crappy plot points in fairy tales include: a Palestinian tale about an anthropomorphized pot who steals riches until a neighbor poops in her; an Italian tale featuring a cockroach who crawls into a man's butt to insert a laxative; and a tale noted in the ATU Index I've yet to track down where a woman tricks her mate into believing she is actually a pile of shit. This is a great alternative to the tired bedroom excuse of "I have a headache." I can't do the nasty tonight, babe. I feel like shit, cuz I've turned into a literal pile of it.

The misti clapped his hands. "Excellent. I see where this is going, but please, continue."

"An elderly angel, with hard, wrinkled feet, brought forth the stinking can, dragging his raggedy wings behind him," Anku continued. "Saint Francis ordered the old angel to cover me much in the same way you were, but with the pot of waste. The old angel did not take the care your attendants did. He slapped it on hastily, caking the mess onto me with his rough, scaly hands." Anku shuddered. "I can smell it still."

The misti bellowed. "Marvelous! A turd covered in turds! I love a story with a happy ending."

Anku spoke up, bolder than he even expected of himself. "That was not the end of my dream, my lord."

"Oh?" The change in Anku surprised the misti too. He narrowed his eyes. "Tell me."

"Saint Francis stood before us, you radiating sugar and light, and I grisly and stinking to high heaven." Anku drew the story out, daring for the first time in his life to lift his gaze level to his superior's. "He was still weighing our souls, you see. At last, he dismissed the beautiful angels and summoned the elderly one. That bent, creaky angel straightened to his full height. His wings fluttered, then swelled with strength. The age melted from his face until he was even more gorgeous than the honey-toting angels."

He turned to the workers, including them in the story. "Saint Francis ordered, 'This honeyed noble did not act so sweetly in life. He used his lofty position to degrade and divide his underlings. Yet this small sad and soiled man worked hard, remained humble, and did his best to care for his people. Thus, you will enforce the following fate between the two of them.'"

The misti waited. "What was our fate?" he cried.

Anku turned back to the misti and allowed himself a small smile. "Saint Francis decreed that you and I would be forever bound to each other. Henceforth, we were to lick each other's bodies—slowly—for all eternity."

Why tell your scummy landlord to eat shit and die, when he could die and eat shit . . . forever?

* * *

SOURCE: José María Arguedas, "The Pongo's Dream."

Want to read more Quechuan folktales? Pick up *The She-Calf and Other Quechua Folk Tales*, edited by Johnny Payne.

References

Introduction

Cox, Marian Roalfe. *Cinderella: Three Hundred and Forty-Five Variants of Cinderella, Catskin, and Cap O' Rushes, Abstracted and Tabulated, with a Discussion of Medieval Analogues and Notes.* Folk-lore Society, 1892.

Friedler, Delilah. "Being in the Middle of a Story Is a Really Hard Place." *High Country News.* May 29, 2020.

Heiner, Heidi Anne, ed. *Sleeping Beauties: Sleeping Beauty and Snow White Tales from Around the World.* SurLaLune Press, 2010.

Heiner, Heidi Anne, ed. "Little Saddleslut." In *Cinderella Tales from Around the World.* SurLaLune Press, 2010.

Jacobs, Joseph, comp. "Gold-Tree and Silver-Tree." In *Celtic Fairy Tales.* London: David Nutt, 1892.

Mason, J. Alden, and Aurelio M. Espinosa. "Porto Rican Folklore: Folktales." *Journal of American Folklore* 38 (1925).

McNeill, Lynne S. *Folklore Rules: A Fun, Quick, and Useful Introduction to the Field of Academic Folklore Studies.* Utah State University Press, 2013.

Nuwayhiḍ, Jamāl Salīm. "Rummana." In *Abu Jmeel's Daughter and Other Stories: Arab Folk Tales from Palestine and Lebanon.* Interlink, 2002.

Rooth, Anna Birgitta. *The Cinderella Cycle.* Lund, 1951.

Wood, Pete Jordi. *Tales from Beyond the Rainbow: Ten LGBTQ+ Fairy Tales Proudly Reclaimed.* Puffin Classics, 2023.

Zalka, Csenge. "The Woodcutter's Luck." In *Dancing on Blades: Rare and Exquisite Folktales from the Carpathian Mountains.* Parkhurst Brothers, 2018.

Zipes, Jack, ed. and trans. "The Story of Grandmother." In *The Trials and Tribulations of Little Red Riding Hood*, 2nd ed. Routledge, 1993.

Zipes, Jack. "What Makes a Repulsive Frog So Appealing: Memetics and Fairy Tales." *Journal of Folklore Research* 45, no. 2 (2008): 109–43.

A Quick Note

Jorgensen, Jeana. *Fairy Tales 101: An Accessible Introduction to Fairy Tales*. 2022.

Jorgensen, Jeana. *Folklore 101: An Accessible Introduction to Folklore Studies*. 2022.

Daddy's Little Donkey-Skin

Heiner, Heidi Anne, ed. "Doralice" and "The She-Bear." In *Cinderella Tales from Around the World*. SurLaLune Press, 2010.

Lang, Andrew, ed. "Donkey Skin." In *The Grey Fairy Book*. Longmans, Green, 1905.

Perrault, Charles. *The Fairy Tales of Charles Perrault*. G. A. Harrap, 1922.

Zipes, Jack, ed. and trans. "All Fur." In *The Complete Fairy Tales of the Brothers Grimm All-New Third Edition*. Random House, 2003.

The Devil Made Her Do It

Andersen, Hans Christian. "The Red Shoes." In *The Annotated Hans Christian Andersen*. Edited and translated by Maria Tatar. W. W. Norton, 2008.

Ashliman, D. L., ed. and trans. *Mother Killed Me, Father Ate Me, Folktales of Aarne-Thompson-Uther Type 720*. https://sites.pitt.edu/~dash/type0720.html.

da Silva, Francisco Vaz. "Red as Blood, White as Snow, Black as Crow: Chromatic Symbolism of Womanhood in Fairy Tales." *Marvels & Tales* 21, no. 2 (2007): 240–52.

Tatar, Maria, editor and translator. *The Annotated Brothers Grimm*. W. W. Norton, 2012.

Tolkien, J. R. R. "On Fairy-Stories." In *Essays Presented to Charles Williams*. Oxford University Press, 1947.

Zipes, Jack, ed. and trans. "Little Snow White" and "Hansel and Gretel." In *The Original Folk and Fairy Tales of the Brothers Grimm: The Complete First Edition*. Princeton University Press, 2014.

Thumberella

D'Penha, Geo. Fr. "Folk-lore in Salsette." In *Indian Antiquary*. Bombay: Education Society's Press, 1891.

Heiner, Heidi Anne, ed. "Cendrillon" and "Little Saddleslut." In *Cinderella Tales from Around the World*. SurLaLune Press, 2010.
Naithani, Sadhana. "The Colonizer-Folklorist." *Journal of Folklore Research* 34, no. 1 (1997): 1–14.
Uther, Hans-Jörg. *The Types of International Folktales: A Classification and Bibliography, Part I*. Folklore Fellows' Communications, 2011.
Zipes, Jack, ed. and trans. "The Six Swans." In *The Original Folk and Fairy Tales of the Brothers Grimm: The Complete First Edition*. Princeton University Press, 2014.
Zipes, Jack, ed. and trans. "The Story of Grandmother." In *The Trials and Tribulations of Little Red Riding Hood*, 2nd ed. Routledge, 1993.

SNAKES WHO CANNOT SHED THEIR KIN

Bierhorst, John, comp. "The Girl Who Joined the Thunders." In *The White Deer and Other Stories Told by the Lenape*. William Morrow, 1995.
Britannica, The Editors of Encyclopedia. "Žaltys." *Encyclopedia Britannica*. 1998.
Dundes, Alan. "The Binary Structure of 'Unsuccessful Repetition' in Lithuanian Folk Tales." *Western Folklore* 21, no. 3 (1962): 165–74.
Forsyth, Kate. "The Rule of Three." *Writing Journal* (blog), April 2022. https://kateforsyth.com.au/writing-journal/the-rule-of-three.
Knowles, James Hinton, comp. and trans. "Nagray and Himal." In *Folktales of Kashmir*. Trübner, 1888.
Myung-sub, Chung, ed. "Divine Serpent Scholar." In *Encyclopedia of Korean Folk Literature*. National Folk Museum of Korea, 2014.
Propp, Vladimir. *Morphology of the Folktale*. University of Texas Press, 1968.
Sergent, Bernard. "Un mythe lithuano-amérindien." *Dialogues d'histoire ancienne* 25, no. 2 (1999): 9–39.
Zheleznova, Irina. *Tales from the Amber Sea*. Progress, 1981.

BLANCA ROSA, MOTHER OF THIEVES

Heiner, Heidi Anne, ed. *Sleeping Beauties: Sleeping Beauty and Snow White Tales from Around the World*. SurLaLune Press, 2010.
Pino Saavedra, Yolando. *Folktales of Chile*. University of Chicago Press, 1967.
Uther, Hans-Jörg. "709—Snow White." In *The Types of International*

Folktales: A Classification and Bibliography, Part I. Folklore Fellows' Communications, 2011.

LOVE IS FOR THE BIRDS

Andersen, Hans Christian. *The Complete Fairy Tales and Stories.* Translated by Erik Christian Haugaard. Anchor Press, 1983.

Nassaar, Christopher S. "Andersen's 'The Shadow' and Wilde's 'The Fisherman and His Soul': A Case of Influence." *Nineteenth-Century Literature* 50, no. 2 (1995): 217–24.

Raby, Peter, ed. *The Cambridge Companion to Oscar Wilde.* Cambridge University Press, 1997.

Wilde, Oscar. "The Nightingale and the Rose." In *The Happy Prince and Other Tales.* London: David Nutt, 1888.

LOVE IS LIKE A TREE

Calvino, Italo. "The Handmade King." In *Italian Folktales.* Translated by George Martin. Harcourt, 1980.

Carter, Angela, ed. "Blubber Boy." In *The Old Wives' Fairy Tale Book.* Pantheon Books, 1990.

Elliot, Aubrey. *Head-dresses of the Xhosa Woman.* Exhibition catalog. Dutywa, South Africa, 1981.

Mandela, Nelson, ed. "Kamiyo of the River." In *Favorite African Folktales.* W. W. Norton, 2004.

Osei-Nyame, Kwadwo Jr., comp. "Of the Fat Woman Who Melted Away," and "The Poor Man and His Wife of Wood." In *African Myths & Tales: Epic Tales.* Simon & Schuster, 2020.

Peires, Jeffrey B. *The House of Phalo: A History of the Xhosa People in the Days of Their Independence.* University of California Press, 1982.

Williams, Mark. "Blodeuwedd: The Woman Made from Flowers." In *The Celtic Myths That Shape the Way We Think.* Thames & Hudson, 2021.

LOVE IS A REVOLUTION

Aquilar-Pollard, Marlene. *Myths and Legends of the Philippines.* Jacoby, 2000.

Lanuza, Michelle. "The Legend of Maria Makiling." *Misteryo at Lohika* (blog). Accessed October 6, 2024. https://misteryolohika2005.blogspot.com/2006/04/mystical-mount-makiling.html.

Rizal, José. "Mariang Makiling." In *La Solidaridad*. 1890. Translated by Arnold H. Warren. The International Philippine Philatelic Society (IPPS), 1968. http://www.theipps.info/Presentations/makiling.pdf.

Santiago, Fernando A., Jr. "Manners of Resistance: Symbolic Defiance of Colonial Authority in Nineteenth Century Philippines." *Philippine Sociological Review* 63 (2015): 137–68.

Love Is a Family Affair

Afanas'ev, A. N. "Prince Danila Govorila." In *Russian Fairy Tales*. Translated by Norman Guterman. Pantheon Books, 2006.

Gardner, Fletcher. "The Sad Story of Juan and Maria." *Journal of American Folklore* 20, no. 77 (1907): 112.

"Hon Vong Phu—The Mountain of the Woman Who Is Waiting for Her Husband." https://www.vietnamtourism.org.vn/attractions/culture/myths-legends-folklores/hon-vong-phu-the-mountain-of-the-woman-who-is-waiting-for-her-husband.html.

Nguyen Thuy Kha. "Proud of 100 years of Vietnamese music: 'Hon vong phu' Le Thuong." *Nguoi Lao Dong*, September 22, 2017.

"Núi Vọng Phu: Những Thiếu Phụ Choờ Chống Muôn Kiếp." https://www.thukhoahuan.com/index.php/lch-s/15861-nui-vng-phu-nhng-thiu-ph-ch-chng-muon-kip.

Randolph, Vance, ed. *Pissing in the Snow & Other Ozark Folktales*. Avon, 1977.

Love Is Dead

Schwartz, Howard, comp. "The Finger" and "The Demon in the Tree." In *Lilith's Cave: Jewish Tales of the Supernatural*. Oxford University Press, 1988.

Till There Was Mew

Cocteau, Jean, dir. *La Belle et la Bête*. DisCina, 1946.

d'Aulnoy, Marie-Catherine. "The White Cat." In *Fairy Tales by the Countess d'Aulnoy*. Translated by James Robinson Planché. G. Routledge & Co., 1856.

de Villeneuve, Gabrielle-Suzanne Barbot. *The Story of Beauty & the Beast: The Complete Fairy Story*. Translated by Ernest Downson. John Lane, 1908.

Heiner, Heidi Anne, ed. "Persinette," "Parsilette," and "Petronisella." In *Rapunzel and Other Maiden in the Tower Tales from Around the World*. SurLaLune Press, 2010.

WHEN A BIRD LOVES A WOMAN

Benson, Elizabeth Polk. "The Vulture: The Sky and the Earth." In *Eighth Palenque Round Table, 1993*. Pre-Columbian Art Research Institute, 1996.

Bierhorst, John, ed. "The Buzzard Husband." In *Latin American Folktales: Stories from Hispanic and Indian Traditions*. Pantheon Books, 2002.

Mejia, Shirley. "The Tzotzil People." *HistoricalMX* (blog). Accessed September 2, 2024. https://historicalmx.org/items/show/86.

MULE BE IN MY HEART

Bawadi, Mohammed. "Tunisia—El M'Rabet, Oldest Café in the World." A24 News Agency, March 30, 2017.

Fermé, A. "Contes Recueillis a Tunis—IV." *Revue des Traditions Populaires* 8, no. 2. (1893): 80–84.

Hejaiej, Monia. "Women's Oral Narratives in Tunis." Ph.D. dissertation. University of London (1992): 382–86.

Koskas, Sonia. *Contes des Juifs de Tunisie*. Aux origines du monde 13 (2015): 83–93.

Moors, Annelies. "Wearing Gold, Owning Gold: The Multiple Meanings of Gold Jewelry." *Etnofoor* 25, no. 1 (2013): 78–89.

Nunnally, Tiina, trans. "East of the Sun and West of the Moon." In *The Complete and Original Norwegian Folktales of Asbjørnsen and Moe*. University of Minnesota Press, 2019.

Sadeh, Pinḥas, and Hillel Halkin. *Jewish Folktales*. Anchor Books, 1989.

Zipes, Jack, ed. and trans. "A Tale About the Boy Who Went Forth to Learn What Fear Was." In *The Complete Fairy Tales of the Brothers Grimm All-New Third Edition*. Random House, 2003.

MY CARP WILL GO ON

Comhaire-Sylvain, Suzanne. "Creole Tales from Haiti." *Journal of American Folklore* 51, no. 201 (1939): 329–32.

Comhaire-Sylvain, Suzanne. "Thézin." *Bulletin of the Pan American Union* 71, no. 1–12 (1937): 169–72.

Flood, Bo, Beret E. Strong, and William Flood, eds. "The Island of the Dolphin Girls." In *Pacific Island Legends: Tales from Micronesia, Melanesia, Polynesia, and Australia.* Bess Press, 1999.

Heiner, Heidi Anne, ed. "The Fish Prince" and "Mankarikadi." In *Beauty and the Beast Tales from Around the World.* SurLaLune Press, 2013.

Lynch, Patricia Ann, and Jeremy Roberts, eds. "Chipfalamfula from Mozambique." In *African Mythology, A to Z,* 2nd edition. Infobase, 2010.

Mayer, Fanny Hagin, ed. and trans. "The Fish Wife." In *The Yanagita Kunio Guide to the Japanese Folk Tale.* Indiana University Press, 1986.

Szeles, Ursula. "Sea Secret Rising: The Lwa Lasirenn in Haitian Vodou." *Journal of Haitian Studies* 17, no. 1 (2011): 193–210.

Subramanian, Sushma. "The Dolphin Myth That Refuses to Die." *Atlantic,* November 12, 2020.

Wolkstein, Diane. *The Magic Orange Tree, and Other Haitian Folktales.* Schocken Books, 1980.

MASTER AND SERPENT

Dasent, Sir George, trans. "Prince Lindworm." In *East of the Sun and West of the Moon: Old Tales from the North.* G. H. Doran, 1920.

Grundtvig, Svend. *Kong Lindorm.* (Collected from Maren Mathisdatter.) Copenhagen: C. G. Eversens Forlag, 1854.

Lang, Andrew, ed. "King Lindorm." In *The Pink Fairy Book.* Longmans, Green, 1897.

Lindow, John. "Transforming the Monster: Notes on Bengt Holbek's Interpretation of Kong Lindorm." In *Telling Reality: Folklore Studies in Memory of Bengt Holbek.* Department of Folklore, University of Copenhagen, 1993.

Pettitt, Thomas, trans. "King Serpent (Kong Lindorm): A Wondertale from Danish Folk Tradition (Working Paper)." University of Southern Denmark, 2023. https://www.researchgate.net/publication/376809684.

THE X-TREME SPORT OF GIANT KILLING

Campbell, J. F. *Popular Tales of the West Highlands, Volume 1.* Edinburgh: Edmonston and Douglas, 1860.

Chase, Richard, ed. *The Jack Tales: Folk Tales from the Southern Appalachians.* Houghton Mifflin, 1943.

Jacobs, Joseph. *English Fairy Tales*, London: W. Scott, 1890.

HOW TO TRICK FRIENDS AND EXECUTE PEOPLE

Andersen, Hans Christian. "Little Claus and Big Claus." Translated by Jean Hersholt. Hans Christian Andersen Centre. https://andersen.sdu.dk/vaerk/hersholt/LittleClausAndBigClaus_e.html.

Frank, Diane Crone, and Jeffrey Frank, eds. *The Stories of Hans Christian Andersen: A New Translation from the Danish*. Duke University Press, 2005.

Singer, Isaac Bashevis, comp. and trans. "Wise Men of Chelm." In *Zlateh the Goat and Other Stories*. Harper & Row, 1966.

Thompson, Stith. "J1703. Town (Country) of Fools." In *Motif-Index of Folk-Literature: A Classification of Narrative Elements in Folktales, Ballads, Myths, Fables, Mediaeval Romances, Exempla, Fabliaux, Jest-Books, and Local Legends*. Indiana University Press, 1955–1958.

Zipes, Jack, ed. and trans. "The Three Little Gnomes in the Forest." In *The Complete Fairy Tales of the Brothers Grimm, All-New Third Edition*. Random House, 2003.

NEVER CROSS A CINDERELLA

Han, Hee-sook. "Women's Life during the Chosŏn Dynasty." *International Journal of Korean History* 6 (2004).

Heiner, Heidi Anne, ed. "Greasy Matty" and "Slut-Sweeps-the-Oven." In *Cinderella Tales from Around the World*. SurLaLune Press, 2010.

Korean Culture and Information Service (KOCIS). "Kongjwi and Patjwi: Cinderella Tale Offers Insight into Old Korea," Korea.Net. July 17, 2014.

Myung-sub, Chung, ed. "Kongjwi and Patjwi," "Why Tree Frogs Croak." and "Fairy and the Woodsman." In *Encyclopedia of Korean Folk Literature*. National Folk Museum of Korea, 2014.

Yang, Su Jin. "Adapting Korean Cinderella Folklore as Fairy Tales for Children." Ph.D. dissertation. University of Louisiana at Lafayette, 2014.

SKIN-DEEP

Basile, Giambattista. "The Old Woman Discovered." In *Il Pentamerone: Or the Tale of Tales*. New York: Henry, 1893.

No Small Peat

Afanas'ev, A. N. "Maria Morevna" and "The Robbers." In *Russian Fairy Tales*. Translated by Norman Guterman. Pantheon Books, 2006.

Calvino, Italo. "The One-Handed Murderer." In *Italian Folktales*. Translated by George Martin. Harcourt, 1980.

Dawkins, R. M., comp. "The Robber Captain" (abstract only). Cited in *More Greek Folktales*. Clarendon Press, 1955.

Hubert, Jürgen. *Sunken Castles, Evil Poodles: Commentaries on German Folklore*. 2020.

Muche, Carla Lea. "A Short History About Peatlands." Mission to Marsh, May 2024. http://missiontomarsh.org/en/a-short-history-about-peatlands.

Pröhle, Heinrich. "The Girl in the Wegsmühle Mill." Translated by Jürgen Hubert. In *Harzsagen zum Teil in der Mundart der Gebirgsbewohner*. 1886, 150.

Schwartz, Howard, comp. "The Pirate Princess." In *Elijah's Violin and Other Jewish Fairy Tales*. Oxford University Press, 1994.

Zalka, Csenge, trans. *The Multicolored Diary* (blog). http://multicoloreddiary.blogspot.com.

Zipes, Jack, ed. and trans. "The Seven Ravens" and "The Robber Bridegroom." In *The Complete Fairy Tales of the Brothers Grimm, All-New Third Edition*. Random House, 2003.

Good Soup

Kasschau, Anne, and Susumu Eguchi. *Using Japanese Slang: A Comprehensive Guide*. Yenbooks, 1995.

Mayer, Fanny Hagin, ed. and trans. *The Yanagita Kunio Guide to the Japanese Folk Tale*. Indiana University Press, 1986.

The Stench of Embarrassment

Blank, Trevor J. "Cheeky Behavior: The Meaning and Function of 'Fartlore' in Childhood and Adolescence." *Children's Folklore Review* 32 (2010): 61–86.

Burton, Richard, trans. *The Book of the Thousand Nights and a Night: A Plain and Literal Translation of the Arabian Nights Entertainments*. Burton Club Society, 1885.

Horta, Paulo Lemos, ed. *The Annotated Arabian Nights: Tales from 1001 Nights.* Translated by Yasmine Seale. Liveright, 2021.

Knapp, Mary, and Herbert Knapp. *One Potato, Two Potato . . . : The Secret Education of American Children.* W. W. Norton, 1976.

Legman, G. *The Horn Book: Studies in Erotic Folklore and Bibliography.* University Books, 1964.

Mahdi, Mushsin, ed. *The Arabian Nights.* Translated by Hussein Haddaway. W. W. Norton, 1990.

It Snot What You Think

Burton, Richard, comp. and trans. "The Three Wishes, or the Man Who Longed to See the Night of Power." In *The Book of the Thousand Nights and a Night: A Plain and Literal Translation of the Arabian Nights Entertainments.* Burton Club, 1885.

Carroll, Michael P. "The Trickster as Selfish-Buffoon and Culture Hero." *Ethos* 12, no. 2 (1984): 105–31.

Dorson, Richard M., comp. "Three Wishes." In *American Negro Folktales.* Fawcett, 1967.

Myung-sub, Chung, ed. *Encyclopedia of Korean Folk Literature.* National Folk Museum of Korea, 2014.

Rasmussen, Ann Marie. "Wandering Genitalia: Sexuality and the Body in German Culture between the Late Middle Ages and Early Modernity." *Kings College London Centre for Late Antique & Medieval Studies,* Occasional Publications, vol. 2, 2009.

"Sonmalmyeong." In *Encyclopedia of Korean Culture.* (Google Translate.) Aks.ac.kr, 2024, http://encykorea.aks.ac.kr/Article/E0030464.

Kalendrin, the Party Princess

Elwin, Verrier. *The Muria and Their Ghotul.* Bombay Press, 1947.

Elwin, Verrier. "The Story of Kalendrin." In *Folk Tales of Mahakoshal.* Oxford University Press, 1944.

Irwin, John C. "The Sacred Anthill and the Cult of the Primordial Mound." *History of Religions* 21, no. 4 (1982).

Lele, Teja. "Thandai: An Ancient Cannabis Drink for Celebrating Holi." BBC.com, March 25, 2024, http://www.bbc.com/travel/article/20240325-thandai-an-ancient-cannabis-drink-for-celebrating-holi.

The Pongo's Prophecy

Arguedas, José María. "The Pongo's Dream." In *The Peru Reader: History, Culture, Politics*. Duke University Press, 2005.

Basile, Giambattista. "The Cockroach, the Mouse, and the Cricket." In *The Tale of Tales*. Translated and edited by Nancy L. Canepa. Penguin, 2016.

Gil, Cecilia Castillo. "Aproximaciones a la sátira y el sueño del pongo." *Tierra Nuestra* 9, no. 1 (2012): 87–102.

Payne, Johnny, ed. *The She-Calf and Other Quechua Folk Tales*. University of New Mexico Press, 2000.

Muhawi, Ibrahim, and Sharif Kanaana "Ṭunjur, Ṭunjur." In *Speak, Bird, Speak Again: Palestinian Arab Folktales*. University of California Press, 1989.

Tantaleán-Castañeda, Romina. "The Pongo's Dream—Sensitivity Reader Report." Ph.D. dissertation. The Social Justice Institute (GRSJ), University of British Columbia, 2024.

Uther, Hans-Jörg. "1441*—Old Woman Substitute" cited in The Types of International Folktales: A Classification and Bibliography, Part I. Folklore Fellows' Communications, 2011, 222.

Recommended Reading

Andersen, Hans Christian. *The Annotated Hans Christian Andersen.* Edited by Maria Tatar. W. W. Norton, 2007.

Badman, Stephen. *Folk and Fairy Tales from Denmark, Volumes I and II.* 2015.

Bang, Im. *Tales of Korea: 53 Enchanting Stories of Ghosts, Goblins, Princes, Fairies and More!* Tuttle, 2023.

Basile, Giambattista. *The Tale of Tales.* Translated and edited by Nancy L. Canepa. Penguin, 2016.

Calvino, Italo. *Italian Folktales.* Translated by George Martin. Harcourt, 1980.

Codrescu, Andrei, ed. *Japanese Tales of Lafcadio Hearn.* Princeton University Press, 2019.

Druchunas, Donna. *Folktales of Lithuania: Six Comics Inspired by Traditional Stories.* 2023.

Esperon, Maria Garcia. *The Sea-Ringed World: Sacred Stories of the Americas.* Levine Querido, 2022.

Frank, Natalie, ed. *The Island of Happiness: Tales of Madame d'Aulnoy.* Translated by Jack Zipes. Princeton University Press, 2021.

Hanh, Thich Nhat. *The Dragon Prince: Stories and Legends from Vietnam.* Parallax Press, 2003.

Horta, Paulo Lemos, ed. *The Annotated Arabian Nights: Tales from 1001 Nights.* Translated by Yasmine Seale. Liveright, 2021.

Hubert, Jürgen. *Lurkers at the Threshold: 100 Ghost Tales from German Folklore.* 2022.

Jackson, J. K., ed. *Scottish Folk & Fairy Tales: Fables, Folklore & Ancient Stories.* Flame Tree, 2022.

Jackson, J. K., ed. *Southern African Folktales.* Flame Tree, 2023.

Kohli, Svabhu. *Tales of India: Folk Tales from Bengal, Punjab, and Tamil Nadu.* Chronicle Books, 2018.

Louis, Liliane. *When Night Falls, Kric! Krac!: Haitian Folktales*. Libraries Unlimited, 1993.

Mahdi, Mushin, ed. *The Arabian Nights*. Translated by Hussein Haddaway. W. W. Norton, 1990.

Nuwayhiḍ, Jamāl Salīm, comp. *Abu Jmeel's Daughter and Other Stories: Arab Folk Tales from Palestine and Lebanon*. Interlink Books, 2002.

Paterno, Maria Elena, Neni S. Romana-Cruz, and Sylvia Mendez Ventura. *A Treasury of Philippine Folk Tales*. Paperworks.

Payne, Johnny, ed. *The She-Calf and Other Quechua Folk Tales*. University of New Mexico Press, 2000.

Pino Saavedra, Yolando. *Folktales of Chile*. University of Chicago Press, 1967.

Ramanujan, A. K. *Folktales from India*. Pantheon Books, 1994.

Russell, P. Craig. *Fairy Tales of Oscar Wilde*. NBM Comics, 1998.

Schwartz, Howard. *Lilith's Cave: Jewish Tales of the Supernatural*. Oxford University Press, 1988.

So-Un, Kim. *Korean Folktales: Classic Stories from Korea's Enchanted Past*. Tuttle, 2024.

Tatar, Maria, ed. and trans. *The Annotated Brothers Grimm*. W. W. Norton, 2012.

Zipes, Jack, ed. and trans. *Beauties, Beasts and Enchantment: Classic French Fairy Tales*. New American Library, 1989.

Acknowledgments

Building a folklore anthology is like cooking up a pot of stone soup; it takes a village! I started with a rock, albeit a very cool rock, and ended up with this delicious meal thanks to the contributions of many smart, talented, and kind people.

Pete Jordi Wood was the first to ask, "So when are you writing a fairy tale book?" He held my hand through the query process, prepared me for the highs and lows of authorship with frankness and enthusiasm, and gave me the jump-start I needed to move my work off of TikTok and onto the page. Thank you for that, and for one day giving me a grand tour of Cornwall, home of the Greenwitch.

I'm so lucky my agent Ronald Gerber spied my query in the weeds of his inbox and agreed that our partnership could be a fruitful one. He wears the towering stack of hats required of a literary agent with panache: editor, cheerleader, pitchman, literary matchmaker, negotiator, occasional therapist. . . . Apparently being a literary agent is being a human hat stand! Thank you for all of that, and for geeking out on musicals between shop talk.

My editor Tom Mayer added me to his roster of Very Important Writers and almost made me believe I deserve to be among them. He knows how to turn straw into gold and knows when to point out the gold already hiding under the straw. He understands the subtleties of what makes one dick joke art and another just plain bad. Tom's an instrumental person to have in your corner. Plus, he doesn't make fun of me for not knowing what any word actually means. Thanks, Tom!

Thank you to Nneoma Amadiobi, Rebecca Springer, Dave Cole, Sarahmay Wilkinson, Delaney Adams, and Brian Mulligan at W. W. Norton for cleaning up my book and making it beautiful. Thank you to my marketing team Elizabeth Riley and Lara Drzik. I'm sure I'm forgetting people. Names escape, but the sentiment holds.

To my glittering web of sensitivity readers and fact-checkers: Brittany Warman, Sara Cleto, Jeana Jorgensen, and Jürgen Hubert; Antara Dutt and the folks at Tessera Editorial; Mandy Ballard, Victoria Cho, Fatin Marini, Erin Olds, Tova Seltzer, Sachiko Suzuki, and the staff at Salt and Sage Books; Adwoa and Soloman of Adeche Atelier; Kenny Boyle, Isabelle Felix, Hagar Moawad, Stef, Romina Tantaleán-Castañeda, Georgina Tena, and Lwazi Vazhure! I couldn't have done it without you. I couldn't have done it *right*, at least.

All of my friends have all held me up at various points of the process, but special thanks to Jillian Blevins, Beth Hicks, and KA Simon for your feedback and perspective.

Thanks to librarians David Bernardo and Elizabeth Karageorge for delving into databases and juggling about a hundred-thousand inter-library loan requests. Thank you to both my supervisors and my staff at the Cumberland Public Library for picking up the pieces I dropped while juggling author duties between librarian ones.

Thank you to my followers and friends on TikTok et al., who show that you can in fact be a nice person on the Internet. Thank YOU reader, for loving this book so much, you even read the thank-yous!

Thanks to my "leetle seester" Jade for putting your heart and soul into the artwork for this book, and for being the Jiminy Cricket to my Pinocchio. Thank you to my mom, who introduced me to all my favorite cultural objects, and whose support for me is so hardcore, she once told me she'd be proud of me if I pooped on stage. Thank you to my dad for teaching me how to laugh loudly and hug hard, and for understanding why I wanted my work to be for love over money. Thank you to my stepfamily Ning and Vincent for being the antithesis of fairytale stepfamilies. And thank you to my number one guy Dan for patiently waiting while I was cooped up in the solitary tower of writing, for being the #1 fellow who can make this princess laugh, and for treating me like a beauty even when I'm feeling extra-beastly.

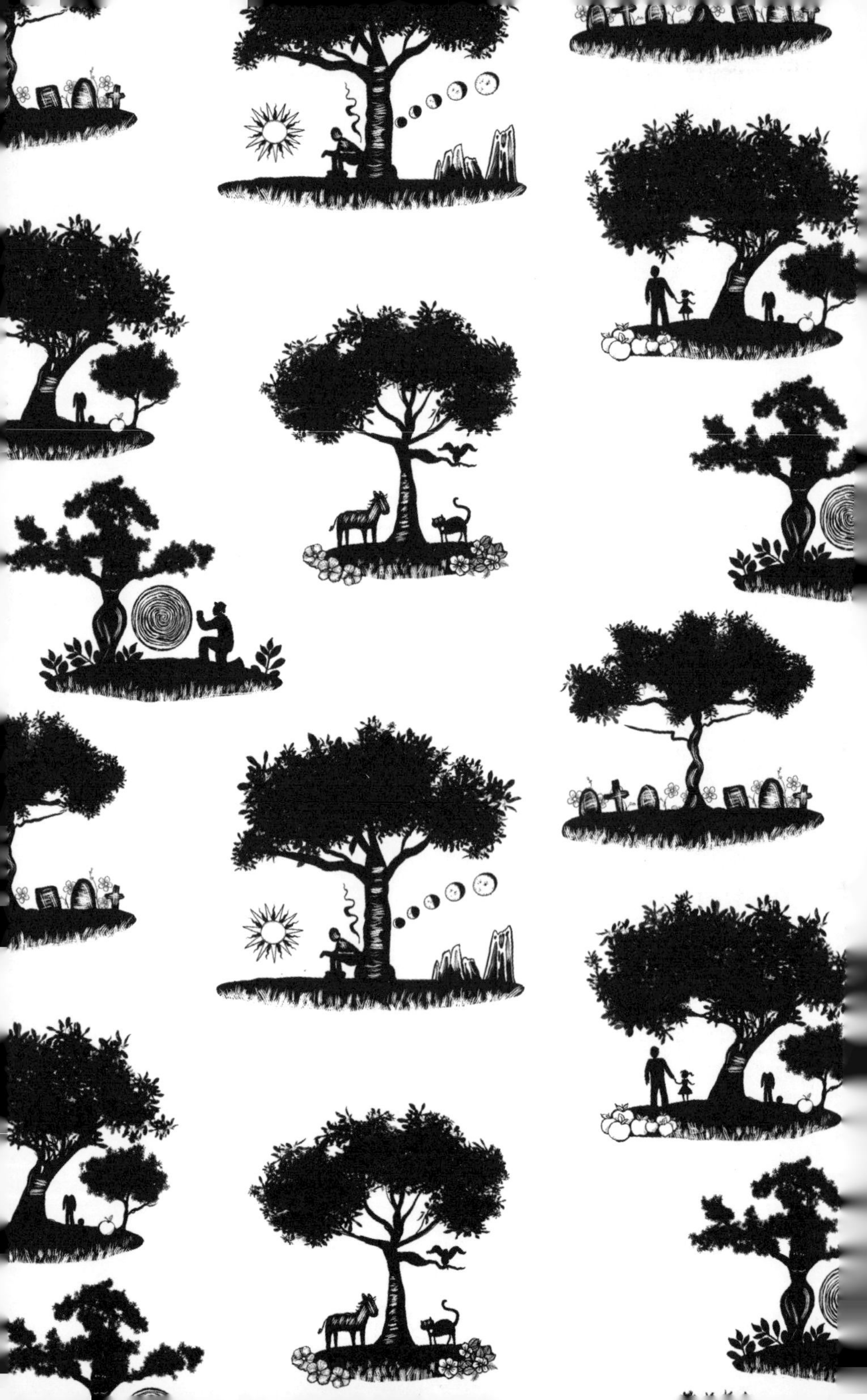